The Survivors

Also by Katherine Ginbey

The Valkyrie Ellis Trilogy

Valkyrie's Sight

God Save The Prom Queen

Fresher

For the one in every three.

It does not define you.

It is important to remember that the following chapters may trigger readers. They are written in a way that if they are skipped then you will not miss any core information as factors and context are littered throughout the book to give the essential plotlines enough background for it to be understood.

Trigger warnings include rape, assault, torture, paedophilia and racism.

Chapters with graphic rape and assault scenes include twenty-four, twenty-five, twenty-six and fifty.

The Survivors

Katherine Ginbey

Prologue

Annie

"Rapist or Murderer?" I call as I hear the front door softly close.

Grace and Cleo turned in hours ago. They had a long day at university and then drinks afterwards. Grace had popped her head in to say goodnight to me before Cleo had whisked her upstairs. Weak rays of sunlight started to peak through the windows. Lola was cutting it close.

When she doesn't answer I pull myself out of my armchair and head down the hall towards the downstairs bathroom. I run my fingers across the polished wooden walls in no particular hurry to get to Lola. I hear the tap turn on. Faucet as Lola says. She has lived in Europe on and off for almost two decades but some phrases we simply can't wean her off using.

She has left the door wide open for me as she unceremoniously scrubs at the dried blood on her face and neck with a cloth. Her fangs are still out as she grimaces. Her bleach-blonde hair is now scraped back into a bun. Recently, if the random streaks of blood in it and on the back of her neck are anything to go by.

"Messy," I comment softly. She lets out a small amused nose. Streaks of pink water run down her tanned skin and start to stain her white crop top. She hasn't been a gymnast since 2003 but she was changed in her prime. Her stomach is flat and the rest of her is toned. She looked healthy and human, especially with the spray tans she goes for every week. The Californian party girl was still thriving, forever frozen at twenty-one.

"Whatever happened to vamp etiquette?" Lola grumbles. She drops the now ruined washcloth onto the side of the sink with a wet thump. She starts to dry herself with the hand towel on the rack. I had turned it to 'warming' earlier. New York in the fall was always so cold.

"What happened?"

"That ass Owen. I was mid-bite and he just swoops in." Lola growled, tossing the towel to the side without even looking. I tut and reach down to pick it up as she continues, putting on a gruff Brooklyn accent as she mimics her rival. *"Lemme guess OC. Big bag man said you had a nice ass."*

"Owen is going to get himself caught one day," I reply bluntly. "He hunts recklessly and he is impulsive."

"If he was human," Lola begins slowly.

"We have had this discussion." I cut her off with a snarl. Lola retreats into herself and I wince. It is so rare that I have to police her now: she has improved so much in the last decade that it makes my heart hurt at the look on her face. I reach out and gently cup the side of it. I use my thumb to gently rub away a fleck of dried blood that she missed.

"We do not hurt other vampires, Lola," I whisper. "It puts us at too much of a risk. But we have to eat, and so…"

"And so we eat the monsters that wear human skins," Lola finishes our family's unofficial mantra.

"Exactly." I place a gentle kiss on her forehead.

"I hate him." Lola hisses. "I just hate him."

"We all hate him," I reassure her as I pull away. "He's a prick."

Lola laughs loudly as I knew she would. She loves it when I use my 'English swears,'

"He actually had a message for you." Lola rolls her eyes. "He said to tell you that your teddy bear misses you. Pretentious, sexist-Annie?"

Her voice echoes around the halls behind me as I bolt from the room and up the three flights of stars. This townhouse was lovely. It had enough room for all of us so that we would not clash heads. It had an outdated kitchen and a chimney. I would miss it.

"Wake up," I yell as I flick the old-fashioned light switch. Grace and Cleo are a tangle of bodies barely covered by blankets. Pillows are scattered around the floor along with their clothes. Grace's eyes flutter open, but she just blinks at me. Cleo starts slurring Arabic at me as she props herself up on her elbows.

"Get dressed. It's time to go." My voice comes out as a hoarse whisper. "Pack light."

"Who's here?" Grace rubs her eyes.

"No one. We just need to go."

"Go where?" Cleo grunts as she covers herself.

I lock eyes with Grace as my throat tightens. The nearly five centuries we have spent together come in handy as she knows my answer before I have to say it.

"Home." Grace sighs.

Chapter One

Three months later

Lola

"I have said I am sorry Cleo." I snarl as I continue to pace back and forth. The fire is crackling but it doesn't drown out the rain. Nothing drowns out an English rainstorm, as I have learnt these past few weeks. "How was I supposed to know?"

"You could have used your brain." Cleo plays with the strings on her dark grey hoodie. Grace's hoodie. I remember buying it for her as a joke when we first arrived in this grey country. The large heart-shaped union jack that covered the chest seemed in poor taste for Cleo.

"Cleo," Grace chastises softly. She stands next to the large windows, arms crossed as she watches Annie outside. The estate we are inhabiting is well-maintained and massive. I used to make fun of Annie for her posh accent. I didn't realise how close to the mark I had always been. To me, a 'Tudor Lady' just meant she was old.

"What?" Cleo's tone was softer. It always was when she was speaking to Grace. Not for the first time, I wonder how Annie coped with them like this for the eighty years before she turned me. Grace claimed that she and Cleo had love at first sight all the way back in Egypt, 1922. "Is it not true?"

Cleo's accent was lighter than it had been when I first met her in 2003. You could only really tell where she was from by how she pronounced her R's or when she got angry and tired enough to speak in Arabic.

"There is no way Lola could have known that Owen was talking about Edward." Grace moves over to behind the couch-*sofa*- and starts to gently massage her shoulders. Hot jealousy rises in my throat and I have to look away.

"None of you ever told me his name." I remind them bluntly. "Grace only ever told me that Annie had a brother, and she never knew exactly what happened to him or why he was turned. He could have been called John or Henry or Richard or-"

"I am aware you know multiple male names, Lola." Cleo drawls. I glance back and find her leaning into her girlfriend's embrace. I feel my face flush thanks to the pervert I drained this morning.

We have to take it in turns out here in the countryside. The population is smaller, the choice of criminals limited. Maybe that was why Cleo was so grumpy. She wouldn't get to feed until tomorrow. Her and Grace were going to have to travel over an hour away to shrug off any suspicion. We had already had people knock on the doors, delighted the estate had been 'bought' and was getting renovated. Nosey old cranks.

"How long will we stay here?" Cleo murmurs in Grace's ear. Grace shrugs her shoulders, her gorgeous jet-black hair cascading down her shoulders in waves.

They are the complete opposite in looks and personality. Grace is like Snow White with bright red lips and pale skin. She is charitable and forgiving. She wears her heart on her sleeve. Not exactly the personality I would have expected from a girl raised in a Tudor brothel.

Cleo is brash and bold, her skin a gorgeous brown with light caramel eyes. She looked like a delicious dark chocolate candy bar. When she opened her mouth, that opinion changed to a small, sour chewable vitamin. Good for you but an acquired taste.

"I don't know my love." Grace gently stroked Cleo's hair. "A little while longer. Maybe. Edward clearly hasn't been here. I think we all just need to give her some time."

That feels personal. It always does when one of them says 'we all.' Sometimes it feels like Cleo and Grace have their own secret little language and they only say things out loud for mine and Annie's benefit. I know for a fact that it is Grace's unwavering loyalty to Annie that keeps them from leaving us behind. She doesn't relish in the killing as I do, and Cleo finds the rules more restricting than motivating.

"I'm going to go get her. It can't be comfortable out there." I say it out loud, running the idea through Grace. I hate myself for it. I'm the youngest in our 'family' but I wasn't turned yesterday. I have been by Annie's side for twenty years. I know her well enough to decide to check on her as she stands for hours in the pouring rain.

When neither of them says anything, I stalk silently from the room.

Chapter Two

Annie

I missed the English rain. American rain smelt different and never soaked me through to my bones in the same way. The grounds of my family's old estate are turning almost swamp-like. My boots are caked with mud and grass, and I am constantly having to shift my feet in order to not get sucked into one spot. I wrinkle my nose as the wind whips the smell of manure from the farm next door over the rolling fields.

"Annie?" Lola's American drawl is almost drowned out by the pounding raindrops and the whipping wind. If I were human, I wouldn't have heard her. She is standing on the backdoors stone steps, staying under the slanted roof. She styled her hair nicely this morning. It would be a shame for her to ruin it for the sake of my mental breakdown.

"I'm okay," I say loud enough for her super hearing to pick it up. "Has Cleo picked what we are watching tonight?"

"I think they are going to have an early night. They think because we are in the countryside they get to have at it like rabbits." Lola laughs and I can't help but chuckle along with her. "But…we can still watch something together. If you want."

I decide then that I need to be more of a presence for Lola. With Grace, it was easy. I had clung to her for centuries until we stumbled across Cleo. With Cleo, it had been only a small adjustment. I had to accept I was no longer Grace's whole universe, and I would need to give them some alone time. I had moved that lesson onto Lola when perhaps it was the other way around. Lola needed more one-on-one time from me than Cleo ever had.

"I would really like that, Lol." I respond. I stay facing away from her as I slowly smile. I can almost hear her inner turmoil as she debated whether or not to let the nickname go without a 'polite' correction. Lola's first bonding experience with us all had been to teach us texting.

There was a moment of silence between us again. I take in a final deep gulp of the freezing air before I turn on my heel and head back towards the house. The whistle of wind that follows me sounds like an echo of my brother's laugh.

You'll never catch me! Not when you run like a girl!

I am a girl Teddy and I am still going to beat you!

"It's really beautiful here." Lola brings me out of my reminiscing. "So green."

"Not much green in California." I agree.

"Not this type of green anyway." Lola steps back into the warm house and opens the door as wide as possible for me. I scrape my boots against the rug on the outside of the door. That wasn't here before. Small things have been altered and added by the people I paid to maintain the property. I would have signed off on the major changes, although I couldn't remember when. Things like installing a shower were not high on my memories priority list.

I hear a high-pitched giggle echoing from the top floor. We had given that to Grace and Cleo so they would have some semblance of privacy. I now wish I had added soundproofing to the list of improvements. I might yet have time if I could just keep up my resolve.

Owen had been less than helpful when I visited him that night three months ago. He was a typical bully, lashing out at Lola with whatever information he had overheard. He had never spoke to Teddy. He had overheard a rumour at one of his secret boy's clubs that a vampire called Teddy was looking for me. He had twisted that into a sharp knife Lola had mistakenly dug into me. I had dug literal knives into him in retaliation.

I tell Lola to pick whatever she wants to watch as I dash upstairs to change from my wet clothes. I move at vampire speed because wet denim is uncomfortable to everyone. The day we arrived, I sent the other three to the largest town nearby to get supplies. Lola had gotten us all fluffy pyjamas to keep warm during the 'big English storms.' race said she was so excited to get us all matching sets that she didn't have the heart to tell her it would only be some annoying spatters of rain.

I hear Lola switch on the TV from rooms away and then rush through the house to change into her own onesie. I smile softly as I pull the zip all the way up. Lola was a much-needed breath of fresh air. Only months after turning her I had wondered how I had ever lived without her. How any of us had lived without her until then? We needed her perkiness. It brought me and Grace out of our sedation. It was so hard to feel when you were over five hundred years old. It was even harder to let that fact terrify me.

Another giggle echoed through the house quickly followed by a hush. I take it back. I needed Lola's perkiness. Grace just needed Cleo. I flash back downstairs to try and give them as much privacy as possible.

Lola must have had the same idea. She beats me downstairs although when two laughs follow us down she stops. She stares up at the ceiling. Her mouth is tilted down into the slightest frown. I squeeze her shoulder as I pass her and throw myself down onto the sofa. Lola has left the TV set up on the guide.

I have no idea if Lola has ever truly been in love. I know she has had a string of lovers and infatuations. I know Owen hates her because he wasn't one of them. She is gorgeous and bold and if I get the chance then I would happily give her what I had accidentally given Grace.

"What was he like? Your brother?" Lola asks tentatively from the doorway. Her onesie is so baggy that we could easily both fit inside it. An unusual choice for her. I focus on the snowflake pattern stamped on it as I debate how to answer.

"Progressive." I decide on the right word. "For the time. He was a man in favour with the royal court in the Tudor era. He could have got away with pretty much anything he wanted."

"With a sister like you, I doubt he had any other choice." Lola tells me kindly. I let out a small amused noise and stare down at my hands.

"I was different back then." I think back as far as I can remember. It's all flashes of uncomfortable corsets, jewels, and Anne. My cheek has a phantom weight to it as I remember the thick lead-based makeup that would be smeared onto my face. I scratch at it. "I was...obsessed with doing all the right things and marrying the right man. It's just how it was back then."

"Grace...Grace said you were a handmaiden to the Queen."

"I was a friend of the Queen. The true Queen." Even after all this time, I cannot keep the bite from my voice. I cannot talk about her without my gut twisting and my fangs prickling in my mouth.

"I thought...look I didn't get taught your version of history at my high school. If ya wanna talk about the civil war or the declaration of independence I could probably root around in my brain for a fact or two. But English Queens...I got nothing. Less than nothing since they all have the same names." Lola moved into the room, settling next to me with her hands hidden underneath her thighs.

"You never said you wanted to learn about any of it." I'm more curious than anything else. I rest my elbow on the arm of the sofa and study her face. She looks so young, especially as she kicks her legs back and forth.

"I thought you would open up eventually," Lola admits. "But here we are. We are finally in England in this beautiful house, and you look terrified to be here. I want to understand why. I want to be there for you like you are for me."

"Oh Lola. You're making me all gooey." I tease her, reaching out to pinch her cheek

"You can be such a bitch." She bats me off and rolls her eyes.

"Yeah. But that's not news to you." I wink. "You called me a lot worse the night we met."

"I thought you were murdering me."

"You weren't entirely wrong."

"Yes I was. I'm more alive now than I ever was when my heart was beating." Lola stares at me with her bright blue eyes as wide as saucers. They are begging me to believe her and to let her in.

"And what a beautiful heart it is." I whisper. I adjust myself into a more comfortable position and face her. "Ask away, Lola."

Chapter Three

Grace

"You have to be more patient with Lola." I whisper into the shell of Cleo's ear. I place a delicate kiss there as she grunts her response. I continue down her jaw, my hand running through her thick black hair. Where mine was simply dark, hers was onyx. I would kill to find a crystal that deep a black. She loved her collection. I could make her earrings, maybe a necklace, depending on the rock's size.

"It is not my fault that she is so naïve." Cleo's fingers run tauntingly up my bare thigh. "You treat her like a babe. She would be forty by now."

"And you would be over one hundred."

"Carry on insulting me." Cleo huffed. "And you can find a different bed to sleep in."

"Don't be like that, my love," I whisper even as I pull away and prop myself against the pillows. "It would just make it easier if you finally started to warm up to Lola. It's been twenty years, Cle."

"Oh, you would just love that wouldn't you? Getting me and the American all friendly," Cleo asks hotly as she pulls herself completely out of my reach. I finally snap.

"For the last time Cleo, I am *not attracted to-*"

"Shhhhhhh." Cleo hisses, throwing her hand over my mouth. I'm tempted to let my fangs down and slice at her for it. She knows I hate it. She only ever does it in these moments when we are walking this dangerously thin line. It's almost like she is goading me.

In our darker moments, I think it's to make me hate her. To make it so she has a reason to leave. But those moments are decades in between, small blips in our otherwise complete bliss. "Someone is outside."

I freeze for a half second and then prick my ears. Cleo has better hearing than me in the same way that Annie is better at hypnosis. We all have our talents. Lola is the fastest runner and I...I make good cups of tea. A few seconds later, I can now hear the stranger stomping their boots against the welcome mat.

Male. Definitely male. Their breathing is normal as they knock twice on the front door. They had to be fast. Cleo can hear people all the way across the field from up here. A human couldn't have moved that quickly and this had to be a human. His heartbeat echoed in my ears. My fangs itch as they lengthen and my throat feels impossibly dry. Cleo stops breathing to try and make it easier on herself.

Footsteps that I recognise as Annie's make their way to the front door. She doesn't rush. She is almost stomping. I pull myself slowly out of bed, throwing on my shirt as I get into a crouch. The plan, if we are ever under attack, is to leave her behind and get the other two to safety. It has never been a plan I intended to follow.

Annie's footsteps stop. The heartbeat of the human that isn't human speeds up slightly. I assume he is looking through the glass at her. His next breath is significantly longer. I can't help but smile as I realise who it is.

"Thomas."

Chapter Four

Cleo

"Do not be a fool." I hiss at Grace as she moves at human speed towards the door. "She has not given the signal."

"It's Thomas." Grace's response is blunt. She does not even look at me as she searches for her other clothes.

"The witch boy?" I scowl. "You said they have not seen each other since-"

"Exactly." Grace cuts me off. She sits on the corner of our bed to carefully pull on a pair of white fluffy socks. I scrunch my nose up at the sight of them. Such itchy things.

"So why would you want to go and ruin their reunion?" I tug on the corner of the covers. She tuts at me but still does not turn.

"Just…get dressed." She begs me softly before leaving the room. I wait until she is out the door before I begrudgingly do as she asked. I grab a hoodie from her side of the wardrobe and drape it around myself.

There is no noise from downstairs, not even Lola's usual high-pitched drivel. They are at a standstill with the witch boy waiting to be let in. As I close the door to our bedroom behind me, I think of everything Grace has told me about Thomas.

He is a part of the cursed coven, meaning he was as immortal as any of us. He had never told Grace what it was his coven had done to receive that curse. This was not surprising, considering his coven had never told anyone. They had long conversations when he would visit her in the brothel she had grown up in as a human. He never hired her. He was just there to check in on Annie. Grace suspected he was behind the annual flowers on Annie's birthday and the random 'leads' towards the more despicable people we have hunted. Thomas was never a subject Annie would talk about.

He had been (and still was according to his heartbeat) romantically interested in Annie. In the winter of 1914, eight years before they saved me, Annie had reciprocated them. Once. Annie and Grace had moved countries the next morning. They never talk about it.

I doubt Lola knows who Thomas is. I only know because Grace mentioned him as I drunkenly insisted we get Annie a partner back in 1983. Apparently, Thomas and Annie were quite adorable. I didn't see how that could be the case. He sounded like a supernatural stalker. It was strange that he would go to a brothel and ask about her when he knew that she wasn't in the building.

Cleo and Lola, stay out of sight. Annie's voice cuts through my thoughts and I stand still on the top step. I can't see anything important from up here. The staircase spirals around a corner. I can see a tenth of the door at best.

He will sense us anyway, I snip back.

Stay. Annie's tone makes me flinch. The bond between a vampire and their maker was intense and infuriating. This was not the first time I wished it had been Grace's blood and bite to turn me. She would never be so casually demanding. There is a slight whoosh as Lola moves at hyper speed to the other side of the house like an obedient puppy.

I settle myself into a crouch and wrap my fingers around the end pole of the balcony. This way I can throw myself down the stairs and down to Grace's side when needed. At some point, it would be needed.

Chapter Five

Annie

Thomas is still annoyingly attractive. Thick dark hair cut short with slightly curly ends. Plump pink lips and sharp cheekbones. His eyelashes were longer than mine and his stormy grey eyes had a blue tint to them, a reminder of the colour they used to be. Those were especially beautiful when he fluttered them at me from under his brow as he was doing now.

"Am I not even invited in?" His voice is soft and lilting. He is so classically beautiful-

"Stop it." I snap at him. He grins at me, showing me a slightly crooked right incisor.

"I'm not doing anything." Thomas insists.

"You are using that witch charisma trick on me. I told you never to do that."

"Or you would kill me. Yes I remember." Thomas puts his hands in his pockets, clearly quite amused at how quickly he has managed to irritate me. He is wearing dark jeans and a tight-fitting white t-shirt. A black leather jacket completes the classic look. A simple rucksack is thrown over his shoulders.

"Yet you start to do it. On my very doorstep." I crossed my arms.

A strange look crosses Thomas's face but it is quickly replaced with resilience. His lips press together and his eyes turn serious. "I have an offer for you."

"You always do." My fingers twitch as I debate opening that door. This isn't his usual offer. This isn't him sending me flowers for my birthday or offering up the police files of someone particularly vile. This is to do with Teddy. The lump in my throat tastes suspiciously like pride.

"You always say no." Thomas raised an eyebrow.

"I'm…more lenient this century." I swallow down my desperation to know the terms I will be agreeing to. We both know I will be agreeing just like we both know I have purposely kept the latest additions to my family away from him. Grace has known him since she was human. I cannot change that. I can keep Cleo and Lola as close to enigmas as possible.

Thomas's eyes flicker over my shoulder. His face splits into a grin. "Hello, Grace."

"Hello, Thomas." Grace beams. "How have you been? It's been a few decades."

"It would be better if I could get out of this drizzle." Thomas joked. "You look good, Grace. Being in love suits you."

I hear Cleo shift her weight upstairs. I have already pushed my luck with her today. I need to leave her to it, or she will run down here out of sheer spite even though it would hurt her to defy me so blatantly. Grace blushes as she moves to stand next to me.

She wants to tell him all about Cleo, about her last century with her soulmate. Thomas would have the patience for it. He would nod and smile at her throughout before shifting those eyes to me when he thought I wasn't looking. My problem was that I was always looking.

"I suppose you better come in." I finally sigh. I move slowly to open the door for him, but he moves quickly through the gap as if I was going to change my mind. I might have if the stakes were different. His act of insecurity tricks the part of my brain screaming at me to change my mind. I almost smile as a whiff of his scent, sharp and fresh like a woodland, washes over me.

Grace immediately goes to hug him. She moves at human speed and Thomas smiles slightly. He wraps her arm around her in a bear hug, lifting her in the air. She squeals but hold back her strength as she hugs him back. Always so careful.

"Is this when I get to meet the elusive new members of the family?" Thomas puts her down with a soft thud.

"No." I snap. "Not until we discuss the terms."

"You haven't even offered me a cup of tea yet, Annie." Thomas's eyes seem to twinkle as they focus on me again.

"We have no teabags." I tell him bluntly.

"Liar."

"I didn't realise you were with me when I did the shopping."

"It's you. You always have tea."

"Except right now. When I do not have any."

"Okay okay. No tea." Thomas is still smiling as if this is all an elaborate joke. As if he isn't about to offer me something he had always kept out of my reach.

As if he didn't know that I would agree to literally anything for the information he is about to dangle over my head.

I can put the kettle on. Lola's soft American lilt worms its way gently around my brain.

No Lola. This prick doesn't get a cup of tea. My mouth twitches as I fight back a smile. *But thank you.*

"It's impolite to use telepathy in front of guests." Thomas tuts.

"It's rude to turn up uninvited." I say as I make my way slowly down the corridor and into the living room. He follows as he always does. Grace skips at his side.

She was forever stuck in an eighteen-year-old's body, halfway between an adult and child, but occasionally there would be a few seconds where I saw her as she had been when I first met her. Six years old with tight plaited hair and wide wonderous eyes.

She had never belonged in the brothel she had been born into and I had fought tooth and nail to let her keep a small shred of innocence. Five hundred years down the line, that innocence had turned into compassion. Compassion even for the cursed coven and its desperate yet attractive members. Thomas would never deserve the trustful beaming smiles she sent his way even if he lived until the world was turning to ash.

"I am so sorry for the interruption. You were clearly very busy." Thomas is pushing his luck with that one.

"How do you spend your days, Lord Thomas?" I drawl as I settle myself in the armchair by the fire. Thomas flinches quickly before lounging across my sofa, arms thrown over the back of it as if he owned it. My fangs prickle in my mouth.

"Staring at your portrait quoting Shakespeare." Thomas jests. "Sometimes writing heartfelt poetry about your auburn hair."

"Never show it to me. You're as creative as a gibbet." I say softly as Grace curls up into the armchair on the other side of the fireplace. Her bare feet hang near the flames. Thomas's lips twist into a crooked smile.

What's a gibbet? Lola interrupts again.

Look it up on your little box. Cleo snarls. *I want to know why he is here.*

I don't even know who he is! But he's cute.

Would you both be quiet. I snarl down the bond.

If you two wouldn't mind. Annie looks like she is going to have an aneurysm. Oh…and it's nice to meet you too, Lola. Thomas's voice drifts through our minds as smoothly as a hot knife through butter.

Chapter Six

Grace

Annie is across the room in a flash. I don't even have time to blink before Thomas is against the wall, Annie's hand wrapped around his throat and her fangs extended.

"How did you do that?" Annie whispered. Her tone was low and curious, almost seductive. I don't think she knows how she changes when he is around. Thomas must just assume that it's how she always is.

Cleo and Lola crash into each other in the doorway, both in a rush to come and help. I bite back a snort. It's sweet but Thomas would rather carve his own heart out with a plastic spoon than hurt any of us.

"You're not the only one with tricks, Annie." Thomas stares straight into her eyes. He doesn't so much as glance at the pointed teeth that were only inches from his jugular.

"Not an answer." Annie growled. I can see her fingers tense slightly. Thomas breathes in sharply through his nose but says nothing else.

"She told me about you." Lola interrupts slowly. She looks like a child playing at protector, chin held up in the air and her hands in loose fists. It warms my heart. The fact Cleo slides so easily in front of Lola, acting as an extra barrier, sets it on fire. My love is all fire and passion but confused at how to show it. Lola has yet to learn that when Cleo is horrible, it comes from a place of love. A place of family.

"Did she?" Thomas cocks an eyebrow.

"She said you knew her back when she was human." Lola continued. She moved her head around Cleo to get a better look at him. "That you are a part of the cursed coven."

"Did she tell you what that means, young one?" Thomas finally turns his gaze towards her.

"That you know what happened. But you just won't tell her. That if anyone knows why we can do what we can do, then it's you."

"And she thinks I've been holding out on her."

"So, you do know what we can do." Lola smirked. She thinks she is triumphant in her comment. I sigh softly.

"Thomas has always known." I tell her softly. Cleo scowls in my vague direction. I'll pay for not telling her that later. "His coven got us out of London all those years ago. He has never told anyone about us."

"That we know of." Annie grumbles under her breath. Thomas looks wounded at the insinuation.

"Why is he here now?" Cleo asks bluntly. She puts on more of an accent than she has normally. She is trying to throw him off, to change his perception of her. There is no use. Thomas knows better and is a better person than to judge someone for their ethnicity.

"I come with an offer." Thomas has turned his attention back to Annie. I think he does it subconsciously most times. I like to think he loves her so much he can't bring himself to ever really look away from her whenever they are in the same room. She deserves that kind of love. She deserves romance. She deserves more than we as a family can give her.

"You always come with an offer. You haven't answered my question." Annie finally lets go of him, taking a step back as she flexes her fingers. Thomas stays pressed against the wall.

"I don't know why, Annie." Thomas shrugs. "I've been able to since 1914."

1914. The year that we had fled from Paris. Annie had been covered in soot and blood when she came home. There had been streaks on her face from tears. She had started to pack a bag, moving at such speeds that I had only heard her in a room once she had left it and things fell from the walls. We had run straight to Italy.

"You have access to the witch archives." Annie crosses her arms and ignores my pointed glance. "You could figure it out."

"That's not a priority for me." Thomas said dismissively. "Is it a priority for you?"

"You are never a priority to me, Thomas." Annie says it so matter-of-fact that even I almost believe it. "Now what is the offer?"

Thomas's eyes flicker over us all. He is weighing the room. He doesn't know Lola and Cleo like he knows me and Annie. He doesn't know how they will take the news. The heavy news, because if he has come himself, empty-handed and in person, then it's a large offer.

"I need you to turn someone." Thomas's eyes focus on the fire over Annie's shoulder. My stomach drops.

"Which someone?" Annie voice is calm like the eye of a storm.

"Crown Prince Alistair." Thomas barely breathes the name.

The room explodes with sound.

Chapter Seven

Lola

"You think I am going to turn *the crown prince of England.*" Annie snarls at Thomas, almost bent in half with her fury.

Cleo is spitting insults in Arabic. I recognise a few words. None of them are pleasant. Grace is at her side in a second, whispering Arabic at her in a reassuring tone.

"Why?" I ask Thomas. "Why him? Why Annie?" *Why Why Why.* I feel like a toddler, too young and naïve to see the bigger picture.

"He needs to be a daywalker." Thomas keeps his eyes on Cleo. Smart. If anyone is going to attack him, then it would be her. Not that he would be able to move quick enough- or would he? He could infiltrate our telepathic bond. That was supposed to be sacred between companion vampires.

"He does not *need* anything." Annie hisses. A thoughtful look crosses Grace's face as she stares at Thomas. She now has a tight grip on Cleo's arm.

"He is dying, Annie." Thomas finally snaps.

"Good."

"You don't mean that. He is an innocent boy-"

"That 'innocent boy' has been in the papers every single day he has been alive. Drugs. Drunken behaviour at balls. Scandalous affairs with married nobles. He does not deserve what you are asking." Annie shouts back, counting off the offenses on her fingers. Her focus is solely on Thomas. They look so much like my parents that I balk.

My mother would scream in my father's face, usually in perfect makeup and holding something sharp. My father wouldn't yell back right away. He would wait until she was a blubbering mess and then say something cold and calculating. I would always sneak out during the screaming when they were more distracted. Annie had that same look in her eye now. A look of being so angry that her eyes watered, so betrayed it was as if she was choking on the pieces of her shattered heart.

"You cannot blame him for what his ancestor did." Thomas keeps calm as he cuts right to the deeper issue and the real reason Annie is so passionately refusing.

"His entire family are the same. They raise their children with the same entitled attitudes. They never changed. They never will." Annie scowls.

"Prince Alistair did not cut Anne's head off, Annie. Do not punish him as if he did."

"If you are going to talk about her, you do it properly." Annie growled. "You use her title like you just used his. You give her that respect."

"Annie." Grace says gently. "He didn't mean it like that. We should hear him out."

"You could offer me the entire empire." Annie took one step towards Thomas. "And I will still tell you to fuck off."

"I am not here to offer you that." Thomas doesn't so much as flinch. "I am here to offer you something greater. Something you actually want."

He is taunting her, I realise. It's all a game. He knows the answer he will get. He came here tonight, tracked us all down, so that he could see it first-hand. He doesn't care that the room has three other vampires in it. He is only here for Annie.

"I can get you Edward and I can get you answers. All you have to do is say yes."

Annie swallows her initial answer, swallows those shattered pieces and stares at him. She swallows again before clearly deciding she cannot speak. She closes her eyes and gives the briefest nod.

Thomas's shoulders droop in relief. He wasn't sure she would say yes. I was wrong. That realisation feels me with a sick sense of smug pride. Even I know that she would agree to this.

She would do anything to finally find out why we always needed to run, why her bite and her blood is so special, why she had to be so picky with who she turned. But not for her. She wanted to find out for us. We were her priority from now until the end of time. Just as she would be mine.

"Where are we going?" I ask, breaking the silence. Annie's head snaps to the side and she shots me the softest of smiles.

"London." Annie and Thomas answer at the same time.

"Make sure to get a nice dress. You'll be bowing to pratts in crowns as soon as we get out of the car." Annie's voice is matter-of-fact. The anger that was there only a second ago is gone. She walks calmly out of the room without a backwards glance at any of us.

Thomas lets out a deep breath. He looks at Grace and gives her a tentative smile. "Can I have that cup of tea now?"

Chapter Eight

Cleo

"You look so stunning." Grace purrs into my ear as her hand moves further up my thigh. The cursed coven had deep pockets and they had dipped into them to get us a fleet of private cars. Each of us were given our own but I had refused to move from Grace's side. Thomas had unsubtly sat himself in the same one as Annie. Lola was the only one alone, if you could call two guards armed with silver bullets sitting across from her being alone.

The two guards in our car have stayed silent the whole drive. For humans that's impressive considering it was a six-hour drive from Annie's estate. There had not been a single cough or shuffle. If their heartbeats were not filling the car with noise, then I would assume they were also immortal. Their focus is mainly on me. I like to think it is more for my natural violent aura than because of my skin colour.

We were driving under the cover of night, the ruse forever being held. It felt like a cruel trick from the god who had turned his back on me that night. I did not burn to ash in the sun, but I was not allowed to stroll through it either.

Grace nuzzles her face into the side of mine. Her bare shoulder brushes against mine. We are both in thin strappy dresses that flow around our knees. Grace because that is the style she loves, me because I love to match her. I want to make it clear to all of them that she is mine. Her dress is a lovely pale green. Mine is dark blue.

The car slows. The windows are completely blacked out. My ears twitch. There is basic city noise. The scuttering of rats, the snores of homeless men and the whistling of air trapped between two buildings. There is one group of drunken women stumbling around a few hundred feet away.

"This will all be fine, my love." Grace kisses my cheek as the car stops. I hear the slightest creak as iron gates open and we are moving through them even slower than before. I know the gates. I stared at their picture all of last night. I studied this palace for hours as Grace slept beside me. The information hadn't been complete, obviously, but thanks to 'vlogs' and Instagram I was now intimately familiar with the public areas of the palace.

They were only public when the royal family was away, of course. The British royals had a selfish amount of homes across the nation. This palace right in the centre of London was the most popular. It had previously been known as Buckingham. Grace said it was renamed after the original owner died. His son-in-law sounded like a pretentious prick.

Kelner Palace had nearly a thousand rooms after a major extension in the 1950's. Most of them were for the servants or functionality. Its gardens were spread over almost forty acres. There were hundreds of photo shoots and videos of the royal family taking strolls through them. Prince Alistair had been suspiciously missing from quite a few of them.

PR from the royal family all included the same videos of him running in those gardens at maximum thirteen years old. Anything past that, he was basically stationary. He was stood on the balcony or in a stately room. He walked the halls before it cut to his father waving to an adoring crowd. Anything past that was newspaper scandals, videos, and grainy pictures of him stumbling or collapsed in a corner.

The Royals all looked so averagely human it made me sick. Their skin was pale, hair and eyes brown. Grace looked more regal than any of them. Maybe I would buy her a crown with the money I planned on demanding from this bargain. If Annie was going to throw away her rulebook then we may as well get a small fortune out of it. Maybe I would simply steal one instead.

The car comes to a final stop. Grace reaches out to open the handle with a soft smile on her face. She's excited. She is about to meet royalty, about to save a young boy's life. Those kind of things make her undead heart beat a little faster. The guard on the left moves to stop her. I grab his wrist before its even halfway towards her.

"You don't touch her." I hiss.

"Cleo." Grace tuts as she makes me let go. "It's fine. It'll be a protocol. Right?" Grace looks to the guard with a kind smile on her face. The guard doesn't even blink in her direction. His dull green eyes are staring straight at me, almost daring me to break his wrist. He probably has at least four silver weapons on him that he is itching to use.

"Annie Dawson is to be escorted inside." The other guard was completely neutral as he turned his face to the window. "Should she send for you, you will be escorted inside after."

"*Should* she send for us?" I scoff. Annie couldn't stand to be more than a town away from Grace on a normal day. She was not going to leave us in this car with armed royal guards inside of having Grace at her side. Not willingly.

"After the offer has been negotiated, then you will be allowed inside." The guard continued as if he hadn't heard me. "If the offer is rejected then you are to be escorted back to the estate in which you were found."

"With Annie." Grace added quickly. When the guards did not answer she looked between the two of them. "Right?"

"Of course, my love." I finally let go of the guard's wrist and run my thumb over the back of her hand. "We will not be leaving without Annie." It was a promise and a threat. I had no doubt in my mind that this car was bugged.

Chapter Nine

Annie

"You still haven't told me how you have been these past hundred-odd years." Thomas speaks in near whispers, which is how I know we are being recorded. They are not as dumb as I thought. This tiny truck is loaded with silver. I can almost taste it in the air. The driver's keychain. The gun and bullets hidden away in his jacket. The necklace on the guard in the front passenger seat. None of it was on Thomas. He is in tight-fitting casual black clothes. The fact we accidentally match makes my stomach roll.

It was supposed to be an insult. I would wear no dress or jewellery. I would not curtsey for them. I would wear all black as I did for two years after their ancestor cut off my friend's head. I would declare myself in mourning and remind them that they needed me more than I needed them. They were the one with a dying child and I had all the time in the world to find my answers. I had all the leverage here.

When Thomas had come swaggering out of my guest bathroom in almost identical black skinny jeans and a tight-fitting long sleeve I wanted to throw him through the window. He even wore similar thick black outdoor boots. The only difference was our jackets. His was the same as it had been the night before, sleek black leather. Mine was red leather with black sleeves. My hair was up in a practical ponytail. The edges of my fringe flickered around the edge of my eyeline. I needed to cut it again soon.

"Ignoring me. How refreshing." Thomas says sarcastically as he rests his forehead against the window.

"I have been sat in this stationary car for ten minutes now. Surely they knew we were coming. All those secret little phone calls of yours had to have had some purpose." I bang my head against the hard leather headrest.

"You cannot rush royalty, Annie." Thomas says it as a soft warning. I'm sure I will hear it echo around my brain as I tell the King of England I will not be a loyal subject from the goodness of my heart. He wants my blood, and his family would pay in every sense of the word for even a single drop of it.

"I am over five hundred years old, Thomas. I don't rush. But I do grow impatient." I flex my fingers out in front of me. Lola had painted little flames on top of the black I had originally chosen. They were quite good.

"Lola…is not what I would have picked for you." Thomas shifts in his seat.

"Stay out of my head if you want yours to stay on your shoulders." I snap. I could open the door, but I would not make it out of the car. Thomas would bind me in magic so fast even I wouldn't see it coming.

"You would really hurt me, Annie?" Thomas cocks his head to the side and stares at me. A coldness runs through me as if those steel eyes were looking straight at my soul. Every time he looks at me like that I pray it is the last.

"What will happen to the others when I am taken inside?" I demand bluntly.

"They will be safe."

"A vague answer to a specific question."

"You used to like it when I did that."

"Don't be crass."

Thomas's responding laugh makes me smile. Not because it makes me happy that I have made him laugh or that it speaks to some secret part of my soul. His laugh makes me smile because Thomas had the annoying privilege of being the most charismatic man to exist. If he laughed, then you smiled. If he frowned, you wanted to rip whatever saddened him to shreds. It was a fundamental instinct that came to the surface whenever anyone was around him. I couldn't even hate him for it.

Thomas stops laughing. The smile drops from his face as he reaches for the doorhandle. It's time. He is out the door in one fluid motion and then holds his hand out for me to take. Despite myself, I accept it.

The palace is dark. All the front-facing windows have the lights turned completely off. We have been dropped off right by the steps leading into the main doorway. I don't know if that's to block anyone from seeing who has arrived or if it's to block whoever lets us in from being seen. Either way, it makes me uneasy even as I can hear Cleo arguing from her car. They must have multiple back entrances. Why choose the front?

Settle. I hiss down the bond. I don't risk saying anything more while Thomas is here. I'm not sure how his new mind trick works. They all know the plan for if we ever get separated like this. They will be fine. Cleo growls but does not say anything else.

Thomas acts as if he cannot hear us. He simply strolls up the steps as if he were the rightful owner of the palace and opens the door. I clench my jaw and move at a sluggish human pace after him.

The inside is equally as dark. The sharp scent of fake lemon attacks my nostrils. They probably used it in all their cleaning products. Everything looks sleek and polished. I briefly wonder how many staff work the night shift.

Thomas's eyes are not as sharp as mine, but he moves throughout the hall as if its brightly lit. He doesn't walk too close to the vases lining the small tables across the walls. He automatically turns away from the petals of the dropping lilies as they threaten to run across his shoulders.

"How often do you come here?" I breathe as I follow him down a sharp left corridor and out of the entrance hall. Thomas doesn't respond. His heartbeat stays steady. We come to a crossroads. One set of marble steps leads downwards while another leads upwards. Everything looks like it's made of bloody marble. I sniff slightly. The steps lead down to the kitchens.

Thomas takes a hold of the end of the banister and twirls himself up the stairs two at a time. I raise my eyebrows but follow after him, still at a human pace. There are no guards following after us, but I doubt that would still be the case if I were to start speeding around. Thomas almost definitely has orders to keep me in line.

I run my tongue over my fangs as we reach the top of the stairs. Everything is white and gold with a splash of red. The carpet would be obnoxiously bright in the daytime. The lemon scent is much stronger now but not strong enough. Underneath it all is a thick smell of sickness. It is so close to the haunting smell from a few centuries ago that I almost recall.

"You never told me how sick he was." My lips pull back in revulsion. "This may not even-"

It will work. Thomas's voice cuts through my thoughts.

Wishful thinking is for children, Thomas.

Thomas comes to an abrupt stop and lets out an agitated breath. He licks his lips as he turns to me. I stop a few feet away from him, the idea of drinking any of the blood from that decaying person in the room opposite turning my stomach.

I have drunk infected blood before. I have tried to save children from dying of the plague. It did not work. Their death was swifter than it would have been, but they were still buried in the piles of burning flesh whose ash refused to wash from my hair. I had been bedridden for weeks. Grace had brought me deer and dogs and I would simply throw up bloody foam. It had almost got us caught.

"This is not the 1600s, Annie. This is not the plague." Thomas half reaches out for me before realising what a poor decision that would be.

"There is something not right in that room." I respond bluntly.

"Something…unclean."

"Maybe we should have had this conversation in the car." Thomas sighs.

"Maybe." I repeat. "There are a lot of maybes here."

"Your bite and your blood will work Annie. Trust me. I just…could you at least meet him first?" Thomas takes the few remaining steps to the bedroom door and places his hand on the pure gold doorknob. I bare my teeth at him out of pure instinct. He doesn't flinch.

He simply opens the door and steps inside. I curse at him in my head and for the first time hope he can hear it. I walk in after him.

Chapter Ten

Alistair

Vampires were noisier than I imagined.

I could hear her arguing in the hall with Thomas. I didn't realise I smelt that bad. I knew sick people smelt bad, but considering I was bathed daily, I didn't think I smelt *unclean*.

The two guards standing by my nightstands shifted slightly at the insult. I ignore them. They weren't ones I recognised, which means they were new to the king's guard. Brand new, vampire hunter king's guards, in case this all turned ugly. Would vampires be ugly? Would there be something repulsive about me, something fundamentally and subconsciously terrifying for the rest of my existence? They must be worse than these hunters, who even my servant Lyra feels skittish around. She is hiding out in my en suite, pretending to clean instead of standing next to them.

The chandelier above my bed has one flickering light. I stare straight up at that as the door opens. The light burns into my retinas and leaves strange coloured squiggles, but hey, at least I'm feeling something. I've had so many blood tests and IVs, the pricks of needles just blend in with the usual aches in my bones.

"Evening, Your Grace." Thomas greets me. He's smiling. I can hear it in his voice. He always smiles when he talks about Annie the vampire, so I would guess it was an outright grin around now. I turn my head on my freshly plumped pillows to look. No grin. How interesting.

"I told you not to call me that." My voice sounds like two pieces of sandpaper rubbing together. I wince. I should have downed the glass of water when I heard them in the hall. Lyra appears at my side in an instant, moving the near-empty IV stand out of the way so she can bring the glass to my lips.

"And I told you that until you put that as a royal decree, you have to suck it up." Thomas pretends not to notice as Lyra smooths my hair down and adjusts my blankets. I pretend not to notice how he shifts closer to the ginger girl that steps next to him in the doorway.

She is pretty in a predatorial sort of way. The sort of way that a cheetah is cute until you try to cuddle it. She looks human with her delicate features. A 'classic' face my mother would call it. I wonder if that word still counts if this face was around back when it was the norm. It would be like time travelling back to the 80s and calling a cassette 'vintage' wouldn't it?

"This is Lady Annie Dawson." Thomas's smile does turn into a grin then.

"Don't call me that." Annie's hands are in her jacket pockets. Even from here, I can see that they are clearly set into fists.

"I like her." I laugh. My attempt at a connection with my potential saviour is cut humiliatingly short as that laugh turns into a coughing fit. I try and sit up as my chest tightens but Lyra holds me down. Blood dribbles from my mouth after a particularly gross hack. I wipe at it with my hand.

"Sorr-" I cut myself off with a strangled sound as Annie is suddenly sat on my bed and cupping my bloodied hand gently between her own. She leans forward so her nose almost touches the gross pool of my fluids. She takes a gentle sniff.

"Oh." She breaths. She turns her head to look at Thomas. He simply smirks at her in a 'told you so' type of way. It's the smirk he gives Bruce every time I prove the training master wrong and make it more than five steps from my bed.

Lyra lets out a small whimpering sound and I turn my head back to her. She said she volunteered for this shift, which was stupid considering how frightened she was of everything supernatural. I open my mouth to tell her that it's okay, but a different phrase leaves my mouth.

"Put. That. Down." I command the guards. Both of them have their weapons out and have them pointed straight at Annie's head. "If she wanted to kill me, she would have. You're about six seconds too slow."

The guards once again shift. My heart sinks as I think they may not listen to me. I didn't exactly look very princely right now. The one on the right obeys immediately. The guard on the left nods slowly and puts his gun away while his eyes stay focussed on Annie. She winks at him. I press my lips together to stop from smiling.

I lose the urge to smile as she turns those eyes to me. Those deep green eyes that seem almost primitive. Those eyes tell me that she is a murderer, that she has seen things that would make armies of men weep and has come out the other side with a smile on her face. Okay, maybe her eyes don't tell me all of that, but they definitely scare the shit out of me.

"You are a little young to be the alcoholic drug addict I see splattered on the news." Annie smiles at me. A wave of calm runs over me. I feel my face grin goofily back at her as if the jab at my character is hilarious.

"Annie." Thomas warns. "You don't have to do that."

Annie turns away from me and the feeling fades. Oh. Vampire hypnosis. Cool.

"She can do whatever she wants if she's going to save me." I tell Thomas.

"I haven't agreed yet." Annie tells me slowly although she keeps her eyes on Thomas. My friend stares back at her without taking a breath. I am tempted to tell them to get a room. This place has plenty of spares.

"I don't drink or do drugs. Well. My pain meds made me loopy, and we had to come up with an excuse." I tell Annie quickly. I don't know what it will take to make her agree to change me. I don't know if anything will change her mind. I just know that if I don't, then I won't make it to Christmas.

"And those scandalous affairs…hospital trips?" Annie lounges back on my bed as if she owns it. Lyra whimpers again. The vampire lolls her head back to look at her and gives her a reassuring smile. Lyra shoots a weak one back.

"What's your name?" Annie asks her softly.

"L-Lyra." The brunette stutters. "Ma'am."

"Well Lyra. You have no reason to be afraid of me or of my family. We don't hurt innocent girls. Okay?"

While the vampire reassures Lyra, I glance over at Thomas. He set all this up for me. He was the one who promised me that I would be able to run in the sun. I would finally be able to drink and dance at balls. I would only get a few years before a faked 'tragic' death. The line of succession would hold, as by then I would have a younger sibling, and should the supernatural finally overcome us, the line would survive. There was a plan, and I would live. Live and not just survive with tubes running in and out of me.

He isn't looking at me. He is watching Lyra and Annie. The vampire has reached over to take Lyra's hand.

"He's a good person." Lyra blurts out. "Really good."

"He treats you well?" Annie asks. I realise then that this is an interview but it's not for me. Lyra will decide my fate. A quick glance at Annie's hand show me that she isn't feeling for a pulse. She isn't checking for a lie. Does she just know? Is it some extra vampire sense?

"Very well, Ma'am." Lyra nods and then it's as if a dam inside of her breaks. "He's always kind to all of us, even when we are giving him his medicine. He ain't ever yelled at us. He always tries to make us laugh. He looks for the silver lining every single day and he knows Ma'am, he really does know, that he is lucky to be born as he is and he ain't never held it above any of us."

Lyra's chest is quickly moving up and down as if she had run a mile. My heart breaks.

"Lyra." I say softly. I don't know how to finish the sentence, but she shakes her head at me as her eyes water. She focuses those eyes on the immortal blood drinker in front of her.

"Please…Please save him." Lyra begged softly. "This country needs him, Ma'am. Even for a little while. We…We need him. I need him to be okay."

"Lyra." I began again. "Lyra you don't have to-"

"Yes I do." She snaps at me. Her tears finally start to fall but she stays still. Her hands grip at Annie's so tightly I can see them going white. "I want you to live, Ali. Alistair. Your Grace."

"You call me Ali." I tell her. "You can always call me Ali. I mean, you've had to wash me, Lyra. We are well past the title stage." The weak attempt of a joke makes her smile, so I press on. "You are my friend. I may not be yours, which is fine, because let's face it: you have a whole life outside looking after me, but you are mine. So, if this is too much, then you can leave, and I will not blame you. I will still be your friend, even if you tell this vampire you were lying and to rip my throat out."

"You're my friend." Lyra sniffs softly. "I…I would be really honoured to call you my friend, Ali. Now shut your gob and let me beg for your life."

I laugh. It hurts but I laugh.

Annie doesn't breathe. She doesn't move. She is a living statue for thirty seconds before she leans her head down and she gently kisses Lyra's calloused hands.

"Okay, Lyra." Annie agrees. "I'll save your friend."

Chapter Eleven
Lola

The guards refused to speak to me while we were in the car. I tried to get them to. I asked questions and made jokes. I showed them cute dog videos that popped up on my screen as I scrolled through my phone. It was all futile. They didn't even smile.

I had set up a burner account on all major social media sites. There was no identifying features on it. The profile picture was a coffee cup. There were no posts with my face in it. It could be anyone's. Perfect to use to stalk the people from my past.

My ex-boyfriend Zach owns an unsuccessful surfboard company. My frenemy Melissa is part of four MLM schemes. My first crush Jackson is now a doctor. He lives in Ohio with his husband and three kids. It's strange to watch them all slowly age in a way I never will. In a hundred years I may look back on these profiles and compare them to their grandchildren's.

"Okay." The driver said. My head snaps up. "She is good to go."

"I'm going in?" I ask. The guards do not answer me. They just nod at each other and open up the doors. I don't question them again. I don't want to spook them either so I move slowly, showing my hands and smiling with my normal teeth as I exit the truck. I already know that Cleo would not give them the same curtesy.

Cleo and Grace stand staring up at the palace in front of them, their arms entangled with each other's. I move to stand next to them.

Follow Thomas. Annie's voice is like a beacon. We start moving in unison towards the door. All of the guards follow after us. *We have work to do.*

The main doors open for us as if by magic. Thomas stands in the centre of the entrance hall with his hands in his pockets and a relieved look on his face. He wraps his arms over Grace's shoulders and leads us onwards.

"I knew she would do it." Thomas whispers to her proudly. "As soon as she met him. He reminds me of you when you were younger. She was never going to let him die."

Thomas speaks to Grace as if we are not there. For once I feel like me and Cleo are on the same page. We are both the outsiders in this scenario, both permanently young in comparison to them. Cleo drops Grace's arm and scowls as the other girl doesn't even notice. Grace is beaming up at Thomas with her arm looped around his waist as they walk ahead.

I do not like it here. Cleo declares to us all. She is staring daggers at the back of Thomas's head. Grace turns back to look at us – at Cleo – and sighs.

Cleo, please. Grace begs. *This place is gorgeous. Annie is going to save someone. This is a good thing.*

If you two are going to bicker, Annie interrupts, *could you at least do it verbally and in private? We are about to have a very important meeting.*

Sorry. Grace apologises immediately. Cleo simply huffs.

"This place really is pretty." I say conversationally as we end up down a corridor with solid oak flooring. Cleo glares at me.

"This is one of the older wings. It's mostly studies and meeting rooms." Thomas tells me with a smile. I have known him barely twenty-four hours, but it seems to be his natural reaction to most things.

"We are going into the meeting now?" Cleo's accent is back to being thick. I understand how she uses it as a shield most times, but with Thomas it feels a little too late.

"Why do you think I told you all to look nice?" Thomas's arm drops from Grace's shoulders as we move towards a thick silver door with a digital keypad next to it. Every other door was wooden with a classic handle. This…This was a panic room. A vampire-proof safe haven.

Thomas stops us so quickly that my shoulder bangs into Cleo. The girl recoils away from me and into Grace's side.

You must bow when he walks in. You call him Your Highness. Annie is the only one he wants to hear speak. I will be the mediator and whatever you think, I am *on your side. You all need to watch yourselves and trust me. Okay?*

Okay. Grace is the first to respond.

We have no other choice. Cleo responds dryly.

I trust you. I add on quickly.

I love you all. Annie's response almost breaks my heart.

Even me? Thomas' response is so soft and so private that it seems wrong for it to echo in all of our heads.

Shut up Thomas. Annie snaps half-heartedly.

Chapter Twelve

Annie

The King struts into the room in a well-tailored suit. His wife is at his side in a blue dress that was so dark it may as well have been black. I expected them to be wearing their crowns, to have shoved large rings embedded with jewels onto their fingers.

Instead, the Queen consort is plain-faced with her blonde hair scraped back from her face. It is held in place by bobby pins. Her eyes are red and puffy as if she has been crying. She settles into the seat opposite me and splays her hands on the table. I tilt myself back slightly as some of that near-constant blazing anger in my stomach sputters. I can be angry at her husband and his ancestors, but I cannot be angry at an upset mother of a dying child.

The room is clearly meant to be anti-vampire. Silver lines the walls and the door is made of it. There is a large ornate cross hanging from the wall above the three large water coolers, most likely filled with holy water. Directly above the long wooden table is a skylight. Silver, crosses, wood, sunlight, and holy water. It must make them feel better since only two of those things can harm the vampires in this room.

"You saw him." The Queen consort's voice cracks slightly.

"Emily." The King stands behind her and places his hands on her shoulders. I press my lips together to stop from snarling. He is tall with thick brown hair and a short beard. He is an average weight. He is nothing special, not really. He exudes self-importance which I begrudgingly accept as he is yet to drive this country to war, but he wasn't alive to fix the last one either.

His wife is beautiful. Alistair looks more like her than his father. Her hair is honey blonde and her eyes so wide and so blue that they remind me of a child's. She is ten years younger than him and so much thinner. A single tap of my finger may just break her. But those wide eyes show her for what she really is.

She is a survivor just like me, Grace, Cleo, and Lola. She is surviving the slow death of her child. She is fighting to keep him alive in any way she can. I can respect that. I can almost like it.

My girls are at the far end of the table, and they did as Thomas had asked. They had all showed respect to the King as they entered. Lola had bowed lowly, Grace had curtseyed, and Cleo had ducked her head. I had done nothing until now, when I slowly bowed my head at the Queen and the Queen only.

"You said you would save him." Queen Emily voice evens out. She takes a deep breath as she looks me in the eye.

"I did." I keep the eye contact.

"Did you mean it?"

"I did. As long as I get what I was promised." The phrase feels dirty coming out of my mouth, but I could not turn soft now. I could not throw Teddy away. I could not let the opportunity to know why we are daywalkers slip past me.

"You will." The Queen tells me.

"Those terms are what we are here to discuss." The King interjected far too late. I do not even glance at him. I keep my eyes on Emily.

"The terms are simple." I whisper. "I get my information. Your son gets eternal life."

"Thomas said that you wanted information on someone. You can-" Queen Emily began.

"Once Alistair is turned and trained, you can have any information you need." The King interrupted. My lips twitch but I still do not look at him.

"Training a newborn vampire is hard work." I tell Emily gently to try and soften the blow of what I'm about to say. "He will go insane trying to fight his urges. He will fail a few times. It could be years before he is ready to be in a room with you without someone there that can stop him."

"I will pay you anything. I will give you and your coven anything." The Queen pleaded.

"Within reason." The King added.

"No." The Queen turned to look at her husband and shook her head. "*Anything,* Gerald."

"Emily we talked about this before we came in here-"

"Do you honestly think she does not know how desperate we are?" Emily laughed without humour. "That she does not understand I would carve my own heart out and offer it to her on a silver platter just to have her think about saving Alistair? We have no high ground here. It is stupid to pretend we do."

I finally turn my eyes to King Gerald. The complete despair and humiliation on his face does not make me as happy as I thought it would. He is not a two-dimensional direct descendant of the vilest man I have ever met. He is a king that came here without his crown, a father grasping at supernatural straws.

"My family are free to come and go as they please." I begin to list my demands. "I will stay as long as needed until Ali has recovered and in control enough to live alone."

"Annie." Grace gasps but I don't dare to look at her.

"I get all the information I requested as soon as I turn Ali. I am not to be a prisoner here. I am not to stay under lock and key." I turn back to the Queen. "And you both need to understand that if anything happens to my family, to Thomas, or to me while this agreement is in place, then I will burn this whole place down to the ground."

The Queen does not hesitate to agree.

Chapter Thirteen

Grace

She cannot expect us to leave her. I stare up the table at my closest friend as I stop breathing. My throat tightens and tears start to prickle in the back of my eyes. I have to stop myself from gripping at the table and ripping it in half. I am expected to stay silent, as are Cleo and Lola. Annie is sat there, deciding her fate, and that was fine until she decided she would be a martyr and stay behind at the royals' mercy.

Wherever I go, you will always be by my side. That is what she had promised me in that brothel centuries ago, and yet now here she was, making this deal, all for a human boy. I go to open my mouth to argue but my jaw will not budge. It feels as if an invisible grip is keeping it shut. I hiss through my nose.

Don't fight it. Thomas tells me.

She is going to regret this. I know that Cleo would be jumping to my defence if she could hear this. Which means Thomas has made this a private conversation. That was probably for his own sake.

She is doing very well. Thomas argues.

She is offering too much. They haven't even said they know anything.

It is not the King who will be telling her about Teddy. My coven will.

That revelation rolls through me. I turn to look at him but as always, Thomas is looking at her. Thomas knows where Teddy is. Thomas knows why we are what we are and he never told her. Never told me. The thick silver walls around us suddenly feel like they were closing in on us. This is a trap a trap a trap.

I grip Cleo's hand so tightly that I feel her fingers snap. Annie glances over at me.

We should go. I beg her softly.

You can. Annie responds even as her mouth says something completely different to the King. They are getting down to the gritty details now. Annie is smart: she won't let there be a loophole that would trap her here. I tell myself that over and over as I refuse to leave. Cleo starts to flex her fingers, which are in my grip. They had healed quickly. Everyone except Annie went hunting this morning. She wouldn't leave Thomas alone in the house.

Cleo gives our hands a subtle shift towards the door. She will lead me out of here if I give her the signal. She wouldn't care about it being rude. She would claw through the silver to make me comfortable. I know that. But I refuse to move.

It will be an argument later. It will be the same argument we have every five years. The argument where we go in cycles trying to avoid the truth that we both know- that I will never leave Annie. I will not leave her here. I will not leave her when we end up home. I will not leave her even when the earth beneath our feet starts to crumble and the oceans start to bubble.

My eyes move to focus on King Gerald of the United Kingdom, first of his name, protector of all that live under his flag. I had never met his ancestors. I was too lowborn and the brothel I grew up in not popular enough with nobility. I had only seen their portraits and then on the television when that was invented. I couldn't tell if Gerald looked anything like them.

Annie had hired a painter to draw a portrait of me for my fifteenth birthday. I don't think it looked anything like me. The one she commissioned for my fiftieth birthday was much better. By then, I had finished growing up, emotionally and physically. My face then matched the idea of the adult women I was being treated as by the time that first portrait was commissioned.

The trauma and the starvation had made sure of that. They had made sure that when Annie was forced to turn me or lose me, I was a stick figure with hollowed cheeks and cracked lips. The process of the turning had made my skin and hair look healthier. A predator plus point, as Lola calls them. I would never put on weight, but I would always look alluring. It was something to do with the chemicals that we exude.

The royal couple in front of me were naturally gorgeous, the king in a gruff masculine way. If he changed from his suit into a red plaid shirt and a beanie, then I wouldn't even blink twice at him. His arms were as thick as trees. When he was older, that muscle would all turn to fat, but for now he was probably working out constantly to maintain it. As the king, he could probably run on a treadmill and have a servant read out his important papers to him.

The Queen (or Queen Consort as Annie would insist on calling her) was youthfully pretty. She was not as pretty as Cleo. Her skin is as pale as milk making the pink blush on her cheeks even more prominent. She was like a grown-up porcelain doll, a real-life English rose. Even her voice was perfect. She was from Oxford, if I remembered correctly. The newspapers had gone near feral as their at-the-time future king started to court the daughter of knighted actor Sir Avery Reynolds.

Annie finished speaking. I tried to zone back in, but I was so lost in my spiralling thoughts that I had no idea what point in the negotiations we were in. The King stands from his chair abruptly. Thomas ducks his head. I follow his lead. When I looked back up after hearing no footsteps, I see the Queen holding Annie's hands in her own. The Queen of the United Kingdom kisses Annie's hands and rests her chin upon them.

"Thank you." She whispers to Annie. "Thank you."

"You do not need to thank me, Emily." Annie responds. I feel as well as see the King stiffen at the lack of title. The Queen simply smiles.

"Yes, I do. I will spend the rest of my life thanking you because I will get to spend the rest of my life with my son. That is a gift I can never repay."

"I will go see Alistair in the morning. Explain to him the risks and the life he will need to lead." I know Annie well enough to hear the next part before she says it. "But this is his choice. I will not force this on him."

"My son wants to live." The Queen places Annie's hands back on the table as if they are made of glass. As if she could ever hurt her. "He hasn't ever truly lived."

That is when I know that Annie will not be leaving this place. I don't think that she knows it or even if Thomas knows it, but Annie is drawn to broken people in a way I have never seen in anyone else. She adopts us and revives us in every possible way. The prince will be no exception.

"When do we meet him?" I interrupt the sweet moment. Annie and the Queen both look at me in unison but neither answer. The King simply scoffs as if this was a stupid question.

"When?" I press for an answer.

"In the morning with Annie." Thomas answers for them. "He is sedated now. He needs his rest."

"What…What exactly is he dying from?" Lola's voice shakes like a child's. Her eyes are focussed on the table as her head is still ducked.

"A very rare combination of a blood and bone disease. I've only ever seen it in two bloodlines." Annie almost seems to find it funny. Her lip curls into a soft smile. "King Henry had it. He passed it onto one of his bastard sons. It never manifested in either of his daughters. I never thought that Margaret may have been a carrier. It seemed like the men were more susceptible."

"A royal disease." Cleo hums from beside me.

"No. Not quite. I said two bloodlines." Annie corrects her gently. The smile on her face starts to worry me. It isn't genuine but it isn't fake either. It's a twisted sort of in-between as if the universe were forcing it upon her. She looks right past me and focuses on Cleo. For the first time in a long time, that bothers me. I want to scream at her to look at me, to tell me what she is about to tell all of us at once. I want her to confide in me first.

"Which one of them?" The King demands as if we are not even here. Annie does not answer. Her smirk just grows and she shakes her head. "I am your King. You answer me when I speak to you." He stands over Annie. He thinks that because she was soft with his wife that she will be soft with him. He is terribly wrong.

I blink and Annie has him pinned to the wall by his throat. Her fangs are out and so close to his face that for a second I think she is kissing his cheek. I hear a gasp leave the King's mouth. She moved him so quickly that a breath had caught in his throat.

"I do not recognise you as my king." Annie cooed at him, as softly as if she were telling a child a bedtime story. "I stopped recognising your bloodline when it cut off my friend's head so it could use the promise of a throne to screw other women. I am not here to serve my country. I am here to get what I want. Nod if you understand me, Gerald."

The King's nostrils flared. He was putting on a brave face, but his heart was beating loud and hard. He's scared.

"Annie." Thomas's voice booms through the room. I hold my breath as my best friend pretends not to have heard him. Cleo's nails dig into my hand. Her eyes were narrowed at the Queen, who is watching Annie and her husband with her heart only slightly erratic. I get the sick sense that she would let Annie rip out her husband's throat as long as she still saved her son afterwards.

"Nod." Annie flexed her fingers around his throat, a reminder that a slight twitch from her would have him dead in a half second. "If you understand."

"For God's sake, Gerald, just nod." The Queen hissed. The King had enough pride in him to sneer as he followed the command. The Queen slumped in her chair as Annie let the King go. Cleo snickers as The King almost slides down the wall.

"If you wouldn't mind, Thomas." Annie lolls her head to look at him. "I think you should show us our rooms now."

Thomas stares at the King, who is quickly righting himself and moving to stand behind his wife's chair. His large hands settled on her shoulders. A smarter move than before, but still not smart. Any one of us could be across the room in a second, our teeth in his jugular and the Queen unscathed if we wanted.

"Go, Thomas." The Queen places her hand on top of her husbands. "We will see you in the morning."

"Your highness." Thomas bowed in their general direction before quickly heading from the room. Lola follows at his heels. Cleo and I move in a flash, ending up in the corridor well ahead of Thomas. We turn to look at them.

Annie has her arm wrapped reassuringly around Lola. Lola shoots her a shaky smile as the silver door slides shuts behind them. Thomas storms right past them and right past us with a face like thunder. We have no choice but to follow.

Chapter Fourteen

Annie

Thomas doesn't speak to me until we are alone. He takes Lola to her room first and she heads in without a word. Cleo and Grace have their own set of rooms two floors down. Grace says a curt goodnight before shutting the door in my face. I try not to take that personally. It was a big day.

"You have been alive half a millennium and you still cannot control your temper." Thomas faces straight ahead as he chastises me. He is heading towards another flight of stairs. A pathetic attempt to keep us all separated. I would almost be worried about that if I hadn't seen how clearly we are underestimated here.

"Do not try and goad me Thomas. I will not apologise." I drawl. I shove my hands in my pockets as I follow him upwards. He scoffs but says nothing else for six flights of stairs.

He opens my door for me, throwing it wide to reveal a king-size bed with plush blankets and a pyramid of pillows all decorated in a deep red. Everything in here is made of a dark polished oak. On the footstall at the end of the bed is a large gift basket. It is full of blood bags and dog-shaped shortbread. I cannot stop the laugh that bursts out of my throat. I am still grinning as I turn to look at him.

"You are only half Scottish." I accuse him mockingly.

"And that stops you liking shortbread?" He leans against the doorframe. I mirror him, resting my back against it. We stare at each other for a moment with the anger all gone, wiped away by my laugh.

"That's a lot of shortbread." I whisper. I can hear human heartbeats in the other rooms down this hall. There is no point disturbing them. Dawn was still hours away.

"Wishful thinking." Thomas slowly blinks at me. This feels too familiar. This feels like back when I was human, and we would lock eyes across a feast. Back then, I would duck my head with a soft smile and look back up at him a second later. More often than not, he would be looking back at me. Then he smirks and that mood is broken.

"This is the part where you offer me some shortbread." He stage-whispers, leaning forward so he is halfway across the door. I lean forward to meet him. Our faces are only centimetres apart. His breath smells like stale peppermint.

"This is the part where you tell me what I want to know." I stage-whisper back.

"Racing right ahead." Thomas sighs.

"I meant it, Tommy. I am not here because I'm a good and loyal subject. I'm here because I want to be a good sister."

"You are a good sister, Annie." Thomas sighs again but this time it's more irritated. "But that doesn't start or end with Edward."

"I left him behind. I spent the first fifteen years of my immortal life hiding in a brothel in London. I didn't look for him until it was too late." I snap back.

"He was in France. He left *you* to go and try his luck in France." Thomas pulls away from me and looks into the room. "Maybe I should have asked them to put a pedestal in there for when you find him."

"You are not funny." I whisper. "That was not funny."

"But what you did in that meeting was? He could have ordered you dead right then and there and I...I would have had to have done it."

"You would not kill me, Thomas." I know that in my very soul. He did not kill me back in 1914, and he would not have killed me today. His eyes meet mine. In this light they are such a dark grey they are almost black.

"No." He agrees. "I wouldn't have. But I would have killed today."

I don't respond, at least not verbally. I reach out for his hand and entangle our fingers. He is so warm to my touch, I am tempted to check him for a fever. He goes still and stares down at our fingers.

"Would you like to come in for some shortbread, Tommy?" I ask the question even as I am gently moving us into the room.

"That sounds like a euphemism." Thomas mutters as he shuts the door behind him.

"You aren't that lucky." I lie even as I continue walking backwards.

"Here I was thinking we would make it a centennial event." Thomas takes my other hand in his. I gently detangle our fingers and press our palms together.

"I don't remember your hands being so much bigger than mine." I sigh playfully. "Weird, considering how easily I could break them."

"I'm very scared." Thomas plays along. "Terrified, really."

"You should be." I drop my hands. They fall uselessly down to my sides. "You've just invited four day-walking vampires into the heart of Britain."

"I should be." Thomas nods. "I would be if I hadn't invited a day-walking vampire into my heart a very long time ago." He pulls me towards him, wrapping his arms around my waist. It doesn't cross my mind to resist. I have agreed to stay here for the foreseeable future. Why couldn't that foreseeable future finally be the one where I had Thomas?

"I have missed you." I breathe into his chest.

"You missed me because you ran." Thomas nuzzles his face into the top of my head. I hear his heartbeat speed up as he takes in a deep breath of me. "I understand why you did…but please, Annie. Please never run from me again."

"Don't ask me to make a promise you know I can't keep."

"I'm not asking you not to run. I'm asking you not to run from me."

We stand still for a moment and then because I am what I am, I have to break that silence once again. "But that's one of my favourite hobbies. I've spent 487 years doing it. I'm relatively good at it, you know."

"I do." Thomas's chest rumbles as he chuckles. "Although you've slipped up once or twice."

"Once." I correct him.

"I was talking about all the gifts from me that you accept. But if we are talking about all the times you've slipped into my bed, then you're right. It's once."

I move my chin to rest against his chest and stare up at him. He pulls his neck back to meet my eyes. It would be an unflattering angle for anyone else, but Thomas is as breathtakingly beautiful as ever.

"Hardened criminals for me to gnaw on are gifts, are they?"

"Would you have preferred sticks of rock?" Thomas decides to move us. He lifts me and I wrap my legs around him. He walks slowly towards the bed.

"Yes, actually." I say pettily. "At least they come in different flavours."

"Oh, I am sorry." Thomas purrs against my neck. He places a taunting kiss on where my pulse used to be before throwing me off of him. I bounce on the mattress. It's almost too soft and definitely top of the range. "Next time I'll send you a strawberry-flavoured serial killer."

"Very thoughtful of you." I lounge backwards so I am resting on my elbows. "Now come here. I've almost forgotten what you taste like."

"Tempting." Thomas looks down at me with hungry eyes. His lips have a ghost of a smirk on them. He clicks his teeth before turning on his heel and walking to the door.

"Wh-Where are you going?" I stare at him in disbelief.

"I have shortbread in my own room." He shoots me a wicked grin over his shoulder. "Goodnight Annie. Try not to dream of me."

The door shuts a single second before the pillow hits it. I hear his chuckle and his heartbeat as he retreats down the hall.

Chapter Fifteen

Lola

Annie looks pissed. She looks even more pissed than Cleo, which is strange because no one ever looks more pissed than Cleo. Her hair is pulled back into a messy bun, and she gulps down a full mug of coffee.

"We are going to be late." Grace tells us all softly. She is wearing another dress but the rest of us have taken Annie's lead from yesterday and gone with casual trousers and shirts. I feel like I am pushing that boundary, considering my 'trousers' are yoga pants.

"So?" Cleo pouts at her as she stares out of the window. The gardens here were beautiful with all sorts of vibrant flowers growing in them. I had a great view from my bedroom window and the room was so far away from the others that my ears were mercifully saved from Grace's whimpering moans. I had only realised the downside when I woke up and had no idea where to go to meet them. Not that it mattered as the three of them had strolled into my room barely ten minutes later.

"He is still getting ready." Annie nips that argument in the bud. She turns the page in her book without a glance at us. I try to focus but I have no idea how she knows that as I can't hear anything out of the ordinary. The palace is full of the usual background babble of heartbeats, breathing and clumsiness. There was a maid humming to herself as she cleans a room down the hall. Someone in another room was showering.

"Thomas will let me know when it's time to go." Annie told us all. The next page flip felt passive-aggressive.

"Was he really angry with you?" Grace asks sympathetically.

"No." Annie's fingers trail over the page as if she was actually reading it. She isn't. Her eyes are glazing over the pages. Her nails have held up nicely. I always end up chipping mine as soon as they are dry, but Annie's tiny little flames look exactly like they did when I was applying the topcoat.

"Oh please." Cleo drawls sarcastically. "Stop giving us so many details."

"When my private conversations with Thomas become vital to your survival, I will give you all the details you want." Annie sounds almost bored.

"I doubt your sex life will ever be vital to my survival." Cleo scoffs. My mouth drops open. I go to snap at her not to talk to Annie that way, not to be so vulgar about it when we all know how much Annie needed someone to love like that. Then I see Annie shoot Cleo a filthy grin. I realise then that she must speak to us all so differently in private and that there would always be so much history that I have missed. I would never catch up even if we outlasted the universe.

How depressing.

"So there was sex?" I interrupt and then internally die. Annie shoots me a small smile. I hope I am overthinking the pity in it.

"Did you all have nothing better to do last night than think up questions to ask me about my sex life?" Annie shakes her head at us all.

"Of course we did. Some of us had sex." Cleo smirks. Grace tuts at her from her place by the empty fireplace. One day I would be brave enough to ask her why she always moved to sit near one. It would probably just be something simple like she grew up before thermostats were a thing but it could also be a nice bonding moment. I could tell her all about how my father always needed it to be 63 degrees no matter the season. She would at least pretend to be interested in the fact.

"I knew that's all girls talked about when they are together." Thomas's voice cuts through the room. Me and Cleo spin on our heels and stare at him with wide eyes. We didn't hear him or the five people of various ages behind him approach. They had no heartbeats. Except I know that Thomas has one because I have heard in over the last two days. They are masking them.

"I hate it when you do that." Annie sighs. She doesn't look up at any of us. She aggressively turns another page. "Is the big bad cursed coven coming to give me a list of rules I won't follow?"

"You will not be allowed near the crown prince without agreeing to them." The man's voice is like gravel. I take a good look at all of them.

The man that spoke looks to be in his sixties, with deep lines cutting through his face. His eyes are the exact same as Thomas's eyes, so grey that it is almost as if they have been leeched of their colour. They all have those eyes and they are all in matching black tunics, like this is some low-budget fantasy movie.

Well. I suppose it's more fantasy horror if I'm here. Is that a genre? It's been so long since I have watched anything but medical dramas and soaps that I'm not even sure.

The coven has three men and three women. The final man is in his late twenties at a complete push. His hair is a near unnatural bright blonde, almost pure white. Behind him, hiding or being hidden, was a preteen girl. Her black hair was up in pigtails. She looked like a mini female Thomas. They had the same nose, ears, and lips. A sister, maybe?

The two other girls were clearly twins. Their skin was as dark and as flawless as ebony. Their hair was set into identical braided ponytails. Their faces were indifferent but the one on the left's eyes are focussed on Grace rather than Annie.

"Hello, you." Annie's voice turns playful as she now leans forward and peers around the blonde boy. That wicked grin is back as she stares at the girl. "Not still mad at me, are you?"

"Yes." The girl says sullenly, but a smile plays on her lips.

"It was an honest mistake."

The girl scoffs and crosses her arms. Annie opens up her own in a gesture for a hug and the girl laughs before bolting over and hugging her tightly.

"You are still the best hugger in the family." Annie holds the girl tightly to her. The girl's laugh is muffled against her collarbone. It's harsh and loud, the opposite of what I would expect from such a small petite thing.

"I'll pretend to be insulted later." Thomas watches the two with a soft smile on his face. He doesn't blink. I'm thankful that they are using some kind of magic to cover their heartbeats. I don't want the moment ruined by the embarrassment of us all overhearing.

"I'll be genuinely insulted." The blonde boy purrs as he sticks his hands into his trouser pockets. They are all British, which makes sense, although the witches had a different lilt to them. Scottish, I think Annie said. They were all friends (if that's the right word) with Annie before she turned. They would have lived nearby.

"Go ahead, Elias. I never cared for your feelings anyway." Annie and the girl separate. She may be older than I initially thought, more mid-teens than pre-teens, but that could be because I know she's really centuries old.

"It is good to see you again, Lady Annie." The ebony-skinned beauty on the left says. "But William is right. We do need to cover the ground rules."

"You think I would be stupid enough to drain him instead of turn him, Corsi? Now *I'm* genuinely offended." Annie finally puts the book down. Corsi shoots an unsubtle look in my direction.

"Lola," Annie says bluntly, "has adjusted incredibly well."

"She is still an infant." The other beauty states. I can't help but be a little irritated by that. I would be in my forties by now- and they are hanging round with a permanent child!

"She is going in that room, Mary. They all are." Annie stared the girl right in the eyes. I would have backed down, but Mary raised a delicate eyebrow as if to dare my maker to try.

"There are things we have to consider Annie." The old man's voice is softer now.

"This is not one of those things, William." Annie responded in a mocking mimic of it. "My girls go with me. They meet him. They will be linked to him-"

"That is another thing." William interrupts her. Anger at the rudeness shoots through my veins. Annie was the one that was asked here to save their prince. We had the meeting last night where the terms were laid out. There could be no contract because there could be no written confirmation that we were turning the crown prince of Britain into a vampire. That did not give them the right to suddenly change the deal now.

"No. It isn't." I hear my own voice snap. The blond witch jolts and looks at me as if he wasn't aware I could talk. That anger burns brighter. "The terms were laid out last night. That's the end of it."

"You do not speak for her." William says dismissively.

"Oh, she does now." Annie leans back in her chair with a grin on her face. "She's right. If you wanted to throw a spanner in the works, you should have done it before I promised the queen consort I would save her son. Take the win, Wills."

William's jaw clenches at the nickname. I fight back a smile.

"Once you have turned him." Thomas takes the lead and tries to steer the conversation back to getting what he wants. "You need to break the maker's bond."

Annie laughs harshly twice and as she stares him straight in his face. The smile slips off of mine as we all realise he is serious.

"You can't." I shake my head. "A newborn vampire without a maker's bond? You are asking for a massacre. He could kill everyone in this place and then get out onto the streets. London would be swimming in red."

"For once, she is not being dramatic." Cleo comes to my defence...I think. "That is a stupid idea thought up by clearly stupid men."

"Told you." The teenage girl who has still not been introduced turns to William with a wicked grin. "Not everyone can be Annie."

I latch onto that piece of information, that link between them. Annie had told me that the last human memory she had was her attack and that she wished it had been something nicer. She had woken up afterwards in the back room of a Tudor brothel house with no maker's bond and no idea who had saved her. She said she never wanted to know. This little girl must know that and so Thomas must know that.

Annie winks at her before turning her steely gaze to the three witch boys. "Once he is trained. Once I know he will not rip out Lyra's throat the second she gets within a mile of him. Then I will think about getting rid of the maker's bond."

"You know we need more than 'think' Annie." Thomas gestures for the teenager to come back over to him. The girl smirks at him and doesn't move. Definitely related.

"You can't have more than think." Annie sighs. "You either have a day-walking prince who is guided into avoiding mass murder every time he is peckish via the nurturing nature of a maker's bond, or you have a night-time vampire who has to be locked into a silver box and can never go in public, but he has no maker's bond. It's not your choice. It's his. I know which one he will pick."

"Well, when you put it like that." Elias rolls his eyes. "This whole meeting was a waste of time. The prince isn't getting any better while we bicker."

"You are the ones that came to bicker. I just wanted breakfast." Annie put her hands up in a mock surrender before swiping at the large plate of croissants laid out on a silver tray. Cleo had scoffed all of the pan au chocolate and then complained they weren't as good as ones from Paris. I had no idea how the servants knew to bring enough for all four of us. They had almost run from the room after putting the tray down.

"Aren't you about to eat?" Elias smirked. Annie shot him the middle finger as her teeth ripped away a section of the pastry.

"Attractive." Thomas smirked. "Can we go, now you've had your little breakfast?"

"Your friend can have a few more heartbeats while I finish my tea. Would you like a croissant, Christiana?" Annie brought a delicate china teacup to her lips and stared at him as she sipped. It felt like we were all invading on some private bickering moment between the two. I have never wanted to leave a room to go and watch someone die more than I did right now.

The young girl looked up at Thomas with wide eyes and she reached over for a croissant. Thomas sighed, William tutted, Elias smirked. The two other girls smiled. They clearly all doted on her. She was their Grace, I realise with a jolt. I wonder which one of them was their version of me.

I drag my eyes away from her and look around my room again. It's all thick carpets and blankets in deep red colours. The furniture is all dark polished oak. It was exactly what I would have thought a room in a British royal palace would look like. I knew I had been wrong about a lot of British culture before, so I was quite pleased with myself about that one.

Normally Cleo would be using our group telepathy to judge everyone without them hearing. Since we knew that Thomas could hear us, there was no reason to think the others in the coven couldn't. Smart, although I miss those extra voices in my head. I want to know if Cleo noticed the resemblances between them, I want Grace to delicately add information only she knows and do a beautiful job of acting as if she had only just remembered.

"Okay." Annie pushes herself to her feet and wraps her arm around Christiana's shoulders. The girl beams. "Let's go."

Chapter Sixteen

Grace

Christiana looks so big now, even though I know it's only in my head. The girl has forever been frozen two days before her sixteenth birthday. She will never get taller, and she will never fully mature. She fits underneath Annie's arm the exact same way she always had, so why did the sight of her send a pang through my heart now?

Elias is as cocky and easy to smile as ever, William just as gruff. Corsi and Mary do not look at me. A pang shoots through my heart again. The witches flank us as we walk down the halls. William and Thomas follow closely at Christiana and Annie's heels, ever the doting father and brother.

Lola follows after them. Elias slides into the space beside her to introduce himself. He makes it look natural and less of a strategy. Corsi and Mary follow behind me and Cleo.

It might be subtle if we hadn't all been through what we had been through. We all knew what it was like to be herded into one direction, either from personal experience like Cleo or from stalking those who did it when we were hungry. I reach out and take my girlfriend's hand in mine. Her fingers twitch, but then her hand goes limp in mine. She is staring a hole in the back of Elias's head.

I fight back a smile. Cleo will swat at Lola and judge every breath that left her lungs, but when there was a genuine threat near her, she would not be distracted from glaring at it. If Elias made so much as a passive-aggressive twitch in Lola's direction, then he would lose his throat for it. Maybe then Lola would realise that Cleo does in fact care about her.

I can hear the prince's heartbeat now. It's so much weaker than the other ones in this part of the palace. There are three other heartbeats in the room. Two of them were average while the other one was elevated. Maybe his mother? Surely she would want to be there for this. Although it would be a terrible idea. My own mother had never looked at me the same after seeing Annie change me. I swallow the lump in my throat. I don't want to have to manhandle the Queen out of the room.

That worry is gone as soon as Christiana opens the door. Neither the King or Queen are here. The prince is lying in bed, looking three breaths away from death with no family- no blood relation, rather- by his side. The closest person to him was the guard, clearly holding a silver dagger. My heart cracks a little.

The prince has inherited his mother's looks, even in the state he is in. His hair is stringy and stuck to his head from cold sweat, shades darker than it would be when dry. His skin is almost blue, and his body is gently shivering. Each breath looked like it took all of his strength. Despite all that he turned to look at us with alert green eyes. He looked at each of us in turn. His eyes quickly moved from Cleo back to Lola. His lips cracked as he smiled.

"Hi." He croaks.

Astounding. Cleo snorts. *Even on his deathbed.*

Be nice. I sigh with my eyes still locked onto him. *He looks so small.*

He's nineteen. Thomas interrupts us. His eyes are locked onto Annie as she moves away from Christiana and settles herself on the end of the prince's bed.

Nineteen forever. There are worse things to be. Lola's face is stuck in a smile.

Put it back in your pants, Lola. Cleo said bluntly. *You're old enough to be his mother.*

And what does that make Grace to you? Lola's response is uncharacteristically harsh. I press my lips together to stop from smiling.

Shut up. All of you. Annie snarls. *Or I will take William's advice and kick you all out of here.*

That's my girl. Thomas coos.

Shut up, Thomas.

"What?" The prince asks. "Something wrong?"

My heart breaks again at the panic in his voice. He thinks this final chance has been snatched away from him.

"No." I tell him with a wide smile. I place my hand over my heart and bow my head. "It is nice to meet you, Your Highness. I'm Grace."

"Cleo." Cleo introduces herself after I give her hand a squeeze. The prince smiles at us. He blinks and struggles to open his eyes again. I almost yell at Annie to turn him already. When his eyes do open they are focussed on Lola.

"I'm Lola." She smiles. She hesitates for a second before awkwardly bowing. "Your Grace."

The Prince goes to speak but only a cough comes out. The servant girl hidden away behind the guard rushes to him to help him sit up.

"Hello, Lyra." Annie greets softly. "I thought your shift would have finished by now. You can't have slept."

"I wanna stay." Lyra insists as the prince finally catches his breath and leans back against his pillows. I open my mouth to argue, but Annie beats me to it.

"It is a hard thing to witness." Annie warns. "It's painful. It will look like I'm killing him. I *will* be killing him. This needs to go perfectly, and I can't risk-"

"His parents aren't here- their majesties. They aren't here." Lyra quickly amended her sentence and her face turned red. "If ya gonna kill him, then he can't be alone."

"Lyra." The prince rasped. "If it's not safe for you-"

"She would be safe." Lola tells them quickly. Annie snaps her head to look at her. "I could hold her…well, not back, but I could keep her safe. In case he needs her."

"Deal." Lyra says quickly. Her heartbeat gives her fear away.

"Lyra, no." Prince Alistair wheezes. "Go home. We talked about this. When I'm okay…Thomas will come get you."

"You can't be alone." Lyra says fiercely. Her hand slides down to hold his.

"He won't be." Annie reaches over to cover both Lyra and Alistair's hands. "Thomas will be here every step of the way. I promise."

Lyra takes an angry breath before her head snaps up. Her face is set in a scowl as she stares at the cursed coven. She doesn't even flinch. Brave girl. "Promise me." Lyra grounds out as she looks at Thomas.

"I promise."

Lyra releases a shaky breath and nods to herself. She is still nodding as she walks straight past us all out of the door. She didn't look at any of us as she passes. Half of me wants to follow her and give her a hug. The other half reminds me that would only scare her worse.

"So," Annie turns back to the prince. I hold my breath as a familiar speech begins. "This is going to hurt. I'm not going to lie to you about that. My bite is going to hurt. You are going to be out of it once I start to drink. You will feel woozy and nauseous-"

"No change there, then." Prince Alistair tries to smile. I let out a soft amused noise. He turns that smile to me. A few weeks helping him may not be too terrible. He is a lot more frail then I had imagined he would be. Maybe that had taken away the arrogance princes stereotypically exuded. People did tend to change when they stared death in the eye. Usually too late.

"When you wake up, you may not remember this next part clearly. That's normal. I will be here waiting for you." Annie continued. With Cleo, that had been where the speech ended. Annie had rushed to bite her and replace that blood with her own. Lola had it all whispered to her during her medical coma.

"We will be linked. All of us." Annie says it almost as a warning. I notice the prince's eyes flicker over to Lola once again. "It takes a while to get used to it all. Your thoughts may not be your own. You will want to rip the throat out of anything with a pulse every time you are slightly hungry. You will move too fast and break things you touch."

Annie pauses before adding, "If any of that sounds worse than what you will live with for the next few months- and in complete honesty I don't think you will live that long- tell me now."

"I thought you would ask if I had any questions." Alistair rests his head back against his pillow. A look of pain crosses his face as he swallows a lump in his throat. He would not last the next few months.

"We can get to those when you are able to hold your own head up. But I will take that as the go ahead." Annie runs her fingers down his arm. He shivers delicately as they find his pulse. Annie brings his wrist to her lips. I close my eyes as Alistair lets out a scream.

Chapter Seventeen

Annie

His blood was disgusting. It was like sludge running through his veins, far too thick and far too grainy. He would have been dead in hours. As I choke it down, I wonder if Thomas knew, if that was why he had come himself rather than try sending a gift or even an official summons. He knew he did not have the time to spare.

The boy must have been in agony for most of his life, only getting worse as his body grew and his heart fought harder to push this poor attempt at blood around him. It was a miracle he had made it to adulthood. I can only think that magic helped that along. It would be typical William to force a boy through that agony just to make sure nothing like what happened to Chrissie would happen to him. I can't bring myself to hate him for that. I can still hate him for everything else.

After one more painful swallow, I pull back. Alistair has collapsed into his pillows, eyes closed and chest barely moving. I swallow back the vomit rising in my throat, force the blood back down. I nearly fail. My body is screaming that this was wrong wrong wrong. I bring my wrist to my mouth and rip it open with my fangs. The blood the flows like a river out of my wound. I press it to Alistair's mouth and force his mouth open.

The blood stays in his mouth, pooling in it as if it had nowhere to go. "Drink." I snarl. When Alistair still makes no move to finish the transition, I add on, "For Lyra. For your mother. Drink for them."

It works. His throat gives a pathetic attempt at a swallow, but it works enough for me to know the rest will be easy. Alistair is just like Grace. He is motivated by loved ones and that, I can work with. That, I can train. It is much better than the alternative. I didn't want to have to explain to Thomas that I beat his friend's arrogance out of him.

The more that trickles down his throat, the more eager he is to drink. My blood has an almost drug-like effect. It has to. Every species has an instinct for reproduction and while no vampire will ever carry a child, we can make people eager to be one of us. One sip of blood and it drives a human into a frenzy for more.

That's enough Annie. Thomas cuts through my thoughts.

Forgive me for not agreeing with you. I think back sarcastically. *But you have never done this before. I have.*

Silence. He has no response to that. He never does when I bring up what I have done in my long life. He is happy to send me criminals. He is not happy to be reminded that I am one.

A moment later, I agree with him and pull my wrist away. Alistair's head tries to follow it, but I give him a shove back down onto his pillows. He hisses at me, but his eyes are closed. It's instinct, nothing personal in it. I press my other hand against the wrist, pushing the edges of broken skin together to help it heal. I then turn to my audience. I focus on my family first.

Lola looks horrified. That's fair. She had been hooked up to all sorts of machines and painkillers when I had turned her. She hadn't been able to agree. She hadn't been able to consent. The guilt still soured my stomach.

Cleo was tilted forward on her tiptoes to try and get a better look. That should have been expected. Cleo always liked horror films, had always been interested in the process, and had never seen it happen before. Grace's eyes were focused on Alistair's face and a sad frown pulled at her lips. I had to force myself to not look to Thomas.

"We will take shifts with him." I decide. My stomach is churning, and my mouth and throat are grainy as if I had eaten wet sand. I could feel the two bloods fighting each other in my system. My body was trying to adjust and take the energy and nutrients from Alistair's blood, but it had barely any. My mind was already going cloudy and my skin prickling with heat. I needed to get back to my room as soon as possible.

"Grace." I gesture for her to take my spot. The transition was most risky in the beginning. She knew what to look for. Grace drifts over to the bed. Cleo moves quickly behind her. I latch onto her arm to hide my stumble. Cleo's eyes flash with rare worry. She grabs onto my elbows as my knees start to give out.

"Annie." A male voice bounces around the room so loud that it makes me wince. I don't answer as my vision goes back and I drop into Cleo's arms.

Chapter Eighteen

Cleo

I bare my fangs as the two younger witch boys both step forward. Annie is dead weight in my arms, but I shift her into an easier hold.

"Don't even think about it." I growl.

"Give her to me." Thomas demands, opening out his arms for me to place Annie in them.

"Not a chance in hell." I scoff. Speaking with my fangs out gives me a slight speech impediment but the message is clear. Thomas clenches his jaw and does not argue.

"You should at least take her to her room. There is fresh blood in there." Thomas speaks to me softly like I am a panicked little girl. It infuriates me more.

"I'm foreign. Not an idiot." I shift Annie's body once again, this time twisting her so I could walk out of the room with her.

"I didn't- I don't think you are." Thomas balks. "I just…Can I at least show you the way?"

I sneer at him for a second. He is still masking his heartbeat, but his eyes are focused on Annie's far-too-pale face. If he thought he could, then he would rip her from my arms right now. My hold tightens.

"Bad blood makes us sick." I remind him tauntingly. "And you just got her to down four pints of pure poison."

Thomas flinches as if I physically hit him. His fingers twitch as I turn to Lola and offer Annie out to her. Lola hesitates and glances at Grace.

"Show her." Grace tells Thomas. "I'll be fine, Cleo. You'll be able to hear me."

Her tone is reassuring but final. I feel like I am the one swallowing poison as I am dismissed from the room. She isn't wrong, but that doesn't reassure me. I slink from the room behind Thomas. The rest of the witches move to let me pass.

I sulk silently as we walk. Every time Thomas looks over his shoulder at us, I show him my fangs again. I can hear Annie's breathing getting better with each step, but she remains unconscious.

Grace had told me about Annie during the plague seasons. I knew she needed clean blood and rest. But my head was screaming that I shouldn't have left Grace and Lola back there, surrounded by a group of witches who had done something so terrible they were called the cursed coven. It felt like there was a thin metal cord lassoed around my heart and it was sharply tugging me backwards.

Thomas opens the door and walks straight into Annie's room as if it was his own. It is larger than mine and Grace's, but the colour scheme is the same. It must be the same throughout this entire wretched place. Lola's is a smaller version of this one.

I gently set Annie down on top of the covers. I grab one of the folded blankets from next to a gift basket at the end of the bed. I swallow the sarcastic comment that flew up into my mouth. We received no such basket, just a note informing us we would be getting blood deliveries each morning.

"I can stay with her." Thomas offers as he places wood into the fireplace. Once he decides there is enough in there, he snaps his fingers and they burst into flames.

"No." I tell him as I move to fill one of the empty glasses on the bedside tablet with a blood bag. I pick the bag up and find them too warm; not as if they had been out all night but as if the blood were still running through a human body. I tilt my head to look at Thomas. "Did you spell these blood bags?"

"She doesn't like cold blood."

I purse my lips but turn my attention back to Annie.

"Why won't you leave me alone with her?" Thomas asks softly.

"She can decide if she wants you here when she wakes up."

"Oh." Thomas breathes. I freeze for a second. I prepare for the wave of pity, but it doesn't come, even as I turn to look at him. He isn't looking at me, not really. He is looking through me straight at Annie.

"Oh." I repeat back bluntly.

Thomas settles himself into one of the armchairs and rests his head against his splayed fingers. The fire crackles behind him. I sit down by Annie's feet. We both listen to her breathe, waiting for a hitch or a rattle. Just in case. Her skin slowly turns less grey as time passes.

"She turned you in the twenties. Didn't she?" Thomas asked once it becomes clear that Annie was almost completely fine.

"Yes."

"In Egypt?"

"Aren't you clever."

"I'm just trying to get to know you." Thomas sighed. "You make Grace very happy."

"Quite an observation when you have known me less than a week."

Thomas pauses. That pause speaks volumes and my fangs lengthen once more. I run my tongue over them as I stare at him.

"She writes to me." Thomas finally admits. "Calls and texts on some rare occasions."

"So, you've been lying." I hiss. "Letting us all believe that-"

"That you can hide things like how old you are?" Thomas scoffs. "Annie knows. She either knows and ignores it or she knows it so deep down inside of herself that her brain knows to shelter her heart from it. She knows I would never have left her and Grace so alone and defenceless."

"You've been watching them for all those centuries? Watching me and Lola too?" I try to get him to clarify.

"You make me sound like a stalker." Thomas's lips twitch into an almost smile. "I suppose I am, in a way." He looks me in the eye. "But if you had known Grace your whole life. If you had adored her since you were children…and then you couldn't save her from what that man did to her…would you have left her alone for centuries?"

No. The response is automatic and straight from my brain, heart, bones, and soul. I had imagined ripping the throat out of every man that had ever looked at Grace growing up. I couldn't know their faces, so they were blurred humanoid shapes or exact copies of my own attackers. I knew that I was damned, but I had prayed to every god, ancient and modern, western and my own, to thank them that Annie had saved her that day. That the boring girl sleeping beside me had heard Grace scream and ripped the cause of it apart. It was a debt I would never be able to repay.

"She will never love you more than she loves Grace." I warn him. The lack of bitterness in my voice surprises me. "Or more than she loves Lola."

"Or more than she loves you." Thomas notices that I purposefully did not add myself to the list. I am Grace's source of happiness not Annie's. I am too rude, blunt, and judging for Annie to adore me as she so clearly does the other two. But it is still a nice lie to hear.

Annie groans and her feet hit my back. I move with supernatural quickness to press a hand to her forehead. Still no fever. Annie moves away from my hand and opens her eyes to glare at me. Three seconds later, the frown on her face turns into a smile. I shove the glass of blood at her before she can speak. She chuckles around the glass.

Thomas has sat up straight in his seat. His face has broken into a grin. I resist the urge to roll my eyes. She wasn't dying.

"Grace and Lola are still in that room." I whisper to her.

"How long have I been out?" Annie frowns.

"An hour and twenty-three minutes." Thomas answers before I can even look at the clock on the wall. Annie and I share a look.

"Are you okay with him being here?" I ask her. "I can make him leave."

"Go back to Grace and Lola." Annie orders although her voice is so rough that it's hard to take her seriously. "This is going to be the gross part anyway." She gives me a gentle shove. Her hand is clammy. "Go."

"I'll stay for the gross part." Thomas encourages me. "And if my family gets a little too much, just call for me. I'll make them behave."

Family. Interesting use of the word. I look back at the person I would loosely call my family as I start to leave.

Chapter Nineteen

Annie

I hold back the bloody vomit until the door closes behind Cleo. I throw myself over the side so it would cover the floor instead of my covers. Thomas is at my side and trying to pull my hair out of the way, but he is too slow. He pulls the blood-covered strands back anyway.

I would like to believe that the thick maroon sludge all over the floor looks worse coming up than going down, but I doubt it. I run my tongue around my mouth and continue to spit out everything I could. I couldn't stay in bed for days this time. Alistair would need me. This was my decision. I couldn't leave it to my girls to pick up the slack.

Thomas rubs gentle circles on my back as I start to gag. A trickle of blood falls out of my mouth. I blindly reach to the side for the glass with the dregs of fresh blood. My fingertips barely brush against the glass. Thomas's hands leave my back. My senses are muted but I can hear him climbing to the other side of the bed and ripping another blood bag open so clumsily that it makes me smile. That smile is ripped off my face as another wave of Alistair's diseased blood leaves my mouth.

"Here." Thomas climbs into the bed beside me, curling around me as I lean off the bed. He holds the glass in front of my face once the second wave has finished. I lean back into his chest and take deep breaths. My fangs prod into my bottom lip as I resist the urge to down it. Instead, I take two small sips and then wait. My stomach twists and rumbles but eventually settles.

I repeat that process painfully slowly. Thomas doesn't complain and he does not move. It works for the most part. The smell of the blood sludge overpowers the room and makes me heave, but I keep down the clean blood. That is the vital thing. My comfort isn't.

"I need to bathe." I finally whisper. My voice is rough even to my own ears. My clothes are sticking uncomfortably to me as if they had merged to my skin once I had fainted. My hair is coated in blood and bile. A bath to scrub the smell of it all off of me would make me feel better.

"I'll run one for you." Thomas tells me softly. "And I'll have the room cleaned and the sheets changed while you are in there."

"I can do it myself." I try to argue even as I sink further back into him.

"You can." He agrees. "But so can I, and that way you can lay down for a few extra minutes. You didn't say that you would get so sick from this."

The last part is an accusation. As if me admitting this would have stopped the need for it, as if my discomfort would have caused him to call the whole thing off and give me what I needed just for considering it.

"It wasn't important." I wave him off. I can't get out of the bed without standing in the vomit or rolling over him. "Grace can look after Alistair for a few hours until I am well enough to sit with him."

"It was important. I wouldn't have tried to demand you go in there alone for one." Thomas argues. He moves off of the bed and picks me up before I can try and follow him. I don't waste my strength pushing away from him. I let myself curl into his chest, into his warmth, for the few steps it takes before we are inside the en suite.

The bathroom is surprisingly modern, made of wide ceramic counters with built in sinks. The bathtub is large enough for four and in the centre of the room. It looks more like a hot tub than a bath. It was so deep that there were three small steps embedded inside it for easy entry. The room is lined with mirrors, floor length on the walls and smaller ones mounted on the cabinet doors.

Thomas places me on the nearest countertop and starts to run the taps. Nausea hits me again and I lean back. The wall is cold against my cheek, and I sigh happily. I close my eyes to focus on my breathing. I can hear Thomas searching for towels and squirting sweet smelling soaps into the bath. I open one eye and stare at him.

"Bubble-gum?" I smile weakly. "Interesting choice."

"It was that or lemon." Thomas splashes his fingers in the water. He turns the heat up. His face is set so seriously that I want to tell him a joke. I can't think of any at the moment. We used to have so many inside ones back when we both had heartbeats. None of them were relevant now.

"Well, when life gives you lemon soap…" I say as my pathetic attempt. It works. He chuckles and his face changes into something more like my usual Thomas.

"You should have told me." Thomas chastises me again.

"But then you wouldn't be able to look after me." I smirk at him as I close my eyes again. "And we both know how much you would love to watch me bathe."

"Don't be a tease."

"Hypocrite."

"Still sour about that, are you?"

"It's been less than twelve hours." I open my eyes as the taps are turned off. The tub is full, probably helped along by magic, with bubbles nearly overflowing from the sides. The room smelt sharp and sweet. It would easily cover the sickening smell of Alistair's blood.

I slide myself off the edge of the counter and start to peel my clothes off. My shirt drops to the floor. I raise my eyebrows at him as I undo the button on my jeans.

"You can't get in fully dressed." I tell him when his eyes remain steadfast on my face. I slowly pull at my zipper.

"You can barely stand." Thomas rests his hip against a counter on the opposite side of the room.

"I wasn't suggesting standing."

"You're being a tease." Thomas half whines as I shimmy out of my jeans. They aren't the most attractive things to strip from but his eyes stare at my chest so intently that I don't think he cares.

"You know." He purrs. "I read this thing on the internet once. If a women wears matching underwear then she is the one deciding to have sex."

"Inviting you into my bath wasn't enough of a hint?" I bat my eyelashes at him.

"We both know damn well that the second I strip, you will change your mind."

"Think you did that bad of a job last time, do you?" I quip, leaning back against the counter as the room starts to blur again.

Thomas throws his head back. His laugh echoes around the room. I grin. When he looks back at me, those grey eyes are sparkling.

"I was expecting a size joke there." He says as he moves towards me.

"Of course, you were. You aren't as witty as I am." I tilt my head up to look at him once he comes to a stop. He makes a small 'humph' sound, corners of his mouth still set in a smile, as he reaches around me and unclips my bra. His fingertips trail around the curve of my breasts and then down my ribs. As they reach the delicate strip of lace at my hips I take a deep breath in through my nose and rest my forehead against his shoulder. I swallow down the urge to take a bite from him both literally and metaphorically.

"See." He whispers tauntingly as he tugs the lace down my legs. He follows them down, going onto his knees and gently lifting my feet to slip them off of me. "Next time this happens, I would like to blame the weak knees on just me and not a prince."

Thomas places quick kisses on each of my knees before shooting up and wrapping his arms around my waist. I let out an involuntary squeal and latch onto his shoulders. Thomas lets out a breathy chuckle in my ear. I nip at his ear lobe with my front teeth, careful not to use my incisors. Thomas grunts slightly before dropping me into the bath water.

I yelp as my ass hits the bottom of the tub, swallowing soapy bath water as I do. I push myself above the waterline, clawing at the side as I cough. Thomas laughs as I shoot him the finger. The mood is almost broken but that just sums up our century-spanning relationship. We are almost in the same city at the same time. We are almost agreeing to stay together from now on. We are almost courting with almost the same heartbeat. This will not be another almost.

With the hand that I had used to shoot him a vulgar gesture, I grab at his shirt and give him a vicious pull forward. He stumbles and nearly falls into the water with me. His fingers grip the edge, overlapping my other one. His fingers dip into the bubbles.

"Wicked thing." He purrs down at me. I look up at him through my lashes. We move in unison. He moves down to crash his lips against mine, hands dipping further into the water. His hands cup the sides of my chest, his thumbs brushing along the underneath of my breasts. I groan into his mouth as my wet hands tangle in his raven hair. I can't hear his heartbeat, but I can hear the blood rushing through him. I whimper as his tongue slips into my mouth.

His hands run up and down me, twisting to stroke down my spine. I moan loudly and give his hair a tug in retaliation. I nearly pull him into the water with me as his teeth nip at my bottom lip.

I have no idea how long we stay like this, attached by the lips and hands running all over each other. His shirt is covered in the bubblegum-scented water, his hair damp and sticking up in every angle. I only know that when he pulls himself completely away from me, it feels like he takes the breath in my lungs with him.

I am back to feeling unsteady and weak. I notice how my stomach feels hollow and my chest too tight. The want for fresh blood hits me like a steam train, battling with the want for him. The solution seems simple. Drag him into this now lukewarm water, strip him down, and screw him as I bite into his shoulder and take a pint or two. We had done it before.

Instead, I throw myself to the opposite side of the bath and avoid looking at him. He walked away last night. He pulled away just now. What we had done before had hurt him. Now he was scared to do it again.

"I wouldn't bite you without permission. Without consent." I tell him thickly, running my hands over the bubbles.

"I know." Thomas breathes. "I just…"

"You don't have to explain." I shake my head. "No is no."

"It's not a no." He tells me quickly. "It's a not right now."

"That is a no." I smile. "And a no is perfectly acceptable, Thomas. I am not going to push you for anything you do not want to give."

Thomas moves over to one of the mirrored cabinets, pulling out two plastic containers full of light purple liquids. He moves around to my side of the bath and places them beside my head. I watch him closely and make sure to move at a slow human pace. My head tilts back to rest on the side of the bath.

"I want to give you everything." He tells me. A lump rises into my throat, but I do not reply. I do not know how. He leans forward to press a gentle kiss to my forehead. "And right now, I am going to wash my friend's regurgitated blood from your hair. If you don't mind."

I smile and reach my hand up to caress his cheek. He plants another kiss on my palm as I sigh. "Okay."

Chapter Twenty

Lola

The witches refuse to leave us alone with the prince. I understand one or two of them taking watch until they trust us, but five of them seems like overkill. Grace and Cleo left when it was my shift. We are taking them two hours at a time. The most exciting thing to have happened was Cleo coming back with the report that Annie was now awake. Grace had visibly relaxed.

Elias had started up a game of 'two truths and a lie.' Only Christiana and I played along with him now. Grace had while she was here, but she was off with Cleo. She said they would be unpacking their things, but I think that they will be having an uncomfortable conversation about their new living arrangements instead. Cleo would not be happy staying here for years.

"I once kissed Queen Mary." Elias began the next round, counting off the options on his fingers. He had settled himself into a chair, legs draped over the side as if this was his own room and there was no dying prince in it. "I had front row seats to the last Olympic swimming event. I think you're only alright on the eyes."

I let out a little giggle as Elias winks at me. I knew from experience, both human and vampire, that the easiest way to get information was to flirt. It helped that Elias was easy on the eyes with a lovely subtle Scottish accent. While the game had made it clear he was centuries older than me, he hadn't said exactly how old he was. He could be older than Annie by a year or by a dozen of them.

"Which Queen Mary?" Christiana said suspiciously. She was settled on the floor, cross legged and squinting at the blonde man. I had taken Cleo's spot on the prince's bed. The body had been still ever since Annie left.

"The true one." Elias smirked.

"Very helpful. She's American, you numpty. At least make it fair on her." Christiana chastised him.

"Oh, I am so sorry." Elias held back a laugh. He turned his greys to me. "I meant Mary Queen of Scots love. Cousin to Elizabeth. Very briefly Queen of France."

I nod along as if that suddenly helps me realise who he meant. The name rang a bell but not from anything factional, just from random TV dramas or historical romance that occasionally got some buzz during award season. "I am just gonna go with the Olympics being a lie."

"Clever." Elias grins and points a finger at me. "Because you are stunning, and I was second row at the swimming."

"You did not make out with Queen Mary!" Christiana scowled at Elias. "I don't even know when you would have met her, you little liar."

"Your father wouldn't like me telling you such stories, little cousin." Elias laughs. I quickly look between the two of them.

"You two are cousins?" I focus on Elias.

"We are all related." Christiana waves my question off. "My turn. I am allergic to strawberries. I was at the execution of Anne Boleyn. My eyes are green."

"Your eyes are grey. All of you." I say immediately.

"Very good." Christiana beams at me. "It happened when we stopped ageing. Since you are going to ask, Thomas is my brother and William is my father. Elias is my cousin. Corsi and Mary are close enough to be considered family, just like Grace and Cleo are to you." Christiana stares up at me with those stormy eyes, waiting for the next question.

"Annie said she knew Thomas when she was human. That means she knew all of you back then too." I stop as Alistair's legs twitch. I put my hand on the pile of covers on top of him. He stills.

"I'm older than I look." Christiana smirks. "How old are you?"

"I would be forty-two this year." I admit, feeling even more like a toddler than I do around Grace. My eyes stay on the prince's face. He is slowly gaining more colour and I think his face is shifting a little. It looks less gaunt than it did before. His dark eyelashes flutter against his cheekbones as he lets out a rattling breath.

"A young one. No wonder we hadn't met you yet. You are still young enough you might end up liking us." Elias spins in his seat so his feet were now firmly on the ground.

"Do you hear yourself when you speak?" William finally joins in the conversation. He had settled himself with the two pretty women on a small table in the corner. I assume they were having private telepathic conversations since they had not spoken at all since Annie and Thomas left.

"You said would be." Corsi turns her hard gaze to me. "You do not consider yourself forty-two?"

"It's not the answer I give whenever someone asks." I admit.

"Well, no, it wouldn't be." Elias says kindly. "You would blow your cover with that. If it helps I only consider myself twenty."

"I consider you an ass." Christiana said in a singsong voice.

Elias gives a flick of his fingers and Christiana's pigtails whip around her face as if stuck in a miniature tornado. Christiana made an aggravated sound and swept it away with a wave of her own hand.

"That is why!" Christiana frowned.

Elias shoots me another wink and I can't help but laugh. I adore Annie, Grace, and Cleo, but I am so rarely included in these moments with them. I am always like William or Mary, looking in on them with a gentle smile.

Alistair kicks out his legs, his foot whacking me in my spine. I jump. His heartbeat had stopped an hour or so ago, which Elias had told me was normal. He also told me that his eventual spasms were his cells and nerves changing. I had no reason to think he was lying. The witches wanted this to work more than I did. If there was something to worry about, they would be the one to do the worrying.

Alistair starts to spasm. All the things I know you are supposed to do when someone has a seizure fly out of my mind. I grip at his feet and keep them pushed down. Christiana is immediately at his head, hands pressing into his shoulders. She is mumbling Latin with her eyes closed.

I don't understand it, I can't translate it, and if my heart could beat, it would be breaking its way out of my chest right now. I could not be the reason that Annie did not get her brother back. I could not be the one on watch when Alistair didn't make it. I needed one of them, any of them to be here with me. I had never seen this before, I had no idea if this was normal, I had no idea *what to do.*

A wave of overwhelming calm seizes my brain. My hands, still held tightly around Alistair's ankles, suddenly feel light and tingly. My lungs take in more oxygen, and I can do this. I can. His seizure has already slowed. I don't know that I didn't have the exact same thing myself twenty years-

The calm disappears along with a bang. A literal bang I realise as I turn my head and find Cleo with her hand wrapped around Elias's throat in a strange mirror of Annie and the King yesterday.

"You do not do that again." Cleo growls at him, fangs breaking the skin on her bottom lip.

"She was panicking." Elias glares at her. Good for him. If our positions were swapped, I would be crying like a baby. "You left her completely alone. She has no idea what is happening to him."

"Cleo." A voice snarls from the doorway. Annie's voice. I let go of Alistair, who was now still, and blink at her. She is dressed only in a towel, hair sopping wet and behind her is a half-drenched Thomas. "Let Elias go."

"He-" Cleo starts to argue.

"I know what he did." Annie's voice is cold, but it shakes. She shakes actually. There is a light tremor all over her body. Thomas reaches out to steady her, but Annie grips the doorframe instead. Her eyes turn to Grace, who had planted herself behind Christiana, hands on the younger girls shoulders as if to rip her away from the prince. Christiana didn't seem to care. She was too busy staring a hole into the back of Cleo's head.

Cleo lets out an angry breath through her nose and drops Elias as if his skin burned her. Elias bites the air in front of her mockingly. She sneers at him.

"You should be in bed." Grace moves to Annie's side in a blink. "Turning him has taken a lot out of you."

Annie tilts herself against the doorframe. I take a sharp breath. I have never seen her look so disappointed in Grace. Not during a hunt when emotions ran high, not during spring cleaning or safe house planning. Never. The look is quickly gone but it was there. I know it.

"I am not leaving Lola." Annie breathes. "She was terrified."

"Alistair will not wake up for hours." Grace insisted. "Let me take your shift. You are not well."

"I'm fine now." I add quickly. "I just…I didn't know. I do now. It's fine."

"It is not fine." Annie shoots me a soft smile.

"She is in safe hands with us, you know." Elias says sulkily. He dramatically rubs at his throat after shooting Cleo a side-eyed glance.

"I know." Annie agrees. She adjusts the towel around her chest. "But I don't want you to have to get inside her head and calm her down when we could be there to help."

"I'm calm. I'm good. I just didn't know seizures were a part of it." I insist. Annie really does look sick. Could the prince's blood have done something like that to her? Taken her out of commission so completely? Had my blood done the same two decades ago?

"There shouldn't be many more." Annie tells me kindly. "It happens as my blood takes over his organs."

"That is very biologically inaccurate." Christiana says playfully. "Really Annie…" Christiana stops herself and then looks to her brother. "Thomas, get her in bed with more blood. I can handle this: you know I can."

Thomas puts his hands up in a surrendering gesture. He would be taking the lead from Annie and Annie only. Annie takes a sharp breath in. I need to convince her I was being stupid. I could be uncomfortable as long as she was getting herself off of death's door. Could this kill her? It hadn't yet. She had lived through it at least three times, but none of us had a blood disease.

"If you are even slightly uncomfortable." Annie visibly swallows as she looks at me. "You call for me."

"Okay." I agree quickly.

"It's my shift again soon anyway." Grace says quickly. "She won't be alone again. I promise."

"Okay." Annie nods, closing her eyes and breathing in through her mouth. "Okay fine."

"Again." Christiana pipes up. "We were always right here."

Annie smiles and rolls her eyes, feigning competence as she moves around Thomas and from the room. Thomas shoots his sister a smile before following after her.

"If they get together-" Elias begins.

"Then it would be about time." Grace finishes. She moves around me and sits on the other side of Alistair's bed. I look at her over my shoulder. We lock eyes. Hers are so vibrant, so alive, that she looks more human than any of us. I smile as she reaches out and places her hand over Alistair's.

Chapter Twenty-One

Two Days Later

Alistair

I have never felt better. It is easier to breathe now. My lungs take in mouthfuls of air rather than slow wheezes. My limbs feel like they aren't even there- no shooting pains or aches coming from deep within my bones. I feel like I am made of air, like when I open my eyes I would be flying in the clouds.

I don't open them just yet. I focus on all the new things I can hear and smell. I assume I am still in my bedroom. There is a sharp smell of bleach from all the medical equipment we keep in it. There is something sweet overtop of it. I would guess it's the flowers my mother has put everywhere to try and make me feel better about being indoors all the time.

I can hear faint thumping heartbeats and even closer breathes. I can only think of one creature that breathes with no heartbeat. My own chest is unnervingly still. The breathing is out of time with everything else. I would guess there are…no. There can't be six of them. There was four vampires. Annie, the two with the dark hair, and the gorgeous blonde. So, I must be wrong. I must be confused.

My head is pounding, and my throat is sore with a sour taste in my mouth. It's the most familiar thing in this whole situation. I needed a drink. I almost laugh but it comes out as a dry hacking sound. The breathing in the room shifts. There are gentle sounds. Fabric rubbing against each other as people moved, items being placed onto the wooden tabletops.

Showtime, I suppose.

I force my eyes open and slowly gasp. The room is far brighter than I had ever seen it. The sunlight has exposed every single fleck against the white ceiling. I can see a thin strand of spiderweb in the corner, tiny flecks of random stains too high up to be deep cleaned. It was almost painfully clear, like watching a 4K film that was clearly not meant for the format.

Hi there. A voice like smooth caramel with an American twang drifts into my head. I jolt up onto my elbows, snapping my head to look at the cause of all that breathing. The blonde is here, right at the end of my bed, and she looks even more breath-taking with my new eyes. Her skin is as smooth as porcelain, not a single blemish or scar on it. She was like a doll. There wasn't even a slight colour difference under her eyes. Mine had always been rimmed with dark purple bruises.

"Hi." I croak out. The blonde smiles. I am tempted to repeat myself just to see if it will get wider.

"How are you feeling?" She whispers. She then pauses and adds on, "Your Grace?" As it she is unsure that's the correct title. I smile this time.

"Ali," I correct her softly, "and…thirsty."

A chuckle comes from the corner. I force myself to look away from the American and see familiar faces in the corner. The witches' council. I notice Thomas is the only one missing. That's disappointing but not a shock. This was his idea. He would be dealing with my mother's panic, my father's anger, and the long-lost vampire girlfriend he fawns over from afar.

"We will get you something to drink soon." Christiana promises me with a reassuring smile. "We just need you checked over first."

"You don't have heartbeats." I blurt. "I just…I thought you would have heartbeats." It sounds stupid to say out loud.

Elias chuckles again. Christiana glares at him. They were always the more chatty members of the council. William was the stick up my father's arse and if he ever looked at me, it was calculating, not emotional. Corsi and Mary only bowed their heads and stayed silent in their seats. I was a prince who would never be king. I was unimportant in the scheme of their long life. I was not worth remembering.

"We thought it would be easier on you and on Lola for us to mask them." Christiana glances over at the blonde.

"Lola." I repeat.

"That's me." The blonde beams. Her eyes are flashing all over my face, taking me in. I wonder how different I look. I wonder if I looked healthier in my undeath, if my skin was as smooth as Lola's or if my eyes would be as bright as Annie's. I hadn't properly looked at the other two, but they had the same aura of unnatural beauty. That would be nice.

"Pretty." I beam back.

"Watch it, princey. I've called dibs." Elias teases me from his spot in the corner. A light blush creeps into Lola's cheeks. My teeth hurt as I stare at it, a slow ache that turns into a slashing pain by my incisors.

"I'm gonna get Annie." Lola whispers to me softly, her wide eyes staring at my mouth. I grab at her arm, so quick that I jump. I didn't think about doing it. I just did. Her gaze turns from my mouth to her arm.

"Sorry." I whisper thickly.

"Don't be." Lola replies instantly. "I'm not going to leave, okay?"

"Okay." I nod. It's so strange to do that and not have a shooting pain down my neck.

"You don't have to let go." Lola adds. "If it makes you feel better. If it makes you feel…grounded to have someone to hold onto."

"Is that normal?"

"It was for me." A smile grows on Lola's lips. "I almost broke Annie in half when I woke up. Annie says that Cleo bit her in a sort of frenzy. She doesn't remember that. Something about her being half starved anyway. So, you only grabbing me is a really good sign."

The babbling is reassuring. It's reassuring that I am not the worst she has ever seen, even as she throws the names at me. She shoots me a wink and I don't know what for until another voice drifts into my head. The voice pulls at a cord somewhere inside of me, some invisible string that splits off into separate directions. One of those directions is Lola. That particular string starts to hum.

Hello Alistair. Annie's voice vibrates down the strings. *Keep calm. We are going to be with you very shortly.*

We? I latch onto the word and recoil as I realise everyone linked with those strings could hear me.

All of us. A softer voice promises. She has a distinctly English tone.

So don't move. A stricter voice with a different accent adds bluntly. *The witches won't want you zooming about this place like an overexcited puppy dog.*

They are nicer than they sound right now. Thomas cuts in. My friend's voice twists around those strings. It doesn't fit in. He is trying to jam himself into it but that's impossible. He is not a part of this, cannot be a part of this, and it is wrong wrong wrong that he is here.

You heard him, witch boy. The one with the accent smirks. I can tell that, even if I'm not sure how. *Get out of here. This is vamp business now.*

Cleo. Annie chastises softly.

You are all overwhelming him. Lola cuts in at the same time. *Less speaking and more moving. He needs a drink.*

The strings fall silent. I let my head fall back against my pillow and look at Lola through half-open eyes. My throat is so dry it hurts to swallow. The door to my room opens seconds later. I loll my head to the side as the sound of breathing seems to take over the room, echoing loudly in my ears. A feeling of comfort washes over me, a feeling of safety. I have no idea why, but I am grateful. I am grateful to feel anything.

Annie and Thomas smile at me. I wonder if they know it was perfectly in time with each other. It would be typical of Thomas to get his soulmate to save my life. He had all the luck. The other two girls walk in after them. They are all walking slowly with exaggerated steps. They don't want to spook me.

They were all pretty, although Lola was the prettiest. They shared perfect skin, thick healthy hair, and plump lips. I assume they are all vampire attributes. They all look soft and gentle and nothing like the predators they are. The predators *we* are.

"He has accepted this remarkably well." The girl with the caramel mocha skin smirks at me. She was the one with the accent. The sarcastic one.

"He is pulling what I lovingly call a Cleo." Annie jokes as she takes another slow step towards me. I look over at Lola to see if she gets the joke, but her face is set in a gentle frown. I'm not the only one waiting for the punchline.

The one that looks like Snow White giggles and kisses the sarcastic one's cheek. The girl's scowl falls from her face. Ah.

"Cleo's bark is…well. Her bite is definitely worse." Annie flashes me a grin, fangs on full display. "But she won't hurt you."

I wouldn't let her. Lola's eyes are focussed on Thomas even as she spoke down that invisible string between us. *And neither would Thomas.*

Thomas a good fighter? I think back.

Not a clue. Lola responds before we both start laughing out loud.

You realise we can all hear you. The sarcastic one- Cleo- snaps at us.

Shhh my love. Snow White responds. *It is nice that he can laugh so quickly afterwards.*

I go to respond that I can also hear them, but Elias gives a dramatic sigh from his space in the corner.

"No telepathic conversations please. Those without the ability find it rude and frustrating."

"I find *you* rude and frustrating." Cleo tells him coldly. Elias ignores her although he does look back at Lola.

"You are still my favourite." Elias tells her. My gums prickle again as a red-hot feeling shoots up my throat.

"Rude." Annie whispers. She comes so close that her legs brush against Lola's. She looks smaller than she did the other night. She isn't the towering figure that I had seen in my haze of pain. She still looks fierce and terrifying, but the string that connects us takes the edge away. Her smile is reassuring just like yesterday, but now it fills me with a sense of warmth. They all fill me with a sense of…home.

"Are we ready to start?" She asks me softly. I nod.

Chapter Twenty-Two

Annie

"You should start with the basics." Elias suggests loudly. I twitch my finger and resist the urge to run him into a wall. There was once a time where I had adored him. His laugh would echo across a banquet hall, and I would look over at him and Thomas with wide eyes and a thumping heart.

Those times were now few and far between. Elias was like a ghost in my life, a figure I briefly see from the corner of my eye at random parties or spend a few hours with at twenty-four-hour food places where no one else could see. *Don't worry. I won't tell Thomas that I saw you.*

"Out." Thomas beats me to the order. "All of you."

"You do not give me orders, boy." William grumbles even as he stands from his seat.

"The prince is fine now." I say bluntly. "But he can hear all of your blood rushing through your body. You can hide your heartbeat, but you cannot stop him smelling you. You want to risk your throat, then fine. But I will not continue while Chrissie is at risk."

Chrissie frowns at me but she leads her old nursemaids, cousin, and father out the door. Thomas stays in the doorway. I raise an eyebrow at him. He raises one right back.

"You really think I would have hurt her?" Alistair's voice cuts through the room.

"Probably not." I answer honestly and turn back to look at him. My heart swells in my chest. He looks more alive now, as an undead soulless monster, than he had before with his damaged heart and bones. "But they are very annoying, and this is about you."

"Oh?" Alistair blinks. "Is there some ceremony or prayer or..."

Alistair cuts himself off as Cleo snorts again. Grace tuts and gives her lover's hand a gentle tug as a gesture to quit it.

"No." I fight back a smile. "But this is where we answer your questions and explain everything. You don't want to, and you shouldn't have to, hold anything back. Any thought that crosses your mind. Nothing is unimportant. No one here is going to judge you."

Alistair glances over at Cleo in disbelief. Cleo sighs and repeats, "Nothing is unimportant, and you will not be judged…I didn't even judge Lola when we turned her."

Alistair slowly nods and then hesitates before taking in a deep breath through his mouth. He winces. My hand reaches behind me towards Thomas and what I had hidden in his jacket pocket as we rushed from my room and away from our very appropriate card game. We had somehow slipped back to how we were back when we were human, even after the bath incident. Everything we did together was physically distant and as appropriate as if we had a thousand witnesses.

Thomas places the blood bag in my hand. He is careful for his fingers not to brush against mine. I gently unravel the tube that we all jokingly call a straw. I settle myself next to Alistair's shoulders. He has to shuffle to the side to make room. His eyes glaze over as he stares at the thick red liquid slushing around in my hand.

"You are going to drink first." I tell him slowly. "And then you can ask as many questions as you like. Understood?"

He nods furiously, fangs poking out between his lips as if he couldn't help himself. He has been remarkably well behaved until now, but this was always going to be a reaction. It may have been hundreds of years since I woke up after my own transition, but I remember the prickling heat of my throat and the emptiness of my stomach in vivid detail.

Alistair's breathing turns to gulps of air as I slowly move the 'straw' towards him. As soon as it touches his lips he goes near feral, gnawing and sucking at the plastic. I hear Lola take a sharp breath.

Alistair finally gets some blood out of the bag, and he lets out a long groan. His eyes are closed. He is slurping the blood down so enthusiastically that some dribbles down his chin and over his hands. The bag is empty in seconds. It wouldn't be enough, but it would take the edge off enough for him to focus. Alistair blinks twice before staring around the room sheepishly. He doesn't look over at Lola. The fresh blood rushes to his cheeks instead.

"We've all been there." Cleo tells him in a rare moment of unconditional kindness.

"It's sweet." Alistair stares down at the empty bag and the mess all over his fingers. "I didn't…I didn't expect it to be sweet." He starts to gently suck at the quickly drying blood on his skin.

"You have some on your chin." Lola whispers to him once he is done. His face goes a deep red again.

"Cleo is right." I tell him kindly. "We have all had a messy first meal. Mine was much much worse actually."

"Does this not…I mean, are you not this hungry?" Alistair looks up and past me, straight at Thomas. I move myself to block his view.

"No. You get better at it. It doesn't always seem so…consuming." Lola says quickly. "I was so terrible for the first three years. I ruined so many shirts. You are already doing better than me."

A look of disbelief crosses Alistair's face. Thomas takes a few steps forward and back into the brand-new vampire's viewpoint. I'm tempted to rip his throat out myself.

"Annie's first time was a mess." Thomas joins the conversation at my expense. I let him continue just so I can see where this goes. I had no idea he had been paying attention to what I did those days, at least outside of his small talks with Grace when she was a little girl. I only knew he came to see me directly five years later. He had avoided me where Chrissie and Elias hadn't.

"I thought he had been killed by an animal. He was torn apart." Thomas stares at the empty blood bag. "He deserved it. He deserved far worse."

"He?" Alistair looks at me.

"He." I repeat firmly.

"What did he do?" Alistair's whole body stretches and twitches as if he wants to bolt from the room. He might do just that when he hears my answer. We would take him out to the grounds when the sun set.

I stare the crown prince in the eye as I answer. "What didn't King Henry the Eighth do?"

Chapter Twenty-Three

Grace

I find myself strangely proud of how Alistair's face falls. My friend, my maker, had shaped the nation with one simple bite. We had never been able to brag about it before, not without having to prove it or someone implying she was exaggerating. I had never been able to outright grin at how greatly she loved. My maker would kill kings for the people she loved, and she loved us more than anything.

"You just admitted to treason." Alistair stutters. "You just…he was my…"

"Somehow I doubt you will hang me for it." Annie smirks. "You never met him, and he was a twat."

Thomas splutters out a laugh from behind her. Alistair snaps his head to look at him.

"He was difficult." Thomas admits with a nod. He forces his face into something failing to be neutral.

"He was a twat." Annie repeats herself with an emphasis on the final T. I can feel Cleo's hand start to silently shake as she holds back her own cackle. I brush my shoulder against hers. Her skin is warm to the touch, which is a good sign. She wouldn't need to go hunting for another day or two. We could go together, make a date night of it. She would look so stunning lit up under the streetlights by St Paul's.

"Anyone else you want to admit to murdering?" Alistair scoffs. "Isaac Newton? The Black Dahlia girl?"

"You act as if I didn't have reason." Annie says belligerently. "The man was a tyrant to women. He created divorce simply to entrap as many women as possible."

"He only had two wives. Modern men have had more." Alistair argues. I wince. Wrong response.

"He was ready for a third and my friend paid the price for it." Annie's voice turns icy. My chest tightens, a sharp pain shooting through my heart. "Of course, we know now that men are the one who choose the sex of babies. Not the women. So, tell me, Prince Alistair, why Catherine of Aragon was separated from her child and why Queen Anne Boleyn was used as a breeding mare for sons. Why were they both punished for their children simply not having an extra external body part? Hm?"

Alistair recoils into his pillows as he stares at her. He stays silent. Definitely the best option if he isn't going to agree with her. Annie would always listen to the other side unless it was about Anne, and then it became too hard to argue with her anyway. The pain was too raw even after all this time. My mind flashes back to my mother hissing at me to be quiet when I asked too loudly about all the former Queens. There was too much discourse around the line of succession for it to be safe.

"Annie." Thomas says so quietly that I think I may have imagined it. His hands start to gently rub her shoulders. I sigh. Has he learnt nothing after all this time? Has he still not realised that Annie is not a fragile doll? Annie glances over at me as she shrugs him off.

"We have a moral code we live and hunt by, Your Highness." I cut straight to the usual speech. "We do not hurt the innocent. We drink rapists, abusers, murderers, and those like them. We may have to make some adjustments for you but that will not change. Understood?"

"You find it that easy to find such people?" Alistair gaps at me. "Enough for all four of you to feed…however often we need to feed."

"One in three women find those types of people." Annie tells him. It takes a few seconds before the realisation of that statistic sets into the crown prince's face. His features harden as he nods that he does, in fact, understand.

"We feed every four days or so. We can go longer but that's the sweet spot between getting too hungry or being too full. You should listen to your body, obviously, but newborn vampires generally feed every two for the first few months. Their bodies need longer adjustment periods." Annie's voice loses its harshness.

"We have organised for you to have blood bags." Thomas injects himself into the conversation, his hands back at his sides. "We can't have you running around ripping into people."

"They will be temporary." Annie warns. "Just for a few days while your body settles a little more. I'm sure you realise how sick you were when I bit you. Your body has a lot of catching up to do even now. It needs to get used to its new strength and speed and wants. Once you can run a few laps of the grounds without collapsing, we will get you a criminal or two."

Alistair hesitates before asking what my most pressing question was when I first turned. His narrowed eyes shift over to the window and the bright yellow light seeping into it. The light was shining on Lola's skin and her blond hair absorbed it until she had a faux halo around her.

"I can really walk in the sun?" Alistair whispers. "I'll be able to go outside in the sun and…run and laugh and swim and…"

"All of it." Annie promises him fiercely, taking his hand in her own.

Alistair's face breaks into a spectacular grin. He is not focussed on the facts from Annie's past. He is focussed on all the things he can now achieve, things his body will finally co-operate with doing. My unbeating heart swells in my chest for him. Was I this positive? Was I staring down the barrel of eternity with such childlike wonder?

"That can't be all your questions." Annie says playfully. "Don't you want to know if you can still drink booze and eat human food?"

"Those were important questions." Lola grumbled from the end of the bed. "Who wants an eternity without pizza?"

Cleo gives a throaty chuckle from beside me. Lola jolts as if our presence had been forgotten completely. I suppose she has had a rough few days. I was a lot calmer seeing her turned than seeing Cleo. She sends Cleo a soft smile. Cleo smiles back.

"That is a good point." Alistair points over at Lola, sending her a smile of his own. "Can I eat human food?"

"As long as you have a steady supply of blood, you have every normal human function." Annie smiles. "You can even get drunk, which Thomas says is something you are excited for."

Blood rushes to Alistair's cheeks again. For a prince, he is awkward and unsure. I had never met a prince before, but I had watched them on the news and read about them in the papers. They were always calm and collected. Alistair looked like any normal, flustered, barely-out-of-adolescence boy.

"Can I see my parents soon?" Alistair's voice falters. I think back to how his parents had reacted in that meeting room. His mother would have given anything for him to be saved. His father seemed more worried about who in the room had the most power. Now his son would have more than him, forever.

"Soon." Annie agrees softly. "You are going to be stuck in here for a few more days like I said. We will bring your mum in first and see how that goes. We may not bring her too close, just in case."

Alistair nods. His chest rises as he takes a deep breath through his nose. His eyes focus on Thomas's throat even as he faces Annie. I tense up, ready to rush over and tackle him back to that bed if he so much as twitches. Thomas notices the look…and his heartbeat starts to echo around the room. Far too loud to be normal. He is amplifying it on purpose.

"Are you insane?" Cleo gapes at him. She shifts herself so she is slightly in front of me. A memory of Lola almost ripping Annie's arm off during her first hunt flashes before my eyes.

"He's not going to hurt me." Thomas's eyes stay focussed on Alistair. The prince's chest starts pistoning up and down, but other than that he stays still. He doesn't attack. He closes his eyes and just…listens.

"Fascinating." I whisper. I go to step forward, but Cleo blocks me. Alistair's eyes shoot open, and he stares at us. He tilts his head to the side. His iris's flare as ours do before feeding and then go back to normal. He was fighting it. He was winning. The least we could do was help him, give him something to focus on. The least we could do was share our stories of this exact same moment.

"I was born in London on May 7th, 1529. I met Annie when I was seven years old." I say slowly. "She turned me after someone hurt me in the brothel I was raised in. Cleo was born in Luxor in 1903. Annie turned her in 1922. Lola was born in Los Angeles in 1982. Annie turned her in 2003."

Chapter Twenty-Four

Grace

London, England

1546

The lace of my dress scratches at my skin, but the idea of taking it off makes me gag. It won't be my choice soon anyway. A winter wind sweeps through the gaps in the window pane. I want to wrap myself in a blanket but the idea of sitting down on that bed makes me shudder. The usual sounds of my home echo louder in my head. The drunken men, the exaggerated moans, and screams. The smell of it all threatens to choke me.

I had been sick before. I had huddled on my meagre bed and emptied my stomach into buckets that Annie dutifully emptied. I had yearned for her to run her cold hands over my forehead and whisper-sing songs to me to get me to sleep. I yearn for that now, for her to burst in and save me from this.

She had tried. I know she had. She had made the matron hold off on this for as long as possible. She had tried even harder than my mother had. But the matron had gotten less scared of Annie over the years she had stayed here. She had caught onto Annie's feeding habits and knew she was not at risk.

Annie was off feeding now. She had pushed herself to her limit waiting, expecting this. She was too hungry to wait any longer and she refused to drink even a drop from me. The locked door behind me wouldn't keep Annie out but it was keeping me in.

The matron had insisted as she locked that door that I would enjoy it eventually. Some girls here did. Carol almost had an obsession for it, caring less about the money than about getting picked first. Annie, when I had asked her, told me that some people get addicted to things other than drink and powders and we should not judge her for it.

Thundering footsteps and the matron's voice echo down the hall. My breath hitches in my throat. I rub my arms and stare at the rotting wood around the thick metal handle. Annie had paid for the lock to be installed when I was smaller. The metal had been a symbol of hope, a symbol of being saved. It had been a barrier between me and the people that knew no boundaries. The scratching and clicking as matron turned the key changed that.

She doesn't even look at me as she opens the door and escorts the man inside. I want to scream at her, make her look me in the eyes as she takes that clinking bag of coins from him. Was I worth gold or only silver? Did he pay extra for my virginity? Some girls were paid extra to be beaten. Would she have added that to my price?

He could probably afford it. His clothes are thick and clean, no tattered flea-ridden rags. His belt is etched with silver and attached to it was a leather sheath. The dagger inside of it gleamed. My heart dropped. It was smart to bring it- this was a dangerous part of the city. He would need protection walking down the streets like that. He looked clean as well. There was no dirt on his face or under his fingernails. At least I wasn't obviously about to catch something.

"A little older than her portrait." He grumbled, sliding his hands into his bag, and taking out three coins for his disappointment. Gold coins. I almost want to be flattered. Matron says nothing still. She just takes the rest of the bag and leaves. The key turns in the lock again. I try not to sob.

He is so much taller than me. Taller and bigger and stronger and armed. My heart feels as if it has stopped beating. My lungs feel full of water as he swaggers towards me.

The room has always been tiny, set aside for me. Annie paid the rent on it. I know that the price went up the more I grew, but she had never complained. I only knew because one of the girls had complained about it when I was close enough to hear.

As soon as he gets within arm's reach, I take a step backwards. My body is moving without my brain knowing why, and suddenly I am up against the wall next to my bed, my spine pressed against the little scale Annie had carved in to measure my height. My fingertips brush against the carved words as he traps me against the wall.

His lips press against mine, somehow slimy and chapped at the same time. I panic. I lash out, shoving him back and yelling. I know the yelling is useless. No one that is here will care or even notice. The only person that would is far out of even supernatural hearing range.

He barely moves so I shove him again. He lets out a laugh as if this is funny to him. As if my lack of consent, my lack of arousal and autonomy in this moment is all a big joke. Anger flares through my veins and when he steps back into my space, I swiftly bring my knee up to smash into that thing between his legs.

He is no longer laughing. Now he is groaning on the floor. I try and hop over him to get to the door, to bang on it and scream. Maybe I would be lucky, and the matron would assume it was that quick and open the door. I know that wouldn't be something out of the ordinary. I don't get that far.

The unnamed man grabs my ankle and yanks me backwards. I hit the floor with a harsh thud and flashes of pain in my shoulder and chest. I start to wildly lash out with my legs, missing him half the time. I scream as I feel something tear into my leg. I look back with watery eyes and find his mouth covered with my blood.

The bastard bit me.

I kick out this time with the aim of his nose. I hear a satisfying crunch and I start to drag myself across the floor. My leg won't take the weight of running. Wood splinters around my fingernails but I don't register the pain. My leg throbs and my shoulder aches but I make it almost to the door before he starts to drag me back.

"Nononononononono." I sob. "pleasenononononono."

He slams my head into the ground. Black spots float around my vision and my ears ring. I can hear him start to speak but the words come through as a mush. I register the sound of tearing and I feel fingers prodding at the top of my thighs. A calm fills me as I realise…I would rather die.

"No." I snarl. I start to kick blindly, twisting myself as he tried to grab my flailing legs again. My eyes focus on that dagger, that new lifeline. His eyes follow mine as I suddenly lunge for it. My fingers fumble on the handle, slipping to the edge. I grunt as the blade cleanly opens up my fingertips. I don't care. I grab it and pull it out of the sheath, ignoring as it slices my palm and fingers. It won't matter soon anyway.

My eyes are still blurry, my ears still ringing but I have a small victory here. My heart thumps louder in my chest. I raise the dagger, still cutting into my hand. I'm scared to let it go to get a better hold, which is ridiculous. This is only ending one way anyway. It's my pride that makes me want it to be myself to end it.

The door behind us crashes and suddenly, the man is gone. There is a flash of ginger hair and I release a wheezing breath. Annie. The black spots in my eyes get wider, threatening to turn it all black. I focus on the orange of her hair as the dagger drops from my hand. It is the last thing I see before it all goes black.

Chapter Twenty-Five

Cleo

Luxor, Egypt

1922

I fucking hate tourists. They are loud and whiny, especially the English ones. All I have heard around the too-full market this week were complaints from people with stupid accents and a language they expected us all to speak. I can speak it, but it is the assumption that irritates me.

They pay stupid prices for staple items and act as if it was greatly entertaining. They complain about the heat as if they were not aware of it when they booked to come here. They have the sheer audacity to discuss how amazing our history is, how giant our pyramids are, as if they are not plundering them. Only earlier this year did a group of white men 'discover' a young boy's tomb. They spent months stealing from it and now more of them flocked to come and see it from afar.

They were even more annoying in the bars than they were the streets. In the market they were at least doing some good by handing over their money for inaccurate figurines. In the dingey little hovel that I had ducked into, they were complaining loudly about the price of the alcohol they did not recognise and not even trying to hide their beady little eyes following the 'exotic' asses as they walked past. Many of their women were cooing at the fact the bar was in a circle in the centre of the room. They reached up to try and touch the decorations and looked shocked when they were loudly told off in Arabic.

I take a gulp of my wine as I hear a particularly loud group of British men start up some chant. Their words are slurring and their glasses spilling over. I can't help but sneer at them. That sneer drops from my face as I catch sight of the women sat on the table next to them. She and her companion are both dressed in the same style as me, thin floral dresses, and headscarves. They are not wearing the overly bright and bejewelled ones either. They can't be tourists, although they blend in with a crowd of them thanks to their alabaster skin.

The women's dark eyes widen as she notices me looking. Her red mouth pops open. She slowly wiggles her fingers in a wave. I wave back before I can stop myself. She smiles, revealing nearly perfectly white teeth. I run my tongue over mine self-consciously. Her companion leans forward to whisper something in her ear, light orange tendrils falling from her headscarf as she does so. The dark-eyed beauty waves her off without breaking eye contact with me.

The ginger girl moves to the bar, on the opposite side of the circle to me. I quickly look her over. She is pretty but not as pretty as her friend. I don't think they are a couple. They look close, but those who did have different sexual tastes tended to not look close in public just in case of an accusation. It is why I go almost everywhere alone nowadays.

Potentially related. Maybe sisters or cousins? They didn't have the same eyes or hair colour. I couldn't see them close enough to check out any slight resemblances in the actual face. The ginger one with the loose headscarf spoke in broken Arabic. If they had lived here, it wasn't for long. She only knew the basics and the pronunciation was off.

"You shouldn't go home alone." A surprisingly unannoying English accent breaks me from my spying. The dark-haired girl is on my right. She is quick. I go to respond, but my voice fails me. I blink at her. Her skin is flawless, eyes deep dark pools of onyx and that mouth…She could claim she was a daughter of Hathor and I would believe her. I would believe the old gods were the real ones just as I had when I was six and praising Osiris. She had a face that could convince me.

"Those men behind me," the human goddess whispers, "plan on coming over here. They are going to ask you offensive things and make offensive comments. It's not dark yet. Trust me."

I silently nod. She thinks it's an agreement, which it is, but not with what she said. It's an agreement with myself that she's a goddess. She is unnaturally beautiful, unnaturally kind, and, from the look she sent over her shoulder as the men cheered again, unnaturally stupid.

I grab her elbow as she moves to leave. Her skin is cold to the touch, even in this humidity. Another thing to add to the protective goddess list. "Don't." I tell her quickly. She stares down at my fingers and smirks. "They are a lot bigger than you and we don't have a no-weapons rule in here."

"We will be fine." The goddess steps out of my grip. A smile graces her lips as she turns away from me. "Get home safe, Cleopatra."

I never told her my name, and I never *ever* use my full one. A pit in my stomach thinks this is all a joke or maybe some subtle racism. That has been coming in waves with the tourists. That thought is pushed from my mind as I see the largest of the men from that group staring at me. Goddess was right. Time to go.

I throw the rest of my wine back and stand from my seat. I slip through the crowds of people and out of the curtain door at the back. I twist around the groups of men puffing on disgusting smelling cigarettes. The sharp smell of them overtakes the simmering spiced fruit smells drifting on the wind. The market would be changing over now, bringing out more wines and oily foods to suck in the drunk tourists.

I don't know how long it is until I notice the sound of the footsteps behind me. I am too obviously distracted, too focused on trying to name the exact red shade of the unknown goddess's lips that they only register when I am halfway down the final alleyway before home. I speed up my steps, reaching into my bag for my pathetic excuse for keys. Mathias had taken the dagger to work after an incident last week.

The other footsteps get louder. Louder and faster. I don't dare waste time looking behind me. I bolt for the light at the end of the alleyway, for the main street where I can hear other people, where my overcrowded house is with my overly loud cousins. I bolt for the light that would mean protection. I do not make it.

I am yanked back by my arm, so harshly that I feel it pop out of its socket. I scream and fall to the floor. I don't get the chance to move. Knees force my legs open and force them down onto the hard floor. A large arm presses into my throat as I hear the frantic sounds of a belt being unbuttoned. I try to scream again but I can't get the breath into my lungs. All that comes out is a pathetic wheeze as my vision starts to swim.

I reach up to try and claw at that arm, scratching at the skin with my pathetic excuse for nails. The sound of the belt pauses and I feel a fist pound into my gut. My arms drop against my will. My legs flail against the ground uselessly. I know I have limited time, but I can't force my body to do what I need it to. I can't get it to do anything, even breathe. I am going to die and I can't do anything about it. I close my eyes and let out a sob.

The pressure and the pain is gone in a second. Heaven still hurts. My chest hurts, my legs hurt, I taste blood in my mouth. I open my eyes to look at whatever afterlife is the right one, if anyone's guess was even close. I find myself staring up at the goddess from the bar.

"Annie!" She calls. Her mouth and chin are coated with blood. I want to reach up to wipe it away but my arms are still not responding. Maybe I am not dead yet. Maybe I am still dying.

"You are going to be okay." The goddess leans forward, gently stroking my hair out of my face. I have no idea where my scarf is or when it fell off. "Okay, Cleopatra? You are going to be okay."

"Cleo." I wheeze. A flash of pain in my chest makes me regret it.

"Cleo." The goddess nods. "Cleo, you are going to be okay."

She is such a lovely liar. I think as my vision blurs even further.

"ANNIE." The goddess screams as my world goes black.

Chapter Twenty-Six

Lola

LA, USA

2003

"That dude is such a creeper. Has been ever since school."

"Right, Lo? Standing at the bar, just watching you. It's weird!"

"Oh my god, no, do not drink that! You have no idea what he's done to it! Freak."

My friends' voices echo in a loop as I lay hidden behind the nightclub bins. I had made every mistake in the book, and I had spent the last several hours dwelling on them. I suppose I was being a little harsh on myself. He hadn't been a true stranger. We had physics class together in high school. I had stayed with my group as long as I was able to. I had organised a lift home with someone I trusted.

But the lift had fallen through, and my group had somehow all split off away from me. Jackie had needed to go home, so Nadia walked her. Arizona had been puking, so she was escorted out with Lucy. I was alone, so I took the drink he had offered and made a lame joke about our teachers. I danced with him after a few shots. I let him walk me home because 'it's not safe out there for a woman alone.'

I had ended up begging him to stop and being ignored, broken and bleeding by piles of vomit and broken bottles in the early hours of the morning. The cuts were deep and painful. I almost wished they had done more damage, that it had been swift, and I died before he was finished. That would have been better.

Instead, I had been beaten black and blue, body slicing against the glass on the floor. I had lost consciousness at some point. Maybe he thought he had killed me. Maybe he hoped I wouldn't be found until it was too late. No one had heard me crying when I woke up, and as tears prickled in my eyes again, I knew that no one would hear me now.

I count to five and then yell again. My chest protests and so does my throat but I cannot just lay here and wait for that pain to win. I'm in pain anyway. I may as well be in more physical pain and convince myself it's helping. I keep going back and forth between wanting to die and wanting to live.

I think of my friends' reactions when they hear the news. I think of how this will push my parents even further apart. I think of how they would use it to hurt the other. The idea of them hurting each other, the idea that my father would use this as a cold calculating comment when my mother wore a dress he deemed too short. I think of how my mother would use it as an excuse to scream and cry in public.

I want to live out of spite. I want to live so they never get the chance to make this about them. I want to live so I can do whatever *I* want with *my* life. I will get married and they won't be invited. I will have children they will never meet. I will go on to have a future they won't be in and the bastard who did this to me will rot in fucking jail. I take a deep breath, wincing at the cold stabs of pain, and I scream as loud as I can. I repeat that action, repeat that harsh scream, until I can no longer take a deep enough breath.

My breaths turn to wheezes. I realise I can no longer feel my hands. I blame the long hours out in the cold. I convince myself it is that and nothing more serious. I am not dying. Not when help is coming…and help would be coming. It would be it would be it would be.

I fight to keep my eyes open. I look up at the early morning light, up at the orange clouds that mean dawn is here. Dawn means people. I just need to…my thought trails off as my eyes win the fight and they close. I jolt as something that feels like a warm hand presses against my shoulder. I do not have the strength to open my eyes again.

Chapter Twenty-Seven

Annie

Now

Alistair looks at all of us with his mouth open in horror. I don't blame him. My own stomach twists as I remember those nights in vivid detail. None of them could agree, not really. They couldn't tell me if they wanted this life or not. I had no other way to save them, and I could not leave them like that. I could not leave Lola to be found lying in that rubbish and then for her to die in that hospital room. I could not leave Cleo to be found in that alleyway when we failed to help her in time. I could not leave Grace's body to be thrown into the street without a care.

"What about you?" Alistair turns to look at me. My throat feels too tight to answer.

"Annie doesn't remember." Thomas answers for me. It is the only time I think I will be happy for him to do it.

"You don't...There's this..." Alistair licks his lips and motions between us all. "This...connection."

"The maker's bond can be cut off at any point." I admit softly. "My maker decided not to keep it. I don't know why. I don't know who turned me. I only remember that man doing what he did to me and his hand around my neck. I woke up in the backroom of a brothel with Elias and Christiana."

"And then killed my ancestor." Alistair's voice is overly playful to show me he means it as a joke. He has already forgiven the slight to his family.

"He really did deserve it." I whisper back, just as playfully.

"There is something important you haven't asked yet." Cleo's voice cuts in. "Your body is in direct sunlight and not burning. This doesn't shock you?"

"Thomas already covered all of that last week." Alistair admits bashfully.

"We did not know we were coming last week." Cleo scowls over at Thomas. He ignores her.

"Well, I am going to cover it all again. Just in case he got anything wrong." I wink at Alistair, although that piece of information digs into me, a sharp slice in my chest. Thomas had *prepped* Alistair before I had even given an answer.

"Silver, crosses, wood, sunshine, and holy water." I count them off on my fingers. "Basic deterrents. They all work on all other vampires. I have seen a vampire burn to ashes in the sun. I have seen their skin peel from their bones after being sprayed with holy water. They cannot hold or look at crosses. Those things are very, very important things to remember because they are things you are going to have to mimic to keep your cover if it ever gets out that you are now what you are."

"They won't work on us?" Alistair raises his eyebrows in almost disbelief. After seeing their meeting room, he must have believed they all would, other than the sunlight. I am the one chosen to turn him because my bite gives the ability to walk in the sun and they had leverage.

"Holy water stings a little. Crosses…They make me uncomfortable but that's more psychological than anything else." I admit.

"She was a believer when she was human." Grace adds. "Tudor noblewomen all went to mass. I never did."

"We have reflections." I smile. "And we can have our picture taken. Silver can hurt us, but the wounds eventually heal. Wood has the same effect as silver. If stakes through the chest work for us as well as everyone else, I am not sure. No one has ever managed that."

"No one ever will." Lola smirks over at him. "Annie forgot to add that we are totally badass. We murder murderers and rapists. We save people. We get to look hot forever. We run super-fast and we are super strong. We are every superhero you have ever seen, but we are real."

"Can we fly?" Alistair smirks back. "Because I always really wanted to fly."

"Well, now you're just being picky." Lola purrs.

Get a room. Cleo pulls a disgusted face at them.

"You are technically in mine." Alistair grumbles before his eyes drift back towards me. "So…why are we different?"

"That is a very good question." I smile. That smile turns into a smirk as I twist in my chair to stare up at my almost everything. "Time to answer it, Thomas."

Those grey eyes darken as they meet mine. *Privately.* He insists. I raise my eyebrows at him.

"If you are talking telepathically," Cleo says, "then we cannot hear you and it is very rude."

"Thomas wants to tell me the story privately." I say dismissively even as a cold feeling spreads through my unbeating heart. I am not going to like this. This is going to be a story and not a simple handing over of a file. This is going to hurt enough that if I had found out before, I may have run. Thomas is about to hurt me and I have never truly prepared for that. Even so, I stand from my seat with my shoulders squared.

"I don't think the prince needs to be watched so closely, but if one of you wouldn't mind sitting with him just for company." My eyes catch on Cleo and Grace's entangled arms. "Or two of you. As long as he isn't alone."

"He won't be." Lola pipes up. "I'll stay."

"I don't want to be a burden." Alistair tells us. We all respond down the bond that he isn't.

"I would rather get to know you than sit in my room trying not to listen to everyone else's private conversations. Your staff are super loud." Lola winks at me. Alistair's responding chuckle echoes behind me as I leave the room. Thomas follows on my heels.

Chapter Twenty-Eight
Annie

The walk to my room is as silent as before. The space between us is thick with tension. He isn't masking his heartbeat and its slightly-too-fast thumps echo in my ears. He isn't scared but he is not comfortable either. I try and think of a reason and find a rhythm in it, but I can't.

All I can think of is that Thomas has not had to check. Thomas has known all along why I am what I am, and he has never told me. Thomas has waited centuries for the moment where he could dangle that information in front of me like a carrot. I bite my tongue as I open the door and strut inside. I ignore him as I pick up a blood bag and pour it into the fresh glass as he shuts the door behind us.

"I am not going to like this. Am I?" I ask without looking at him.

"No." He answers.

"Do you remember what you used to call me?" I change the subject in a roundabout way. "What you started to call me after the day your father threatened me to keep my fangs out of you?"

"My wicked little thing." He answers with a lyrical tilt. "Because you needed to keep your wicked little fangs to yourself."

We both laugh loudly even though it is not that funny. The few run-ins I had had with William over my five long centuries have been judgemental and harsh. Most of them had occurred in the first few years of my immortal life. They wanted to 'check in' on the city's biggest safety risk. All of them except Thomas, actually. He had kept an eye on me from afar.

"I did...for the most part." I remind him softly.

"Despite my begging."

"Your fang fetish will be the death of you one day."

"It hasn't killed me yet."

"Because I stopped." I scoff and finally turn to stare at him. He is pressed against the bedroom door as if he is getting ready to bolt. "And luckily all the other vampires you have stuck your penis in also have. You get one slightly too new…why are you laughing?!"

Thomas is holding his side as he sucks in deep breaths, his laugh so loud and genuine that it makes my heart soar despite my mood. His breaths come in sharp gasps and wheeze out of him in hiccupping laughs. His head is tilted up to the ceiling with his eyes closed but I think they may be watering.

"Are you seriously so childish that you are laughing at the word penis when you are supposed to be telling me the secrets of my past?" I scowl at him, slamming my glass down on the bedside table.

Thomas is still chuckling as he turns those eyes towards me. I was wrong, they are not watering. They are ablaze with emotion, so dark that they looked like shimmering pools of liquid charcoal.

"I am the childish one?" He grins. "When you start poking fun at my sex life the first chance you get?"

"Not the first chance." I snap. I ignore the fluttering rage in my stomach as he does not deny that I am simply a fetish. I am not the only vampire he has screwed, and I have almost certainly not been the last. Thomas's face turns serious as he looks me up and down.

"You really think that's what that night was to me." Thomas sounds hurt. "That what we did meant nothing."

"It meant something." I argue. "It changed everything. I thought that it changed the battlefield. I thought that we were finally on the same page. You didn't admit it to me in words, but it was fine because you admitted it by letting me bite you. You finally let me know who you are."

"My bloodline does not make me who I am." Thomas snarls. "It never has, and it never will. Just as it will never change anything."

"It could have changed everything!" I yell back. "I understood then, while your blood trickled down my chin, I understood why Elias and Christiana helped me kill Henry that night. They did it because he knew. He knew who you were, who your mother was. They did it because *you* were at risk."

This is not the argument we are meant to be having. These are not the things that should be revealed tonight. But I know deep in my heart that if I do not say it first, if I do not admit everything now, then I will never get the chance. If he tells me first then I will not respond in kind. I am petty enough to take my admittance to the grave that will never come.

"Do not put that on me." Thomas begs in a whisper. "Do not make that about me. You did that for Anne."

"I did." I nod as tears prickle behind my eyes. "I did. But that night when I tasted your blood...When I realised you had the same diseased blood as the Tudors...That became a more important reason. It felt like...divine intervention. I suddenly stopped hating that- I suddenly did not mind becoming what I am as long as I thought that it was so I could save you. That I saved you without even realising I had done it. Your life in exchange for my soul. That made sense to me. That night in 1914 made it all make sense. My suffering made sense if it saved you."

Thomas takes a step towards me, and I take a step backwards, my knees hitting the mattress behind me. I do not break eye contact with him even as my vision began to swim.

"Then you told me you were not in Paris of your own free will. You were there...because the King of England had demanded it." I let out a harsh laugh. "And the idea of that...The idea that the nephew of King James V of Scotland had still spent *centuries* at the beck and call of that kingdom...The idea of you bowing and grovelling to the descendants of that man. It was too much."

"You act as if you are Scottish. You talk like Elias, like you would have thrown up banners and declared me a king." Thomas stepped forward again. "I never wanted that. I didn't get to decide where my blood came from. I didn't get to *choose* being Margaret Tudor's illegitimate grandchild. I didn't want it. I didn't want what that would mean for me. I only ever wanted one thing. One future."

"I act as a woman who you proposed to." I whisper back, taking a half step forward, gesturing with my hands. "Who would have shared your home and had your children. Children that would have been at risk if that truth ever came out. I *speak* like a woman who would have declared you king. Who would have fought for that if you had wanted it and would have been prepared for the worst-case scenario if you hadn't. I act as a woman who would have given you *everything*."

"That." Thomas points at me. "That is what I wanted. That future. I wanted you to say yes. I wanted the sound of our children laughing and chasing each other echoing around our estate while we sleep in. I didn't want to throw in a claim to two thrones simply because I was a man. I didn't want to put my neck on the line for it. My grandmother cheating on the King of Scotland was treason. There was no need to drag that all up just to make me miserable for a few decades. England had an heir. Scotland had an heir. They didn't need me."

"I needed you. I needed you to be honest with me. I needed you to have been willing to tell me that back then." I tell him as tears spill down my cheeks. If I was being honest with myself, this was not the first time I had thought about the lost future. I had imagined what our children would look like when I was human, and that image had haunted me the last five centuries. I would never have children now. The closest I will ever have is Grace.

"I wanted to. I was going to." Thomas whispers. His steps towards me are hesitant now, his arms slightly open and outreached towards me. "But then…There was never a good time after that. Never a good time to make it about me."

It is a poor attempt at a lie. The good time would have been after I ripped out King Henry's throat. The good time would have been in the ensuing wars between his two daughters. There would have been ample opportunity. Those visits to the brothel every week when he came to see Grace, the letters, and gifts he sent while I was adjusting. Those were all good times and opportunities.

I hold myself back from going into his arms and letting him take all this rage away. If I let him hold me then I will not want the answers that I truly came here for. I will not want to know the daywalker secret that he has kept from me. I will not want to rush from the room and head straight to my brothers side once I find out where he is. I will want to stay in Thomas's arms for as long as he has stayed in my heart. Forever.

"This is the good time. This is the good time for you to tell me what you know about why…about why I am what I am. Why I can do what I can do." I take a deep breath, but I cannot think of a different way to phrase it. I cannot bring myself to say it out loud, to beg to know the past I had tried to move on from.

"Annie, please." Thomas whispers. "This is not a good time."

"Yes it is. I am saying it is." I snap. "This was the deal. I saved Alistair. I get my answers. Tell me Thomas. Tell me why I have to spend my existence running. Tell me why I have spent the last five hundred years pretending I cannot even stand near an uncovered window. Why I have not been able to give my girls permanent homes. You tell me now because there will never be a better time. There will never be a good time. I will never get that time back, but I can try and fix it going forward."

Thomas stops breathing for a moment. He holds a breath in his lungs as he stares at me and when he releases it, he closes his eyes.

"I'm the reason." He admits.

Chapter Twenty-Nine

Annie

"Do not be cruel." I hiss at him. "That is not funny."

"It's not a joke, Annie." Thomas's hands drop to his side. His gaze follows them. "After you were attacked you were sent to the infirmary. They said the best they could do was make you comfortable, but you were never waking up. Doctors back then were fumbling but they knew you had a head injury and your stab wound and they…"

I stay silent. I didn't know that. I only knew that I had been attacked, raped, and woken up in a private room at a brothel in the city days later. I woke up to the news that my friend, my queen, had lost her head. I woke up with Elias and Christiana by my side. They had told me they found me mid-transition and moved me there to help me. They broke the news that they were witches. They fed me a cup of blood. The knowledge of their lie stings as Thomas continues.

"I couldn't lose you. I couldn't. My father had a spell that he had tried on my mother when she was dying. It hadn't worked then, but I was going to make it work for you." Thomas turns his dark eyes to me. They are shining. "I broke into his study, and I found the spell. I knew what it was missing, what he had not been willing to give up for her but that I would give up in a heartbeat for you."

"Let me guess. A summoning spell. Some lone nomad vampire running around not wanting a coven? You got down on your knees and begged him until he agreed as long as he could strand me with you?" I sneer.

"No." Thomas says hoarsely. "Annie…You have no maker. There was no vampirism before that day in 1536. You were the first."

I freeze. Or rather I mean to. I go so still that I may as well be made of stone. My ears start to ring, and my lungs stop working. I have misbalanced myself and I fall backwards in an almost feint. My ass hits the soft mattress, and my shaking hands reach out to grip the wooden bedpost. It can't be possible. He can't be right. He can't…

He can't have done this to me.

"Please let me finish." Thomas cuts me off before I have a chance to actually say anything. I nod silently. If he finishes, then maybe my assumption is wrong. Maybe he had a good reason for ripping my soul away from me without asking or ever telling me. Maybe there was some witch reason for it. Maybe I could somehow, someway, eventually, maybe, be saved.

"I called my coven. All of them. Corsi and Mary wouldn't listen so Christiana told my father that if we did not do this then she would kill herself so we would do it for her and she could turn you after. She adores you." Thomas crouches down so he can try and look me in the eye. I avoid his gaze.

"The missing piece was a soul." Thomas reveals. "The spell would not work properly if no one was willing to pay that price. I was willing to pay it for you. But for me to do that, we had to summon someone that my father would not summon for my mother. I had to grovel to the devil himself that he let you live. That he let you live until this whole world was ash and to take my soul in place of yours."

"And what did the devil say, dear Thomas? When you begged for the chance at eternity with me?" I try to sneer but it was more of a sarcastic whisper.

"That he was a sucker for a love story." Thomas answers calmly. "But Annie, I never thought that he would…I never expected to live this long with you. I expected to die in exchange. I was happy to die in exchange." I open my mouth to respond but he carries on. "I knew you might hate me for it. I didn't care if you hated me because if you hated me, then you were feeling something, and if you were feeling something…"

"Do you have any idea how pathetic that sounds?" I snarl. I can finally bring myself to look at him. My fangs slide easily through my gums.

Thomas does not flinch. He drops to his knees and waits. He waits for me to hurt him. I am tempted to. I know that he can survive a snapped neck, a ripped throat. He has told me so himself and I know that no member of the cursed coven can truly die. But that will not make me feel better. Making him grovel will.

"I can walk in the sun because I am the first vampire. I am the first vampire because you decided I still had a place in this world. I have spent centuries hiding these abilities and running from vampires that do not have them, making sure they did not find out, because you decided to change my entire biology without my knowledge. You then *abandoned* me to your little sister and cousin. Have I missed anything there?" I ask coldly.

"I did not abandon you." Thomas responds. "When you were transitioning I was sick. It was a side effect. If you did not fully transition, then my soul was stuck between us. I wasn't able to walk for days. I set fire to my chest of drawers in my delirium. You are able to walk in the sun and you aren't affected by things other vampires are because you have my soul. Everyone you turn gets a little slice of it. That's why it's the same for them. That's the theory anyway."

"I have only turned three- now four- people." I speak slowly because if I don't I may just take it all back and rip him apart limb from limb. "Yet there are vampires that exist that I have not turned and neither have they. My brother being one of them. How exactly does that fit into your plan?"

"The spell now works for everyone that used it after I finalised my devil deal. Other covens could now save the dying. All variations of the spell now worked as a sort of universal deal. But they did not have to give up their souls in exchange so...the vampires they create don't get the perks." Thomas shrugs in a 'what can you do' kind of way. I want to break his shoulders.

"I have spent half a millennium thinking I had no soul only to find out that I have someone else's." I whisper. "Only to find out that I have yours."

"I would do it again." He breathes and I finally look him in the eyes. "I would grovel and beg the devil for the next half a millennium, the next five millenniums, if it gave you one more minute in the sun."

My heart splits in two. One half wants to scream and cry and blame him, lash out and throw a pillow or the glass at him. He has lied to me longer than some species have been alive.

The other half wants to pull him into my arms and make him scream in an all too different way. He loves me. He put his soul on the line for me. He was willing to defy creation for me. The betrayal in me is almost swallowed up by that act of love.

I lunge for him.

Chapter Thirty

Annie

I hear a crack as I slam him into the floor. It was probably his legs based on the position. His head hits the floor, and we start to tumble sideways. I end up on top with my fingers digging into the side of his throat. I could pull his entire vocal cord system out in one twitch. I could do it over and over so he could never lie to me again.

But he is staring up at me with a soft smile on his face and as much as I hate him right now, as much as my veins burn with rage, I cannot wipe that off. My hand refuses to obey any thought of it.

"You gave me your soul." I thought saying it out loud again would help take the sting of it away, the way repeating *monsters aren't real* helps little children scared of the dark.

"I did." He struggles to speak.

"You summoned the devil so you could save me."

"I did."

"You got yourself cursed with immortal life in the process. Your entire coven did. That wasn't part of the plan?" I ever so slightly loosen my grip as his families face flashes before my eyes. Christiana. Elias. William. Corsi. Mary. They are all stuck like this because Thomas loved me too much.

"No." Thomas admits. "It was Lucifer's parting gift. After all, how was I supposed to have forever with you if I don't have a forever?"

Thomas laughs once as if it was some type of sick joke. Maybe it is. We were never meant for a centuries-long love story. I was too addicted to setting the world right. I had changed that night from the girl who dreamed of a large wedding and multiple children. I had been broken apart and the pieces hadn't fit the same afterwards.

But Thomas had put me back together. Thomas had fought to get those pieces of me and had used his soul to fuse them back. If I could allow myself to be honest then I could admit that I preferred the pieces like this. I preferred to be vengeful rather than vain. I preferred to be so clearly broken and glued back together than to worry about ever showing a crack.

Thomas had made me *like* myself. Thomas had loved me so much he had changed the face of the world just to keep me in it. My hand completely drops from his throat, and I lean forward to press my forehead against his. Thomas's breath catches in his throat and his heart increases. I can't help but smirk.

"It's not my fault, you know." Thomas grumbles.

"I was three seconds away from killing you and your heart didn't do that. Your heart was steady." I tease him. My nose grazes his. His responding huff tickles me face.

"I would have come back." Thomas reminds me hesitantly. My smile widens.

"I'm counting on that." I trace my lips gently over his in a mockery of a kiss. Thomas lets out a light groan. "I'll give you my version of the I love you speech later."

"I don't think I ever actually said I love you." Thomas tilts his head upwards as I slightly pull back.

"Actions speak louder than words." I smirk. "Now shut up and fuck me like it's 1914."

"Very witty." Thomas chuckles, shifting himself up onto his elbows and trailing his nose up my neck. His breath caresses my skin.

"The devil gave you a sex life, Thomas. Start taking advantage of it." I move my hands up to tangle in his hair. Thomas rests his head against the side of mine and his fingers gently trail down my spine. He lets out a gentle humming sound.

"You're sure?" He whispers.

"I'm sure." I confirm. "But I'm not going to be gentle. I'm still mad."

Of course you are, my wicked little thing. Thomas nips at the corner of my jaw. It is my turn to groan.

Chapter Thirty-One

Annie

The last time we had done this had been intense. We had broken things with our various parts and his magic; the sheets had been stained with blood and sweat. There had been the constant threat of bombs dropping, of being interrupted by a siren or a patrol of guards. I had ended up going home covered in soot and blood. There were no threats this time, no fireplace to make the place a smudged oily mess.

"I won't bite you this time." I whisper before our lips crash together. The kiss is hungry and wild, teeth clashing against each other as we both fight to take control.

"Spoilsport." Thomas growls, one of his hands cupping the side of my face roughly. I tug at his hair as I shift my legs to straddle him more comfortably. I feel him press against me even through both of our jeans. We both moan as I shift against him.

"Bed. Naked. Now." Thomas demands. When I hesitate, he takes my bottom lips between his teeth and pulls at it. I am on my feet and stripping by the bed in a blink of an eye. I had planned for comfort today and a flash of self-conscious shame runs through me as I realise I have no bra and a pair of bright red boxer shorts on.

I tug my shirt off over my head with my back towards him. Before I can even drop it to the floor I feel him press against me. All of him burns hot and it's all skin on skin. His fingers loop into the strap of my boxers and they are on the floor before I can even finish my breath. Suddenly, he slows.

His hands gently pull my hips to rub against his own. He trails soft kisses up and down my shoulders. I am the impatient one. I am the one that tries to reach behind me to feel him in my hand. He is already hard and pressed against my ass but it's not enough.

He grabs my wrist to stop me. He loops both of our hands around to cup the space between my legs. I take a sharp breath as his fingers gently move through the space between my own to trace those delicate parts of me. He bites into my shoulder as I give a jolt when he flicks his finger across my entrance. I hiss in response.

We stand there for an agonising moment as he moves those fingers across me. He trails them up my stomach and around the edges of my breasts but never touching the vital bundles of nerves that I ache for.

Teasing bastard, I shoot through the bond. The bond he can only talk through because he made a ridiculous sacrifice. I lean back against him even more.

Wicked little thing. He thinks back before grazing his teeth against my earlobe. *On the bed.*

You don't give me orders. I huff even as I do exactly as he asks and settle myself on the edge of the bed. Then I stare at him. I stare at his surprisingly comfortable chest, at his flexing fingers and finally down at his length. I am almost ashamed at how quickly my mouth waters and my core throbs. I remind myself that this is Thomas. Thomas, who once begged for me. Thomas, who I have already had. This should be as easy as breathing.

"You obeyed pretty well." Thomas smirks as he walks over to the edge of the bed. He pries open my legs with his own before kneeling in front of me. He places an open-mouthed kiss on the side of my knee and starts to slowly kiss up my thighs. I lay myself down and once again slide my hands into his hair.

I let out a low throttling groan as he reaches his goal. He starts out with gentle little kitten licks before swirling his tongue all around my folds. Every shift and flick has me twirling my hands in his hair and whimpering.

After one particularly delicious lick my hips jolt upwards. He loops an arm over my hips and keeps them forced down. He brings his other hand around and starts to rub fast circles over the bundle of nerves he had ignored earlier. I let out a small yelp and moan as a familiar feeling starts to build in my stomach.

My knees are thrown over his shoulder and I subconsciously start to pull him forward, closer, deeper, if that was even possible. I want to yell at him to skip this part and get to the main event. I wasn't a prude. I have had sex since 1914, but none of them had put me in such a frenzy. I start to wonder if there is a link to the soul we share, but those thoughts are cut off with an eye-rolling scream.

My hips start to buck wildly as I am tipped over the edge. Thomas makes a pained noise as my hands in his hair turn into fists. He continues licking and sucking until my body is done shuddering. My breath leaves me in bursts and my limbs feel heavy. My legs slide off of Thomas's shoulders as he crawls up the bed towards me.

My still shaky arms try and drag him up to face me. Thomas lets out a breathy chuckle that I cut off by smashing my lips against his. I can taste myself on his tongue and it is still not enough. I frantically run my hands down his body and we both groan as my fingertips brush the side of him. I start to blindly guide him to my entrance. I whimper as he slides against my folds.

"I thought you weren't going to be gentle." Thomas teases me, his lips brushing against mine as he refuses to move away. His hips give the tiniest impatient little push into me. I let out a breathy moan.

"Don't be so judgemental." I whisper back, tilting my hips up to take in just his head. Thomas starts to leave sloppy kisses against my jaw. I smirk, moving my hips in tiny circles before I take my vampire speed and strength and flip us over. I hover over him in a sort of straddle and stare him in the eye.

"Cruel wicked thing." Thomas whines.

"You asked for it. Literally. You got on your knees, and you begged the king of Hell for me." I whine back, slowly taking him inch by inch until our hips clash when I finish speaking.

We both stay there for a moment, adjusting to the new position and new era of our relationship. This both was and wasn't new territory for us. We had done this physical act and many more before, but we had never been so close. It made it better in some ways. Now I could stare in his eyes, and I didn't have to ignore the devotion in them. I didn't have to pretend it was pure lust.

I lean down to plant my mouth against his as I shift my hips in slow grinding circles. The kiss is soft and gentle, the opposite of my promise and my actions last time. Last time we broke each other's bones and bit into each other's skin so hard there was blood gushing. This time I make sure I am not holding him too tightly. I make sure to put feelings into the kiss to show him that this is it. This is it for the both of us.

"Mine." I whisper as I quicken the pace of my hips.

"Mine." Thomas repeats with one hard thrust upwards.

When I let out a whimper, he smirks up at me and repeats the action far quicker than before. I throw my head back and start to mutter his name as that pressure builds again. My fingers scratch at his chest and I feel my fangs break through my gums as I teeter on that edge. Thomas catches sight of them and grabs the back of my head, slamming it down in the space between his shoulder and neck.

I moan at the new angle and the tantalising tempting sound of his pulse. I won't bite him. I won't I won't I wo- My fangs slice into his skin accidentally as my mouth opens in my second toe-curling scream of the day. I come back down from my high and Thomas's thrusts turn sloppy. I lick the blood drizzling down his neck as he groans his own release into my ear.

We lay there, panting and sweaty until his heartbeat calms. I collapse to the side of him, hands splayed across his chest and leg hooked over his hip. He runs his hands up and down my back and presses a gentle kiss to my forehead. He decides that isn't close enough and pulls me further into his chest, so my head rests over his heart.

I am happy to stay in this position, close my eyes, and sleep like this until one of the girls wakes me with an emergency. His chest is more comfortable than any pillow.

"I love you." Thomas whispers.

"I love you." I finally say it out loud. "Even though you infuriate me to hell and back."

"I would go to hell and back for you, if that makes it any better." Thomas laughs and starts to play with the ends of my hair. I laugh with him and place a playful nip on his shoulder.

"You need to stop saying such dramatic things." I tell him as I close my eyes. "You witches love a declaration."

"You owe me one of those if I recall. Your dramatic I love you speech." Thomas rests his cheek against my head.

"Later." I promise in a mutter as sleep pulls at the edges of my mind. "Maybe."

"Wicked little tease." Thomas's breath ruffles the baby hairs around my face. I ignore him.

Chapter Thirty-Two

Hell is hot. It's uncomfortable and moist. It fills my lungs and makes them heavy. It is also beautiful. The trees are thick with foliage. There are no laminated papers stapled into their trunks. The flowers that grow beneath them are bright and sweet smelling. The thick green grass tickles my ankles. I look out across a pool of clear blue water.

"There you are, my little day walker." A voice like velvet sings from behind me. "I was wondering when you would finally come see me."

I don't turn around. Instead, I stare as ripples gently move around the surface of the water. I cannot see anything that would cause them and there is no breeze or wind of any kind.

"Don't be petulant."

"Chastised by the devil." I smirk. "I suppose that is quite a thing to add to my list of accomplishments."

"Only until you die. Then you will find out its quite common."

"I can die?" I say it playfully even as another question worms its way to the front of my mind.

"You can. I won't be telling you how." The voice turns soft. I hear no footsteps or heartbeat as he steps in place beside me. I am tempted to look, to gaze upon what was once famously the most gorgeous face in Heaven, but something stops me.

"Don't want to see me living in a studio flat here anytime soon?" I joke. I want to hear him chuckle, to know what it sounds like when the devil laughs.

His laugh zings down my skin, setting the hair on the back of my neck on end. It's deep and rich but there is an after sense of bitterness in it.

"You have a lot more living to do." Was his answer.

"I have lived longer than I should have."

"The world needs you. The girls need you. The newly turned prince needs you. You don't get to give up yet. I made you resilient for a reason."

"You don't get to claim credit for the things I survived."

"You almost didn't survive them."

"Almost." I repeat the world bluntly. "But I did."

"That witch boy got his entire coven to grovel for you to become the world's greatest threat, Annie Dawson. Does he also get no credit?"

"I did not ask him to do that. I did not want him to do that. I took what I was given, and I made a life out of it."

"And your Grace?"

I snap my head to look at him and blink. He looks barely fifteen years old. His hair is the purest gold I had ever seen but his eyes…his eyes are inhuman. They are miniature galaxies swirling around in eye sockets, stars sparkling as he looked at me. At least his face is turned to look at me. There is no way to tell where his eyes are focussed.

He chuckles. Every part of him clashes with my expectations. His face could only be described as adorable, but his voice is deep and adult. He has no giant wings or intense burns. If he had normal eyes, then he would look like a human teenage boy.

"I won't mention her again." He promises. He hold up two fingers in a salute. "Scout's honour."

"It's not a coincidence is it? That you come to me now."

"Clever girl." The devil sighs as he settles himself down on the ground. He wraps his arms around his knees and stares out across the lake.

"Am I going to have to spend the next hundred years waiting for you to tell me why I am here?" I ask irritably.

"I would like to get to know you. I have heard such great things. But no, Annie. You are also not really here. You are still curled up in bed with Thomas." The Devil responded.

"You don't get a lot of visitors. Do you?" I settle myself on the floor next to him.

"Only one." He admits.

I can't bring myself to harass him for an answer to my question. Not when he looks so small and lonely. My bleeding heart has me feeling sorry for the ruler of Hell. Maybe Lola was right, and I should get a therapist.

"You have a long road ahead of you. You have done something that cannot be undone, and I am afraid not everyone is going to make it out. I need you to promise me that my witches will be safe. That you will stay with them."

"That is a vague warning." I scowl. "And...your witches? You mean the cursed coven."

"I prefer the word blessed but yes. Christiana, Thomas, William, Elias, Corsi and Mary. Whatever happens, you make sure they are safe. You stay with them. Understood?"

"Safe from what?" My thoughts flash to Grace, Cleo, Lola, and Alistair. To my family. Alistair is involved in that now. Even when I get rid of the bond I will still check on him.

"I can't tell you that."

"Why?"

"If you find out, it makes it worse." His answer is blunt and now that his warning has been given, the world around me starts to blur like a painting being smeared with water.

"Take care of them, Annie Dawson." His voice sounds far away even as I can feel him still sitting right next to me. I scream "How?" at him but my whole body moves sluggishly. My eyelids force themselves shut and I scream.

Chapter Thirty-Three

Grace

One Week Later

"The Devil?" Cleo repeats for the third time, pacing around the private dining room. The Queen had organised an entire wing of the castle to be vampire friendly. There was a chilled decanter on the table filled with O negative. The cutlery in the room was all plastic. I would guess that the treats scattered on plates around the table were Alistair's favourites. He had scoffed down three custards donuts in a row.

"The Devil. He cares about the cursed coven after what they did." Annie explains. We had barely seen her the last six days. She would check in on Alistair as he rested, get reports from Elias on how he was doing, and then she left. She left the palace and its grounds. She came back each morning before the dawn and she didn't let any of us know why. Now she has called a vamp-only meeting and told us what Thomas told her that day she left to talk with him alone.

"How romantic." Lola whispers softly over her plate of cheesecake. Cleo looks at her as if she had just declared she was moving to Jupiter.

"He damned her. You do understand that, don't you, Lola?" Cleo spat the girls name at her as she paused her pacing. "And in turn she has damned us all. She damned Grace and then she damned us."

Annie winces. I zoom forward and block Cleo's view of the rest of the room. I take her face in my hands and look her in the eye. I match my breaths to hers. It always calms her down.

"Annie did not know." I whisper softly. Cleo's eye twitches. I start to gently move hair from her face. "She had no way of knowing and even if she did, I would still pick this. I would still pick the path that let me meet you."

Cleo's gaze softens and she presses her forehead against mine. She goes still as a statue, and I know that in a moment or two that she will be calm enough to talk again.

"I would pick this too." Lola tells the room quickly. "My life…My life as a vampire is so much better than my life as a human would have been. I never cared about my soul anyway."

"Ditto." Alistair chimes in around a mouthful of biscuit.

Lola could have said she was moving to the top of mount Everest and the crown prince would have asked how long he had to pack. He had been unsuccessfully hiding his lovestruck glances at our American little sister for days now, much to the chagrin of his human servant friend.

Annie shoots him an amused, soft smile. He fits in well with us, which makes remembering the fact we would soon have to abandon him even more heart-breaking. Maybe one day, in a few decades when his advisors had faked his death and someone else was crowned King, he would be able to return to us. I wonder if Lola would miss him until then.

"He didn't tell us exactly what threat the witches are under?" I ask my maker softly. "He came to speak to you and that was all he had to say as warning?"

"Annoying, I know." Annie sighs. "But he said if I knew more, then it would end worse. Doesn't give me a lot of faith for how he thinks it's going to end now."

"The witches can handle themselves. They have made that clear." Cleo grumbles. Annie raises an eyebrow at her as Lola hides her giggle by shoving a cupcake into her mouth.

"Elias and Cleo got into a little bit of a … tiff." Alistair explained diplomatically.

"He froze my jaw shut for nine minutes." Cleo seethed.

"So he could get some peace and quiet." Lola added on with a grin.

"It was because I called you insufferable. Which you were being." Cleo glared at her.

"So, we take it in turns monitoring and protecting the witches." I cut in to stop the same argument from two days ago occurring. It was irritating then, and it was even more so now. Annie nods in agreement.

"But there are more of them than there are us." Alistair points out with a small frown. "There would always be one of them without one of us."

"You are still too new." Annie tells him softly. "We don't start your basic training until tomorrow, let alone combat training. I can't put you on guard duty with one of them if you can't control your own strength. Not to mention that you are the crown prince and so you cannot play bodyguard anyway."

"But then that leaves someone else to pick up the slack." Alistair argued. He ignores the issue of his position. "That's not fair and it leaves a security gap."

"Ali, Annie is right." Lola soothes him. "What if something happens to you or the witch you're guarding? You need to be able to run and to fight."

Alistair pouts and settles back in his seat. He didn't argue any further, but he was clearly not happy about how the conversation had gone.

"He raises a good point though. There are only four of us equipped enough to act as bodyguards." I say softly. "We can't just leave two of them without someone."

"But they aren't completely helpless anyway." Cleo cuts on. "So why do they need extra protection?"

"I don't know, Cleo. Perhaps I should summon the devil to ask him." Annie said as she reached for a biscuit.

"That's not a terrible idea." Lola said hesitantly. "I mean…we know six people who have done it before."

We all turn and look at each other, pondering that for a moment. It isn't a terrible idea, but there is no way that William would allow it. He had caused a riot every time one of us was alone with the prince 'just in case.' The Queen had finally told him to knock it off this morning.

The ritual could involve things we had no access to. The ritual could involve anything. It could need to be performed at a certain time, under a certain constellation or position of the moon. We weren't witches. Could vampires even perform spells?

"William would never allow it." Alistair sighs. "He won't even let my father go to the airport without a small army. He won't let us invite Satan into the palace. He definitely won't tell us how."

"William won't." Annie nodded slowly. Then a slow grin took over her face. She looks straight at Lola as she adds. "But one witch will."

Annie hasn't been as oblivious to us as I thought.

Chapter Thirty-Four

Lola

Elias had invited me to his room multiple times over the last week. Most of those had been joking comparisons when he dropped off a first edition Charles Dickens to my room. How and why he had it, I didn't know. I just jumped at the thought of borrowing it. I hadn't paid much attention to math or science in high school, but I had liked doing the reading for English. My favourite had been Romeo and Juliet. The idea of a warring dysfunctional family had felt depressingly familiar.

The thick wooden door opened three seconds after I knocked. The heartbeat inside was fast and hard, the reason why clear once I took a good look at Elias. His hair was messy, and his body covered in thick droplets of sweat. He is wearing dark blue workout shorts and matching trainers but no shirt.

"Hi." Elias grins as he yanks out a Bluetooth earphone, his chest pistoning up and down as if I caught him mid-marathon. I might have. His abs were gleaming, making it look like he had just stepped right out of a gym commercial. "Finished with the book already?"

"No. No not yet." I smile and awkwardly put my hand on my neck. "Sorry, I didn't mean to interrupt. I can come back?"

"No. No, don't worry about it. Come in." He steps back into his room, and I follow after him. I don't think there is a need to (as Cleo so delicately put it) whore myself out for the information. Elias and I have an easy friendship already.

His room is a mess. Not in an unclean way but in a 'I am comfortable here' way. There was no packed-up suitcase in the corner like there was in mine. His bookshelves were full with books in a variety of conditions. Some looked like brand-new novels and others looked like hundred-year-old notebooks. A large trunk in the corner was covered with a small shoe rack. Storage maybe?

There are also posters and pictures all over the walls. The white paint was almost invisible behind them. He had created a collage of his eras, a wraparound timeline of his life. I take slow steps forward to look at them.

"You don't have to do that, you know." Elias shuts the door with a soft click. "Walk like a human. I can handle a fast woman."

"Habit." I mutter as my eyes catch on a polaroid photo of Elias with a fauxhawk and spiked leather jacket. He looked like a stereotypical punk, but it suited him. Especially the eyeliner. I reach up and gently run my hands over the logo on his t-shirt.

"I've heard of that band." I laugh.

"No one has heard of that band." Elias says through a slurp from his water bottle.

"I have! My first boyfriend was super obsessed with all these underground bands that never went anywhere. Ya know the type who did some local bars and ten years down the line the bassist is a famous actor's dentist."

"That is the most American thing I think I have ever heard." Elias smiles as he comes to stand next to me. "Although I admit that this photo was taken in New York so…"

"Me dating someone who researched underground punk bands is the most American thing you've ever heard? Really?" I scoff, raising my eyebrows at him.

"Okay, point taken." Elias laughs again. "Did you come here just to look at my walls?"

"No." I whisper, all humour leaving my voice as I once again look around at the walls. Centuries and centuries of living, all summed up. Would I ever be allowed such a space? Would I ever feel safe enough, secure enough? Once this whole mess was sorted maybe we could find a way for us to settle down for a while. Maybe now we knew the reason for our gifts we could find a way that we wouldn't have to spend our existence hiding them.

"Thomas finally told Annie. Annie finally told you." Elias guesses. He crosses his arms and follows my gaze. "I don't think you've come to ask if we were all so in love with her that we begged Lucifer for a second chance."

"I don't think you were in love with her." I feel my mouth twitch into a small smile. "But I do think you love her. You and Christiana. The other three…"

"Have always blamed her." Elias finishes my sentence. "And you're right. I do love Annie. I've known her since I was seven years old. She's as much my family as Thomas is. She's just…the distant cousin that is off doing her own thing."

"Does that make me your second cousin?" I cross my arms in a mirror of his pose.

"No." Elias says quickly. "Not a fan of incest."

"We haven't done anything!" I giggle.

"Yet."

"How presumptuous."

"Forever is an awfully long time, Lola." Elias's eyes focus on my face. "I can wait a few more centuries for you to realise I'm one handsome bastard."

I laugh again, so effortlessly that I wonder if this is what it's supposed to be like. I don't fully know what the 'it' is. I just know that I am not on edge with him. I am not paranoid about what he expects from me or if he is looking at me in a certain way. I can't remember the last time I was alone in a room with a boy and I wasn't paranoid about what I looked like or looking to see if he was worth a kill.

"I want to know more." I admit. "About Annie and how it all happened. How you did it. What it all means."

"And you didn't want to ask Thomas?" Elias moves to his bed, a wide thing with minimal pillows and a thick duvet. He pats the space next to him. I am across the room in a heartbeat.

"I find it easier to talk to you." I shrug. "I had more time with you during Alistair's transition than I had with Thomas."

"Christiana was there the whole time." Elias is clearly fishing for a compliment. I give him a side eyed glance as I fight back yet another smile. "I'll tell you what you want to know. Plus a little bit more because I'm a shameful flirt *and* gossip." Elias bumps his shoulder against mine.

"How thoughtful of you." I bump him back. He launches right into a backstory that I was curious about but had been afraid to ask for.

"Thomas has been in love with Annie since the moment he glimpsed her." Elias's eyes glance towards the storage chest. The things from his human life must be in there. "Which was when we were kids. We were so young that we hadn't even heard about sex, not really. We just knew people got married and girls popped out babies soon after. He came home after meeting her at a Christmas festival some other lord was putting on and he declared her his best friend forever."

Elias turns those eyes to look at me. I knew they are the exact same as the rest of his coven but his looked lighter, more playful, a more gorgeous shade of grey. We have somehow ended up with our bodies constantly touching the other. Shoulders, thighs, hands all gently brushing against each other with every breath and twitch. Neither of us pull away.

"She didn't like him. Not in the way he liked her. She found him amusing sometimes but overall, pretty bland. When she turned old enough to get married off and her father put the word out, she thought he was simply being kind when he was the first in line. Kind Thomas running to her rescue so she wouldn't be shipped across the country to a man three times her age." Elias lets out a soft chuckle. "Thomas went near mad with worry that her father would reject his offer. That she would reject him. Annie's father was unusual for the time. He asked her opinion and considered it."

"So, they were engaged when Annie got attacked." My heart sinks in my chest. Their love story was so much sadder than I could have thought.

"Oh no." Elias snorted. "No. Her father considered her opinion, but he didn't make it a priority. She was a handmaiden for the Queen when the Queen was in high favour. She had access to high-ranking people of the time. A lot of rich lords and councilmen. Thomas never stood a chance. He still tried though."

"He couldn't have used magic?" I joke weakly.

"Oh, the councilman who had publicly beaten his first wife got struck with a mystery illness. But I did that one. She was my friend too." Elias shrugs as if it was nothing, as if witchcraft to curse powerful politicians in the 1500s was no big deal.

"Annie eventually begged her father to say yes to Thomas's proposal." Elias continued. "The other suitors had gifted her gold and jewels, dresses and perfumes. They would have raised her station even higher than it was, raised her father and brother with her. But Thomas...Thomas had brought her a book."

"A book?"

"A book." Elias nodded. "Nothing special about it, either. It was just a plain little book. Apparently, she had mentioned it at a feast two years before and well, you know Annie. Actions speak louder than words with her."

"But they didn't get engaged." I frown at him.

"Someone tried to murder her before the official yes."

"Mood killer."

"You should have been there when he found out." Elias grimaced. "He fell apart. He became obsessed with finding a way to save her. It hurt to watch. Christiana was near tears every time she was in the same room with him."

"How long…" I trailed off. I had assumed Annie's attack and her transition had been quick. A day at maximum.

"Almost a week." Elias's voice was grave. I already knew that was unusual for him. "She was in the infirmary the whole time. They just kept…well. It was the sixteenth century. Medicine wasn't exactly medicine."

My mind flashes back to every historic drama show I had ever watched. I think of dirty, blunt knives and leeches and I give a shudder. Poor Annie. I am glad I was born after the invention of sanitiser.

"Then Thomas found a spell in William's office." I prompt him on. "And then you all summoned The Devil?"

"It sounds stupid when you say it out loud but…a witches' coven is sacred." Elias turns his head and stares at a family photo on the wall. "To see Thomas in such blatant despair was unbearable. It was a physical pain in my chest."

"He's your family." I whisper. If something ever happened to Cleo, I had no doubt that Grace would tear it all down. I would help her in any way I could. "Of course, it hurt you to see him like that."

It feels sick to try and tack on a question about the ritual. It would be obvious and cheap. But Annie wanted to know and that small part of me, or maybe the small part of Thomas that lived inside of us all, craved her approval. The idea of disappointing her overrode the shame rising in me as I placed my hand on his knee.

"How did you do it? It can't have been easy." I keep my voice soft and curious. As Elias freezes under my touch I smile reassuringly at him. "If it was Grace or Cleo in that position, I know I would do anything to help them stay together."

"They are pretty intense." Elias's eyes drag over my lips and then latch onto mine. "Does it ever get lonely? Being the last one?"

"I'm not the last one." I answer. "We have Alistair now."

"But the prince will not be leaving with you." Elias pointed out. I know he is avoiding my question. I can bring it all around again later.

"I have Grace and Cleo and Annie. I am not lonely." I pull my hand back from his leg.

"I have Thomas, Christiana, William, Corsi and Mary. I am still lonely." Elias mimics my tone. When I do not respond, his lips twitch into a smile and he raises his eyebrows at me. "So, Lola. I ask again. Does it ever get lonely?"

"Incredibly."

The admission doesn't feel as dramatic as it sounds. Maybe it should have been, but it wasn't. It is simply surprising that I admit it so quickly. That gentle comfort I get just from being near Elias gently pulls it out of me, and the explanation I carry on with.

"Cleo and Grace have each other, and they are…they are a perfect match. They are fire and ice, the moon and the stars. But Annie has this closeness with Grace that even Cleo can't match. Even with the maker's bond I sometimes feel like a spare. Like I am only around to be something different, but they don't always want or need different. They don't always want or need me."

"This is the part where I tell you that's not true." Elias says slowly. "But I will never tell you that your feelings are wrong. I have been with my family for five centuries and sometimes when I'm in a room with Thomas and Christiana I feel spare too."

We share a soft, sad smile. Elias moves his head slightly forward and I expect the rush of panic that usually comes before someone kisses me. But it never comes just like his lips never touch mine. He pauses mere millimetres away. His breath is minty and sharp. It takes over the smell of the sweat on his skin.

"Why did you really come here, Lola?" Elias breathes.

"I want to know how to summon the devil." I breathe back.

Elias's only response is a blink. I still, turning myself into a living statue. I could wait like this all day. I could sit here and let him get angry at me. He probably thinks I've tried to trick him, make a fool of him so I could run back to Annie giggling about how stupid he was.

He doesn't react like that.

He reaches up and gently trails his fingers over my cheeks. He moves them as if he is tucking an invisibly strand of hair behind my ear.

"That's quite dangerous." He warns in a whisper.

"I'm quite the survivalist." I whisper back.

"That you are." Those gorgeous eyes stare into mine, into my very soul and mind. I briefly wonder if he can read it or talk to me through it like Thomas can. But maybe the reason Thomas can is because he gave up his soul for us- for Annie, who then unwittingly shared it.

"Did he suffer?" Elias's next question throws me off guard. An image flashes to the front of my mind, the same image that flashes every time I hear the word *him.* The same image that is accompanied by the feeling of hot wet breaths on my face and searing pain in my shoulder and a sinking feeling in my stomach.

"No." The answer feels like it cuts the inside of my throat. "I couldn't...and then we had to leave after I was turned, and I never went back. He owns a car shop. Got a fiancée and two cats."

"Would you want to hurt him?" Elias probes softly. I know that if I don't answer, he won't hold it against me. He must already know something, even if it was just that everyone in our small found family was bound together by a shared and horrifyingly common trauma.

"Sometimes." I never talked about it anymore. I had a mental snap when I was home alone a few years after turning, but that was it. Those six and a half hours had been my only outburst in twenty years. A slow, tentative conversation may be good. My truth for his would be a fair exchange. The more detailed I allow myself to be, the more details I would get in return.

"Some days I wake up and I'm back in that alley." I swallow the lump in my throat, but I do not move my face away from his. When I breathe in, I breathe in him, and the action calms me. Elias does not smell of spilt tequila and cigarettes. He does not smell like him.

"I am back in that alley, and I am screaming out for someone to help me all over again. Some nights when I'm hunting, I hear a particular song and it takes me back to that dancefloor where I had that one last drink and I let him pick me up to spin me." I close my eyes. "But sometimes...especially when I'm running fast or jumping off of something I couldn't have back then. That's when I think petty things, if I think of him at all. He will never know that feeling. He will never know what it is like to be so effortlessly powerful."

I open my eyes and find Elias still looking. "He will only know what it feels like to take something, to have to beat someone for them to remember him. I won't let him take any more happiness from me. Some days it's easy to say I won't let him take anything else at all. Other days it's easier to admit that that's not possible every day."

Elias's fingers trace my face again. This time he focuses on the edges of my hairline and my jaw. His eyes flicker all over as if he is trying to find any damage. There is something sweet in the pointless gesture.

"Broken ribs. Broken wrist. Broken nose. Dislocated shoulder. There was something wrong with my legs and my hip, but those were already healing when Annie got me to the hospital, so she didn't have to set those in place." I speak softly. These words come a lot more easily than the ones I said before.

"And you never went back to kill him?" Elias asks in disbelief.

"My parents were looking for me. We couldn't stay."

"Murder can take only seconds. Although I understand why you would want this one to take days." Elias's voice is as cold as ice. I reach up and place my hand over his so I am almost caressing my own face.

"How long did it take to summon the devil?" I ask bluntly.

"A conveniently timed full moon." Elias pulls completely away from me. "And however long it took for Christiana to drain the blood of four chickens."

"That's not funny." I grind out. "I answered your question."

"You don't know I'm joking."

"Tell me how."

"Tell me why you want to know."

"That's none of your business."

"Summoning the devil isn't yours."

We scowl at each other, each of us not letting up on our side. If I tell him why, then the whole dynamic and plan would shift. Elias was friendly but I couldn't see him sitting back and letting Cleo protect him from an unknown threat.

"Could you just trust that I have a good reason?" I ask even though we have only known each other less than a month. Back when I was human I wouldn't have even asked him to feed my fish. If I had fish. My parents never let me get them.

"The problem isn't trust." Elias responds. "The problem is William. He has the spell under multiple locks, both physical and mystical. He isn't letting us get those instructions unless I can go to him with a very, very good reason."

I gently rub my hands over the bedsheets as I think that through. William was menacing and clearly the leader of the coven. I had not seen Corsi or Mary without him and he was Thomas and Christiana's father. He was Elias's uncle and the oldest. There was no reason for Elias to be lying about needing to speak to William.

"You aren't going to like this." I warn him.

Chapter Thirty-Five

Alistair

"You are the worst spy in the world." Cleo snaps at Lola as the five of us sit down in the meeting room. I stare at all of the vampire-proofing, focusing on the subtle silver linings and reinforced walls.

"They were never going to just tell us how." I mutter in my new best friend's defence. "No one could have gotten the ritual from William."

"She wasn't trying for William. She was trying for Elias." Cleo doesn't look at me as she snaps. She just paces the length of the room, moving back and forth at various speeds like she can't decide if she wants to pretend to be human or show off how inhuman she was.

"Infighting is not going to help." Annie cuts in between the both of us. Argument ended. Annie turns her eyes over to me and puts on a soft reassuring smile. "You feeling okay?"

It feels strange to hear that question without having to ignore the fact my own body was slowly poisoning me. Annie isn't asking to see if she has to change the doses of my medicine because I don't have to take medicine anymore. Annie is referring to the fact I am about to see my mother for the first time since I changed. Unsurprisingly, my father has a mysterious charity event that means he cannot make it.

Lola had brought me two jugs worth of warm B+ before the meeting so I am full to the point of discomfort. She says that you can taste the difference in blood types over time. Right now they are all the same. But the idea of drinking any more makes me sick and that's good. That's perfect. I won't be tempted to try and gnaw on my mother's jugular.

It does mean that I will be going hunting tomorrow night rather than tonight. I need to be hungry enough to eat and track but full enough not to go feral when I get close to so many people. I have only been around a maximum of three humans at a time since I woke up with my new teeth. The guards have been silent the entire time. Lyra has been talking at me rather than with me. She wasn't scared of the girls, but she wasn't welcoming them with open arms either. She is as uneasy with them as she is the witches.

"I'm here." Lola says from the space beside me. Her hand is warm to the touch. I smile at her as I give it a gentle squeeze of thanks. While I am linked to all of the girls through our maker's bond, my connection to Lola is stronger. If I had to guess, then I would say it was due to the closeness in age. Lola is only two decades older than me instead of the centuries that the other three were. She is the most recently turned and she understands what it's like to grow up in a recent era.

The door opens. My head snaps to it even though I can already hear there are no heartbeats. The witches' coven (cursed coven, as I realise they are called by everyone living outside of this palace) have masked their heartbeats when around me. I know it's a sweet gesture, even though it grates at me. I am not a weak little child anymore. I do not need constant protection from the outside world anymore.

Christiana shoots me an easy smile as she settles into the place at the end of the table. William, as always, sits himself to her immediate left. Thomas takes the spot between her and Annie. He places his arms on the table far enough to the side for them to brush against hers. Subtle.

Corsi and Mary move to take the remaining seats on this side of the table. Elias moves swiftly past them and throws himself down on the other side of Lola. I fight the urge to scowl at him. The only seat left in the room is the one directly opposite me. My mother will be safe, surrounded by the witches and Annie. If I lunge for her, if I lose control, then I will be stopped in time.

"Before her majesty arrives, I want to make one thing crystal clear." William says in a grave voice. "You are not getting that ritual."

"Father." Christiana sighs. "Please-"

"It is non-negotiable." William turns his gaze to Annie and acts as if his daughter had never spoken. "You will not perform that spell."

"I can't perform spells, William." Annie met his gaze with cool indifference. She lets her fangs down and points up at them. "Vampire. Remember? Spells are a witch thing. Drinking blood is a vamp thing. Should I make you some cue cards so you can remember?"

Cleo presses her lips together to stop from outright laughing as William's face turns a dark shade of maroon. We lock eyes and share an almost amused smile.

"You expect me to hand over that ritual over the ridiculous claim that you were given a secret message in your sleep by the lord of death himself?" William asks through clenched teeth.

"No, William." Annie sighs. "I expect you to hand over that ritual because I like 90% of you and I don't want to spend forever plagued by the guilt if I sit back and do nothing when some other supernatural force rips you all apart."

"How very selfish of you." Christiana jokes dryly.

The two girls share a wicked grin. William looks like his head is going to explode. If Thomas and Annie ever truly got together, then William would have a daughter-in-law that would never leave him in peace. I was going to enjoy watching that come around.

"She just wants to help, William." I try and use the most princely voice I have. It sounds weak to my own ears, but I see Lola smile from the corner of my eye. I sit up straighter in my chair.

"That ritual would put you all at greater risk." William immediately changes his tone. He turns his face away from Annie. "Inviting such evil right into the heart of the palace for no reason other than an overactive imagination is impractical."

"An overactive imagination." Annie repeated under her breath with a chuckle. "God I hope it's painful for you, William. Whatever it is."

"Annie." Thomas reprimands sharply.

"Thomas." She shoots back.

The room starts to bristle with tension. The hair on my own arms stands up as we all shift ourselves towards Annie. The witches do the same, adjusting their positions as if to block us should we lunge for their leader. Elias's arm loops over the back of Lola's chair. His hand grips her shoulder. My lips pull back into a silent snarl.

The door opens again. My mother's heartbeat starts to echo around the walls. My face twists into a crooked grin as I look at her. She doesn't look like she has been crying. Whenever she came to my rooms, it was with fresh makeup to cover up the tear tracks. Now she was just smiling.

"Oh, my baby." She whispers, covering her mouth with her hands. I stop breathing and force myself to stay still. She takes two quick steps forward, guards quick on her heels. Their heartbeats start to mix in with hers.

My mother glances over at Annie as she hesitates on step three. Annie gives her a quick nod. I take the cue before she does, standing far too quickly from my chair and moving supernaturally quick to her side. She gasps but does not move away.

"Hi Mummy." I breathe out. When I breath in, I get a mouthful of her floral perfume. It attacks my throat and dries it out. I swirl my tongue around my mouth to try and get rid of the feeling and focus on something else.

"You look…You look so alive." My mother sniffs as she holds herself back from crying again. Her hand hovers over the side of my face as if she is scared to touch me. I hear the shift of people moving behind me, but I do not look. I just take my hand and use it to guide my mother's, so her hand gently holds my face.

"I am." I tell her. The smell of her blood is not as alluring as Cleo warned me it would be. There is not a single part of me that wants to bite her even though her pulse is near deafening. This is my mother. This is the woman who loved me more than life itself. I could never hurt her. "Thank you."

"Thank you?" My mother repeats as she moves her hand away. For a second I panic, my unbeating heart cracking in my chest, until she pulls me forward into a hug. She rests her chin on my shoulder, having to tilt up even though she is wearing heels. "My baby boy, you have nothing to thank me for."

"You saved me." I whisper back, closing my eyes as I take in the sound. My mother is young, barely forty, and I will have decades with her. But I know that eternity stretches forever, and I can feel down the maker's bond how the centuries will weigh on my soul. I want to take in as much of my family, as much of Lyra and my mother and all the distant relatives, as I can before they become a distant memory.

"Annie saved you. Thomas saved you by getting her here. All I did was grovel." My mother doesn't move from our embrace. She gives a sniff as if she is holding back tears. I hug her tightly. She gasps slightly. I am thrown back across the room.

"Corsi!" Annie screeches as I soar through the air. I hit the wall with a crack.

"Alistair!" My mother yells. She runs over to me, but Lola beats her there. Both of them help me up into a standing position. Lola roughly forces me to look at her and scans my face. She runs a hand over the back of my head and seems satisfied when there is no blood on her hand.

"He hurt her." Corsi declares to the table. "You saw it. He would have crushed her."

"It is not your place." Annie snarls as she hunches over the table. She stares Corsi down, but the witch does not budge.

"You were not doing your job." The witch says coldly. "I am part of the royal guard. The Queen's life is my responsibility. I will not have the prince crush her lungs."

"He wasn't." My mother defends me even though we both know that I had been hugging her a little too tightly. "I was fine."

I take a step away from my mother, but she simply walks right over to my side and wraps her arms around me. She has a set look on her face that I have seen only a few times in my life and most of them have been focussed on my father when he forgets to pretend that he likes me.

"He's fine." Annie tells Corsi bluntly. Her eyes flick towards me. "You are doing great, Alistair."

"Thank you." I say softly. It's rude to not say anything at all.

"We should all sit and stay calm." Thomas says, filling the role of the go-between like he always did. Cleo rolls her eyes at him. I gently escort my mother to her seat. She gives me a soft smile and hesitates before craning her neck up to kiss my cheek. I stay still until she is fully in her seat. I go to move back to mine, but I move too fast. I smash into my chair and crash into Lola's side.

"You're still doing great." She whispers as she steadies me. "Moving slow is the hardest thing anyway."

"Thanks." I whisper as I scrap my chair forward, so I am tucked into place. My mother looks between me and Lola. Her smile grows.

"William says that you are going out tomorrow night." My mother talks to me like she did when I was on my sick bed, as if no one else is in the room. As if any moment between us had ever truly been private. There was always a doctor nearby or a guard outside the door. "That's exciting."

"We will be with him the whole time, Emily. I promise." Annie winks at my mother.

"Thomas and Elias will be accompanying them." William is quick to add. Naturally I would not be trusted to just my new mentor for my first taste of freedom. I couldn't go hunting with a small army of guards, but a large group of supernatural creatures was a better protection than anything else I could think of. As soon as I had myself under control, those guards would only be for show anyway. I would be the greatest threat for miles.

"And we will be nearby as backup should anything go wrong with the glamour spell." Mary's voice is gentle, almost too gentle to be taken seriously.

"Glamour spell?" I blurt out.

"The crown prince of the United Kingdom can't be spotted on the dancefloor of a sketchy nightclub in Soho." Elias winks at me. "You won't feel it. You won't even remember it after a few minutes. It'll be the last thing on your mind."

He's probably right. I have never, not even once, been allowed to go outside the palace for *this* kind of thing. I stay at home and have my transfusions and take my medicines. I would go to essential charity events and balls in other countries so that no one else would ever find out. I would limp my way through a dance with my mother and the queen or princess of wherever we were before I would sit to the side and let everyone think I was too drunk or high to do anything more.

"A nightclub. That's where you are taking him to hunt?" My mother looks around the whole table. "That's the best place?"

"We hunt abusers." Annie doesn't sugar coat it. "And rapists and murderers and people that take advantage of vulnerable women. Nightclubs are the most reliable place to find those kinds of people. While Alistair is being trained by us, he will share our diet."

Pride soars through me. My maker, my coven, my second family: they are heroes, and I will soon be one of them. They took the bad hand that life had dealt them, and they turned themselves into something greater. They rose from the ashes.

"He will be put onto blood donations as soon as Annie and the girls leave. We already have a procedure and a stockpile." William talks about it all so carelessly. That is my life he is talking about. These are my friends.

"And if I do not want to go onto blood donations?" I lean forward to rest my elbows onto the tabletop. I even manage to look William in the eye without shrinking backwards. The witch elder's brow furrows.

"Your Grace." The tone he uses causes a physical itch across my skin. It is condescending and yet respectful. It is the way that people talk to toddlers when they throw things from their prams. "With the schedules you will be on when you can go into the public eye you will not have the time, or the security needed to hunt for yourself."

"But eventually he will have to." Lola frowns. She looks over at Grace and Cleo as if she was waiting for them to put the same pieces together. "Eventually he won't be about to go into the public eye anymore. What is he supposed to do then? Haunt these halls and rely on those blood bags for an eternity?"

"Lola." Grace sighs. "That is not for us to decide."

"But it is something we should be thinking about." Lola snaps. "We cannot just leave him here alone until the end of time."

"We can discuss that later." Grace tries to soothe her. "Right now, we need to organise tomorrow."

The scowl that sets itself on Lola's face makes my unbeating heart soar. I have to swallow back the urge to tell her that she could always stay. They could all stay if they wanted to. My mind starts to twist and turn through all sorts of cliché happy-ever-after scenarios.

All of us drinking hot chocolate in front of a crackling fire. All of us drinking and loudly counting down to midnight on New Year's Eve. Sunday car rides through the countryside. Movie nights and game nights and cooking together.

"You'll all be coming with me?" I look around at the other vampires in the room. My gaze lingers over Cleo, who was the one most likely to avoid coming.

"Of course." Cleo bristles. I smile at her.

"If we see anything getting too much, anything at all, then we will be pulling the plug and trying again a few days later." Thomas warns me. "This is a…test drive."

"But as long as you don't crash the car, set it on fire, and slaughter hundreds of people while doing all that, I will consider it a win." Christiana jokes.

"I wouldn't even know how to drive." I grimace at my poor attempt at joining in on the joke. Lola chuckles.

"Annie's your drivers ed teacher." Lola winks.

"Not a thing outside of America." Cleo mutters. I notice how she quickly looks over at Elias after her comment.

"We all know what she meant." I grumble.

"I want pictures." My mother turns to Annie. "If you don't mind."

"Of course." Annie smiles. The two of them together warms my heart to the point it feels like its burning. My maker and my mother have an easy almost friendship. Maybe Annie would stay after all. She can't completely hate it here. This place has Thomas. Those two were definitely up to something.

"Mum." I gape at her. "You cannot have pictures of me doing that."

"Oh, I don't want pictures of that." My mother waves me off. She doesn't even flinch at the idea. I don't know if that's purely her personality or if Corsi has used her magic to keep her calm like she did when my father's affair came to light. I hope it's the first one. "But pictures of you dancing and smiling? Maybe even posing by the Thames?"

"I'll make him pose, your majesty." Lola grins. "Before we put the glamour on."

"The glamour is going on before we step outside." Elias bursts our bubble. Lola's smile drops slightly, and he is quick to add. "But I can spell the camera so the glamour doesn't work on it. Can't have Emily going without something for the family album."

"Do I get to pick what I look like?" Curiosity gets the better of me as the glamour spell gets more and more attention. All the magic I had been exposed to was medicinal or lifestyle. Glamour spells sounded…almost fun.

"Got any preferences?" Christiana asks. "We can tweak it."

I do not know how to answer especially not publicly. Do I want to be ginger? Do I want to be taller? Do I want to ask for more muscles? Do I want to ask to look like Elias and pretend to be twins for the evening?

"Just let me know later." Christiana fights back a smile. "It won't take me too long to edit it."

I feel like I am being humoured, although Christiana is usually nice to me anyway. I thought it was largely pity-based, which it may be, but I am no longer dying. I choose to see this as more of an olive branch towards an eternity as friends than a pity favour.

"Thanks." I smile.

Chapter Thirty-Six

Cleo

"Cleo, stop!" Grace giggles as I pull her back against me. I attach my lips to her collarbone, leaving sloppy kisses as I make my way up to her earlobe.

"We need to get dressed." Grace whispers even as she cranes her neck to give me better access.

"You're already dressed." I complain as I nip at where her pulse should be.

"I haven't done my hair or my makeup. I've just slipped a dress on." Grace tugs the short black dress further down her thighs.

"You already look perfect." I scowl. "We have the time."

"We don't."

"They'll wait for us."

"Cleo."

"Grace."

Grace spins in my arms and presses a hard kiss to my lips. I melt into it, my hands gripping into her hips and tugging her back with me towards the bed. I haven't put my own dress on. The witches had some delivered to us earlier, not that we needed them to. We had many options in our suitcases. We had packed for every occasion.

"Nonononono." Grace giggles into my mouth as we teeter on the edge of falling into the mattress. She kisses me again, much more gentle than before and steps away from me. "Tonight is about Alistair."

"Tonight will be about Lola being in the centre of Elias and Alistair." I correct her. "With a side act of Thomas looking at Annie with eyes as wide as saucers."

"It is nice that they have found people." Grace crosses her arms.

"Lola has found two."

"And they are both lovely. Whichever one she chooses, if she has to choose at all, then we will both be happy for her."

"I never said you wouldn't be."

Grace cannot hide her smirk as she walks over to the makeup dresser and sits down to unnecessarily edit her face. "But you are the same woman who has constantly gotten jealous that me and the 'insultingly attractive American bimbo' get along."

"I stand by that." I mutter as I run my hands over the dark purple material of my own dress. The neckline cuts down in a sharp triangle all the way to my bellybutton and is held up by two straps looping around my neck. It will be easy to find a sleaze wearing it. I couldn't stomach wearing my more 'exotic' options. There would be enough options in a place like London without me having to do that. A subtle accent would do fine.

"I never rant to you about her being attractive. You always talk to me about it. How do I know that you aren't secretly in love with her?" Grace responds over her shoulder, her top lip gently outlined with bright red lipstick.

"Because I spend 48% of my time with my head between your legs?" I smirk as I change into my dress.

"You think it's only 48%?" Grace runs her fingers through her thick black hair. It shines even under the artificial lighting. I run my own fingers across the golden locket around my neck, the one that holds a small picture of Grace and a lock of her hair. Her wrist has a matching bracelet with a lock of mine inside. A gift from Annie back in 1954.

"2% is touching." I come up behind her, taking the exact same lipstick that Grace had just used and running it over my own mouth. I bring my lips to the shell of her ear and breath. "And you are so delicious."

Grace gives a slight shudder. I have her- or I would if there wasn't an irritatingly familiar heartbeat approaching our door.

"Maybe *he* should put his head between something. Maybe a door and a frame?" I grumble as I search for my shoes. The moving heartbeat comes to a stop outside the door. Grace yells at him to come in before he even knocks.

"You two look lovely." Elias beams. "Glad the dresses fit. You ready to go?"

"You think we need a chaperone to walk downstairs?" I ask bluntly as I zip the sides of my heeled boots.

"I was bored in my room." Elias admits shamelessly.

"And we are your first choice?" I ask sceptically.

"Thomas and Annie are not ready yet." Elias grimaces. "Which I found out by forgetting to knock and now I want at least a thousand beers or a memory-erasing spell."

"You know that is not who I meant." I say bluntly as I twist my hair up into a bun. A few tendrils frame my face. Grace likes it that way and it is easy to hunt in.

"Lola is getting ready with Alistair." Elias shrugs as if that was perfectly fine. If our positions had been swapped and it was Grace getting ready with someone else that clearly wanted her, I would rip that other suitors head from their shoulders. I suppose the key difference here is that Grace is actually mine. Neither of the boys had made an official move on Lola yet. They were not stupid enough to try and claim her either.

"Can you drink tonight?" Grace asks him, perfect face set in a small frown. "Won't that affect the glamour?"

"I can. I won't be getting wasted because this is work, not leisure. I don't make it a habit of spending my Saturdays looking for sexual predators to feed to a prince."

"Not yet anyway." I joke dryly. Grace shoots me a look that tells me to be nice. I bat my eyelids at her innocently.

"Are you two going to be drinking? Alcohol, I mean." Elias ignores me and shoves his hands into his pockets. I take a look at him.

His hair is styled and gelled into a messy faux hawk. His jeans and shoes are plain black, but his t-shirt has some obscure band logo plastered across it in neon colours. Pretentious frat-pledging art boy.

Oh god. I was using Lola terminology.

"It is not fair that we are expected to dress like this, but you can get away with wearing anything and you'll still be let in." I complain as I strut towards the wardrobe and gently pull a thick woollen jacket out for Grace. I take the leather jacket for myself.

"A lot of things in life aren't fair." Elias agrees. "But maybe I can make up for the fact I don't have to wear heels by paying for the first six rounds."

I shoot a wicked grin over my shoulder as I shrug the jacket on. "Just don't expect me to like you at round seven."

"I don't expect you to like me ever." Elias matches my grin.

"I like you both." Grace smiles as she stands. "If that means anything."

I don't respond verbally. I take her face in my hands and place a gentle, sensual kiss on her mouth. I don't stop until Elias awkwardly clears his throat.

Chapter Thirty-Seven

Lola

"You look so amazing." Alistair repeats for a third time as I try and fix my hair again. He had said it when I arrived to his rooms. He had said it again when I changed my hair from its bun to a plait and now once again when I was going for a high ponytail instead.

"Thank you." I smile softly into his mirror. The green silk dress is gorgeous *and* comfortable. It slides across my skin smoothly and doesn't ruffle up at my thighs. It's a perfect dress. It's sad that I may get blood on it.

"This may not ever be an issue for you." I begin my first vampire lesson of the night. "But when you're hunting it's easier to have your hair back or up. It's harder to get blood in it that way. Dried blood is so awkward to wash out completely. If you love those clothes, then I would change. Your first time is going to be messy."

Alistair nodded along as I spoke, his reflection in the corner of the mirror that I was using. I redo my ponytail as I catch sight of a small bubble of hair at the top of my head. Perfection isn't a look that can be achieved, I know that now, but I want to be as close as possible. It is easier to weed out the true animals that way.

"I'm gonna be near you the whole time, okay? Maybe not always at your side so people don't think we are dating. It will be harder to hunt for us that way. People get less open with their creepiness if they think a big strong man is there to protect us. But we should come up with a word you can say so I know to come straight to you in case anything happens. Any suggestions?"

I was talking a mile a minute, but Alistair didn't seem to care. He just sat on the edge of his bed, rubbing his hands together and nodding. He was listening. He was almost over-listening, but the fact he was even trying to listen was a nice change.

"It should probably be something easy to say in conversation right?" Alistair mused. "In case someone hears. It's gonna be kinda weird if I just yell out 'pineapple.'"

"We all have super hearing, Al. You won't have to yell." I remind him, fighting back a smile as I apply a pale gloss to my lips. I shut the gloss with a soft click and place it back in my jacket pocket. I use my vamp speed to go to the door to remind Alistair that he had that too. He is by my side before I can even blink.

We share a grin before racing each other down to the main stairwell of the living quarters. The palace was set up strangely. Half of the castle was lived in by servants and the royals and the other half was fully set up as a public area for balls, feasts, ceremonies, etc., etc. It must have felt like growing up in a fishbowl or a museum, scared to touch anything that wasn't in your own private space.

The others are already here. Cleo and Grace look beautiful, their arms wrapped around each other as always. Cleo looks the most stunning, her dress scandalous and provocative. She looked straight up sexy, but if I say that, she won't take it well.

Annie and Thomas stand to the side, equally as entangled as Cleo and Grace. Annie's outfit is a dark blue lace crop top and high waisted jeans with her hair in two pigtails. Very modern and alluring. Thomas is in a basic dark blue button up. Seeing them interact tonight is going to be interesting. Especially since he decided to match her colours.

It is Elias that catches my eye. Elias, who is stood with his hands in his pockets, swinging back and forth on his heels and wearing the logo of an obscure 90s grunge band whose lead singer grew up to be a celebrity's dentist. I laugh loudly. Elias grins at the sound.

"Are we all ready to go?" Thomas asks bluntly.

"Unless you are planning on springing another one of you witches on us." Cleo says sassily as she turns to face the door.

"Christiana is a little young." Elias jokes, shooting me a wink before going to push the doors open.

"Wait! Alistair's glamour!" I remind him in a panic. This is just like the sunshine rule. Even a second without the lie could lead us all to ruin.

"Already on." Thomas smiles kindly at me. I frown and spin my head to look next to me. Alistair looks the exact same as before. His blonde hair is neatly combed, his eyes the same light blue as before. Maybe his nose is slightly different? I never really paid attention to his nose. I don't want to call Thomas a liar, but I think he's lying.

"We see him as normal. Don't want him getting lost on the dancefloor." Thomas fights back a smile. He definitely heard what I was thinking.

"Okay." I mutter and follow them out of the palace. Since the glamour is on, we can leave straight out the front door. If there is anyone watching, then they won't see anyone they recognise. Elias starts to mutter something in Latin. I realise the outside of the palace is probably glamoured as well and would have been for when we arrived days ago. I really am an idiot.

There is a London taxi waiting for us. We all clamber into the back of it, Cleo ensuring that Grace gets in first. I smile and end up pressed in between Annie and Alistair. The witches have grabbed the window seats. I lean halfway out of my seat to try and look more closely at what was outside. The city looks quite pretty as we slowly drive down its streets.

On the drive in, I had been too nervous to look out the windows, but now that I could, I saw that the image I had in my head of London at night was somewhat accurate. I spotted red telephone boxes and old-fashioned streetlights lining the main road. There were a lot more statues than I had thought there would be and they looked made of iron rather than granite.

People were everywhere. There were lone walkers, dog walkers, and a few couples even at this time of night. The closer we got into the city proper, the larger the groups get. Some had children no taller than knee height. Their parents posed them in front of the buildings and the large brightly lit posters for musicals. I had always wanted to go to a west end show when I was little. My drama teacher said it was a 'more classical Broadway.' I still think she was talking out of her ass, but I want to see a stage just to be sure.

"I love Mamma Mia." Alistair's lips twitch into a smile as we pass. "My mum got the cast to come and perform for us last Christmas."

"William hated it. It was hilarious." Elias stage-whispered to the whole car as we came to a stoplight.

"I always liked Les Misérables." I admit, eyes still taking in everything outside. Alistair shifts uncomfortably beside me. A little girl is skipping in a circle as she waits for her parents to catch up. Her thin brown hair is falling from its plait.

"My favourite is the Prince of Egypt." Grace rests her head against Cleo's. The middle eastern beauty smirks but says nothing. I imagine her favourite would be some twisted stage play. Probably not a musical.

"Here's fine, mate." Elias booms up to the driver. He pulls into the nearest layby and lets us out. We all move around as Thomas leans forward to pay him.

I take Alistair's helping hand as I step from the taxi. I let out a low appreciative breath. Behind us is a theatre and subway station entrance, to our left the

National Gallery. I never realised that Leicester Square had so many little avenues linking it together. But then I also never realised it had nightclubs.

"It's beautiful." I smile. Annie shoots me a smile back.

"It is." She agrees. "But it's...different."

"Decades do that." Thomas smirks at her. She pinches his arm with a scowl. Disgustingly cute.

"You good?" I turn my attention to Alistair, who I realise hasn't taken a single breathe since we stepped out of the car. Alistair nods and slowly turns to look at everything.

I feel...exposed. He admits down the bond. *It's loud and it smells and...*

And you have us. Grace finishes for him. *You will be fine.*

Better than fine, I add quickly.

You can actually get drunk now. You'll be great. Cleo's addition has us all laughing. Well. Everyone but Thomas, who gives the girl a side-eye, and Elias, who has no idea what just happened.

"Let's go." Thomas commands. Cleo raises her eyebrows at him and waits until Annie starts to move before following. Me and Grace share a grin as we both loop our arms through Alistair's and head after them.

Chapter Thirty-Eight

Alistair

The club is somehow more bearable than the streets. In here the music is loud enough to cover a majority of the sounds. I would have to focus on one particular conversation to hear it all rather than have hundreds of different ones attacking my ears at once. The breathing all blends together. The place was full of a variety of people and most of the men looked like assholes. The girls were right. This was the perfect hunting ground for them.

Annie used hypnosis on the door staff so none of us had to show ID or pay for entry. I have no idea about how this is normally supposed to go but I know the pin to the debit card that was in my pocket. Thomas and Elias had their own. I don't know what to do next. The girls all fanned out as soon as they stepped inside.

Lola had explained that they all had a 'strategy' but they would be going against that tonight. Annie would usually go to the smoking area to find the stalkers, Lola would be overly friendly and accept drinks to find the spikers. Cleo was always a target for racists and Grace always looked a little too young.

Lola and Grace moved to the dancefloor, up a flight of colour changing plastic steps. The dancefloor was set in different coloured squares. Lola played drunk, skipping, and hopping between the squares to get attention. Annie moved straight through the building and out to the balcony where there were clusters of humans smoking. My own nose wrinkles at the idea of standing near all that smoke. Cleo heads to the bar and drapes herself against the corner. She looks more welcoming than I had ever seen her. It works. She is approached by a small, squat body builder within seconds.

Us boys stand awkwardly to the side of the doors. Elias was looking anywhere but the dancefloor and I was fully behind that plan but staring at Cleo would make for uncomfortable comments later and Annie was out of actual eyeline. Not that it was stopping Thomas.

"We should get a drink." I suggest hesitantly. Thomas and Elias had more people skills than me (obviously) and watching them figure out a target for me would help me next time. But we couldn't get to picking a victim if we were stood on the side lines.

"Or five." Elias agreed thickly. Thomas grunts a response. We move to the centre of the bar. I make a point not to glance at Cleo, but I do prick my ears to listen. She is making some sultry comment about how she felt like a little girl playing dress up. I assume she is testing out to see if he's a pervert. I stop listening as he laughs hollowly.

I fucking hate the smoking area. Anne said bluntly down the bond.

That bad huh? Grace giggles back.

A man just pressed his unlit fag against my arm because 'I am hot enough to light it.' Annie's disgust is evident down the bond.

Thomas's entire demeanour changes. He turns to face the bar, a wicked grin on his face. His shoulders relax as he lounges against the sticky metal counter. He has always been interested in Annie, I knew that from listening to him speak about her, but I never realised that he would be so jealous and worried. This was her element. Of all the things that could go wrong tonight, of all the people to worry about, Annie wasn't one of them.

"She'll be fine ya know." I tell him softly after Elias orders us three shots of Sambuca and three draught beers. Not what I wanted to try for my first drink, but I wasn't going to complain. "She's Annie."

Thomas thinks that over for a second before saying kindly. "Your version of Annie and my version of Annie are very different."

"She's not the girl in the estate next door anymore Thomas. She can handle herself in a SoHo smoking area." Elias agrees with me. He shoots the female bartender a grin and a tip as she comes back with a tray of drinks. She grins back. Elias hands us all a shot and a beer.

"To Alistair." Elias declares, holding the shot up into the air. "And our new forever friendship."

"To friendship." I tap my plastic shot glass against his, spilling a little of the clear liquid onto my hand.

"To forever." Thomas taps his shot against ours. Elias is the first to throw his back, Thomas quick on his heels. They slam their plastic glasses onto the bar before I have even taken mine. I quickly follow their lead. The shot is disgusting. It takes like burning liquorice and it makes me tongue feel slimy. I gag.

Elias laughs, slapping me on the back as I quickly take a mouthful of the beer to wash the after taste away. It is not much better.

"First shot." Elias calls to the group of girls next to us. They giggle and smile reassuringly at me as my face turns an ugly shade of maroon.

"What did you have?" The girl in the centre of the group asks me. She is wearing a pink birthday sash.

"Sambuca." I wince. Why isn't the taste going away? I down another mouthful of froth.

"Rough choice." The girl nods. She reaches over for their own tray of drinks, full of bright reds and blues. She hands me a blue shot. "Try this. It's blueberry."

I take it hesitantly. It's rude not to but also, as far as shots go, this looks more friendly. I give it a sniff. It smells sweet and fruity. I look up at her and she winks at me. I throw the shot back.

"That was so much nicer. Thank you." I laugh as I put the empty shot on our tray. Elias and Thomas have started conversations with her friends. One of the girls has her hand on Thomas's arm as she leans down to adjust her perfectly fine shoes. Good luck with that one sweetie. "Do you want another drink?" I ask the girl who gave me a shot. "I'm Alistair by the way."

"Diana." The girl moves to stand beside me. She plays with the thin gold chain around her neck. "And thank you, yeah. I'll take another blueberry shot?"

"Two blueberry shots it is." I feel my fangs start to prickle but I force them back. This is not someone I am going to drain. This is just a girl who was being nice in a random club. She is not a monster. She is not someone that fits the code. I also cannot get too drunk, or I may screw up drinking for real.

This guy is an idiot but not drinkable Cleo sighs, interrupting me ordering the two shots. *Anyone got something for Alistair to nibble on?*

Lola's guy has potential Grace responds. A quick look over my shoulder as the shots are poured show Grace dancing alone by the DJ booth and Lola being manhandled by some twat with face tattoos.

A bit gropey but not really drinkable. Bringing him over to Cleo now. Lola doesn't look over at us as she twirls in his arms and starts to whisper in his ear.

Why Cleo? I think back to them. Diana smiles at me as she takes her shot, and we drink them in unison.

Racists always deserve to die. Cleo responds. *Do you not agree little prince?*

Cleo Annie finally joins the conversation. *Mind your manners. Alistair, I've got one. Whenever you're ready.*

I apparently do not get to decide whenever I am ready. Thomas decides for me. He comes to my side, throws an arm over my shoulder, and loudly declares to Diana that we were off for a smoke. Elias barely glances over at us as I am dragged across the floor.

"It was nice to meet you!" I call back at Diana.

"You too!" She laughs.

Chapter Thirty-Nine

Cleo

Lola's choice is a good one. She introduced me by name before showing me with a flourish of her hand. Within one beer he has asked me if I'm not supposed to be wearing a scarf over my head. Then when I told him I don't practise that religion he nodded gravely and asked me if it was because of 911. That paired with the fact he refused to let go of Lola meant I had to refrain from ripping out his vocal chords right there at the bar.

This one is a yes. Are we sharing with Alistair or are you good? Lola asked Annie as our conquest started to brag about one upping HR at his last job. Yeah, no fucking surprise.

"I mean I now make so much more money *and* I haven't gotta listen to Sharon bitch about her childcare falling through all the time. Total win win." The man I have forgotten the name of -and I'm completely fine not remembering it- gives Lola another squeeze as he sips his vodka soda. I have no idea what Lola said for this guy to be so open with his assholery, but she deserves an award. I don't think he has even asked what we do for a living. He certainly hasn't asked me.

Answer please. I shoot down the bond. *This guy is fifteen seconds away from being paralysed. Gropey little bastard.*

Lola lets out a choked laugh. The douche grins thinking it is for him. I laugh with her. I suppose it isn't too bad having her as a hunting partner. I don't have the intense feelings of jealousy or panic like I do with Grace. We usually take it in turns to be the bait. With the extra bodies needed tonight, Grace and Lola were both needed. Thankfully Grace has taken more of a guardian role and had been patrolling the floor, faking interest in her phone as if trying to find her friends.

All of you need to head back to the palace. Annie's voice was low. *Thomas is going to meet you there with Ali. Get Elias.*

What's happened? My heart freezes in my chest as I look around for Grace. It's pointless. I know that she is with Annie, that she would have sped to her side the second she felt something wrong.

Get back. To the palace. Annie snarls down the bond.

Me and Lola lock eyes. We both decide to move at the same time. I slide from my seat. Lola easily breaks the hold that the sleazeball has on her. His eyes widen and he goes to grab after her, but we are already on the move. I elbow bodies out of the way. Lola weaves and dodges. Elias chases after us and settles on my other side.

"What's wrong?" Elias asks, his eyes flicking back and forth at everyone coming and going from the smoking area.

"Annie wants us to leave. She won't say why." I grind out as we get to the doorway. The balcony is full of people, humans laughing and joking and begging each other for lighters. Their sounds are near deafening. The five people in the corner's lack of heartbeats stick out like a sore thumb.

Annie, her face set in a disinterested sneer. Thomas, his hand wrapped around the balcony's iron fence. Grace stuck between the both of them with her arms wrapped around herself. Alistair, half-drunk beer in his hand as he tries to nonchalantly look around the balcony. He looks straight at Lola and gives his head a gentle shake.

It is the fifth person that causes my mouth to pull back and show my teeth. My stupid, useless, human teeth because I cannot show my fangs here. The dark wavy hair that brushes his shoulders. The dark eyes under thick eyebrows and a patchy beard.

"Owen." Lola growls.

Chapter Forty

Annie

I should have fucking killed him. I shouldn't have stopped with taking his tongue, which has grown back. I should have ripped the head from his shoulders, shoved a stake through his heart and burned it all in some shitty rural woodland. Instead, I had followed one of the rules that I had insisted on setting for my girls.

Vampires do not kill other Vampires. It makes enemies that cannot be unmade. Enemies that would spend forever waiting for you to have a moment of weakness. Hurting each other could be forgiven over a few decades and frankly I had assumed that Owen was a face I would not see for at least a century if I ever did see him again.

I was wrong.

He had swanned into the smoking area and called out my name in his usual thick Brooklyn accent. I had frozen for a second before spinning and yelling his name back in an overexcited call. I had privately told Thomas to take Alistair from where they were watching me work and to *go* and then sent a message to the other three. Owen had pulled me into a tight hug and snarled in my ear that he had been looking for me, just as Grace had appeared. She was at my side the second I pulled away.

This was a mess.

"You have some new ones. Haven't you been busy?" Owen taunts me softly. "And boy ones! Very much not your MO."

"Long way from home aren't you?" I ask softly. I hear the other three enter the smoking area and hold back a sigh. Owen tilts his head to look at them. A sick smile crosses his face as he catches sight of Lola.

"Little Lola." He coos. "Don't you look stunning?"

The three of them shuffle through the crowd towards us. Elias slips his hand into Lola's and positions her behind him as he stops next to Alistair and Thomas.

"Owen." Lola greets him bluntly. "What a shame. You've caught us just as we were leaving."

"Without what you came for?" Owen completely ignores me now.

*Get Alistair back to the **fucking palace*** I snarl down the bond to Thomas.

Who is he Annie? Thomas doesn't even twitch.

Someone who will more than happily rip out the prince of the United Kingdom's throat. Get. Moving. We will meet you there.

"We ate yesterday." Lola lies. "This was just for fun."

"Your boyfriend likes watching you get pawed at in bars does he?" Owen says sarcastically as his eyes land on Elias. Owen frowns and takes a long sniff. "Oh." He chuckles. "A witch. That explains it."

"Like she said." Elias looks over at Thomas and Alistair. "We were just going. You guys coming with us?"

I could kiss him. Elias is playing along and acting like the three of them arriving right now was pure coincidence. He was going to get them out. He was going to get Thomas out of here before Owen had a chance to hurt him.

"You already called the car?" Thomas loops his arm around my waist. "Cause I think me and Annie are gonna hang back. I've got a song coming up."

"I'm ready to leave." I shrug and turn my face to look at him. "We can catch up with Owen another time. Can't we girls?"

"Unless he runs back to Brooklyn." Cleo smirks. She drops the façade and places her hand on Grace's ass.

"I'm in London for a while. Got some unfinished business. I want to get it sorted before I leave this shithole of a city." Owen finally drags those dark slits of eyes to look at me.

"Oh?" I feign interest as I adjust my jacket. "Well, I wish you luck with that. And a safe journey home."

"You too." Owen looks us all over for a moment. His gaze finally stops on Lola's chest. "And be careful Lola. It would be such a shame for you to end up cursed and alone."

"Eat a tumour." Lola snaps at him. The two stare at each other as Thomas leads everyone else to the exit. I have to give her a gentle push after them.

"You're lucky I'm so forgiving." He calls. Lola gives a shudder of disgust, but I know he wasn't talking to her. Lucky indeed.

Chapter Forty-One

Grace

"Who was that?" Alistair stares at us as we lead the way out of the club and down the nearest dark alley. It wasn't ideal for hunting but if we waited here with everything in sight then we could grab our targets on their way home if Annie didn't make us leave. Hopefully they wouldn't be too drunk. The hangover from that was always horrible.

"A vampire from Brooklyn." Annie answers bluntly.

"An asshole from Brooklyn." Lola amends. "Who is *lucky* we have a no killing vampire rule. I would have staked his ass a decade ago."

"Lola. Breathe." I whisper softly as we settle down out of sight. Lola sits as close to the open street as we can dare too. She doesn't like doing this. I think it's from flashbacks to her last night as a human. I wouldn't like nightclub alley ways either if I had endured what she had.

"We could stake him now." Alistair suggests, going off of Lola's emotions. It would be sweet if it wasn't so naïve that I wanted to sigh.

"There's an unspoken rule that vampires don't kill other vampires." I explain. "It causes eternity long grudges. It never ends well. Same reason why no one can ever know that…" I trail off as I realise Owen could get into hearing range at any time. I make a little walking gesture with my fingers. Alistair nods his understanding.

"Because people would want to know why." Alistair sighs. "And the easiest way to figure that out is-"

"Brutal torture in the name of science." Cleo cuts him off with a scowl. "Yes."

"Maybe we should all just head home." Elias glances over at Lola. "Try again in a few days."

"No." Annie decides. "We grab a target as they leave. Alistair knows the gist and he deserves some fresh food. He must be starving being so surrounded and not touching any of it."

"He can have food at home." Thomas sides with Elias.

"He will have food here." Annie snarls at him with her fangs out. "You want to leave then you can leave."

Thomas's jaw clenches so hard than I am worried his teeth will crack. He throws himself down to the floor and holds his hand up in a silent, displeased surrender. Elias looks down at him with a scowl, expecting more of a fight from him. Thomas was never going to win that fight and he knew it. Vampire business was Annie business and Annie business was always going to be something Thomas was interested in.

Cleo gently runs her hand down my bare arms. I shudder and rest against her. This could be a long night. The club was open for hours more and a majority of the people inside were still half sober. The two boys that Annie and Lola had picked would more than likely stay until the end and 'pull' the drunkest girls they could find.

"How bad was he?" I ask Cleo so softly that the others would barely hear it.

"Not the worst but I won't feel guilty either." Cleo responds. I notice her glance over at Lola who has her back to all of us. She is staring at the nightclub doors, eyes taking in every slight movement coming from them.

"He's still at the bar Lola." Cleo tells her kindly. "I can hear him."

"You can?" Alistair turns to look at us. "Even through all that noise?"

"She has the best ears." I tell him proudly. "She can tell us when he's about to leave."

"It takes a little focus." Cleo turns her head in the direction of Alistair, but her eyes remain on the silent Lola. "Some vampires have an…edge. My hearing is better. Grace is a better tracker than the rest of us. Lola is the fastest."

Cleo leaves out what Annie can do. Annie is the best at hypnosis. She can walk into a room and have people wrapped around her finger. Now that we know what we know, I would assume it was because she is the first vampire. To me she has always oozed confidence and power but I had never been an enemy. She had always been in my corner. She had never had to turn that switch on with me.

"Does every vampire have something like that? Have an extra biological advantage?" Alistair cocks his head to the side like a curious animal.

"Pretty much." Annie answers for Cleo. "It's like humans. Some of them have twenty twenty vision, some don't. Lola used to be a gymnast when she was a human, so her body was in better shape when she was turned. My blood just gave her an extra boost. Growing up, Grace used to watch the punters from her hiding spot behind the bar. She got really good at watching people. The blood took what we already had and it amplified it. Used it to make us better predators."

Alistair mulls that over for a moment before staring down at himself. The poor boy had been stuck downing pain meds and being injected with IVs. He never had a chance to know what he was good at.

"You don't think I have a high tolerance or anything cause of my history do you?" Alistair asks us glumly. "Cause I really don't feel like I've drunk anything at all."

"Wait till you drink from a drunk human." I laugh slightly. "Drinking from a human is rich and delicious but when they have a decent blood alcohol level? It's like the world's best cocktail."

"I'm going back in." Lola declares as she pushes herself to her feet.

"Lola!" Cleo looks appalled. I take that small realisation and hold back a smile. Day by day Cleo is showing that she really does like Lola. It's a little sad that it has taken her twenty years to be so open about it.

Lola ignores her. Lola ignores all of us as she struts right out into the street and across to the security at the doors. Cleo looks over at Annie, her face twisting into rage.

"Why didn't you stop her?" She demands. "Owen could still be in there. She is clearly upset."

"Lola wants to drink and go home." Annie sighs. "And we both know that she is the last person on Owen's list."

"But she is still on the list." Cleo snarls.

"Do you want me to run after her and drag her out?" Annie finally snaps. "Do you want me to put more attention onto what we were doing here tonight? If Elias had not put that glamour on, we would be knee deep in blood by now. Let Lola go and get the racist pervert and then we all. Go. Home."

Cleo and Annie both bare their fangs at the other, eyes locked and shoulders stiff. Annie could force her to submit if she wanted to. The makers bond could take Cleo's will to fight away. Annie would never do it but from the fire in Cleo's eyes, my girlfriend was almost daring her too.

"Lola will be back any moment." I whisper in Cleo's ear. "Then Alistair can eat and we can go home and warm up some blood bags. I don't mind waiting a few more days."

"Is...Is one not enough for all of us?" Alistair asks with a sheepish smile.

"Not for five of us when we are really hungry." Annie is the one that relents, moving across the alley to throw her arm over Alistair's shoulder. It is a sweet sight, somewhere between sisterly and motherly. I see Thomas smile from the corner of my eye.

"Your first drink, you're going to want all of it." Annie warns him. "That's fine. That's natural and you do whatever you like okay? I'll be here to stop anything going wrong."

Even I feel a sense of calm washing over me at Annie's words. Annie will look after us. Annie will smooth it all over. Annie can make it so that this whole situation works out. The moment is broken as Lola's fake laugh echoes down the street. A quick glance tells me that Lola is leading the man by the hand, straight towards the alley we were in. Her lip-gloss is smudged around her mouth. His lips glisten as they pass under a streetlight. Oh.

As soon as Lola leads him across the street, she spins him so he is walking backwards into the alley. I glance over at Annie and Alistair but find Elias and Thomas have hidden themselves even further back into the alley. They don't want to see this. They don't want to be part of this. I do not expect the wave of anger that flashes through me. They are the reason we exist. They have no right to be disgusted.

"You aren't going to be scared." Lola's whole demeanour changes. She stares the unnamed man in the eye. "You aren't going to move. You aren't going to scream."

"I'm not going to be scared. I'm not going to move. I'm not going to scream." The man repeats in a monotone voice. Lola's face splits into a brilliant grin.

"Good job Lola." Annie praises her, gently moving the unnamed man further back into the alley and then positioning Alistair and Lola in front of him. "Show him how it's done."

As Lola gently tilts the man's head up and points to all the places on the neck where Alistair should bite, Annie moves over to the two witches. I watch her stand toe to toe with Thomas and tilt her chin towards the sky. I assume they are having another private conversation. Thomas flinches but does not look away from her. Annie's face changes and her eyes turn pleading. The moment between them only breaks as Elias releases a shaky breath. The sharp smell of blood hits my nostrils.

Lola and Alistair have both taken a bite of the unnamed man, one of them on each side with their eyes closed. Alistair lets out a deep groan which only emphasises how sexual this looks to everyone on the outside.

It was a position that I have been in with Cleo more times than I could count but then, we are actual lovers. My eyes drift to focus on a small trickle of blood falling from Alistair's side. He's messier than Lola, blood smearing across his cheeks as he takes thick gulps. Lola is almost kitten licking around her bite, holding back from fully drinking again in case Alistair wanted more. It was almost loving.

The body drops as the man's heart stops. Lola catches it and twists herself to hold it up from behind. Alistair doesn't notice or if he does then he doesn't care. He just continues sucking and getting it all over himself like a baby. Which he is in the scheme of things. I should stop being so judgemental.

It feels like an age until he is done although I know it only takes five minutes for a body to be completely drained by one of us. Half of that time for a newborn in a frenzy and with Lola added to the mix, we were probably only watching them for a minute and a half.

Alistair eventually pulls away, eyes still closed as he takes in deep gulps of air instead. Lola smiles again. She has a little smear of blood around her mouth but that is nothing compared to the state of Alistair. He has it on his shirt, hands, and neck. The princes eyes flutter open and he stares at us all. His shoulder hunch and he starts to awkwardly wipe his hands on his jeans.

Lola reaches out, taking one finger and trailing it across the blood on his chin. She brings the now covered finger up to her lips and sucks it off. Alistair watches her with wide eyes before laughing shakily as she winks at him.

"Are we ready to go?" Lola calls back to Annie and the boys without looking back. Annie is smiling proudly at them both, smiling like a mother watching two of her children at the school nativity. Thomas is pale but his arm is now loosely wrapped around Annie's waist. It is Elias that worries me.

Elias is staring at Alistair and Lola with narrowed eyes. He swallows down a lump in his throat. He is angry or scared, probably both. I suppose it depends.

I had heard over the centuries that Elias and Thomas had both been quite the supernatural playboys. Thomas because he didn't have to be celibate while waiting centuries for Annie and Elias because…well. He was Elias. Surely he had been bitten or had seen a vampire bite before.

"Let's go home." Annie nods. She moves from Thomas's grip and holds out her hand for Alistair to take. "You run with me."

Alistair takes Annie's hand with a grateful smile. Annie turns back to look at us three girls. She grins.

Two of you need to grab a witch. After they get rid of the body. She tells us before zooming off. Us girls look at each other and all raise an eyebrow. We could all easily pick them up and run. It just wouldn't be comfortable.

"Pick a ride boys." Cleo turns to the boys and sighs. "After you burn the body of course."

"I don't remember you becoming the boss of me." Thomas says in a forced playful tone. He steps towards the body anyway and starts to search him. He pulls a leather wallet from the pocket of the jeans and throws it to Elias. The blonde lets it drop to the floor as he watches his cousin.

"Keep talking like that and I'll drop you." Cleo purrs at him. Thomas smirks up at her. If these two become friends than I will never know a moments peace again.

"I can carry you." Lola smiles over at Elias. He ignores her instead choosing to reach down and pick up the wallet. He opens it with a faint popping noise and scans the ID in the see-through pocket.

"Rest in peace Connor Parkinson." Elias says. Cleo snorts from beside me but says nothing. Elias takes the cash from the wallet and shoves it into his pockets. I raise my eyebrows at him but say nothing. He throws the wallet back to the body as Thomas takes a step back from it.

"I said I can carry you. If you want." Lola repeats, pulling her arms around herself as if she were effected by a sudden chill. Elias doesn't look at her as he starts to mumble three quick words of Latin. The body bursts into flames, the air around us turning hot. The flames only last a few seconds and then they are gone, the body replaced with a pile of ash.

"I am going to go out. Don't wait up cousin. I will not be back before sunrise." Elias declares to us all. He rubs his hands together before walking straight past us. Lola watches him go with a hurt look on her face. Thomas opens his mouth to say something before deciding against it. We lock eyes and I open up my arms for him.

Chapter Forty-Two

Alistair

"You did very well tonight." Annie tells me once again. We are sat in my rooms, a small bowl of warm water and a wet cloth on the table beside us. Annie gives the cloth another rinse before bringing it back to my neck.

"Lola wasn't as covered in it as I was." I whisper shamefully, trying to stay as still as possible. I could do this myself and I was tempted to insist that I should, but it felt nice to have my makers attention. It felt nice to have access to someone who would answer all my questions without pity or hiding something because I 'couldn't take it'.

"Lola has been a vampire two whole decades longer than you have." Annie tells me softly. The rag dips into the water again, turning it a darker pink than before. "We were all much worse than you when we started. You did very well to only drink that much."

I wanted to drink more. I wanted to go back in like Lola did and grab someone. I don't think I would have even cared enough to drag that person back to the alley. The thing that had stopped me was the fear I would pick the wrong person. I would go for the easy bite; I would go for a girl like Diana who didn't deserve it. I couldn't let those urges control me. Not when it came to being a vampire. Not when it came to being a prince and potentially a King.

"It's going to be harder for me to find people like that." I gently prod at the glaring flaw in their plan. "Not impossible but harder. I may not find one every time."

"Which is why it's important for you to get used to blood bags. With what your schedule might be I can't guarantee you will be able to hunt too often." Annie admits.

"But its best that I do hunt. Right?" I frown.

"It is better for your control and ability. If you spend the next thousand years only drinking from blood bags or even from animals then I don't know what that will do to you when you are surrounded by humans. Something that you with all your balls and charity events will need to be perfect at. There can be no slip ups for you. No one can ever know what you are." Annie drops the rag into the bowl one final time.

I know that. I know that if I make one slip up then I put more than just myself in danger. I put everyone in this castle, this country in danger. Thomas and the other witches, Annie, Grace, Cleo, Lola, even my parents and Lyra. All of them were at risk. If my parents were at risk than this country's stability was gone. A country with weak or no leaders was ripe for the taking. That knowledge felt heavy in my heart and on my shoulders.

"Thomas will make sure you hunt. I just can't say how often that will be." Annie says after taking a long look at me. I force a smile on my face.

"I think I made them uncomfortable tonight." I admit.

"That wasn't your fault." Annie starts to check my hair for any blood. "They didn't fully think the witnessing of tonight through, and the Owen encounter had them on edge."

"Lola…" I trail off before I can ask an actual question.

"Lola has never and will never like Owen." Annie says firmly. "He became a little obsessed with her back when we lived in Brooklyn. She never even glanced at him like that. It's driven him a little crazy."

"There's something else though isn't there." I say before I can stop myself. "Another reason Owen is here."

Annie pauses her searching. She sighs and pulls her arm back. She doesn't respond as she picks up the bloody water bowl and heads into my bathroom. I sit there on the edge of my bed, hands together in my lap like a scolded child.

"I have a brother." Annie says as she re-enters the room. "His name is Edward, but I always called him Teddy. I haven't seen him in centuries. He was turned by someone else back when I was still…newish."

Annie doesn't sit back down on the bed next to me. She slowly paces around my room, picking up random little knickknacks that have been placed in here to fill the space now there is no medical equipment.

"Lola came home one morning and said that Owen had a message for me from Teddy. I went and I found Owen. He was lying. I didn't take it well." Annie runs her fingers over a small ceramic lion. "We left for my families estate here in England. Thomas arrived with a deal. I find out why I am a daywalker and where Teddy is in exchange for turning you."

Annie focusses those dark green eyes on me. I have to force in my next breath. That sounds about right. Sounds like the kind of deal Thomas would make in exchange for my life. But it also sounds a little too good to be true.

"So where is Teddy?" I ask hesitantly.

"Christiana is searching for him now." Annie's tone drops. "The intel they thought they had was old. It could take a while to find him again. He has a way of disappearing without a trace. Handy when you are with him. Annoying when you aren't."

"Wouldn't he want you to find him? You're his sister." I frown. Annie lets out a humourless laugh.

"We were only close for the first few years." She admits. "As soon as I was of marrying age the dynamic between us shifted. We were suddenly adults and we lashed out at each other. We both said things we didn't mean and taking the job at court…It wasn't something I would have had the luxury of declining. If you are chosen as a handmaiden for a favoured lady at court, you are the handmaiden for a favoured lady at court."

"I didn't…I didn't realise you…" I struggle to find the correct sentence.

"You thought I just snuck into court and murdered your ancestor for fun?" Annie shoots me an amused smile. "No Alistair. I knew him relatively well by that point. He married my best friend. She thought he loved her. How could she not? He broke the entire world order to be by her side because he thought she was his world. Then he took her head when he decided she wasn't anymore."

I had heard that story more times than I could count. I had tried to wrap my head around it when Annie had first let it slip she was behind it all. I knew there had to be a reason and that this friend had to be someone important. But back then the kings were a little too happy with beheadings and I just hadn't realised until now that her friend had been the second wife of King Henry VIII.

"Your friend was Anne Boleyn?" I gape at her.

"She called us Anne and Annie. Not really a nickname I know but the way she said it…I had never felt so seen." Annie moves on from the ceramic lion to a small metal yorkie statue. "When Anne smiled at you it was as if the sun itself noticed you. She was beautiful and graceful and so compassionate. All she wanted was to be loved. She didn't want to marry him. Her father wanted her to marry him and as a woman in the 1500s she had no choice but to obey. So, she did. She was flawless in her role."

Anne was beheaded for treason and adultery. She cheated on the King and only had stillborn sons. Even when I was learning this history it was clear the lack of sons was the real crime. I remember actually laughing at such a weak excuse. Shame fills my stomach.

"So, when she started to fall from grace I would have done anything to help her. She was my Queen, my lady and above all that, my friend." Annie picks up a small wooden box and checks it over for engravings. Her voice is unnaturally neutral. "I didn't get the chance to. I won't bore you with the details of my plan but when it became time to enact it, I was raped and almost murdered. You know the rest."

"You don't think those things are linked?" I look at her horrified. "Like someone knew?"

Annie shakes her head, and she finally starts to look at me. "I was courting more than one suitor at the time. My father wanted me to have a backup in case anything happened to Anne. He never trusted her position. Never trusted Henry."

"The timing seems a little..." I once again do not finish. I do not want to call her traumatic experience 'convenient.'

"So few people knew." Annie insists. "Only the ones I desperately needed to know to help me. No other ladies of the court. Only one other handmaiden. Only the people who could hide her away. Only..."

This time Annie trails off. She closes her eyes and takes a long breath through her nose. Her fingers run through her hair, and she starts to pace in a small circle, muttering to herself so softly that her lips are barely moving.

"Annie?" I say softly when I realise that she is shaking. She scrapes her hands across her face, letting out a deep hiss before swearing softly. "Annie I didn't mean to upset you. We should drop it."

Annie turns to look at me, her face set in a sad expression. She doesn't come any closer and she doesn't respond. She just looks me up and down, silently debating something. She lets out another deep breath and nods once.

"I need you to find Lola and the others. Tell them to pack the essentials and wait for my signal. If you all do not hear from me within two hours, you stay with Grace and you run. Do you understand?" Annie speaks slowly, calmly even though her words send a spike of fear through my heart.

"Why?" I breathe out.

"Because I think the Devil played a trick on me your highness." Annie's voice hardens. "And I need to see if it's still safe for us here. You are bound by blood to them. They will look after you no matter what. No matter if I am wrong or right. So, stay with them." Her fingers brush against my face and then she is gone in a blink of the eye.

Crap.

I close my eyes and start to blindly reach out with my mind down the bond. *Lola? Cleo? Grace? Are you there? Are you home?*

What's wrong Alistair? Thomas's voice answers me and for the life of me I do not know why I hesitate to answer him. I just see a flash of Annie's face as she paces, hear the hidden panic in her voice as she left with a vague goodbye.

I want to speak to Lola. I answer diplomatically.

We've stopped on the way home. We'll be back soon. Thomas chuckles.

I need them back now. I snap. *Girls. Girls please can you hear me?*

Are you okay your grace? Grace asks softly. I do not answer for a moment. Would Annie want Thomas to know we were clearly getting ready to run? Would Thomas be able to stop us anyway? Annie didn't mention him. Maybe she had made a point not to.

Annie said I needed to speak to you. I think back slowly and then I lie. *I think that guy took something before we drank him. She thinks Lola might be feeling what I am.*

They had talked about a blood hangover, as if we could get drunk from the booze in the person's blood. Why wouldn't we be able to get high from them as well? If it wasn't possible or if Lola would have tasted it, they will hopefully know that I am lying while Thomas wont. If they don't realise then they would rush home to talk to me. Either way, it should work.

We will be home in three. Grace replies grimly. *Stay in your room.*

Chapter Forty-Three

Annie

I should have fed tonight. I make a brief pitstop at my own rooms and down the bags that I have left. They are warm, still spelled by Thomas in some romantic gesture. The thought that he knew what I had just pieced together almost makes me spit it out. It would not be the first time he has lied to me.

The main problem I have is that the cursed coven cannot be killed. Neither can I. This stand-off will be painful, but it will not truly end. I will need to keep killing them over and over until I can get them into a place where I can keep them. Finding that place could take months. Finding a witch strong enough to ward the place so I do not have to worry every second of the day that they have escaped could take years. But there is no other option.

I will not sit back and do nothing. Not when they could be doing so much worse. Not when I do not know if Thomas is a part of it. Not when Lola is only getting closer to Elias who could also be a part of it. Not when Christiana is looking for my brother. I will not lay back and sleep with the enemy when I do not know if I have the time for the long game. I certainly do not have the stomach for it.

My room has very little practical weapons in it. Multiple things with sharp corners or items heavy enough to have an impact when thrown but nothing that I can easily take with me. Fangs and nails it is.

All the witches stay in the same part of the palace. Thomas's rooms are right next to Elias's which are next to Christiana's. The other three live on the opposite side of the corridor. I know from earlier today that their rooms are sound proofed. As long as she is alone when I get there, this will be fine. The odds of her being alone are minimal.

I move with my supernatural speed down to the halls. Servants only come down this section at set times. Two o clock in the morning is not one of those times. I take a long sniff as I tread carefully down the hall. Neither Elias or Thomas have been down here in hours. Christiana even longer than that.

I pause as a familiar salty scent hits my nose right in front of William's door. Another sniff and I can almost taste rotten eggs mixing in with the sharp iron of blood.

There was a baby making spell some hack had tried to promote centuries ago that needed sulphur. Only the mortals had bought into it. Even magic could not change someone's fertility. The spell had ended up being forbidden due to the botching of it. The witch who created it locked away for the rest of his life. The spell had needed sulphur, blood and…

I kick the door in. I may not like William and had more than once imagined wrapping my hands around his throat and choking the life out of him myself, but like hell was I going to let him be the victim of back-alley fertility ritual bullshit.

William is not the one tied down.

"Oh my god." I blurt out, taking a step backwards back into the hallway as if that is going to stop the images from searing themselves into my brain. All thoughts of revenge are gone as I debate gouging out my eyeballs.

Mary is spread like an eagle, handcuffed to every post of the bed as William viciously pumps his hips into her. He doesn't even stop now he knows he is being watched. He turns his head to look at who has interrupted them and grunts. The eye contact makes me shudder, but I have nowhere else to look. It's either at William as he humps a girl I had always called 'sweet' or at Corsi who is positioned over Mary's mouth with her head thrown back in a scream. Mary's own sounds are squashed by Corsi's thighs thank Christ. All of them are slick with sweat and other juices I do not want to think about.

I want to run away. I am not a prude by any means, but I am clearly not supposed to be here and the idea of taking on three naked cursed coven witches at once has even my flight reflex kicking in.

Instead, I stand and continue to stare at this continuing horror show like a child does when a car is heading towards them. I want to scream at them to stop it. I feel bile rising in my throat and an intense feeling in my stomach that this is something that cannot be taken back. This is wrong for some reason, and I cannot pinpoint the exact reason why. I have no way to explain the intense fear this causes to run through me, until my eyes catch onto the small alter with two photographs in the corner of the room.

The door slams in my face as Thomas calls my name down the bond.

Chapter Forty-Four

Grace

Annie asked Alistair to lie. I don't know why and the two minutes it takes to snarl at Lola to get up and start running home feel like forever. My body feels like an unco-operative ice statue, moving too sluggishly to be of any use even though no one, not even Lola beats me to those hidden back gates to the palace gardens.

Cleo is holding Thomas and is the last to meet us, seconds apart from Lola as I rip those gates open and rush forward again. If Alistair is hurt I will burn this place to the ground. If Annie is hurt then I will burn the entire empire. I do not care if I scare the servants as I throw open doors and vases sway as I move too closely to them.

I get to Alistair's room and almost rip the door from its hinges. I stop mere centimetres from him as I look around the room. Lola is hot on my heels. Cleo must have dropped Thomas somewhere before rushing in and slamming the door shut after her. Alistair jumps at our sudden appearance.

"Where's Annie?" I demand. He looks up at me with wild panicked eyes. I am tempted to shake him until he speaks.

"I don't know." He admits. "She just said to tell you that we need to pack the essentials. If we don't hear from her in two hours then we need to run, and I need to stay with you."

My heart drops to my feet. The edges of my eyeline start to go fuzzy and I suddenly cannot take a deep breath. I can barely breath at all. Cleo's voice in my ear is just a fluctuating ringing noise.

"No." I wheeze and shake my head so hard that I accidentally headbutt Cleo. "No. Where is she?" I demand again.

"I don't- she didn't say!" Alistair says in a panic. "We were talking, and she just-she thought she figured something out and she just-she just said that and left!"

"What did she figure out Alistair?" Lola sits next to him on the bed and forces the prince to look her in the eye. "What were you talking about?"

"Anne Boleyn."

My heart feels like he kicked it across the room. I rip his face from Lola's hands and stare down at him.

"Tell me *everything*." I snarl.

Chapter Forty-Five

Annie

I need a plan. I need a plan to take a scouring pad to my brain while keeping the vital information in it and I need a plan to figure out if I can trust Thomas. Ninety four percent of my body screams at me that I can, that he never would have been a part of what happened to me. The other six percent is floating images of my family, of my girls and Alistair, and that part screams that if it's not related then why the fuck was William screwing Corsi and Mary next to a picture of my brother.

By your rooms I reply softly down the bond. I take the four steps forward to his door and lounge against it as I wait for him. I take deep breaths as I think through what my options are. As sad as it sounds it would be easy to play with Thomas. It will only take a few kisses and embraces, if I can stomach them right now, and he would answer my questions. If I phrase my questions correctly then I will not be given a well-practised answer. I can throw the other portrait in his face and gauge his reaction. He will not be able to hide that one.

Thomas struts around the corner with his hands in his pockets and a wide grin on his face. That ninety-four percent shoots up to ninety-nine. No man that had been behind what happened to me could look at me with his eyes so full of love.

"Hi." He breathes before planting his lips against mine hungrily. I kiss back despite myself. As his lips press mine open I frown and pull back to look at him. He didn't drink a lot tonight and I didn't think he had drunk vodka at all.

"Cleo bought me a small bottle from an off license." Thomas admits with a sheepish grin. I don't care to scold him for holding the girls up from coming home. I just want answers and away from the things I know are happening in the room opposite.

"Come on then." I force a slight smile onto my face as I open the door and drag him inside.

"We only got about halfway through it before Alistair called us home." Thomas babbles as I shut the door behind him. I want to kiss Cleo the next time I see her. She has made this even easier.

"I think I scared him while we were talking." I half lie as I slowly move to lounge across his bed. He hurries to my side and settles himself on his right side to face me. "I was talking about Anne."

"You carry such blame for that. It wasn't your fault." Thomas coos as he reaches out to gently stroke my face. His thumb tugs at my lip.

"She was my friend. I loved her." I whisper back, relaxing into his touch and trying to convince myself it was all a part of the ploy and not my body's natural reaction.

"I know." Thomas replaces his thumb with his lips, gently running them over mine before resting his forehead against mine. "But when you love, you love fiercely. That can be quite terrifying even to the person that is the object of that love."

"Was that supposed to be some deep thoughtful comment?" I ask thickly.

"It was supposed to be me telling you that I know you love me." Thomas smirks, his next kiss more passionate.

"Oh really?" I smirk, looping my leg over his hip and slowly twisting us so he was fully beneath me. "How noble of you to tell me what I feel."

"I think you feel something else right now." Thomas grins cheekily up at me as his hands run up my thighs and grab my ass.

"Cute." I smirk down at him even though he is right. He presses against me even as I fully sit back. Halfway drunk and incredibly horny. Even easier to get information from.

"You're cute." He retorts. "Although right now you look super sexy. Even if you are wearing your 'hit on me so I can rip out your throat' clothes."

"I thought we had this conversation." I frown even as I take his hands in my own and start to play with his fingers. "Back in the alley."

"You scolded me like a child." Thomas pouts.

"You and Elias were behaving like children." I respond as I bring one of his hands up to my face and start to slowly kiss them. "Acting like what we were doing was evil when you are the ones that cursed us like this. Like we aren't making the best of a bad situation you put us in."

"I know." Thomas whispers as his eyes laser focus on my mouth. "So, I watched. Like you said. You were right, as always."

I make a small humming noise as I bring one of my fingers halfway into my mouth. Thomas's breath hitches and then he makes a whining nose as I pull away from his fingers and look down at him instead.

"Before we rip each other's clothes off and put your sound blocking spell to the test again, I have a question for you." I make my tone almost bashful. It feels a little too much, but Thomas's senses are flooded and he doesn't notice.

"Anything." He promises, trying to lean up to kiss me. I keep him down, holding his hands above his head on the mattress. He lets out a soft chuckle as my face is inches above his.

"Why does your father have an alter with pictures of my brother and your mother on it?" I stare into his eyes. The confusion that passes through them is real as is the horror that follows.

"What are you talking about?" He rips his hands from my grip. I let him. He pushes us both up into a sitting position, hips still pressed together as we stare at each other.

"When it was all going south for Anne." I began in a soft snarl. "I created a plan. I needed the servants to disguise her and sneak her out. I needed Corsi."

"What the hell does that-"

"Interrupt me again and I'll rip your throat out so you have to lay there and listen." I move my hand to grip his hair, yanking it back to give me easy access. Thomas clenches his jaw and his throat bobs as he swallows. He says nothing.

"Good boy." I purr sarcastically at him but keep my hold and continue.

"Corsi was to organise Anne's trip back to your estate. Your family were not there. She would stay there for a day before travelling to my estate where she would pretend to be a servant and I would meet her when I returned home. Then I would accept your proposal officially and I would tell you. We would help her leave the country and get a new name. You would have done that for me."

Thomas's eyes do not leave my face as I speak. His expression changes from confusion to anger and then full circle back to the love as he had in the hall. My heart slowly lifts in my chest, expanding and rising like a too full balloon getting ready to burst. I wet my lips before continuing.

"Corsi agreed to help. She agreed that you would help because of your noble heart and that all I would need to do is go and pay for a room at an inn just outside the city under the name of Viviane. Anne would use the room when Corsi smuggled her out." I pause and then feel the need to explain, to brag to him about how clever it all was.

"An inn inside the city meant people were too likely to have seen her or her portrait. Anne always loved to go out and see her people. So I took the gold and I left on an errand. Anne thought I was coming to see you to tell you that I accepted. She told me I could take as long as I liked and to come back to her with all the romantic details." I can't help but smile softly as I remember my friend's delighted face. Thomas's face starts to swim as I blink back tears.

"Oh Annie." He whispers despite my order to stay quiet. He has pieced it together. The way his voice breaks, the way he closes his eyes and takes a ragged breath…He did not know. He did not know about this deal with Corsi. He did not know that she betrayed me. I finish the story even though I do not need to.

"I took no escort. I took a carriage as far as I dared and then walked. I was so focussed on the plan, on completing this first vital part that I never even heard him. I never saw him and I never…I never even thought that Corsi might have told someone my plan." My voice breaks into a sob as the betrayal finally sets in now I have said it out loud.

Corsi not only made me this way and ripped my soul from me. She ripped my innocence and my life from under me as well. I was more than willing to die for Anne. I had known it had been a risk. I knew I would have been hung or tortured or my head cut off. I had made peace with those outcomes. I had been so careful with my choice of confidant because of that. Even five hundred years later, it had not ever crossed my mind that I had been wrong in my choice.

I do not know when I start crying or when I let his wrists go. I just know that he has moved us, so I am gently tucked into the side of chest and his arms are wrapped around me. Guilt and shame rises in me as my balloon heart explodes.

I doubted Thomas. I doubted him and here he was, as constant as the stars in the sky. He was holding me as if I hadn't just threatened him, as if I were small and weak. No. No not like that. He had never made me feel like that. Thomas was holding me as if I were precious. As if I needed to be protected. The thought makes me sob harder.

Thomas moves a hand to gently run down my hair and starts to place gentle kisses to my forehead. He does not make shushing noises. He does not tell me to calm down. He does not tell me that it is okay. He just holds me. He just loves me.

"Call for Grace." He whispers to me once my sobs have turned to hiccups. "I know you. Call for her."

He does know me. He knows I would have sent Grace and the girls away and I would have gone after Corsi. Which leads to a very very awkward conversation now.

"Before I do.." I shift in his arms so I can stare up at him. "You really aren't going to like what I'm about to say."

"I haven't liked what you've had to say all day." Thomas points out. I decide to rip the plaster off.

"I saw that alter when I opened the door and found your dad, Mary and Corsi having a threesome."

Thomas slowly blinks at me, waiting for me to say I am joking. As I press my lips together in a sorry excuse for a smile, Thomas gags. His whole body shudders.

"I will need you to hypnotise the images I just thought of out of my brain." Thomas says as he shakes his head, "cause your wrong. My dad doesn't…not with Corsi and Mary. They are like family. They may as well be blood related."

"There is no way I misunderstood what I saw." I insist. "Not the actual action. I'll admit I thought Corsi was performing some back street fertility ritual-" I cut myself off at the look on his face. Maybe that was a little too much information.

"I am really going to regret this." Thomas sighs. "But you are going to have to tell me everything. After you tell Grace to come back and before we call Elias."

"We can't call Elias." I shake my head. "Or Christiana."

"You can't be…" Thomas cuts himself off and closes his eyes. "He was the one that told me you were hurt. Christiana was the one who told him."

"We don't know who else knew." I whisper sadly.

"You can't ask Alistair to get involved in this." Thomas gives me a squeeze but does not pull away. He is waiting for me to pull away first. I snuggle further into his chest.

"He is already involved in this. They are his witches council. They won't leave him alone if they come for me." I say sadly.

"If they come for us." Thomas amends and places one more kiss to my temple.

"Us." I repeat.

Chapter Forty-Six

Elias

The Diamond Lion was a stupidly named supernatural bar with a suspicious menu and even more suspicious women in it. Even I was having second thoughts about talking to any of them and I was now eight shots deep. There were too many groups of sirens, all of the women with lilting voices staring at each newcomer as if she was going to eat them.

The bar is lit with neon lights and decorated with all metal and glass. No wood around because of the vampires. No silver because of the werewolves. Everything and every creature had a safe place here. If anyone was going to fight, they did it in the lower levels.

Normally I would love the challenge of surviving the night. Even if I didn't technically survive I would still wake up the next morning and out of all the times my heart has officially stopped, I had never quite been fucked to death. Yet every time I try to turn my head to look at the group and take my pick, I imagine a tiny blonde ponytail whipping in the other direction. I hear her fake laugh echoing around the room.

She thinks I hate her. That's easier. I can avoid her for a little while, just until I have shaken off this itching need to be near her, and then I can swan back in and we can be actual friends. Actual forever friends stuck watching as she seduces men just to survive. That would be fine. Totally fine. As long as I never had to watch her and Alistair share someone ever again.

I wrinkle my nose as I stare down at my empty cocktail glass. It was some slimy frozen green drink that the bartender had called a 'witch special'. I didn't ask what was in it. I just slurped it down. The end of the drink was gritty, and I run my tongue over my teeth to get the feeling out of my mouth.

"Elias? Is that you?" A thick French accent giggles from behind me. I close my eyes and hold back a groan. I then plaster on a smile and then spin on my barstool.

"Francis! Long-time no see." I stare at the vampire for a few seconds and refuse to admit it is because my eyes are starting to blur. He looks the same as he had back in 1801. The same slightly curled brown hair that covered his ears. The same unfortunately thick eyebrows and the same sun kissed skin. He was alright looking I suppose. Back in the day it had really been his accent that pulled the ladies in. I imagine that hadn't changed.

"You have been in England too long my friend. We have missed you in Paris." Francis settles himself next to me.

"Yet here you are in London. What is it this time?" I gesture for the bartender to come over.

"Business." Francis sighs and runs his hands roughly through his hair. "It is looking like I will be here longer than expected. We should organise a…as you English people say 'proper piss up' when you are free."

I grin back at him. "That sounds like the perfect next night out. What are you drinking? They have a vampire special."

"What is so special about it?" He asks.

"Maybe no one else likes the O negative they put in it." I joked. Francis laughs louder than I expected or even deserve but I appreciate it. Francis orders the special and when it comes it looks like a bloody Mary. Typical. He takes a long pull and then pulls a face at it.

"Horrible?" I guess as I get a refill on my weird frozen drink.

"Not as horrible as this English prick I have to deal with." Francis gets straight to complaining. The business couldn't be that secret if he was telling me anything at all, even if it was just that his partner was English.

"You always used to say you loved the English." I taunt him playfully, remembering the constant drunken rants every time there was a royal wedding or funeral. "And their blind faith in their pompous monarchy?"

"Ha Ha." Francis scowls at me. "You are English."

"Only cause my mother gave birth on the wrong side of the border."

"After marrying an Englishman."

"I always preferred living in Scotland."

"That's because of your taste for druid girls."

"Watch it sharp teeth. You have a taste for anything." I laugh, running my fingers down the side of my cold glass. Maybe it was the shots finally catching up with me, but I felt too hot in my skin, too uneasy in my seat. The Thames wasn't far and the breeze coming off of it always helped to shock me sober. I should do that before I go home, go stand and watch the world go by.

"Seriously. This one takes the proverbial cake. I have never seen someone with such little reputation be so full of himself. He thinks-Well." Francis cackles. "You will never believe this old friend."

Francis leans forward, glances up at the bartender and then over at the nearest group to us, a bunch of werewolves with their claws half out. "He thinks that he knows where to find the daywalkers."

My body runs from burning hot to freezing cold. No. Not possible. I force myself to scoff and take a long pull from my drink. It really is too hot in here.

"Daywalkers do not exist Francis." I remind him slowly, like telling a child that two plus two equals four. "They are a figment of vampire imagination, created by people turned against their will who miss the feeling of the sun on their skin."

"I know, I know." Francis shrugs in a 'what can you do' gesture. "But he's convinced my boss that he can find them. Brought all sorts of 'proof' that no one else was allowed to see. Whatever it is he obviously faked it and faked it well. I'll humour him for a few weeks before it all comes to a dead end."

The obvious glaring issue is that the proof may not be faked. If Francis were an imaginative man he may have latched onto this Englishman and followed the trail all the way back to me and Thomas. Back to Annie. Back to Lola. If this random Englishman had the right proof. If Annie and the girls had not been as careful as they thought.

"Want any help?" I offer after a sip of my drink. "My job is getting a little stagnant lately. Could use the fresh air."

"The secret job of the cursed coven is finally taking its toll. Only took a few centuries." Francis shoves the bloody Mary mockery to the side and orders a beer. "How are your cousins? Thomas still mooning after Annie?"

"I forget you know Annie." I chuckle. "Christiana is still an angsty little bookworm."

"Everyone knows about the survivors Elias." Francis tuts at me.

"I hate that nickname."

"So does she. But she made that big speech about surviving worse than Winston before she ripped his arm off so she is stuck with it. That and only turning female victims. People notice patterns. I heard she's had two more join her since I saw her last. Have you met them yet?" Francis's tone turns curious. I should move over to water so I don't slip up. I cannot let the booze and general sense of friendship convince me that I can speak freely.

"Winston was a gropey little bastard who got his arm back. I made sure of it." I remind him bluntly. "And if she didn't do it, I would have done it for her."

"Yes you and your blood magic. Uncle William still not approving?" Francis asks yet another question. If he wasn't like this every time we found each other I would assume it was linked to his daywalker errands. I cannot afford to be paranoid or skittish around Francis. He would sense it and all the survivors would be doomed.

"Uncle William doesn't approve of anything." I smirk. My phone starts to vibrate in my pocket. I pull it half out and then decline the call. How Grace got my number I don't know, and I don't care. They can handle Alistair tonight. He was home safe now and that is where my duty for the night ended.

"Someone waiting on you?" Francis stretches in his chair. "It is probably about time you settled down."

"Bite me." I mutter at him. Then it is my turn for questions. "How is Natalie?"

"Dumped me when I agreed to come to England. She didn't want to come with." Francis shrugs again. "Usual ten-year cycle."

"She's not even two hundred." I shake my head. "Hardly a soulmate if you spend half the time fighting with the other."

"Love is pain my friend. It bleeds and it scars but Natalie…How could I forever leave someone like her?" Francis smiles softly, pulling his own phone from his pocket. His home screen is a beaming picture of Natalie, her hair now dyed a bright blue where it once had been a thin brown. She was curled up on what was undoubtably an expensive couch holding a plain white mug. Her smile made her eyes crinkle. My home screen was one of the palace dogs. "We will live until the very world implodes. What is a decade in the scheme of things?"

"You sound so much like Thomas." I can't keep the bitterness from my voice as my phone rings again. "Putting your women on pedestals and letting them lash out at you while you grovel on your knees at the bottom of them."

"When you fall in love Elias, I really hope I am there to see it." Francis replies.

"Didn't you just say that you will live until the world implodes?" I snap at him.

"I will. But I have no idea on how long a cursed witch lives and either way, I want to see you stumble and fall to your knees. Right next to me and Thomas." Francis grins at me. My phone rings for a third time. He gestures for me to answer it. I scowl and answer without looking at the screen.

"What?" I snap, expecting Grace's sweet tone. Everyone else was saved as a contact and no one else would need to call.

"It's Lola." The whispered voice is like an arrow through my chest.

"I'm out right now. I'll be back in a few hours." I glance over at Francis who is grinning like a chesire cat.

"I can't wait a few hours." Lola's voice gets even lower. I have six different ways I want to respond to that, but I don't say any of them as I hear her softly shut a door.

"Are you okay?" I turn completely away from Francis and lower my own voice. "Has something happened?"

"You need to come back, and you need to talk to Annie." Lola is being purposefully vague. Fuck. I stand to my feet and the whole world spins. Double fuck.

"I'm at the Diamond Lion. It's on the Southbank." I say lowly and try to swallow my pride. "I am a little too drunk to walk."

"I'll carry you back. I'll be there in less than five." Lola promises before the line goes dead.

"Well, well well." Francis hides his grin behind his bottle. "Maybe I've already missed it."

I shoot him the finger as I shove my cocktail away and ask for a glass of water.

Chapter Forty-Seven

Lola

I take a little longer than the five minutes I promised. I would rush around the Southbank and miss all the tiny little avenues and signs and have to double back. London is confusing, especially at night. Eventually I stopped and asked people for directions. Most of them had no idea. The little old woman who pointed me in the right direction shot me a wink afterwards. I realised why when I saw the hidden symbol behind the neon name. It was supernatural creatures only.

I have to show my fangs after I pass the initial security guard. Just a quick flash of them is fine. The girl has hers out permanently and tells me she likes my outfit. She recommends the special. I thank her and go to head inside. This place is huge. The staircase to the left of her goes both up and down. I put on a smile and turn back to her.

"I'm actually looking for someone." I admit sheepishly. "He's a witch. Tall, blonde, wearing a band shirt?"

"Oh!" The girls eyes twinkle as she looks me up and down. "You're looking for Elias! Go straight through here and follow the bar around. He likes to sit by the mirrored part."

"Thank you!" I call over my shoulder as I step through the thick red curtains into the main bar. It's loud. The curtains must have been spelled to keep the sound in.

I ignore all the typical club conversations as I follow the girls instructions and follow the bar around. The bar is in a giant L shape and made of thick metal. The section by the curtains is full of plush seats and tables. The windows above them are completely covered. Maybe this place is open twenty-four hours?

There is a variety of smells and heartbeat sounds. I can smell saltwater coming from the girls dancing by the covered windows. I wrinkle my nose as I walk past a particularly gross wet dog smell drifting from an older werewolf. The longest part of the bar showcases a dance floor and, as the girl said, it is full of mirrors. There are mirrors on the bar, on the counters, on the walls and on the floors. The dancefloor is full of six dancing women but the way they spin makes it seem as if there are six hundred of them.

Elias is not alone at the bar. The man next to him is thin and pale with almost too pronounced cheekbones. He is wearing a tailored suit. The whole place is full of people in various types of clothes. Some girls are wearing mini dresses others baggy hoodies and sweatpants. I wish I had known that before I raced over here. Not that I would have had time to change. We were on a ticking clock.

Elias catches sight of me and waves. I smile and zoom over, feeling oddly free to do such a thing inside and around complete strangers. I ignore the fact that Elias's lips twitch, but he does not fully smile back.

"Hi." I turn to his friend instead. I hold out my hand. My father's voice hisses in my ear. *Polite even in crisis, Lola. Do you understand me?* "I'm Lola."

"Francis." The man takes my hand and instead of shaking it, twists it so he can kiss the top of it. "An old friend of Elias."

"Emphasis on the old." Elias grumbles. He takes a deep gulp of water.

"I am a new friend of Elias." I joke back.

"Must be quite new." Francis gestures for me to take a seat next to him. I glance over at Elias. I don't have the time, but he does not look anywhere near sober.

"I'm in a rush." I apologise. "We need to get home Elias. Annie needs to speak to you."

"You know Annie?" Francis's whole demeanour changes. He gives Elias a long look and then drifts his eyes to look me up and down. Not in a creepy or appreciative way but as if he was checking for something. His eyes linger on my neck, at my lack of a pulse, and his face drops.

"You are one of Annie's." He corrects himself. "I am so sorry, mon cheri."

I frown at him. *One of Annie's.* Elias breaks the silence by slamming his now empty glass down on the bar. It makes me jump slightly and I am suddenly aware of everything my body is doing. I can feel how my hands hang limply at my sides and how the end of my ponytail is tickling the back of my neck. I feel exposed and branded as if everyone in this room that glances at me knows what happened. Knows why I was turned. Why I was saved.

"Let me know when you are next free Elias." Francis tells the witch softly although his sad eyes do not leave my face. "And bring the lovely Lola with you."

"Don't bet on that." Elias moves slowly from his seat and takes uneasy steps towards me. I hold out my arm for him to take so I can walk him outside, but he takes my hand instead. "I know what you are like around blondes."

Francis's sad smile changes to a grin as we slowly move away from him. I shoot him a smile over my shoulder.

"Make sure to wear some knee guards Elias." Francis calls after us playfully. "Would hate for them to get hurt."

I pause mid step and whip my head around. Elias gives my hand a gentle but fierce hug as he visibly swallows.

"Not a threat. Keep walking." He mutters. "And while I puke in the Thames you can tell me exactly why you need me back."

"You aren't going to like it."

"Motto of the evening."

"I wasn't even supposed to come and get you ya know." Lola tells me hotly as we pass through the thick red curtains. I wave to Rachel at reception as we pass. I wait until we are out onto the street, in the dark cold night broken up by cheap flickering lamps. Then I answer and it is as pathetic out loud as it was in my head.

"Then why did you?"

"Because." Lola stalls over her words as I let go of her hand and bolt over to the thick black iron railing around this part of the river. The Diamond Lion's entrance leads right out to the walkway and is nestled between three other pubs. Those pubs aren't spelled to repulse humans or to make them forget they had even walked past them. They did quite well in the scheme of things.

I start to hack and gag over the railing as the reek of the river fully hits me. Christiana once teased me with the statistics of how many dead bodies are in there. The thought was less than comforting as I stare into its inky blackness. One noisy wave and the frozen cocktail makes its way back up my throat.

"It's okay." Lola whispers as her hand rubs gentle circles on my back, her fingers as hot as flames through my thin t-shirt. "Get it all up."

I resist the urge to shrug her off. She's stronger than me and it's an oddly comforting feeling. No one has rubbed my back while I threw up in a very, very long time.

"What's going on Lola?" I ask with a sore throat as I wipe at my mouth. Gross but no other option.

"I trust you." Lola answers as she looks at me although she is answering my other question. Probably not a good sign. I am shaking from the cold and from puking, but she steps closer to me and holds out her arms anyway.

"You aren't taking me anywhere until you explain what's gone wrong and why, exactly, you weren't supposed to come get me." I tell her coldly. She flinches at my tone. I want to take it back. She takes a deep breath and looks me dead in the eye as she answers.

"Because one of you tried to murder Annie back in 1536."

Chapter Forty-Eight

Cleo

I am going to die in England.

The thought washes over me as Grace insists to Alistair that we will not be running without Annie. Lola takes Grace's phone and leaves the room. She says it is to make travel arrangements. I half believe her. She will be calling Elias even if it is just to say goodbye. Not that it matters. Grace will not leave without Annie. I will not leave without Grace. We are not leaving as a family. Lola can get her goodbye and run off. She deserves to have closure before she is alone forever.

"We need to find Annie." I interrupt. "Before we get ourselves crazed for a suicide mission that may not be necessary."

"If one of them did that to her, if she is right, then it will be necessary." My love snarls at me, her perfect face twisted into a grotesque rage. I get it. I do. But I must try and coax her out of this blinding mindset. She will never survive if we do not think this through. That is not an option I am willing to consider.

"I do not disagree." I tell her softly as I move one step towards her. She continues to pace around the princes rooms. "But we cannot go in blindly or one at a time. If we face the devil witches then we face them together or not at all."

The prince stays silent the entire time. He just watches Grace and waits for her lead. Annie must have truly rattled him, instilled in him a deep-rooted need to follow Grace. That would be helpful if we did manage to run. It will be a hindrance when we don't.

"They did that to her." Grace's voice cracks. "What she went through that night. What she has been through since. That was them. They have spent centuries watching us and mocking us and it was them. They are going to pay for that."

"They will. But we have to live through it." I take another step towards her. "They are powerful. They are smart. They are strong. We need a plan."

"We are more powerful." Grace insists. "We are smarter. We are stronger."

"Meaning a plan will only help us win." I snap. "I will not lose you because you want to rush in and fight the six most powerful witches on the planet without one."

"You think it was all six?" Grace looks at me. "You think Thomas was in on it too?"

"We cannot know for sure. Not until it is done." My heart breaks as I see a light inside of her die at the realisation. My body floods with rage, rage at all of those witches for breaking a piece of her. I cannot be angry at them for creating the vampire curse. Without it I would have never met Grace. But everything else...everything else I could kill them for. I could kill them slowly and painfully one at a time.

"We just need to get Annie and think of a plan." I whisper to her as I take in the gorgeous flecks of gold in her irises. How many times had I stared into her eyes over the past century? How many times had I taken it for granted, assumed I would be able to look into them a thousand more times? Time was never certain even when you had the promise of all of it and especially not when you had someone you love so deeply that all you wanted was more of it.

Grace closes her eyes and nods slowly, not breathing as she comes to her decision.

Annie. Graces voice echoes down the bond. *Annie we are not leaving you. Annie. Annie please.*

Annie. I join in. *Me and Grace are staying. We are staying with you. Where are you?*

I'm staying too. Alistair's voice is weaker than the rest of ours, but it is clear.

And I am picking us up an ally. Lola's tone is as bubbly as ever. It almost makes me smile.

Funny. Thomas responds. Grace's eyes shoot open in horror as the same realisation makes my breath hitch. Thomas is in our bond. We had forgotten somehow, distracted by our fear and our deep-rooted instinct to use it. None of us move. None of us speak. We all wait with bated breath for him to finish.

Annie is currently with an ally of her own. Aren't you Annie? Thomas's voice is as friendly as ever. There is no hint of this being anything but a normal day.

You all really should have run. Annie's voice sends a wave of relief through all of us. *Safer for all of you if you had.*

I don't want to just be safe. Grace's response is desperate. It is yet another dagger through my heart. *I want all of us safe. All of us together.*

My saving Grace. We can hear Annie's smile down the bond. *Together it is. Thomas's rooms. As soon as you can.*

But please wait for me. Ally number two is a little shaky on his legs. Lola says sheepishly. A bad feeling settings in my stomach.

Who exactly is this Ally Lola? My thought is sharp and cutting even though I know the answer. She cannot have been that fucking stupid.

We can trust Elias. Lola's defence is blunt. *I trust him. With everything.*

That's the hole between your legs talking. Snap his neck and run home right now I demand.

You are not in cha-

Both of you shut up It is Grace that interrupts us. I do not look over at her. I can feel her disappointment already. *Annie?* Grace continues. *Do you think we can trust Elias?*

I think we have no choice but to trust him. Annie's response comes a whole moment later. She was probably talking to Thomas about it. The fact he didn't rush to defend his cousin to us all is not reassuring. I take Grace's hand in my own and gesture for Alistair to head to the door. No time like the present.

Chapter Forty-Nine

Annie

Thomas stays silent until the rest of my family arrives. He drinks some water and changes into more comfortable clothes. When the door opens, he flexes his fingers as if getting ready to fight but he lets them hang loosely at his side when he sees it is only Alistair, Grace, and Cleo.

Grace pulls me into a tight hug as soon as she is through the doorway. I hide my head in the crook of her neck and take in a deep breath as I hug her back. Grace. My Grace who was as reliable and calm as a sunrise. She had not left me behind. The panic I feel at that is suffocated by an overwhelming sense of comfort.

"You know the plan." I whisper in her ear.

"It was never a good plan." She whispers back. We both let out tiny chuckles as we pull away. I turn my gaze to the other two. Cleo is staying because Grace is staying. She would have stuck to the plan if Grace had. I shoot her a thankful smile anyway. Alistair stands completely straight with his hands clasped behind him. Such a royal pose.

"You don't have to be a part of this." I tell him softly. "If you walk out that door and back to your rooms I will not blame you."

"I'm staying." He tells me in a tone that I do not argue with. He would have made a good king one day if his circumstances had been different. If he had not needed my blood to survive. If the United Kingdom could ever have an undead king.

"Okay." I move forward to brush his hair from his eyes. "Then I thank you for staying, Prince Alistair."

"I am so sorry." Alistair whispers. "That I am the reason you were brought here, Annie Dawson."

"I am not." I look back over my shoulder at Thomas. "Saving you has brought me some peace. It has brought me home. I think after five hundred years it is time for the truth to come out."

"There is no way to kill a cursed witch. The devil himself has told you to protect them." Cleo reminds me bluntly. "Killing them, torturing them, these are temporary solutions. You will bring the wrath of the devil himself onto us."

"You said we just needed a plan." Grace gapes at her soulmate. "You acted as if you were on our side."

"I am always on your side. That is why I do not want Lucifer to reach up and drag you down to Hell for going after his witches." Cleo hisses at her. "Who is to say that we are not the threat? That he did not warn Annie as some sick perverted way of keeping us from doing this? That we need to protect those witches from ourselves?"

"You do not need to stay." I snarl at Cleo. "I am more than willing to die alone."

"The issue is you will not be alone." Cleo's lip trembles as she looks at me. She points one finger over Grace and whispers gently. "She does not deserve hell."

"She will not be going to hell." Thomas finally speaks in a monotone voice. "If the devil wants Corsi to be protected then he can tell us that himself."

My stomach twists. It was our only choice I suppose. Our only way of knowing what we would be going into and any weaknesses they would have. But my palms are sweaty at the thought of summoning the devil. A chill runs down my spine at the idea of staring into those galaxies in place of his eyes. Would they appear that way in the real world? Would he look anything like the form he had chosen in my dream?

"You plan on summoning the devil so that you can yell at him. Is that it? Is that the plan here?" Cleo spins on her heel to look at him. "You wouldn't even tell us how to do it!"

"You need a witch. I wasn't willing to do it again." Thomas shrugs as if she just asked him what the plan was for dinner. But his words cut deeply into me. He does not mean that he wasn't willing to ever do it again. He means he wasn't willing to do it again to help himself. I was the only reason that Thomas Bradford would ever summon the devil. That was true then, it is true now and it would be true if we survived this. I resist the urge to lunge across the room and kiss him.

"When can we do it?" Alistair looks up at Thomas without a trace of fear. Brave boy.

"After I speak to Elias." Thomas frowns slightly. "And figure out exactly where he stands on it all."

"You would think," A voice cuts in from the doorway. None of us had heard the door open but we all spin to look. Lola and Elias stood there, resting against the other as they stare at our secret meeting. "That helping to kill a racist pervert with you all earlier would have bought me some confidence."

Lola frowns delicately and hovers with one foot inside the room and the other out as if she is not sure where she belongs. That hurts. Elias moves to take the same step but hits an invisible barrier.

"Thomas." I mutter. The room across the hall has at least one, if not all three of our potential targets still inside. We cannot cause a scene in the corridor. He grunts and quickly waves two of his fingers in the air. The barrier falls and Elias stumbles in. He shuts the door behind him and Lola.

I expected Elias to be angry when he came to see us. I expected anger and petulance, maybe some pettiness. I did not expect him to look at me with such hurt, silver pooling in his eyes.

"You don't honestly think that I would have done that to you." Elias says thickly. "You don't think so low of me. You don't think that I would ever, even for a second, have stood by and let someone hurt you."

"Elias-" I sigh.

"I cast curses on half the men that showed an interest in you." Elias takes my lack of an immediate no to heart. "The ones that were unkind or beat their first wives or made worrying comments when they were drunk. I did that. ME." Elias points at his chest, right over his heart as he continues to stare me in the eye.

"I protected you when even Thomas wouldn't. When Edward wouldn't. You were- you are family to me. I would sooner carve out my own heart with a wooden spoon then so much as give you a papercut." Elias's face twists into something that is still not rage. It is despair. That look breaks me.

"Elias." My own eyes pinprick with tears as I stare at him.

Throughout the years he had been a friend. He had not made me feel guilty when we did not speak for decades. He had always welcomed me with open arms and brotherly comments. We had partied and we had sent letters. We had thrown pillows at each other when we stayed at the same hotels, and we had never let our supernatural habits get in the way. We avoided certain subjects and doing certain things, but we had always been friends. We had always cared if the other was safe. How had I not known about his hidden acts of affection? How had I ever, even for a second, thought that Elias would have hurt me?

185

It was the same with Christiana although with her, conversation of Thomas always eventually arrived. In another reality I would have been their family in more than just spirit. I would have been Christiana's sister. Elias would have been my children's godfather. We would have lived our lives together. How could I ever think that either of them would purposefully have put mine in danger?

"Thomas. Can you go and get your sister please?" I ask hoarsely before I throw myself into Elias's arms.

"I am so sorry." I mutter into his ear. He does not hug me back immediately. I do not blame him. He freezes with my chin rested on his shoulder blade. "I never should have doubted you. Never."

"I would have helped you." Elias mutters back as his arms slowly wrap around me. "If you had come to me back then. I would have helped you. You only needed to ask."

Both of our tears start to fall. I hear the door behind me softly click as it opens and closes. The girls and Alistair do not say anything as I embrace Elias. They barely breathe. I calm my breathing before I pull away and I tell them all the story of what happened that night in 1536.

Chapter Fifty

Annie

Outskirts of London, England

1536

The gold feels heavy. I try not to walk differently but the pouch is hidden under my dress by my right hip and if I try and focus on how I am walking then I know I will end up walking weirdly. I already had to stop myself from reaching down to check it was still there, tied there by a thin leather strap. The less attention I bring to it the better. I have already had to walk further than I would have liked. I couldn't risk bringing a royal branded carriage all the way out here. Anne had been gracious to offer it, but I couldn't have anyone remembering it just in case.

The streets get progressively dirtier and full of people the closer to the edge of London I get. The houses here are cheaper after all but they are close enough to travel into the city for work. Most people that live here do what my mother politely calls 'the grunt work'. They are undertakers and maids, stool boys and stable muckers, which leads them to drink and snort. I would certainly appreciate whiskey at the end of each day if my days consisted of shovelling manure or dead bodies. The odd mouthful of wine at a ball always made me feel less stressed.

I turn a corner, daintily stepping to the side of a pile of suspicious brown liquid and run into a small pop-up market of sorts. The majority had no tables. Most were selling their items on threadbare blankets laid out on the cobblestones while one or two had travelling carts with long faded paint. Those seemed to be medical based. The people manning them, some as little as eight, screamed about hair growth tonics and face creams.

I move around the teeming crowds, side stepping people and items, trying to move as fast as I could. I follow the coach drivers directions to the letter. If I couldn't find it after I thought I had followed them, then I would ask someone for directions. Until then I would keep my head down and get the gold to the innkeeper. It was a simple enough goal. Gold to the innkeeper and keep Anne safe.

Anne Anne Anne.

The shouting gets louder in my ears as the two medical carts started to fight over who had the best prices on a foot ointment. I quickly shuffle to the side of the path, but I am still suddenly surrounded by people as the bystanders make room for a brawl. I am pressed against unfamiliar people who are so much bigger and stronger than I am. My mind flashes to the gold and my hands immediately clutch at my hip. I feel myself being dragged backwards and I let out a yell, but it simply joins the screams of the fight and those placing quick bets.

"It's okay. It's okay." A voice whistles into my ear even as a thick dirty hand covers my mouth, and I am dragged even further backwards. I bite into it, tasting soot and something sharp and chemically. The hand is removed with a yell.

I lunge forward, back towards the crowded street that seems so torturously close. A useless attempt. The hand now just grabs at my loose hair and yanks me back so hard I hit the wall and see stars. I let out an animalistic yell that is swiftly cut off as the man's other hand punches into my stomach.

I slid down the wall moaning in pain but still my hands grip at the gold hidden under my dress. He cannot get the gold. He can't. He can't, he ca-

My thoughts are interrupted as I am dragged across the filthy cobblestones. My dress will be ruined but as long as it hid the gold it was fine. The gold was Anne's lifeline. The gold and what the gold meant was more valuable than my own life or dignity.

My attacker seems pleased with how far into this filthy cut-through we are in. I wait for him to demand my money, for me to respond that I don't have any. He will then hit me, maybe break a few bones and I will stumble into the inn, book a room for Viviane, and send a messenger back to the castle. I will find a way to explain the injuries to Thomas and to Anne.

But he does not ask the question.

Instead, he presses his lips against mine. They are slimy and I realise then that the gold is not the most important thing. I am suddenly cold as if I had been doused in frozen water and my body starts to thrash and to kick all by itself. I will get out of here. I will. I have to. This cannot happen. I cannot fail.

My hands connect uselessly against his shoulders and arms, my legs pinned down by his own. His hands start to rip at my dress, ripping at the fabric as I try to scream against his mouth. I feel his teeth tear my lip apart to keep anyone from hearing. My mouth fills with blood. It starts to choke me. I faintly hear the gold clash against the ground as my dress takes further damage.

His hands are cold on my thighs. I imagine the dirty marks that he will leave, that I will have to scrub off of myself. His hands move, one up to my chest and one to his own trousers. I stop fighting and start to sob, blood squirting up where it was still pooling in my mouth from my half torn off lip. I sob even louder as he pushes my legs open.

The sharp white-hot pain of the knife in my stomach is a relief.

Chapter Fifty-One

Lola

Alistair and I somehow ended up the only two sat on the bed. Grace and Cleo were not as entangled as they usually were. Instead, they just seemed to be stuck in each other's gravity, always within arm's reach and moving in unison. Their aggressively public love is comforting.

Elias and Annie have stopped embracing and crying but Thomas has not come back with Christiana. The room is oddly quiet as we all wait for their entrance. There didn't seem to be anything to say after Annie's story. The lump in my throat would not let me speak even if I could think of something good enough to say out loud. My mind is rushed with words and yet I know none of them were the right ones. They were ones I would hate to hear if I shared my story out loud to so many people at once. They were clichéd lies stolen from TV shows and bad lifetime movies.

"Corsi is going to die. Painfully." Elias's voice is low and terrifying. I go to look at him but only get as far as his shoulders. I don't want to see the devastation on his face, the raw anger that is radiating off of him in waves.

"Elias." Annie's voice creaks. She clears her throat before she continues. "Calm. We cannot be impulsive and angry for this next part."

"This next part is the perfect time to be angry and impulsive." Elias responds sullenly. "This is the part where I should be kicking in Corsi's door and boiling the blood that runs through her veins."

"We have a plan." I offer helpfully. "We do the summoning and then we do the…blood boiling."

"We have the idea of the beginnings of a plan." Cleo rolls her eyes. "We have the little crayon square on a bit of paper when what we need is six rolls of architect drawings."

"I've always been good with a sketchpad." Christiana's lilting voice scratches at my brain as yet another cursed witch walks in without us realising. That is not reassuring for our future crayon house.

"Can you all please start announcing your arrival?" I frown. "It is very unnerving. Even if you just stop hiding your heartbeats. Please?"

"Well. Elias hides his for an obvious reason." Christiana smiles at him, winking as if we are friends. I scowl in response. Thomas can't have told her yet. Not if she is this perky. I change my mind as I see her face turn cold as she turns to Annie.

"She is going to pay." Christiana's voice is as sharp as sliced steel. "With her life and with her own soul."

Annie's responding smile breaks my heart, if there are pieces that are still big enough to break. She is so clearly flooded with relief at the young girls response that it also makes me worry. The Survivors may not survive this.

The thought cuts through everything else, takes away everything until I am filled with calm. I had twenty more years than I was supposed to. That would have to be enough. My eyes trail over the people in this room, trail over my friends both new and old. The people in this room had so many memories and so few of them would involve me. All I can hope is that whoever does survive will have at least one good one.

Elias claps once before rubbing his hands together. The sound drags me from my depressing thoughts. "Let's get this started then."

"We have something we have to talk about first." Thomas grimaces in disgust.

"Something more important than summoning the devil for a centuries old wrong?" Elias scoffs.

"I think it depends on your point of view." Annie drawls, propping herself against the wall with crossed arms as if this is a normal day, a normal meeting to be having. "But it's definitely relevant and definitely gross."

"My favourite combination." Elias scowls. He was good at this, at taking the attention off of Annie and breaking the tension. My lips twitch into a smile as he dramatically throws himself down on the bed next to me. The mattress bounces underneath us all. "What is it?"

Annie turns to Thomas who opens his mouth to speak. When nothing comes out, Annie decides to rip off the proverbial band aid.

"William was fucking Mary in front of Lady Bradford's portrait and a picture of Edward." Annie says it matter of factly even though Elias recoils at the statement. "I saw them."

"What's that got to do with Corsi?" Elias wrinkles his nose.

"She was on Mary's face." Annie glances over at Christiana whose face was set in a grim frown. Elias gives a dramatic shudder.

"You." Cleo speeds over to Christiana and points a finger in her face. Her voice is low and curious even though her body is near vibrating with rage. "Are not even slightly shocked by that."

Cleo is right. Christiana is not phased. Her bright eyes slowly take in Cleo's face as she releases a slow breath through her nose. The young girls eyes turn to look at her brother and her cousin. She places her hands on her hips and acts as if Cleo isn't fully fanged in front of her.

"We share a spell book." Christiana's voice is the opposite of Cleo's. It is full of snarling anger, her lips tilting into a sneer as she spoke. "Yet neither of you know what this means? Are you both that dense that you do not remember – you *specifically Elias* – What part of the grimoire that is in?"

"Now is not the time to preach your own cleverness Chrissie." Elias snaps. "Tell us so we can try and stop it."

"It's too late for that." Christiana sighs. "Probably. I don't- I would have to read it again."

"Read what again little witch?" Cleo scowls. She always hates being ignored and being ignored now? It would be driving her insane. This whole interaction was driving us all insane. We were all twitching and shifting as we wait for the answer. Except Annie. Annie is staring at Thomas with a sad look on her face as if she is sorry this is all happening at all.

"That spell is a reincarnation spell. It has never worked before not properly. The alter has a picture of the deceased and the theory is that the women is impregnated during the ritual. The baby that is born is the reincarnation of the deceased. The closest anyone has ever gotten is a doppelganger. The soul never transferred over." Christiana explains slowly, eyes now on her brother. "He's trying to bring mum back."

"Reincarnation is dark magic. It's playing with the universal rules. We messed those up before. No way would they be allowed to do it again." Elias argues. His shoulder brushes against mine as he gestures with his hands. He doesn't look at me. "They aren't stupid. They know that."

"That's what the picture of Edward was for." Annie realises in a hoarse whisper. "As a transfer. That's what magic is all about. A balance. They sacrifice a cosmic mistake in order to get Lady Bradford back."

"That's sick." The words tumble from my mouth. "And wrong. He would have a baby just to raise it to be his wife again?"

"And why Edward?" Grace's voice makes me jump. I was so focussed on the warmth radiating off of Elias and on Alistair's steady breathing as he stayed silent that I almost forgot she was in the corner of her room. Christiana glances over at the other two witches. When she sees their blank faces she scoffs.

"Corsi and Edward were involved back when we all had an expiration date." Christiana avoids looking at Annie. "Then Edward left. Corsi was a servant and she wasn't stupid. She knew that it wouldn't last but I think that it hurt her more than she expected it to."

"Then he became a vampire, and he never came back for her. Sounds familiar." Annie's voice is hollow as she stares at the floor. Grace is at her side in less than a second. Thomas is not far behind. They both wrap their arms around her. When Annie looks up her fangs are out, and her brow is furrowed. Christiana meets her gaze. Bold girl. I would be cowering in the corner.

"Where is he Chris?" Annie asks softly. A look flashes across Christiana's face. I force myself to start breathing again as the witch closes her eyes.

"He's here in London. He has always been here in London."

Annie nods her head slowly before stepping out of her friends arms. Should I have gone to comfort her as well? I had never met Edward (obviously) and I had never had more than a basic curiosity about him. I did not know how turbulent their relationship had been and I had no sibling relationship to compare it to either. But I should have done something.

"Then lets summon the devil and save him. So I can beat him black and blue afterwards." Annie's comment cuts through me and I cannot help but let out a laugh. When she looks at me I am still laughing. She smiles and lets out a short laugh of her own. The laugh is interrupted as the room's lights turn red. Thomas swears softly. Everyone glances over at him, Elias with a cocked eyebrow.

"Someone just broke into Annie's rooms." Thomas explains.

"Ignoring how creepy that is," Cleo sneers. She is holding Grace's arm before she finishes her sentence. "I think that means it's time to run."

"Time indeed." Elias agrees. He and Alistair grab my hands at the same time. I take both as we stand from the bed.

Chapter Fifty-Two

Grace

Edward was involved in what had happened to Annie. I know that even though I had never met him. Everything Christiana had said in that room lead up to it and Annie was completing some complex mental gymnastics to avoid landing on that particular grenade. He has *always* been in London.

But I am a coward and I do not bring that choice of words up as we rush from the palace. They should not be the focus right now. Edward should not be the focus right now even if Annie has taken the thought of him and used it to fuel her fire for the fight ahead. There would be a fight and it would be soon. There is no way we would risk running in the sunlight if we had any other choice.

We run all the way to Whitechapel. The safe house is smaller than our others, bought back when we only needed two bedrooms. It was above a popular fish and chip shop with a cartoon cod on its windows. Over the years, the purpose of that shop had changed. It was once a small solicitors office and then an accountant. The kitchen was put in when it had a short stint as a café. I smile at the small children in the window seat as Annie types in the keycode on our front door. The boy closest grins back revealing two missing teeth. Cleo prods me forward through the doorway.

We all climb the stairs in silence. They smell of vinegar. Lola's nose wrinkles as Alistair pulls her up the stairs after him. Elias is still trailing after her, holding her hand loosely. Cleo shoots me a knowing smile. I roll my eyes even as it sends a wave of comfort through me. The world has turned on its axis, but Cleo remains the same. We as a couple will remain the same.

The stairs finally end but the vinegar smell only slightly lessens as we enter the flat. The flat is immaculate. Annie must still pay the cleaner to come. There is no dust or cobwebs. The interior design has changed though. The grey satin sofas are new and aside from the small ornaments and scented candles they were the only colour in the otherwise obnoxiously white room. The light coming in through the windows reflected off of nearly every surface.

Thomas clicks his fingers and the candles splutter to life. Annie rolls her eyes as she flicks the light switch instead. Lola moves over and quickly shuts all the curtains. Just in case.

"What do we need to summon the devil?" Cleo asks, getting straight to business. "I assume it is not safe to simply wave your hands and get him to stand still in here?"

"Wave our hands?" Thomas looks at her. "You think it's that simple?"

"I think it better be that quick." Cleo almost purrs back. "The clock has started. They are coming for Annie. Your lovestruck ass should already be halfway done getting this place ready."

"I can go and get the things." Christiana cuts in-between them before I have a chance to. "We aren't using him for a spell this time around, so it cuts the ingredient list in half."

Ingredients as if we were baking a devil's food cake rather than asking the devil to come over. I smile.

"How long?" Cleo presses.

"Cleo." Annie says softly. "This isn't Christiana's fault, and they can't rush this. Lucifer could get here and decide not to help at all."

"And that is when we run. Right?" Cleo does not give up. "That is when we give up."

"There is no giving up." Christiana says bluntly. "Corsi does not get away with this."

"Revenge is not worth our lives. This is what you always say." Cleo turns to look at Annie. "So, this is the final time I am going to beg you. This is the final chance. Tell me right now that if the devil cannot help us then we call it the end and we keep running like we always have." The unspoken intent behind her pleading causes my breath to catch in my throat. Cleo hates running but she hates the idea of me dying even more.

"You are always free to run. I will never blame you." Annie speaks slowly making sure we all hear her sincerity. "But I did all of this for Edward. I can't just leave him as an unknowing part of their ritual. I can't just leave him to die."

"You have not spoken to him in five centuries. He really means more to you then Grace? Then me or Lola?" Cleo gapes her. Annie flinches.

"He is my brother Cleo. That's the end of it." Annie says it with such finality that Cleo now flinches. That is the end of it. Annie has not agreed to what Cleo wanted her too and the outcome is the exact same as it was back at the palace. We are summoning the devil and preparing to fight half of the cursed coven. If we die then we die. I would rather go out fighting as I had before but that is something Cleo will not hear.

"I can get the things within the hour." Christiana declares. "Me and Elias. Thomas will stay here."

"I can come with you." Thomas frowns. "It'll be quicker with the three of us."

"Elias's questionable friendships will be speedy enough. He'll be getting all of the more disgusting things big brother don't worry." Christiana walks over to the bookcase and scans the spines. She grabs a thick paperback and flicks through the pages. She pulls a wad of fifties from the back pages.

"You really need to get better tricks." Christiana smiles at Annie over her shoulder. "It's a miracle this has been left here by your maid."

"Lecture me later." Annie settles herself on the corner of the sofa. She's probably the first person to sit on it. Thomas moves to sit by her side, resting his hand on her knee.

"We will knock four times." Elias drags his eyes from Lola over to Annie. "No more. No less."

"I can count." Annie tells him with a forced smile. "And I know what you sound like. Just if there are any small body parts, please don't tell me where you got them."

"Deal." Elias calls back to her as Christiana leads him from the room.

Annie slumps backwards, bravado leaving her as she is left alone with us all. Her head rests itself on Thomas's shoulder. He gently rubs his cheek against her head as he pulls her closer.

Cleo's boots make a stomping sound as she walks past them to get to the kitchen. The tap turns on and then the kettle. Lola lets out an awkward breath as no one else speaks.

"She's just trying to keep me safe." I whisper to them. "It's not that she doesn't want to do this."

"I know." Annie whispers back. Lola and Alistair only nod. The prince had been oddly silent this whole time. If anyone had a reason to run and never look back it was him. Then again, he also had the second biggest reason to fight. The cursed coven were his families trusted advisors. If this coven splintered it would affect his parents rule for certain and whatever future he had. His true family's survival depended on this win.

Hopefully Lola had figured that out as well. We would need her head as focussed on this as it could be. She could be crueller than any of us when she wanted to be.

Cleo comes back in with a singular steaming mug. The steam coming from it smells sweet and floral. My jasmine tea. Cleo places the mug in my hands and a gentle kiss to my brow.

I won't let anything happen to any of you. Thomas tells us.

I will let something happen to you if it means keeping her safe. Cleo moves to stand behind me, her hands trailing to cover my hips as she rests her chin on my shoulder. I can already sense that her eyes are focussed on the witch, and they would remain that way for hours.

Understood. Thomas smiles.

I sip at my tea. The underlying bitterness is soothing.

Chapter Fifty-Three

Elias

"You really didn't know?" Christiana asks me once again as we find two seats on the tube. There were a few other patrons scattered around the carriage, but it was late morning on a weekday. They were mostly tourists.

"That Corsi was porking Annie's prick of a brother? No Chris. How do you even know?"

"Because I was living with a constant chaperone. I knew everything that was going on in that house, so I knew exactly how to sneak away." Christiana shrugs. "And he wasn't a prick."

"He was a massive prick!" I gape at her. "And you know it."

"You're a massive prick and I put up with you." Christiana says hotly. She has a point.

"You love me. I'm your favourite cousin. I do all the nasty dirty black magic stuff so you don't have to." I nudge her with my shoulder.

"You also create very awkward situations with women that I have to clean up. I don't think the lovely Lola is going to buy the excuse that you have to leave to drop me off at school." Christiana gives me a disapproving look as the automated voice announces we are approaching our changeover station.

"Bold to assume I would be leaving Lola in the morning." I say haughtily as I push myself to my feet and swing on the pole by the door.

"You always leave in the morning." Christiana follows me onto the platform. I huff but do not respond as I lead the way up the stairs and across to the other side of the station. She doesn't continue until we are once again settled in a pair of seats.

"If you aren't going to be serious with her then do not bother." Christiana warns me lowly as she watches a group of girls that look around her age rush to get through the closing doors.

"Everyone has gotten very interested in my love life lately." I settle back and rest my head against the window. "You wouldn't like it if I asked about yours."

"I am permanently stuck in a minors body. The only people interested in me are paedophiles and vampires. I'm not interested in either."

"You don't think I'm stupid enough to think you've been celibate for five hundred years."

"I think you're clearly desperate enough to not talk about Lola that you're trying to make me uncomfortable. You're failing."

"My relationship or lack of one with Lola is no one else's business." I drag my hands across my jeans as I watch the world rushing past through the windows.

"It will soon be Alistair's if you don't make your mind up. Pick her or don't. But be all in on your decision." Christiana speaks with that far too familiar tone that she had inherited from her father. The 'I am the one that's in charge here' tone.

I submit to it and stay silent even if it is mostly to avoid the ugly truth of my current situation. I huff again and start to jingle my leg up and down as the stations move sluggishly past. Every time the train slows or stops for the doors to open I can almost feel the others closing in. They must have checked for the rest of us by now. If I was in their shoes and couldn't find Annie I would assume she was with Thomas. When I couldn't find Thomas I would look for Chrissie. They would eventually come looking for me and realise that we had all picked our side.

"You get the baby bones." Christiana whispers to me as we follow half of the carriage out onto the platform of our final stop. "I'll get the other stuff. Meet back here in twenty."

I nod at her as the sound of the market hits us. Camden station is full of tourists who were bumbling around in front of the turnstiles as they tried to figure out where they were going. We both twist around them. Christiana takes the left turn into the busier streets towards the market to buy the herbs and stones. She'll stop by the butchers and pay extra for some bags of blood. I take the right, heading down the quieter streets towards a sketchy closed shopfront to pay through the nose for the bones of a day-old baby.

Chapter Fifty-Four

Annie

The six of us ended up splitting into couples. Grace and Cleo were the first to leave for their old bedroom. I heard Cleo mutter comments about the lack of modern things in it. I purposefully kept it old fashioned and how Grace liked it. We have not been here for so long that Cleo and Lola had not been thought of in the room planning.

Thomas had gently led me from the room as well, claiming the other bedroom and leaving Alistair and Lola alone in the living room. I went to whisper down our private bond that it wasn't a good idea before his lips crashed against mine. All thoughts of chaperoning left my mind.

"I meant what I said in there." Thomas mutters against my lips. "I won't let anything happen to any of them Annie. Your family is going to be safe."

That familiar feeling of my heart soaring and breaking at the same time hits yet again. Thomas's own family life has shattered yet here he was vowing to keep mine intact.

"If something has to happen to me to keep them safe you let it." I beg him as my fingers gently trace his face. "If something has to happen to me to keep any of you safe. You let it."

"If you think I am going to let anything short of the universe collapsing keep me from you ever again, you're incredibly mistaken." Thomas presses his forehead against mine. "Nothing is going to separate us. Not my father. Not Corsi. Not death. There will be no space between us, no more time wasted. We are going to survive this. All of us."

We had wasted so much time already. There had been so many decades I had lived without seeing his face in person, so many centuries I had celebrated the end of without him there to celebrate with me. I wanted the mundane Christmases. I wanted the going out for dinner just because we can weeknights. I wanted to argue with him for the next five hundred years about what we were wearing on Halloween. I wanted this.

If Edward were not on the line, if Alistair would be okay, if there were not a thousand other reasons for doing this, then I would back out of this fight. I would take my prize, my Thomas, and I would get out of town. I would swallow my pride and my morals and continue to run away forever. Run from the vampires who could never know about our abilities, run from the witches who killed me and keep myself sane, keep myself happy, with the witch who saved me.

"I love you." I whisper. I place a chaste kiss to his lips. "Forever."

"Forever.," Thomas repeats the word. "Is exactly how long I've been waiting to hear you say that."

"And I'll say it again." I promise as I hear four knocks on the front door. "I'll say it every day."

"Then let's go get us some days." Thomas brushes a strand of hair that rests against my cheek. It calms my nerves even though his phrasing should do the opposite. His phrasing reminds me that we either win or we die. The conversation with the devil will just tell us the odds.

Chapter Fifty-Five

Grace

The four knocks at the door cuts through my deceptively hazy brain. I pause with my mouth still on Cleo's bellybutton, her shirt discarded in the corner.

"You've got to be kidding me." Cleo grumbles as she sits up. I kiss her cheek before grabbing her shirt for her.

"We will continue tonight after we win." I promise her, holding her face in my hands to stop her getting dressed in a hurry. Cleo grunts and kisses me, dragging it out as we hear Elias and Christiana climbing up the steps.

"Promise me that you won't do anything rash." Cleo doesn't move her mouth from mine as she speaks. Tease.

"Promise me that *you* won't do anything rash." I counteroffer.

"I am not the one willing to jump in front of a stake for Annie."

"But you would willingly jump in front of a stake for me." I point out. "And I do not want you doing that either."

"It does not count as rash if I think about it before hand. Before you try and use wordplay to convince me, saving you would not be stupid or naïve or wasteful. Your life *is* worth more than mine and yes, I would need to do it because I refuse to live in a world without you Grace. There has not been a minute I have lived when you have not, and I do not plan on that ever changing."

I press my lips together as she ticks off answers to all the comments I planned to make. She pulls away and finishes dressing as I sit there and sulk. There were few things she would not relent on, that she would argue with me about until neither of us were satisfied with the answer. This would be added onto the list.

Elias calls out to us all that they are home. Cleo shoots me a knowing smile and mouths 'Ali and Lola are alone in the living room'. It's more of a peace gesture than information I would desperately need. Cleo wouldn't fight anymore. She would tease Lola and grumble about Thomas being lovesick, but she wouldn't argue for us to run anymore. She was all in.

The smell of cooked fish drifts even stronger through the hall. As I exit our bedroom hand in hand with Cleo I see that Christiana is holding a large bag of takeaway containers dripping with grease.

"You had time to stop downstairs?" Cleo scoffs at them. "Or are overly salted chips part of the ritual."

"Magic takes energy. This is going to be a lot of magic and so a lot of energy." Christiana speaks slowly as if she is lecturing a child. I feel Cleo bristle besides me. "We need energy, so we need to eat. We got enough for all of you in case you want it."

"I'll get plates." Lola jumps up and practically runs from the room. Alistair stands to follow her but Elias hands him a can of red spray paint and a piece of paper instead.

"Draw these on the stairwell and the inside of the front door." Elias commands. "It'll keep everyone else out while we do this."

"And what about keeping…him…in?" I ask softly as I take one of the containers. The paper crinkles under my fingers. It would be rude to not take it even though my stomach is in knots as we take what I count as the first step.

"There is a separate set of runes for that." Elias promises me.

"Good. I would hate to get fallen angel feathers all over my sofa." Annie jokes as she strides in the room. She takes two of the paper wrapped containers and hands one over to Thomas. He rips it open like he is half-starved.

Lola comes back with a pile of mismatched plates. She hands them out to everyone and instructs us to take a fork from the top plate. Cleo scowls but does not argue. She drags me over to the sofa so we can be comfortable as we pretend to eat.

Alistair zooms into the room coming to a stop in the centre of the room. His fingertips are stained red. A thin line of paint oozes from the nozzle of the can. A single drop lands on the wooden floor.

"Sorry." Alistair smiles sheepishly over at Annie.

"Elias can clean it when he cleans up my walls." Annie waves him off. I laugh before taking a small bite of a chip.

"You're welcome for the extra protection." Elias says around a mouthful of a burger. Christiana sends him a disgusted look from her place in the corner chair as Annie rolls her eyes. Alistair takes the final plate and sets himself down on the floor. Thomas leads Annie over to us and places her next to me. Lola remains standing which cannot have been comfortable.

We all eat in relative silence. The ticking from the clock on the wall worms its way under my skin and reverberates in my skull. How many more ticks would we have? How many more precious seconds would fly by with Cleo's arm pressed against mine? How many would we have after this meal was finished, after half of the cursed coven once again begged the devil to do their bidding? Would it even be one more? Or would he consider this the highest insult and kill us all before we could blink?

Once we are all done, Annie comes around and takes all of our plates. I hear her dump them all in the sink. No point doing the dishes right now I suppose. Annie doesn't join us again. Instead, she leans against the doorway and looks over all of us slowly with a gentle smile on her face.

"Okay." Christiana finally sighs. "Let's do this."

Chapter Fifty-Six

Lola

Elias has not looked at me since he came back. Alistair cannot stop looking at me. It would be an awkward situation if I was not convinced that we weren't going to make it out of this. The thought doesn't scare me, not even deep down in some hidden part of my heart. I had been ready to die before. I was ready to die now. Some vampire and blood witch love triangle should be the least of my problems.

But as we move all the furniture to the very edges of the room and the witches all take a can of spray paint and start to draw a wide circle of runes on the floor, I can't take my eyes off Grace and Cleo. The rest of us had all clambered onto the couch. Cleo and Grace in their original spot pressed into the corner, Alistair next to them and Annie beside me on the end. I am perched on the armrest.

Cleo stares at the witches intently although her fingers run gently through Grace's raven locks. Grace tilts her head into that touch looking completely at peace despite the situation. A love like that would have been nice even if I would only have had twenty years of it. Twenty years I shouldn't have had anyway.

Elias finishes his runes first. He comes to a stop next to me and crouches down to look through the plastic bag he brought in with him. He pauses and decides against taking it all out here. He takes it to the kitchen. I hear him search in the cupboards for something, ceramic items scrapping against each other. He comes back a moment later with a metal mixing bowl filled with what is undoubtably blood. The iron sting of it fills my nostrils and takes over the lingering smell of vinegar. I sense Alistair freeze.

Annie and Grace each take one of his hands in their own. He takes a deep shaky breath but does not move to drink. It's impressive and I make a mental note to tell him later. If we get one. He deserves one. He deserves a thousand and one laters.

Elias places the blood bowl down on one of the largest runes. The four large ruins were spaced out across the circle like a compass. Smaller ruins and candles link them. The bowl of blood was facing north, towards the closed and covered windows. Christiana pulls out a bundle of roses that were on the edge of death from the second bag. They had a slight whiff of decay to them and their petals had a slight dark tinge to them. She rips off the reduced-price sticker and throws it towards the bag without a glance to see if it went in. The flowers were placed at the south, towards the kitchen door where Elias has disappeared once again.

He comes back with a smaller bowl, this one porcelain and clinking. My stomach rolls at the idea of what is inside that bowl. I am thankful when he places it on the 'east' position furthest away from me and I can pretend I didn't see how tiny those bones were.

I take that back as soon as I see what the fourth object is. I jump from my seat and zoom across the room as Christiana places a stuffed rat on the rune. The teenage looking witch frowns at me.

"It's not alive." She uses the same tone she used with Cleo earlier. My face flushes red.

"I don't like rats." I mutter. I swear I can hear it twitching and squeaking in my ear, nibbling at trash behind me as I am back in that alley all over again.

"You can stand with me." Elias offers softly as the three of them take their positions. Elias stands outside the circle of ruins, with his arm stretched out towards me.

"Thomas and Annie." Christiana interrupts out moment to gesture to the bowl of blood. "You go there. Alistair come stand with me and the bones. Cleo and Grace stand by the rat."

Everyone moves at once to take their positions. I take Elias's hand and stand with him. The three witches all look at each other and solemnly nod. Thomas turns his head and plants a long, sensual kiss on Annie's lips. She returns it. Grace and Cleo turn to each other and simply smile. They must have already had their last kiss, just in case. Smart.

"When this is over." Elias's voice is gravelly as if he is forcing the words from his mouth. He doesn't look me directly in the eye. He stares at my chin. "You should let me know what your coffee order is."

"Oh lord." Christiana whispers under her breath. I frown.

"So that I can buy you a coffee. If you want to go and get one with me." Elias continues when I don't answer. I realise that he is making his move now at the most inopportune time and despite myself I feel my face break into a grin.

"I prefer hot chocolate." I whisper.

"Hot chocolate it is." Elias grins back.

"If you two could be done," Christiana snaps. "I would like to summon Satan before the end of the millennia."

"Then go ahead and start little cousin." Elias turns to face the rest of the circle. He doesn't drop my hand. Christiana glares at him before closing her eyes and starting to chant softly in Latin. Ten seconds later, Thomas and Elias join in. They start to repeat themselves.

With each set of chanting, a candle would magically alight. The flames flicker higher as the spell continues. The boy's voices never overtake Christiana's. Instead, they all flow together like a horrifyingly enchanting melody. I wished I understood what they were saying but that might just ruin it.

Elias's Latin was soothing, running over my skin, and filling me with calm. Christiana's is perfectly pronounced, everything she says coming out crystal clear. Thomas's is low and almost clunky in comparison but his eyes, the dark look on his face...Thomas was terrifying as he stared into the circle. The candlelight causes shadows to whisper over his face and those grey eyes that they all share look black. A glance over at Elias show his grey blue eyes were shining with an unnatural inner light.

The Latin turns to shouting. The flames of the candle shoot high enough to scorch the ceiling before going out all at once. Even with my vampire eyes I cannot see anything in the darkness. But I can hear- and there is one too many people breathing in this room.

Chapter Fifty-Seven

Annie

The candles splutter back to life and reveal the blonde boy with the galaxy eyes. I don't know what I expected him to be wearing or if he would look different but a sense of dread washes through me. He is wearing clothes I would expect to be worn to a ball held back when I was human, a thick black tunic with red accents and matching trousers. Leather boots that shine even in the weak candlelight. He's dressed to impress.

"Hello again." The Devil smiles as he spins in a slow circle to take each of us in. He scans the way we are paired off, takes in how close we all are. His gaze pauses on Christiana and Alistair a second longer than anyone else.

"You aren't here to beg again are you?" The Devil finishes his circle looking at Thomas. "I would hope you aren't bored of Annie now you've got her."

"You told me to protect the coven." I cut in coldly. "That is no longer an option."

"Oh?" The fake surprise on his face sends a hot sensation running through my veins. I want to claw those fake wide eyes right out of his sockets for it.

"You knew all along." I let my fangs slide easily from my gums. They may be useless against him, and I am not foolish enough to walk into the circle to try and use them, but they give me a sense of power anyway. They make me feel not quite defenceless.

"I knew she was involved. Truth is that those three were not people I paid much attention to. There were much more interesting people I was watching back in the sixteenth century. I only realised later when she was willing to offer her soul to make it right. She wasn't willing to do that for Lady Bradford." He seems almost apologetic. The fire in my veins turns cold.

"What did you just say?" The question comes from Christiana. The young girl is staring at him in horror, her voice a hoarse whisper. The Devil turns his head towards her, but he does not answer.

"Corsi's soul was not a part of the original bargain." Thomas growls from beside me. "It was mine. My soul for Annie's life."

"No," The Devil frowns. "The bargain and the spell state it clearly. For each revival there would be a sacrifice- there would be a balance. The original spell takes the victims soul as that sacrifice. But you wanted Annie brought back as close as possible to what she was, for her to be able to live and breathe, walk in the sun, swim in the lakes and everything a human woman could. I asked if you were all sure. You all agreed. I was clear that a soul was the price of that."

"Oh no." Christiana gasps. Her hands shoot to cover her mouth. Everything slows down like it does when I am running at supernatural speeds. Elias's face drops. Thomas's hands close into fists. The Devil's mouth opens as he stares at Christiana. A look of pain shoots across his face.

"I thought that it was clear." He tells her softly, taking one step towards her but remaining in the circle. "I thought you all knew."

"Which one?" Christiana snarls at him and her hands drop to her sides. "Which one of them has *my* soul?"

Lola gasps but I do not look at her. I stare at Christiana as she stares down at the king of Hell and wins.

"Grace." He answers in a soft whisper. "Grace has your soul."

Christiana closes her eyes and takes in a deep breath. Her fingers flex at her side. Everyone else's attention shifts to Grace as my oldest companion lets out a shuddering breath. My own breath catches in my throat as I watch The Devil instead.

His young face is twisted in pain and longing as he takes in as much of Christiana as he can, almost drinking her pain into him. It was a look I was familiar with. He snaps his head towards me. I wink at him. He scowls.

"Get away from her. Back in the centre." Elias drags his attention away. The Devil hangs his head and returns to the centre of the circle. I look at Elias. His eyes are hard, and his jaw clenched. His nostrils are flaring. I think Lola might be the only thing holding him back from lunging after him.

"Tell us whose soul went to who," Cleo demands with her head held high. "Now."

"The souls were given out in the order they were taken." The Devil explains slowly as he turns his attention back to me and Thomas. "In the order that you all entered the circle."

"Mary never entered the circle." Thomas realises with a groan. "She remained the spells anchor as I stepped inside."

"Dad was supposed to go next. But I stumbled. I fell in after you." Christiana's eyes are still closed as if she is replaying that night on the back of her eyelids. "Elias caught me."

Cleo snaps her head to look over at Elias only to find he has done the exact same thing. Maybe that will become an inside joke in another five hundred years. For now, none of this is funny.

"Corsi went to catch you, but she was across the circle. Lola has hers and Alistair has Williams." Elias's voice is hollow.

"Do they know?" I ask the room. "If you three didn't realise then there is a chance they didn't either."

"With the ritual they were performing and the fact it was Mary they were trying to impregnant? It's a safe bet that they have figured it out." Christiana says irritably. Cleo swears softly.

"Their ritual will fail." The Devil says confidently. "I'll make sure of that."

"That bargain made the witches indestructible." I steer the conversation back to our major question. "How do we change that?"

"You can't." The Devil shakes his head and shoves his hands into his tunic pockets. The picture of nonchalance. "It's also irreversible. They all understood that part. No way to misunderstand my warning there."

"There has to be a way to keep them down." I insist. "Magic needs a balance. Even I know that."

"There is no way to kill them." Those galaxies in the shape of eyes focus in on me. I force myself to keep the eye contact even as it makes a small part of my brain start to scream and beg for me to run. "But there is a way I can help take them off of the chess board."

"What is the price?" Christiana opens her eyes as she asks him. He doesn't look directly at her, only in her vague direction.

"Nothing." He promises her in a seductive whisper.

"There is always a price when a deal is made with you."

"Not this time." He insists. "Take it…take these as a gift."

He pulls his hands from his pocket and opens his fist to reveal three large, heavy looking iron coins in his palm. They are engraved in the centre with pentagrams and their ridges etched with runes similar to the ones painted on my floor. He holds them out to Christiana with a sincere, sad smile. When she does not reach for them, he takes two large steps forward so his toes test the boundary of the circle.

"A gift." He repeats. "Or an apology if you prefer. For letting this all happen."

"How will they help?" Christiana stares down at the coins.

"Once you have them down, ripped out throats or snapped necks or however you plan on doing it, put these on them. I'll come and collect them. They won't be a problem for you anymore."

"What will you do with them?" Lola speaks for the first time. Her hand is still in Elias's and her voice shakes.

"I will take them to my home." The King of Hell tells her without taking his eyes off Christiana's ashen face. "And keep them there."

"This coin will drag my father to Hell?" Christiana clarifies. The Devil almost flinches before he nods. Christiana snatches all three from his palm, fingers grazing against his. He gently curls his fingers upwards as if to briefly catch them.

"Annie. Do you have any other questions for Satan?" Christiana finally looks him in the eyes even though her words are to me.

"You'll stop their ritual. Edward will be safe from them?" I phrase it carefully so there is no way for him to worm around it. He couldn't respond that Edward would only be safe from their ritual.

"Edward will be safe from Corsi, William, Mary and their combined ritual." The Devil tells me slowly. His mouth twitches into a smile. That should not be as reassuring as it was.

"You are dismissed from this realm." Christiana tells him coldly. Lucifer does wince then and stumbles back a step.

"Until next time." He promises in a whisper. I have a sinking suspicion that he didn't mean it only for Christiana. He disappears in the blink of an eye. The lights turn back on, and the candles splutter out.

"Well. That was fun." Elias jokes dryly. "Can we – once again – promise to never do that again?"

Chapter Fifty-Eight

Annie

Christiana hands me the coins before I can even ask. She strides through the now useless circle, slams them into my palms and then storms out of the room. She slams the bathroom door seconds later.

"Please tell me we are going people hunting before we go witch hunting." Cleo cuts through the tension as she throws herself down onto the sofa cushions. "I'm in the mood for some easy murder."

"We should be as strong as possible." Lola agrees. "But maybe some blood bags? Probably safer."

"There aren't any here. Too risky to leave a fridge full." I say softly as I examine the coins more carefully. The runes etched into them are almost beautiful, smooth lines and swirls without any hitch. The pentagram lines are perfectly straight. The magic in them is so strong that they are warm to the touch. The longer I hold them the hotter they get.

"I think that we should go for them tonight." Alistair suggests, swinging his arms at his sides. "No point waiting now we have a secret devil weapon, right?"

"It gives them less time to plan anything." Lola agrees.

"Can you stop saying yes to anything that gets said right now?" Cleo scowls at her. "It is making you more irritating than usual."

"Back off. She's trying to help." Elias bristles. Lola shrinks in on herself, running her hands over her arms as she stays silent.

"Make me." Cleo bares her fangs at him, leaning forward in her seat.

"I'll take that soul right back." Elias takes a step forward.

"It took you five centuries to realise it had even been taken. I think I'm safe."

"Could you please both shut up?!" Thomas snaps at them. "This isn't helping anything."

"Taking the urge to kill humans away." Cleo grumbles. Her eyes remain on Elias and Lola. "Although…how long would it take you to come back if I drain you, little blood witch?"

"You heard Thomas. Knock it off." Lola bares her own fangs back.

"That was a genuine question." Cleo puts her hands up in mock surrender. "IF we need to stock up then we have three witches who can't permanently die on our hands. How strong could we get from a couple gallons of that?"

"We are not going to drain the Bradford's." Grace looks at her in horror.

"Don't look at me like that. If it would give you the edge, I would make you drink all three and not let anyone else get a drop." Cleo's voice changes, still holding a hardness in its centre but its sharpness was blunted by a layer of love.

"It's not exactly a bad idea. If we have the time." Thomas relents. Elias stares at him. "Not to drain us. But our blood is full of magic. It would give them a certain boost."

"Excuse me if I'm not going to agree with the guy who has a fang fetish." Elias scoffs. "Not when it comes to biting. I'm not opening up a vein mere hours before we potentially have to fight our family. We need our strength too."

"Elias." Thomas says slowly as his eyes lock onto his cousins. "They are faster. They are stronger. They are deadlier."

"Only deadlier than you." Elias promised in a thick whisper.

"And them." Christiana's voice wavers as she re-enters the room. "They don't care if its black or blood magic Elias. They may never have cared. Even if me and Thomas wanted to start to practise that, we would lose. We don't have centuries to get good at it."

"You are stronger than any of us. You always have been." Elias continues to argue. Pointless. Christiana knows her powers and her limits. Black magic is a dangerous tightrope of a path, blood magic a messy trail with various hidden holes to fall into. Elias had lasted this long due to immortality and our enemies would have the same advantage. Thomas and Christiana would not have the luxury of time for them to fall into the obvious traps.

"We will not feed from any of you." I decree, looking at all my girls and Alistair. Cleo frowns and clenches her jaw but does not argue. Lola nods frantically, Grace more delicately but Alistair's nod is slow and his gaze set on Elias's neck.

"Annie-" Thomas tries to argue.

"No one is giving up any of their strength." I hiss. "And this is going to happen tonight. We cannot give them any more time to plan. We cannot give them even an inch of mercy. These coins are our answer, and we don't know that The Devil won't just turn around and give them some as well."

"You think he would do that?" Lola asks slowly. "After all he said about them being an apology?"

"A gift." Christiana corrects her. She looks so small standing in that doorway, like a normal teenage girl rather than the witch powerhouse she truly was. This summoning has taken more out of her than she let on. Her skin is pale and her hands shaking. I think she may have thrown up. She is hiding her heartbeat from us all once again.

"Don't trust Satan seems like a good rule to follow." Alistair mutters.

"We have to get them somewhere small. Somewhere we can control. Somewhere they won't put other people in danger to try and get us to stop." Christiana runs a hand over her face. The three witches then all turn to look at me.

"What?" I frown.

"We are assuming you have yet another safe house. One that fits that description." Thomas's lips twitch as he holds back a smile.

"You find it funny that I have multiple safe houses?" I scoff up at him, shoving the demon coins into my pockets.

"It's a little paranoid."

"How many years have you spent on the run because you're the only ones of your kind that can walk in the sun?" I raise my eyebrows at him. He stares at me for two seconds before nodding once.

"Fair point." He concedes.

"Do you have a safe house that will work?" Christiana presses. "Because if you don't then that becomes the major problem."

I turn my gaze to Grace and find her already smiling sadly. We both release a breath. We need somewhere close but not in the city. It would be a little bit of a travel but the farm could work. Grace glances purposefully over at Alistair. That would be the only problem.

"Alistair needs to go back to the palace." I say slowly. "We can't drag the Crown Prince of the United Kingdom to a deadly witch fight."

"No!" Alistair yells. "I'm coming with you all."

"Your Grace-" Grace begins kindly. Alistair glares at her and she halts.

"Don't call me that. I'm coming with you. This fight is my fight too."

"It's too risky." I tell him softly. "If anything happens to you then the whole line of succession, the whole monarchy will shift. I didn't save your life only to have you die by the hands of a witch not even a month later. You aren't coming with us."

"So, you expect me to sit back in my palace, sipping some o negative and trying to ignore the fact my future witch council is tearing itself apart and my new immortal family may be being ripped to shreds?" Alistair stares me dead in the eyes.

"No." Thomas answers for me. "Not completely."

"Oh, I'll just partially panic then." Alistair drawls.

"Keep that fiery attitude little prince. I think you are going to need it." Cleo purrs at him. A small smile plays at my lips as I realise that Cleo is only a half-step behind me and Thomas. Alistair shoots her a confused frown.

"You are going to tell Corsi exactly how to find us." Thomas tells his friend. Alistair mulls on that for a few seconds before appearing to decide that it was an acceptable role.

"Is that safe for him?" Lola demands. "For him to go back, alone and try to trick them into coming after us? What if they don't believe him? What if they know it's a trap?"

"I'm not that bad of a liar." Alistair pouts. "And it's William. It won't take much for him to think I'm scared of him and spilling our secrets because I'm a naïve little boy."

"He has a point." Christiana agrees. "It won't even cross Dad's mind that Alistair is playing him. He's gotten overconfident with the royals the last few generations. Unless Alistair outright says that it's a trap, his ego will take over." Christiana moves to look Alistair in the face. "Just don't overdo it."

"That's the advice I'm getting?" Alistair jokes weakly. "Don't overdo it? Anyone else got anything for me?"

"Don't die?" Cleo smirks.

"Don't eat them." Grace smiles.

"Don't be scared." Lola moves next to him again and gives him a gentle hug. "And remember you can use the bond. Those three can't hear us."

"And good luck." I add finally. "Not that you'll need it."

"We have jumped so far forward that I can't remember where our actual plan stopped." Elias runs both hands over his face. "Is this what it's like being with you people all the time? Everyone else is two steps behind?"

"Don't be pouty Elias." I smirk at him. "Alistair is going to go home and tell them where we are going while we go and get the farm ready to kick their ass. That's the plan."

"That's a guideline."

"That's not a helpful comment." Thomas sighs.

"You boys don't have a plan. Us girls all know exactly what revenge we want." Christiana's voice was soft, but it sent a chill down my spine. She wasn't wrong. I had a long list of things I wanted to do before putting those coins on their bodies.

"That is strangely reassuring." Elias sighs.

Chapter Fifty-Nine
Alistair

The palace was completely normal which sets my skin crawling. I'm not a complete idiot, I know that the supernatural keeps itself hidden, but the servants lack of fear makes me want to take them by the shoulders and scream. How could they not know? How could they not realise that more than one of the pillars of that hidden world were crumbling and it could bring the real world down with it?

"Alistair." My mother's voice calls down the hall after me, full of relief and hope. I must have walked right past her in my hurry to get to the witches rooms. Unnecessary since two of them are flocking my mother as she rushes to hug me.

"They said Annie took you away, that they couldn't find you with a spell. We have been so worried." My mother's arms wrap around me so tightly that the breath is knocked from my lungs. She pulls back a heartbeat later, cupping my face in her hands as she scans me over for injuries. "Are you okay? Did she hurt you?"

"Mum." I breathe softly, placing one of my hands overtop hers and taking deep calming breaths. "It's very, very hard to hurt me now. Remember?"

"But they would know how," Corsi shoves herself brutally into the conversation. "Just as they would know how to hurt the rest of our coven. Were they with you, wherever she took you?"

The witch sounds full of concern and behind her Mary's lips are wobbling as she stares at me. The picture of a worried family member. If I didn't know that it was fake, if I didn't know the things that they were capable of, my heart might have bled for them. But Annie's face as she ran from my room earlier, Lola's poorly hidden panic as she hugged me goodbye moments ago flash across my mind and remind me that its game time.

"I need to speak to William." I tell the two of them coarsely.

"That is not an answer." Corsi gapes at me as Mary lets out a gentle sob.

"Alistair...tell them." My mother whispers to me. She moves phantoms hairs from my forehead. I play along and lean into that touch before sighing. I scan my mother's face as she just did mine, taking in the tiny lines around her eyes and mouth, the tiny spot forming in the crease of her nose. She looks so fragile in comparison to us and yet she was the most calm. The most steady. My mother deserved to be more constant than any of us. She deserved more than the sick liar of a child she had been given.

"I didn't see anyone else there." I force myself to shrink into my mother's side like a scared child. "They kept me separate from everything and I didn't check for anyone on the way out."

"How did you get out?" Corsi presses. "Christiana and the others could get out the same way."

"Maybe we should have this conversation in private." Mary moves to place her hands on me and Corsi. "With William."

"Lola." I practically spit the word. "Lola let me out."

Corsi and Mary share a look. I fight for my own face not to give away the intense relief at the fact they believe me. They think I was taken, which was the assumption we were banking on, and now they think I was let out by the goodness of Lola's heart which is also something they will think of when they attack.

"I ran all the way from Surrey." I keep my voice low, throwing paranoid glances in the direction of every heartbeat I can hear. "Annie has this farm in the countryside there. Nobody lives near it but there's a bunch of buildings. If Christiana or anyone else is missing, then I suppose they could be in those."

"I am going to need to know exactly where." Corsi tells me slowly, making it abundantly obvious that she was reaching out to touch my head so not to spook me. I flinch anyway. She pauses.

"You don't have to do that. He'll tell you everything he knows." My mother chastises her.

"It would be quicker, your grace." Mary explains gently. "With half of our family gone, it is a miracle that Prince Alistair is home. I would like the others back with us as well."

"Neither of you are to go into my sons head." My mother uses her regal voice. Corsi's hands drop, and her head briefly bows. They are so good at acting like that, like doting servants of the crown. If I had never met Annie and the others, if I had been born healthy, would I have ever known it was all fake?

"I took a picture of the town sign after I got out. I figured it would come in handy." I offer up after a moment, as if the photo Lola sent to me a few seconds before I walked through the backdoors to the gardens had only just occurred to me.

"The town will narrow it down. Thank you, your grace." Mary says kindly. She always sounds so kind and sincere. Maybe she was the best actor out of all of us. I pull my phone from my pocket and swear genuinely as it refuses to turn on. I can't remember the last time I charged it and I was too preoccupied saving the photo to check the battery percentage.

"My phones dead." I scowl.

"They won't be running off straight away." My mother starts to lead me back down the hall. We take the familiar left towards my rooms. "You can put the phone on charge and eat something while your father and William finish their meeting."

Alarm bells started to ring in my head at that sentence. Corsi and Mary follow after us with their footsteps near silent. They could easily sneak up on me and plunge a giant wooden stake in me. That realisation nearly makes me shiver. If I were a religious man, I would pray for my friends. Instead, I remind myself that we have the second-best thing to a god on our side and that we are faster, stronger, more bloodthirsty. All they have is the element of surprise and we will be taking that away.

"William and father have a meeting today?" I ask my mother as we walk.

"An emergency one when we realised you were missing. The girls went to Annie's room and found that she had taken you. We need to call the guards back." My mother shoots the order over her shoulder at the witches. Corsi grunts in acknowledgement and starts to mutter under her breath. I don't understand the Latin.

"You're not going to send the guards after the girls?" I gape at her.

"Just your personal ones." My mother brings us to a stop in front of my bedroom and gently runs her knuckles over my cheek. "I am so sorry my little bird. I should never have brought them here into our home. I just wanted you to be able to go in the sunlight."

"This is not your fault mum." I whisper back to her as I open my door. "I don't blame you. Never even thought to."

"Stay inside. I'll get you some food sent over and I'll come back with your father. Okay?"

"Okay." I breathe in relief, stepping into my room as Corsi and Mary are joined by two royal guards in thick black fighting leathers and take their positions either side of the door. I am definitely not leaving, even though I want to. I look at the two witches as I start to shut my bedroom door behind me. My insides are screaming at me to drag my mother inside as well, to get them away from her. I resist.

"I hope you find Christiana." I tell them earnestly. Mary smiles at me as the door shuts.

I wait a few more seconds. My mother's heartbeat starts to move down the hall. I hear Mary talking to her softly. It sounds like they are discussing the meeting, then discussing how easy it would be to catch Annie. The two guards outside are breathing steadily but they are human. Highly skilled humans, but humans.

Okay. They'll be there soon. You sure you don't need me?

We need you to stay alive little prince. It is Cleo that responds to me. That's not as shocking as it would have been yesterday. *We will see you soon.*

Stay safe Ali. Lola's gentle wish seems to echo in my room.

You too. All of you. I send back. The silence that follows is heavier than any I had ever experienced before, even the one that hovered before my diagnosis. When the servant knocks on the door with food, I flinch.

Chapter Sixty

Annie

"You owe me a sofa." I scowl at Elias. I had come into the living room of the main house on the farm and found the blonde blood witch on his stomach, carving and burning things into the white leather sofa that had remained pristine since it had been brought in by an interior designer in the late 80's.

"I'm booby trapping your house, Annie. Things are gonna get damaged." Elias tells me in a sing song voice, not stopping what he was doing.

"You think that when they come to kill us, they will sit down on the sofa and have a cuppa first?" I bristle.

"I think one of you strong vampire girls could throw them onto it and my magic will keep them on it long enough for us to shove the devil coin down their throat."

"So we are doing all the heavy lifting are we?" Lola giggles as she zooms into place beside me. There is a tiny flake of dried blood on her bottom lip. She must have downed her blood bags already. Strange since she was the one who had most recently fed from the vein. She must be stress drinking.

Cleo and Grace were probably savouring their own bags or savouring each other until the trouble arrived. I couldn't blame them. I was acutely aware of where Thomas was on the property at all times. Currently, that was drawing protective runes around the smaller house used for storage. Christiana was searching the same house for helpful relics.

Elias finally turns his head, shooting Lola his signature charismatic grin. He taps his lip twice. Lola shoots him an incredulous look as I press my own lips together.

"No, I'm not asking for- You have blood on your lip." Elias mutters, turning his head back to his runes to try and hide the sudden flush of blood in his cheeks. I had not seen Elias so awkward and embarrassed in centuries. We had to survive this simply so I could tease him about it.

"The witches can be quite terrifying when they want to be." I tell Lola. "They have their own defences. But we are quicker and physically stronger so we will do the initial heavy lifting."

"And the coin things." Lola adds.

"I will do the coin thing. The witches will keep them still long enough for me to do it." I reach out and give her shoulder a squeeze. "It's not a detailed plan but it is a plan."

"I mean it's a better plan than shouting attack." Lola winks at me. I laugh and give her a gentle push towards one of the armchairs.

"No!" Elias yells as she takes a step. We both look at him. That smile has turned sheepish. "I've already done that one."

"But it…Obviously it looks fine." Lola sighs. "Or it would be pointless."

"Is there anywhere that is safe to sit?" I cross my arms. "Or is all of my furniture forever doomed?"

"I am trying to keep us all safe." Elias shrugs. "I'll buy you new furniture as long as we are all alive to use it."

"So that's a no then?"

"Yeah. It's a no."

"I don't mind the floor." Lola waves us off as she drops down into a crossed leg position. "It's not like we aren't sacrificing the chairs for something useful."

"How many more traps are you planning?" I ask Elias. I reach out my hand and gently smooth down the out of place strands of fringe on top of Lola's head.

"This is the final one for this house." Elias twists awkwardly to begin a new rune in the corner of the arm. "Which is where we are planning on facing them. Unless you want to change course and fight them in your storage mansion?"

"I have a lot of memories and a lot of things I want to keep Elias. Don't act like you aren't the same." I scowl.

"Elias doesn't have every dress he has ever worn put away." Thomas's voice drifts from behind me. I grin over at him. He is leaning against the doorframe, scrubbing at his stained red hands with a tea towel and his hoodie looped around his waist.

Everyone had gotten changed at the previous safe house after hot showers. The options for the boys had been somewhat limited. Luckily Lola and Grace liked baggy hoodies and shirts, so they shopped in the men's section for 'comfort clothes'. Elias and Thomas would be fighting for our lives in matching bright red tracksuit bottoms, but it was better than grease and blood covered jeans.

"But he would look lovely in my eighties one pieces." I snicker. "So would you."

"I was happy staying inside with my leather jacket for that decade." Thomas wrinkles his nose.

"I thought the eighties would have been fun to be immortal in." Lola frowns up at us all. "They were fun to grow up in."

"You were very young in the eighties." I smirk down at her. "You grew up in the nineties."

"Still." Lola shrugs. "My 80s family photos look super cute."

"Your family photos from the last two decades look super cute too." Thomas grins wickedly at me. I gasp playfully.

"You had time to snoop through my photo albums while putting those ruins up?" I ask sceptically.

"No. Christiana found them while looking for some handy little magic relics she gave you centuries ago. Do you always wear such ugly pyjamas on Christmas?" Thomas pinches my side. I whack his hand.

"Stay alive for the next one and you can find out." I tell him in a whisper, leaning up on my tiptoes to press a gentle kiss to his lips.

"Deal." He hums before kissing me back.

"Cousin present!" Elias yells as he pushes himself from the sofa.

"Cousin would also be invited." I roll my eyes at him. "If he wanted to come."

"I dunno. How much blood pudding do you people add onto your Christmas dinner? Not a fan myself." Elias takes the tea towel from Thomas and rubs at his own hands.

"No black pudding." Lola promises him with a grin. "My plate is 85% those little sausages wrapped in bacon though. Best thing you guys ever created. We also have Thanksgiving if you want to celebrate that with us."

"Oh, you mean a Sunday roast but on some random Thursday?" Elias sits down on the floor next to her. "With some fake promises to be more thankful for the little things?"

Lola's face drops for a second before she plasters on a fake smile as she nods. Elias opens his mouth to apologise or make another comment but in the blink of an eye, the air in the rooms turns cold enough to see our breath. The first warning spell had been activated.

Grace. Cleo. Main house. Now. I nearly snarl down the bond.

We are with Christiana. Grace whispers back. *She says to stay put. We will come to you and get them from behind.*

Why did you... I trail off. Cleo had a weapons chest stored away in there. Between me and Grace we had gifted her nearly all of them. Swords and daggers, crossbows and what would now be considered antique guns. They must have been looking through those.

All the lights in the house flicker twice. Warning spell number two. Lola is up in a flash and moving herself and Elias out of the room. They end up upstairs near one of the giant bay windows. They will come down when needed and attack from the side.

Me and Thomas are the bait. We are the giant flashy come and get us neon sign to attract them to the right spot. I turn to face the doorway which leads to the hall and ends with the giant oak front door. I reach out and intertwine our fingers.

"I love you." I whisper as a flash of fire runs over our skin. Final warning.

"I love you." He whispers back.

Chapter Sixty-One

Annie

The door slowly creaks open, the opposite of the dramatic slamming I expected. There is only one witch silhouette in the doorway. Corsi takes one large step inside. No one breathes as we lock eyes. She stops with her hands splayed at her sides. It is more terrifying than if she was holding a weapon.

"Please." I say coldly. "Come in."

Corsi scoffs but the next five steps that move her into the living room are fluid and calm. She stops just inside the entrance to the room and tilts her head in Thomas's direction.

"Your father is so disappointed in you." She chastises softly.

"The feeling is mutual." Thomas grinds out.

"But you could come home with us." Corsi continues speaking as if Thomas had not replied and I was not standing here. "Kill Annie and you, your sister and Elias can all come home. You will have to face your punishment, but you will all live."

"Funny." I cut in, trying to drag her attention to me to give Thomas a second's respite. "But there isn't a way to kill a member of your coven. That's not exactly mercy."

"But you and your disgusting little sidekicks can be killed. That will be how this ends. Even if we must keep the Bradford's permanently tortured in a dungeon, your bodies will feed the worms. If even they would want you." Corsi still does not look at me as she speaks. Fire flares in my veins.

"You have done much worse things to me." I remind her slowly. Her eyes finally flicker over to me and her face changes, softens. She looks almost apologetic as the understanding runs through her immediately.

"He was only supposed to kill you." Corsi says in what is almost an apology.

"Maybe that will comfort you when I rip your throat out sixty-seven times in a row. Or maybe I'll stab you sixty-seven times. That seems more poetic, don't you think?" I take a step forward. Corsi visibly swallows as the meaning of my comment hits that small, sympathetic nerve that all women have. The one that responds when we hear phrases like 'she deserved it' and 'well what were you wearing'. It is not that Corsi truly cares about what she put me through that night. It's that I made her face the horror of it for a brief second.

"You will not get close enough." Corsi shrugs. I go to scoff but a blinding pain shoots through my neck and skull. The breath whooshes from my lungs as I can't help but fall down to my knees. Every cell in my body feels as if it was spit roasted over a furnace, twisting, and being torn away from the other. A scream chokes its way between my lips as my hands claw at my head. Blood drips between my fingers as my nails cut through the skin of my cheeks.

Sweet breath fills my lungs seconds later as a crash echoes throughout the house. Corsi had been sent flying backwards through the door and I am not sure if it was by Thomas whose palms are raised outward or by Lola, who now stands in front of me with her shoulders tense and hands in fists.

"I have your soul bitch." Lola purrs, her gaze set on Corsi as the witch pushes herself to her feet. "Come and get it back."

Corsi grins at her, blood staining her teeth and making her look near feral. The witch moves her hands in two swift gestures. Thomas flies backwards. I lunge for him, nearly dislocating his arm as I yank him towards me and stop him from landing on the booby-trapped sofa.

"Three versus one." Corsi takes a slow step forward. "How very typical of you all."

Lola doesn't move. She doesn't even twitch in our direction as she essentially plants herself as a human shield between Corsi and me. My heart breaks and I let go of Thomas's arm. Before I can rush to her side, Corsi collapses to the floor clutching her hands together. A strange smell reaches my nose, harsh enough that I nearly gag. Once I realise what the smell is, I gag twice.

Corsi's skin is literally melting from her bones. The first few layers of skin on her fingers peel back and something similar to fat and muscle drips from between the white flashes of bone that I can see as Corsi cradles them to her chest and screams. Tears join the skin and blood on the floor, sizzling along with everything else. She is burning from the inside out. The skin still on her hands is red and bubbling, as if the blood running beneath them is boiling in her veins.

A quick glance shows me that this isn't Thomas. He is staring down at Corsi with wide eyes and all the blood leeched from his face. His mouth isn't moving so he can't be performing a spell, not one of this magnitude.

"Elias." Lola breathes out, the word a ragged sound. I frown and follow her gaze, grateful to look away as blood starts to gurgle from Corsi's throat. I don't think that was part of the spell. I think that she is simply screaming so hard that she has torn her throat apart.

Elias stands at the bottom of the staircase, half hidden in the shadow of the doorframe. His hands are splayed, those signature Bradford eyes narrowed as his mouth moved nearly soundlessly. Corsi manages to suck in a shaky breath before spitting more foaming blood onto the floor. Elias takes that as a challenge and takes another step forward.

"Elias!" I snarl. The blonde witches eye twitches but he does not stop. He just gets louder; the spell now audible as he blankly watches Corsi start to writhe on the floor.

"Enough." Thomas booms. Elias finally drops his hands. Corsi stays on the floor, moaning and spluttering but alive. Barely. Her body shudders at the sudden loss of the unbearable heat or perhaps because her nerve endings are now fried. A small part of my brain screams that she should have suspected this. Had she not thought of using a protection spell? The part is quickly soothed by a deep, male voice reminding me that we had the devil on our side.

"The coin." Elias tilts his head in my direction, but his eyes remain on the tortured woman on the floor. I reach into my pockets and hiss slightly. The coins are hot to the touch, burning my palm as I grasp them. I pull only one out and flip it between my fingers as I hesitantly step forward and crouch within arms distance of her.

Her dark eyes narrow as she takes me in. I stare back down at her and release a long breath. This woman ruined my life. She is the reason I am what I am, the reason Thomas was driven to the point of near insanity and threw away his soul for me. She is the catalyst for the worst day of my existence, the hidden villain behind every flinch and shudder that takes over my body when I cut through a market. She is the first chapter in the story of why I am a monster.

"I don't know what the rest of your years will be like." I tell her softly, in a tone gentler than any I had ever used before. "But I hope they are agony."

I slam the coin into her mouth, cracking teeth as I push it to the back of her throat. She screams around the metal, but more blood pours out of her mouth. The torrent of red comes out of her with such ferocity that it foams and spills over my shoes. Corsi doesn't die without a fight- she swings her arm out and knocks me off balance.

The wrestling that follows its pathetic. She is too weak, her skin too raw and fragile for her to win. Every time she touches me, she lets out a small, pained sound. But she tries. The tiniest part of me respects that. The larger part hits her harder.

Corsi collapses as I rip her fingers away from a feeble grab of my throat. I slam her head against the hardwood floors once, twice, three times until I hear a distinctive crack. I shove myself to my feet and wrinkle my nose at the state of my hands. I scrub them on my jeans.

"One down."

Chapter Sixty-Two

Grace

Mary was never menacing. She always appeared soft spoken and kind even though she was a part of the cursed coven. There was always an overwhelming sense of innocence around her. Now, staring her in the eyes as Christiana bleeds out on the floor, there is only a sense of rippling anger.

Christiana had not stood a chance. The witch had frantically started to draw different ruins on the walls once she realised that we were stuck in here when Mary had sent her flying through the air in a sneak attack. Even Cleo had not heard her.

Christiana had landed on the still open trunk of our antique weapons. Multiple things had sliced and stabbed into the young girls body. I crouched in front of her in a defensive pose, refusing to take a proper look at her but I could smell it all over the room. Christiana was slipping away as those wounds turned the floor around us into a crimson lake.

I knew she would come back, that her wounds wound heal and eventually her eyes would open again. It did not quell the lava like feeling of rage that flowed through me as Mary barely even glanced at her. Her eyes were focused on Cleo who paced back and forth in front of me and Christiana like a lion protecting its den.

"Where is Annie?" Mary asks her bluntly. "She is usually attached to your mates' side."

"Mate?" Cleo echoes. She comes to a stop and blocks me from view. "Like we are a pair of god damn mongrels?"

"You are barbaric fanged beasts that fornicate constantly. Do you not like the comparison?" Mary swirled her fingers around the air and sparks fly from them.

"I am going to enjoy killing you." Cleo snarls.

"You will go through a lot of pain trying." Mary finally looks down at Christiana. Her face does not change from her cool indifference. Even her eyes only have the barest flick of emotion. My stomach drops as I recognise it as hatred.

"Fuck you." Christiana gags on the words. Her breaths are uneven and ragged. The agony she must be in… I reach behind, trailing my fingers through the pools of warm blood until I finally brush against her arm. I shuffle myself with my eyes still locked on the witch, running my fingers across Christiana's worrying cold and clammy skin until my hand covers hers.

"Where. Is. Annie?" Mary asks us again.

"She is going to get you." Christiana coughs. Her hand gently shakes in mine. "And I hope its soon. I want to watch."

"Why are you holding on for such an impossibility little one?" Mary taunts her. "It must be so painful. Just let go."

"Painful?" Cleo smirks. "You don't know the meaning of that word yet."

"Such a large mouth saying such silly little things." Mary gestures for Cleo to come at her. "I promised Corsi I would let her kill you. But I suppose she will forgive me pinning you to the floor while I rip Grace apart."

Cleo's growl rips through the room as she zooms forward. She does not make it to Mary. The witch twists her hand. Cleo screams and falls to the floor as her spine cracks. Cleo takes hissing breaths as she tries to twist herself into a healable position. I do not look over at her as I lunge at Mary.

The witch twists her hands again, but she is not fast enough. Her air spell flashes past my ear, I can feel the heat of it against my cheek, as I hit her in the middle and tackle her to the ground. Her body hits the hardwood with a crack. I press the advantage.

My fangs lengthen as my hands pin her shoulders to the ground. My lips are two inches from her throat when my head feels like it is exploding. I let out a yell, my hands instinctively reaching to press against my temples.

Mary slams her palm into my throat, and I tumble backwards off her as that exploding pain turns into a searing cold sensation running through my major arteries and veins. It hurts to breathe, and any breathe that does leave me causes a cloud to linger in the air above my mouth.

My ears start to hurt like they do if I go out in winter without a hat. My toes tingle. I scrape together the energy to loll my head to the side and look at Cleo, to reach my hand towards her. My lips twitch but fail to smile properly. At least she will have the others when I am gone.

Freezing to death wasn't the best way to go and it wouldn't have been something I thought could happen to me now. But I knew the signs back from when I was little, back when my mother would grip me tight and scream that she needed to do this to give me food and shelter. I could see my fingers turn blue and start shaking even though I couldn't feel any of my limbs.

I see Cleo mouth my name before a shining heeled boot kicks me in the face. I feel no pain which I know is a bad sign. My vision spins again but my head now faces the ceiling. The dark wood blurs around the edges as what feels like acid pools in my mouth and throat. A small part of my brain tells me that it is probably my own blood. Another part starts to ring a warning bell as it gets harder to breathe.

Mary crouches down and looks down at me. She reaches out and roughly squeezes my face between her fingers.

"Poor little Grace." Mary coos before she snaps my neck.

Chapter Sixty-Three

Annie

"Why can't we hear them?" Lola breaks the silence that had settled over us all. I turn to look at her, hands turning sticky as blood cools in the wrinkles of my palms. I briefly wonder if they will ever be truly clean.

"Why isn't the devil swooping in to drag her away?" I focus on the bigger question. The coin is still in Corsi's mouth but there is no sign of our saviour. No flickering lights, subtle smell of sulphur or deep rumbling to say he was even on his way.

"Why was it only her that came?" Elias gestures to Corsi's body but does not look directly at it.

"I'm going to check on Christiana." Thomas strides for the door. He doesn't look at Corsi or at me as he passes.

"I'll come with you." Lola and Elias offer at the same time.

"One of us needs to stay here." I look around the room. "Elias how long did it take your head to re-join your neck when you had your head chopped off?"

"Had his what?" Lola gaped at him.

"A day. But my head was held against the neck." Elias tells me uneasily. "I have no idea what would happen if it wasn't."

"Go to the storage house." I instruct as I move over to the fireplace. The cast iron tools are all neatly in their holder. I hear a gentle whoosh as Lola speeds from the room and seemingly takes both boys with her.

I pick each tool up in turn, weighing them in my hand. One is heavier than the others and has a flat pointed end to its scoop. It is the one I would want chosen if our situations were reversed. I pick the tool that looks the exact opposite. This one has a blunt pointed end, made for poking at the logs rather than clearing the ash afterwards.

"What exactly." I say into thin air as I move back to Corsi's body. "Could the god damned devil be doing to make him late for this?"

I bring the heavy metal tool down using all of my strength. I don't aim for the neck straight away. I let those residual kernels of anger in my stomach flare to life and I hit any part of her I can. I break her legs, knees, arms, spine. The sounds of the assault are a symphony to my ears. Each crack is like a plaster being placed on the deep, still healing cuts to my soul from five hundred years ago. Every trickle of blood that falls from her washes away some of the fear that I have never truly been able to shake away.

The crack of the neck is the sweetest sound of them all. The blood that sprays as the iron rod rips her artery is an even sweeter sight. I go for a third swing-

ANNIE Lola screams down the bond.

I am out the room before the rod hits the floor.

Chapter Sixty-Four

Lola

There is so much blood. The smell is overwhelming even though we come to a stop at the open front door of the smaller house. Thomas might not be able to smell it as I can, but a look of pure panic crosses his face. He bolts through that door quicker than I have ever seen a human move, yelling his sisters name as he skids across the polished wood.

"Thomas!" Elias yells after him. I blink, my hand clawing at Elias's shoulder to stop him from moving any further. Another wave of the tangy iron scent of blood rolls down the stairs. My throat tightens as I realise that I can only hear three people breathing inside.

"Let go." Elias snarls at me, trying to rip himself away from my grasp but my fingers tighten. I don't mean to. I know we should run inside. I know that it's the right thing to do and I also know deep down that if it was just me here, I would.

But as Thomas screams, as that primal roar of pain echoes in my ear, I only know that I will not let Elias put himself in danger. I will not let him go to face what is in that house. Not him. Not now.

I love Grace and Cleo. I would rip my heart out myself in exchange for their safety. But I will not trade Elias for them. That guilt can eat me alive for the next eternity- but it will be an eternity in which Elias lives. In which he is free. Another scream, this one female, has me screaming against my internal dialogue. They need me. My family need me.

"Lola." Elias breathes as a flash of wind moves past us. A flash of Annie scented wind. "Lola, I'll keep you safe. But we need to help them."

"I am not worried about me." I snap at him, nails still digging into him as I prick up my ears. Another set of breathing, this one ragged and angry and then-

Complete silence.

"No." My hand drops from Elias's arm. We both run in, Elias stepping on my heels as we clash in the doorway. I keep him behind me as we bound up the stairs three at a time.

Chapter Sixty-Five

Cleo

Grace's chest stops moving, as my eyes water and the tears pool down my cheeks to tap against the floor, as a figure bursts through the doorway with a pained roar, I cannot help but let out a sob. It is not Annie as it should be. But it is the second-best thing. I will never be happier to see Thomas than I am right now.

Christiana's heartbeat is weak. Something is keeping her here, something not right. Something spiteful. Something more than just her will to live. She should have been dead within seconds. But she lets out a rattling, wet laugh as her brother turns his hard gaze towards Mary. She knows exactly what I do. That the first-born Bradford will not let Mary out of here alive. He will not let her out of here without making her beg for the pain to stop.

The chuckle that leaves me makes my chest hurt, the back of it right underneath my lungs. My spine hasn't healed properly, or it is still healing. I have no idea what she did. It just hurts. My eyes move back to Grace, to her blue tinted skin and lips. She would come back. She had to. I tell myself that over and over as Annie rushes into the room.

Mary lets out a scream. I let that melody sweep over me, taking away the aches and sharp pain shooting down my back. I see blood splatter down onto Grace's body as if it were raining crimson. It stains her face, drizzling all over her. A flash of movement behind her body makes me gasp.

Annie is slowly moving Christiana off all the weapons impaled into her. She is being gentle, soothing the girl in hushed whispers underneath Mary's scream. Christiana's eyes are glazing over but they are pointed towards her brother. Her brother who is making small swift gestures with his index finger. With each little gesture, a corresponding cut slit itself across Mary's skin.

The cuts are not deep but there are already dozens of them. They are debilitating cuts, mostly on the legs but there is a particularly nasty one on the chest. Mary stumbles down to her knees but keeps her eyes on Thomas. She starts to laugh.

Thomas stops his gesturing. Annie does not stop her nurturing of Christiana. I blink twice. When did Lola and Elias get here? Oh. When did my hearing go away, replaced by a loud ringing noise? There was suddenly more blood on the floor than before. Mary's mouth is moving, her face contorted into something wild like a trapped animal. But I cannot hear what she is saying. The ringing is just getting louder.

I feel my lips start to move. My tongue is heavy and feels too big in my mouth. If I make a sound, it is more of a croak than any actual words. But I know what I am trying to say even as my mind focuses on unimportant details.

As I take in the tiny drop of blood spray on the ceiling, the deep brown leather of Lola's boots, the stray strand of spiderweb on the corner of the weapons chest, my mouth forms Grace's name over and over.

Chapter Sixty-Six
Lola

Grace looks so small in death. So small and so cold. When her finger twitches, I nearly cry with happiness. I scramble over to her side and drop into a crouch. Thomas continues torturing Mary behind us. Mary continues to shout at him that he can do whatever he likes to her, the vermin will die etc etc.

William is not here and so he will probably swoop in any second in an ambush. I don't care about that. I care about taking all this anger in my stomach, this hot feeling that is threatening to spill over and burn it all to the ground and doing something with it. If only I could give it to Grace, warm her back up and get her moving again.

"Lola don't touch her." Annie's harsh tone cuts through all the other noise. My hand hovers over Grace's shoulders.

"What? Why?" I move my eyes away from Grace and over to Cleo who is staring at the two of us, her mouth moving in the same formation over and over.

"Because Mary's put a curse on her. Haven't you?" Annie looks over at Mary. She doesn't glance over at Cleo or at Grace. She moves her eyes to purposefully avoid it. Realisation settles in my gut. Annie does not look at them because if she does, she will break. She will be taken over by a rage even deeper than my own and it will consume her. It will overtake all her reasoning and she would lash out. She would make Mary's death far too quick.

Mary coughs a laugh. She is cut off in a gurgle as Thomas makes a dramatic gesture with his hands. A cut scrapes itself across Mary's stomach.

"Answer her." Thomas growls.

"Your mother would be so disappointed in you." Mary ground out. "Throwing your lot in with demons of the night."

"Who made us demons Mary?" Annie asks her softly. "Who was the anchor for the spell that night? How fickle a creator is when they despise their own creations the way you despise me."

"Exactly." Mary locks eyes with Annie. I hold my breathe. "You. I made you. I did not make the rest of them. Your broken, brutish children. You took it too far when you created them."

"No," Annie's eyes burn with emotion, the wall she had put around her fury crumbling. "You have taken it too far. You have hurt them. You have killed them. You have then cursed their bodies and knowing you as I do, knowing how spiteful William can be and how eager you are to please him, I can only guess what will happen if I were to touch them."

"Test it out." Mary taunts her. The fire in my stomach flares, so much that if this were one of the cartoons I had watched as a child, there would be steam blowing from my ears and an overwhelming sound of firecrackers.

"I would rather spend my time with you." Annie purrs menacingly. Mary flinches.

"Take the curse off." Thomas demands bluntly. Just as Annie has not looked at Grace, I had not seen Thomas look over at Christiana. The young girls eyes had now completely glazed over. She was gone. Elias cradles her body to his chest, not bothered as he was soaked in the dark crimson. I jolt as I see that his eyes are on me. Not on Christiana. Not on Thomas or on Annie or even the now slowly moving Cleo. Me. Despite his rush to get in here, to get past me as I tried to keep him out and keep him safe, I was somehow high on his priority list.

"No." Mary snaps at him. "You are going to have to kill me. Over and over and over."

"I plan on that." Annie promises her in the same soft way that mothers promise their babies sweet dreams. "I think first I will get Thomas to cut you a few more times. Then I will take a long iron pole and I'll beat your bones until they separate. I'll beat your head from your shoulders just like I did Corsi."

Mary's nostrils flare as those words sink in. She lets out a guttural cry and despite the deep cuts on her knees and the blood that soaks the floor beneath her, she lunges forward. Annie kicks her in the face.

Mary collapses into a moaning heap on the floor. The blood loss must be getting to her by now. She moves sluggishly into a sitting position. Annie smiles down at her.

"Take the curse off Mary." Elias grounds out. "Before this gets worse for you."

"Oh, there is no worse for Mary. There is only one thing worse than this and I am not that cruel. Neither are you." Annie tuts, slowly turning on her heel and moving towards the weapons chest that is full with Christiana's blood. Annie reaches in and removes five daggers, juggling them in her hands as Thomas once again waves his arm.

This time there are no fresh cuts. This time, Mary's body is forced into a straight position. Annie flashes past me. Mary screams only once as Annie puts four of those daggers into her. One in each hand and one in each thigh. The fifth dagger is still in her hand.

"Elias. Take Lola and Christiana outside." Annie orders.

"I'm staying." I argue, the words out of my mouth even as I stand.

"You need to protect Elias." Annie turns her usually bright green eyes towards me. They were so dark now, almost leeched of their colour as if to match the fact that Annie had now been leeched of all her kindness.

I did not recognise this woman in front of me. This was not a woman that would sit with me and watch bad sitcoms. This was not a woman who would wake us up with pancakes and milkshakes on Valentines day. This was not the women who instilled in us a strict moral code.

This was the world's first vampire intent on causing pain and spilling blood. This was a girl who had brought the monarchy down to its knees by becoming a king killer.

"Lola," Elias gently calls to me. "Come on."

"Go," Cleo wheezes from behind me. She is speaking now. She is healing and twitching and moving. Those were all good signs. I keep my eyes on Annie as I force myself to walk away from them. The screams start as soon as I shut the door behind us.

Chapter Sixty-Seven

Annie

I had never learnt how to skin someone. It wasn't as easy as I had imagined it would be. The thing that made my failure more satisfying was the fact this clearly hurt more. Mary never stopped screaming. Thomas used some sort of magic to keep her conscious and alive. A part of my brain registers the fact that Cleo is moving. I can hear her shifting on the wood, shuffling across the floor to be closer to Grace. Her breathes are pained hisses but she is alive. Grace will be too. She has to be.

The bloody stumps of flesh that I peel from Mary get dumped to the side of me. Each twist and slice of the dagger is therapeutic. They match up perfectly in my mind to every single significant cut from my own memories. This slice on Mary's arm was from when Edward accidentally sliced my own with a pair of scissors growing up. This slice on Mary's stomach was my rapist delivering what should have been a killing blow. Each slice takes a weight from my shoulders that I had not been aware I was carrying.

Thomas does not stop me. He doesn't say anything. He always keeps himself on such a refined leash, attaching that leash to the marble pedestal he puts me on. He doesn't want to join in even after seeing what Mary did to Christiana. That's fine. I can be his executioner, his attack dog, his secret weapon. I have more of a taste for it than he does. The amusing part, if I could find it in myself to think anything was amusing right now, was that it was his love for me that gave me this appetite.

"Annie." Grace's voice cuts through me. The dagger drops from my hand. She had not said my name like that, so gentle and so full of awe, in centuries. Not since she was half my height and she needed me to plait her hair back.

"Gracie?" I turn my head, the silence now that Mary had stopped screaming even louder than before.

She still looked cold, but the blue tint of her skin had nearly gone. She was shuddering and wincing, but she was awake. She was alive. Relief like I had never felt before and likely never would again flows through me. I take the second coin from my pocket and shove it deep into a cut in Mary's abdomen without a glance at her face, even as she whimpers. I throw myself across the gap and I wrap my Grace in the tightest hug to ever exist.

While the room reeks of all the mingling blood, Grace still smells like home. Her hair smells faintly like the apple shampoo I bulk bought her over a year ago. There is something natural and sharp underneath that, the specific Grace smell I have never been able to accurately identify or replicate. Her skin, the parts of it that I can feel as her sleeves ride up her arms, is still smooth as satin. Grace has no blemishes. Grace has no flaws. Grace was *alive*.

"Annie." Grace sobs once into my shoulder.

"Gracie." I sob back, the break in her voice causing me to lose my hold on the fragile string keeping my emotions all neatly tied together. We say nothing else. We just hold each other, ignoring the sound of Thomas breaking Mary's neck in the background. A moment later Cleo wraps her arms around us, her hold on me almost hesitant. I adjust my arms to hold her just as close as I am holding Grace.

"I thought I had lost you." I choke out.

"Never." Grace whispers back fiercely. "Neither of you will ever lose me. I promise." Grace gives us both a quick tight squeeze. The breath whooshes from my lungs but the pain of it is the most exquisite thing I have felt in centuries.

Chapter Sixty-Eight

Lola

Christiana is starting to warm up again. Elias had laid her down gently in the grass. I ran around the parameter to check for William under the guise of giving Elias space to close her wounds. In reality, it was so I could scream far away enough that no one else would hear.

I did nothing. Grace and Cleo had been in danger, and I had done nothing. What kind of person was I? I had tried to stop Elias going into the house where his cousin was dying all under the pretence of keeping him safe. I had been willing to leave them all in danger as long as the pretty boy was safe.

How pathetic. How vile. How unforgiveable.

William is not here. He could still be back at the palace, with Alistair. I do not know him well enough to know for sure if he wouldn't hurt the prince. But Alistair would have vampire hunter guards and they would provide at least a second's distraction if needed. He could run away in that second. He would be safe.

Even though William is not yet on the grounds, I cannot risk using anything less than full speed to get back to them. When I come to a stop behind a crouching Elias, the screaming has stopped. The blood on Elias's hands and shirt has gone sticky. I should give him space, give him a moment. I know that. But I immediately change my mind.

"He's not here." I say out loud because I want Elias to look at me. I want him to look at me, see the self-disgust that is rushing like acid through my veins, and to make it all go away. It is an unreasonable ask in any circumstance but especially this one. My emotions were not his responsibility. They were not his burden.

"Christiana will wake up soon. We should get her some fluids but it's just a waiting game now." Elias doesn't turn. He adjusts Christiana's body again, changing her position every few seconds to try and make her more comfortable.

"Has…" I trail off. I don't know which question I want to ask or how I want to phrase any of them. My head is far too full of them for any of them to make sense.

"Grace is going to be fine. Mary will have taken the curse off or she would still be screaming." Elias answers two of those unspoken questions. He still does not look at me. I nod along, pressing my lips together and looking around. The farm was large, green, and held no animals. I imagine the rules and protocols for it are the same as all the other safe houses. People were hired to keep it clean and out of disrepair, but it was otherwise left alone.

"About before," Elias says hesitantly. I keep my eyes focused on the lone bird moving around the corner of the field.

"I would say I'm sorry, but it would be a lie." I say bluntly as I cross my arms.

"I am not asking for an apology." Elias finally turns to look at me fully. I can feel those grey eyes scraping across me, trying to get into my disruptive thoughts and pull away at the porcelain, neutral mask that I have haphazardly thrown into place. He won't find a way in. I have been practising this look since I was in diapers.

"I don't think this is the right time." I say diplomatically. It makes my very soul shudder. That one was straight out of my dad's playbook. It used to be followed with a dramatic, victimised sigh as my mother started to softly cry but say nothing. Then, when she finally caved into her own insecurities and started to speak, he would simply look away with disinterest as if the car crash of a woman in front of him was lower on his priority list than remembering the name of the shade of paint on the wall.

"That sounds like there will never be a right time." Elias sighs.

"If there is then it's certainly not today with Christiana, Grace, Cleo and maybe even Alistair dead." I snap my head to look at the storage house. Footsteps. Footsteps of multiple people. Footsteps of-

The four of them leave the house as a group. Thomas dropped to his knees next to his sister's body but the other three all looked straight at me. Grace smiles wildly. I sob and throw myself at them, arms reaching wide and failing to hold all three of them at once.

"I am so glad you are okay." Grace whispers to me.

"I am so glad you're alive." I whisper back. "You looked so cold. So still."

"We got lucky." Grace pulls away so she can look me in the eye. The smile widens.

"William isn't here." Elias ruins our moment.

"No." Annie sighs. "I doubt he would stay at the palace without a plan. We will need to do a locator spell when one of you is strong enough."

"Can you at least give us until Christiana is awake?" Elias snarls up at her, baring his teeth at her as if he had his own fangs. "Or do you not care about any of us at all? Christiana is dead! Grace was dead! Cleo wasn't far behind! You didn't even look at them."

"Watch yourself Elias." Thomas warns in a low grumble.

"Don't get me started on you." Elias hisses at his cousin. The two boys scowl at each other, shoulders set as if the only thing stopping them from wrestling each other was the young girls' body that was in between them.

"We should tell Alistair that we are all fine. Maybe he knows where William is. He is probably worried." I suggest softly.

"That's a good idea." Grace mutters. She is still smiling. How could she go through all that she had just now and still be smiling? Still be reassuring me? Grace really was far too good for this world.

"I'll do it." Annie tells me bluntly but not unkindly.

"I think Lola is capable of sending a simple message." Cleo is uncharacteristically distant from Grace, her hand hovering over her girlfriends' skin and her body tilted away from her now we were out of the group hug. Interesting.

"If Alistair is panicking then I can use the makers bond to calm him down." Annie moves to Thomas's side, kneeling in the grass. A cool breeze whips around us and brings with it the sharp smell of rotten eggs. I wrinkle my nose. I notice that Annie smiles.

"The devil has finally arrived." My maker purrs as she gently moves Christiana's hair. "Convenient timing."

Chapter Sixty-Nine
Christiana

This afterlife looks like my childhood bedroom. The thick maroon curtains around my hand carved single bed. The porcelain dolls displayed evenly across multiple shelves on the wall. Thin, cloth bound books that were all about insipid young girls acting prim and proper. I take one step forward, expecting the tell-tale squeak of the floorboard that my father didn't want fixed. He thought it would stop me sneaking away. It hadn't.

This was the first time I had been back here in centuries. Every other afterlife had been different. Brighter. Happier memories. A lovely pier I had visited in the seventies. Hyde park on a crisp autumn day.

"I thought you would be more comfortable here." A voice like velvet drifts over my skin. I spin on my heel. The blonde-haired devil cowers in the corner of my room, rubbing his hands together nervously. His eyes flick around my body quickly, never focusing on one part for too long.

"When can I go back?" I ask bluntly. "They need me."

"You were very hurt." The devil swallows a lump in his throat. "I am sorry. That I could not be more helpful. That I was not there to stop it."

"My own mistake led to my own suffering." I say with a dismissive wave of my hand. "I should have struck first. It's a mistake I will not make again. When can I go back to my family?"

"Elias and Thomas are waiting for you." The devil gives me a slow blink. "But your body still needs rest. The wounds are closed. That's good."

"You cannot bring me back now?" I scowl. "You do not have that power?"

"You are always so impatient." The devil smiles at me. Actually smiles. My stomach squirms. "You need to prioritise yourself, Christiana Bradford."

"My family are in danger. My prince, my queen, my king." I hiss at him, tilting my chin up in defiance as I had all those years ago.

"We both know he is not your king." The devil takes a step forward, into the weak grey light that is shining into the room through the two tall windows. *"She is not your queen. You have seen too many live and fail."*

"Alistair will not fail." The statement shocks even me. I had never held any faith in his family line, and he had spent his life in a sickbed. *"He will be a good king. If he gets the chance."*

"Your brother would have been better."

I lock eyes with him, focusing on one of the planets slowly moving around the edges. That truth runs through me as quickly and as cold as if he had injected ice water straight into my veins.

Thomas as king had been a hidden dream locked away since I was learning to walk. When I was younger, more naïve, I had thought that he would become king and make me a princess. Even horrid, satanic little witches wanted a tiara. But as I grew I realised the weight of that dream, the weight of the family secret and the imprint it left upon our souls.

"I am too old to wallow in such childish thoughts." I run my hands over my arms and break the eye contact. *"My brother is alive and happy. That is what he should be best at."*

"I didn't say best. I said better." A smirk pulls at the devil's lips.

"Bradford's do it the best or we do not do it at all." I recite one of the many phrases that my father had drilled into my head. The irony is not lost on me. This fight was Bradford V Bradford and we could not all be the best. The room's temperature drops as if the archangel in front of me can read my thoughts. I don't know if he could or couldn't. The thought is unsettling.

"I have taken Corsi and Mary already." He whispers to me gently. *"Your father did not go with them to the farm."*

I expect a sinking feeling in my stomach or perhaps a tightening feeling in my throat. Neither feeling arrives. I do not even flinch. Mary killed me. Corsi put Annie, my future sister, through a fate some would argue was worse than death. That action led to my brother grovelling for us to save his love, my body to be permanently stuck in this awkward in between, and our souls to be handed out to other victims without our own clear consent. They lied for centuries. They deserved this. My father would deserve this.

"Of course, he didn't. That would imply he cared enough to die with them." I move over to the window and lean forward, nearly pressing my nose to the cold glass as I stare down at my mother's garden.

"Whatever happens I want you to know that he does care about you Christiana." The devil's voice has a near tremble. I choose to believe it's out of fear of me. That hollow thought isn't comforting.

"Not enough." I shrug. I did not need someone else to tell me my father cares about me. I know that. I also know that if it came to a choice then I was the lowest priority on his list. It didn't mean I wasn't a priority. It meant that Thomas was always a bigger one.

"He cared about you enough to perform that ritual again. Even after it had failed to bring his wife back."

"He never loved my mother enough either." I reach out to gently run my fingers over the glass, tracing my mother's initials in the condensation. "William Bradford loves his legacy above all. That's why he did what he did to Annie. He would have helped Corsi with the plan. He had to have approved it. Annie would have brought our house to the ground with her plan to save Anne. She was a threat to him. She is always a threat to Thomas."

"But he did the ritual anyway." The devil insisted. The complete faith the devil had in my father's love for me would have once made my heart soar, sent a fog into my brain to twist and cloud my thoughts until I might have believed it. That time was long gone.

"He did the ritual because when he refused, I threatened to kill myself. He knew that Thomas would do the same, that his heir would not choose to live in a world without me and Annie."

"You do not make it easy to reassure you."

"I do not need reassurance. I need to be home with my brother and cousin, setting this all right."

"This is not your wrong to set right."

"Why are you here, Lucifer the fallen?" I sneer. I do not have the courage to look over my shoulder at him.

"To check on you, Christiana the vengeful."

I like that. I fight to keep my lips from smiling as I roll that name around my thoughts for a second. I had definitely been called worse. Every time someone called me little girl then I would grind my teeth together so hard that I would have to spell them back to normal after.

"Is everyone else okay?" I ask softly, the pale faces of my favourite vampires flashing in my mind. My stomach feels hollow as I realise how far down my friend's wellbeing was on my own priority list. Like father like daughter.

"Grace and Cleo will be." The devil answers diplomatically. I frown and cock an eyebrow in his direction. He is closer to me now, hovering an arm's length away from me with a pained look on his face.

"What happened?" I grind out. Mary was all sweetness and sunlight ninety five percent of the time but that other five was nasty.

"You don't remember?"

"I was a little distracted choking on my own blood."

"Fair enough." The devil winces.

"I remember Thomas coming in." I say in my defence. "I remember knowing I could let go after that. Grace...When I was injured Grace took my hand. I remember speaking to Mary. I heard shuffling and Grace and Cleo were both on the floor...I remember thinking they weren't dead. Just hurt. Was I right?"

"That's very good." The devil forces a smile onto his face. He should be better at faking them than he is.

"Was I right?" I repeat.

"She killed them. Not permanently. Very hard to do that, even for a witch like Mary."

The ice water flowing through my veins suddenly turns hot and starts to bubble. Grace had my soul. An insult and injury to Grace was an insult and injury to me. We were joined.

"How could I never have sensed it?" I blurt out. "The soul connections."

"You and the infamous survivors haven't exactly been best friends these past few centuries. You dealt with Annie if you dealt with them at all. Those meetings were few and far between. It has taken you over a century to meet Cleo, and you only know Lola even exists because of Thomas's spying. Is it really so shocking that you never knew?"

The reminder of the distance between us all makes me grimace. I would have adored spending more time with Annie and the others. Shopping in Paris in the nineteen thirties. Sneaking into sleazy gentlemen's clubs in the early eighteen hundreds. She would have stood by me during that incident during the civil war. Grace would have too. They could have been closer than family.

"Whoever Annie turns from now on-"

"Annie will not turn anyone else." The devil interrupts me.

"You sound sure of that."

"I am."

"You won't tell me why."

"That would be telling. I've learned my lesson about that."

"Only took you a few millennia."

The devil throws his head back as a laugh bursts from his mouth. The laugh is short but deep, the sound echoing around my head long after he is finished. It's a nice laugh.

The devil's face falls for a brief second before settling back into a genuine smile. That was even nicer. He gestures slightly with his head to the direction of the bedroom door.

"Time to go." He tells me. I rush past him, grab onto the iron handle, and then pause. I look over my shoulder at him. The window behind him illuminates his hair into a golden halo.

"Don't be offended." I say dryly. "But I'm hoping not to see you for another five hundred years."

"Only five hundred? I'm touched." The devil places a hand over his heart. Or, I suppose, where I assume his heart would be. He winks at me. I wink back before opening up the door and stepping into the harsh yellow light.

Chapter Seventy

Annie

"You are not coming with me." I repeat for what feels like the thousandth time as we all convene in the farmhouse kitchen. The seven of us crowded around the kitchen island, awkwardly leaning against it as all the stools had been boobytrapped by Elias earlier. Grace is sipping at her fourth mug of sugary tea. I insisted on it, even though I knew she was perfectly fine by now. Cleo takes gulps of her own herbal mixture. That's more to lubricate her throat after lecturing us all for the past forty-five minutes.

Alistair was a panicked mess when I checked in with him but when he heard we had two victories and zero final fatalities he calmed down. I saw no need to tell him about Christiana and Grace's brief lapse of living. He had asked permission to confide in his mother about everything. With only William left, I saw no reason to keep her in the dark. She could help us track the weasel down since the first locator spell had given us no results.

"I still can't believe you let them track you." Lola wrinkles her nose. "Like your animals."

"It was better than the alternative. Besides. I swapped out the amulets for the three of us before we left. I wouldn't be surprised if father did the same. It makes the royals feel better, that's all." Christiana says after swallowing a mouthful of mint hot chocolate. Thomas was doting on her, as he should, and kept adjusting the blanket I had wrapped over her shoulders when she had been led inside.

"There is a worse alternative than being treated like prized cattle?" Lola snorts.

"Can we get back on subject please?" Grace sighs, pushing away her half full cup. Her eyes bore into mine, their bright shade clashing with the dark stubbornness I find in them. "You are not facing William alone."

"I will not put any of you in any more danger today." I grip the edges of the marble countertop. "I will not risk it."

"Bold words for the woman who didn't even look at Grace's corpse earlier." Elias mutters under his breath quietly. Not quietly enough.

In a second, Grace has one hand wrapped around his throat, slamming him into the wall so hard that the paint cracks behind his shoulder.

"Annie loves me." Grace snarls at him, fangs barely an inch from his face. "All your sarcastic, cruel comments do not change that."

"I never said-" Elias is cut off by Grace slamming him again. No one else in the room moves. Those of us that can stop breathing. Grace has more patience than any of us. More patience, love, loyalty, understanding. She is calm and collected. Always.

"I understand why she reacted as she did because I understand her." Grace continues as if she had not been interrupted. "She is my maker. She is my friend. She is my sister and mother and best friend all rolled into one. I will not have you making her feel guilty because she did what she needed to cope in the moment."

"Grace." I whisper with the little breath I was holding in my lungs. "Let him go. He never means what he says."

"I am sorry Grace." Elias tells her. He keeps his grey eyes focussed on her, his face sincere in his apology. "I know she loves you. We all do."

"Never say it again." Grace's voice breaks. "Never."

"I won't." Elias promises her. "Never again."

Grace debates that over for a few seconds, maybe debating if Elias's word was trustworthy after all we had been through today. She nods once, drops him, and spins on her heel. She nuzzles herself into Cleo's side. The Egyptian beauty wraps her arms around her waist and glares at Elias. The blonde blood witch stares at them before smiling gently.

"You deserved that." Christiana breaks the tension with her dry comment. I chuckle, Thomas doing the same at the exact same time. We lock eyes and our smiles deepen.

"Annie is right though. No one else is coming with us." Thomas uses a tone that sends me right back to when we were human, and he had servants at his beck and call. The 'do as I say' arrogance that I knew was always meant well. There is only once small problem.

"I never said you were coming either." I point out. "I can get rid of William by myself."

Thomas looks at me like I've stabbed him in the stomach. Christiana takes a noisy slurp of her hot chocolate as she gives her brother an amused side eyed glance.

"We do this together." Thomas scowls at me. "We do not split up. I do not sit here and let you walk into that danger alone. Maybe you didn't notice, but you have needed a witch both times today."

"I can handle this." I reach for his hand. It is cold to my touch. He had refused a hot drink.

"Together. We can handle it together." Thomas does not let up.

"We had this argument hours ago." Cleo rolls her eyes. "It is exhausting hearing it again. Can we just accept the fact we are all going and finish this?"

"I really do like you." Elias grins slowly at her.

"The feeling is not mutual." Cleo sniffs.

"Grace and Christiana died today." I force the fact from my mouth. It leaves a slimy feeling in my throat, my stomach squirming as if I am about to throw up. "They died. I cannot let that stand and I cannot let that happen to anyone else."

"It didn't even hurt." Christiana shrugs.

"It wasn't your fault." Grace tells me.

"You're both terrible liars." I smile at them.

"Well, that's not true is it? We are all excellent liars. It's what makes us so terrifying." Christiana smirks. "And I would like to get some revenge in now I'm back on the living side." Christiana peers around Grace to look at Cleo. "And I'm betting you do too."

Cleo's response is a slow, devilish grin. My phone gives a shrill beep. Something must be watching over us, I decide as I read the text with William's location. The timing of that was far too perfect to be a coincidence.

Once the girls are up and moving, Elias grabs my arm gently and pulls me back for a private conversation. Lola shoots us a confused frown but Thomas gently leads her away with the others.

"Once this is over, she gets her chance at revenge." Elias whispers to me. I do not need him to tell me who 'she' is.

"If she wants it." I respond immediately. "All she has to do is ask."

"We both know she won't ask. But she deserves it." Elias drops my arm.

"We both know she won't ask because she doesn't want to face him. That's her choice Elias. You can't make it for her."

"He deserves to be punished."

"I know." I slowly grin. "And trust me, there's a lot of ways that can happen. Even from afar."

Elias's eyes light up with understanding as I give his arm a gentle squeeze and then follow everyone else out of the house.

Chapter Seventy-One
Annie

The Diamond Lion looks the exact opposite of where I would expect William to be. The image of William on a nightclub dancefloor, grinding it out to a pop anthem with a plastic cup of sex on the beach makes me shudder. A stuffy state room in a crumbling estate, sucking on the end of an expensive cigar as he nestles into a plush armchair. That was how I imagined William awaiting his fate.

He had to know I was coming for him. He had to have a plan. This place was public enough and enough of a supernatural culture staple that he would cause quite a stir by destroying it. Would that be the plan? To blow me to pieces? Even I probably wouldn't survive that. The urge to insist the others stay back floods me again but one glance at them shows that would be a pointless argument. All of them have set shoulders and faces. Cleo's hands are even balled into fists.

"This place gets even busier during the day." Elias warns us softly as we all strut towards the entrance. The air reeks of the Thames, wind whipping across the water in a frenzy. "People come and wait out the sun in half assed lock ins."

"Oh joy." Cleo drawls.

I pause and step to the side of the doorway. I look at them all in turn. I know it is poor form to say goodbyes before a fight, especially when in potential hearing range of the enemy. But Elias is right and the club sounds busy. I can give the majority of the goodbyes with the makers bond but for Elias and Christiana, I would have to say things out loud.

"I am so proud of you," I tell them both. "I am so proud of how you have grown. How much you have learned. I am honoured to have known you for even a moment, let alone all these years. I love you. No matter what happens next, I love you."

"Aw shucks Annie." Elias smiles, running a hand through his hair and looking down at the floor. His eyes are shiny. "How are we supposed to beat that?"

Christiana takes a step forward and takes my hands in her own. She is so much smaller than me physically, but her personality is the size of a skyscraper. Those Bradford eyes stare up at me, wide and unflinching.

"You may not have married Thomas. But I always saw you as an older sister." She tells me. "I am happy to die again and again for you to get your vengeance. I love you too."

Christiana wraps her thin arms around me. I squeeze her back, letting some of the tension slip as her words cut through me. Christiana saw me as a sister, saw me as family. How the human me would have wept from happiness at hearing that.

"I do hope you have a few more dramatic comments left." Cleo cuts in. "I am desperate to hear how much you love me."

I open my mouth to respond but I am overrun by Lola's sudden, desperate giggle. The American claps her hands over her mouth to stop herself but the sound is simply muffled. She cannot stop.

"Sorry." She giggles. "I just…I really do love you all."

"Even me and Cleo?" Elias leans towards her, speaking in a weirdly husky tone. Subtle.

"Especially Cleo." Lola leans towards him as well, smirking at him.

"Do you love me enough to stop eye fucking the blood witch until after the fight?" Cleo wrinkles her nose in fake disgust. Lola smiles and shoots her a rude hand gesture.

I have no words. I say down the bond as I take a long look at my three girls. *I do not even know where to start. All of you have come so far. Pride is too small of a word. You have persevered and fought and loved. I know these past few weeks have been scary and the revelation of our gifts even more so, but I would willingly give my soul up to save you, again and again and again if it was needed. Love is too small a word for what I feel for you, but I love you all immeasurably.*

The girls all look at me solemnly before, as a group, they pull me into a bone crushingly tight hug.

This is not goodbye. Grace tells us fiercely. *For any of us.*

Of course not. Cleo agrees with her. *We are all far too important to the universe.*

Lola laughs again but this time it sounds on the brink of turning into a sob. She grips us all closer and takes deep breaths.

My own family wasn't worth much. I wanted to thank you all for being my new family. For showing me what the word is really supposed to mean.

All of us tighten our holds in the hug, unsure of who exactly we have the best hold on but showering them with love anyway. Elias clears his throat. We reluctantly pull back. I notice that Cleo is the last to let go, but it is not Grace that she is holding onto. It is Lola. The image makes my throat feel tight.

Finally, I turn to Thomas. I stare into his eyes, latching onto the familiar feeling they send shooting through me as I smile sadly.

For you, my dearest Thomas, I have only one regret. That I spent so long running from you. It may not have seemed like it, but I have always needed you. Maybe not always at my side but I have always needed to know that you are out there. I needed you to still be breathing and feeling and have the potential to randomly pop into my life. I needed to know that if I walked on a path there was always the possibility you could be at the end of it.

Oh, my Annie. Thomas coos back as he gently takes my face in both of his hands. *We will have all the time in the world.* The kiss he gives me knocks my breath from my lungs. It is soft but firm. There is no mature intent behind it. The kiss is as innocent as we once were, back when we were worried about living a righteous life. It is nice to know that we still have a piece of that inside us somewhere.

Thomas is the first to pull back. He rests his forehead against mine. His gentle sigh tickles my face. "Okay. Now let's go kill my father."

Chapter Seventy-Two

Annie

The club is packed full of vampires. I suppose I should have expected that they would be the main clientele for a day long lock in. We make a big show of hiding every inch of our skin behind our jackets and rushing into the reception area with panicked faces. The show starts now.

The girl at reception is a werewolf but she is nice enough as she ushers us inside. The music is set on a low volume. It's some kind of ballad I had heard on the radio multiple times over the last week. No one is paying us too much attention. The groups by the door glance over at us before returning to their pints. The three girls holding wine glasses and slowly swaying smile as they catch sight of us mid spin. I look around the whole first section of the bar. No William.

Round the corner Lola whispers to us. *There is a room full of mirrors.*

I nod and move slowly, taking my time to listen to everyone around us. I wanted no surprises. A familiar scent drifts over and I stall in my walking for a second. I snap my head towards the furthest, darkest corner before we enter the mirrored section.

I should have recognised him immediately, but his hair as changed. Back in the seventies, it had been dyed a bright letterbox red and had been a tangled, shoulder length mess. Now it was a glorious turquoise faux hawk. The lip piercing was still present, as was his eyebrow piercing. He had a few more in his ears now. More patches had been added to his leather jacket.

I quickly turn my head back to the room of mirrors, ignoring the split second of eye contact. No distractions. No pauses. Just revenge.

"Annie!" A purring French voice greeted us from across the hall. People glanced over. I do not smile as Francis throws his hands wide, his own lips set into a devilish grin. "Such a gorgeous face to light up such a dim place."

I don't respond. Francis is always a flirt and considering his black and red themed ruffled outfit, he hadn't changed much since the eighteen hundreds. But he was sat in the corner booth, at a clearly hastily thrown into place table, with two unfamiliar vampires and one William Bradford.

"You." I whisper softly as my eyes latch onto him. I sense my friends spread out on a line behind me. No one will get past them. To his credit, William stands to his feet with grace, side stepping around Francis and undoing his blazer jacket with one hand.

"Children." William chastises gruffly. "You should know better by now."

"Go fuck yourself." Christiana's voice is full of disinterest. To anyone that didn't know her, it would be believable, a part of the cool façade she had perfected over the years. Christiana Bradford had always been a force to be terrified of, the Hyde to Thomas's Jekyll. Tonight would only cement that reputation. It would change all our reputations, for better or for worse.

"Language Christiana. I didn't raise you to be so crude."

"I wouldn't say you raised me at all." Christiana waves her hand up, palms facing forward. "I would need seven hands to count the number of nannies you hired."

"And this is the thanks I get? My own flesh and blood siding with treasonous, murderous whores."

A snarl rips through the room. Cleo's fangs are on proud display, and she is hunched over slightly, ready to pounce on him. William's eyes lazily take her in, flicking over to Grace and Lola before landing back on me.

"Are you not curious William?" I ask as I take three long strides across the room. The rest of the club has gone silent, the sounds of heavy, anxious breathing echoing around the space. Someone had cut the music off. How dramatic.

"What would I be curious of?" The head of the Bradford family asked bluntly. Francis shoots his companions an uneasy frown.

"Where your precious Corsi and Mary have gone of course." I tilt my head to the side and put on a confused frown. I can play pretend. I do it every time I feed, when I am the sheepish nervous girl in the smoking area that drunken men are too aggressive with. Those men never won. This one wouldn't either. We were already two thirds of the way there and we had the devil on our side. I could afford to taunt him. I will enjoy it.

"I assume they are locked away somewhere with some nasty, blood magic booby traps. I will free them once I am done with you." William dismisses me with a wave of his hand. He shrugs out of his blazer and places it behind him on the table in-between glasses of wine.

"Oh no William." I tut, starting to slowly pace around the room in a half circle in front of him. "Well. They may be locked away, but you certainly won't be freeing them. Even you don't have that power."

"You underestimate me. I am not my son. I will not care that it is you begging for mercy." William rolls up the sleeves of his shirt. Anger bubbles in my stomach. He is talking as if Thomas isn't here, as if his son was weak. My lips twitch as I hold back a snarl of my own.

"Thomas is worth one thousand of you." I pause my pacing just as I am in front of Thomas.

"He is certainly worth more than you." William spits at me, the first sign that he is getting angry. Good. I want it to be a fight. I want it to turn bloody and vicious.

"Ask the question William." I smirk. "Don't you want to know what I did to your friends?"

"You will pay for their pain tenfold."

"Corsi's skin melted from her bones. Then I beat her. I took a blunt object, and I broke every bone in her body before I tore her head from her neck." I speak softly, smile growing as I keep my eyes on William. I hear someone behind me swear softly.

"Mary made a grave mistake." I continue. "She went after my children. You should know how angry that made me William."

"You have no children." William clenches his jaw.

"I have four children." I hiss coldly. "All of which you have put in danger. I can't have that."

"Yet you hide behind my children's magic, bringing your so-called children right into the danger with you." William sneers.

"Elias." Francis begs lowly. "Stop this."

"You do not scare me William. Not anymore." I let out a laugh, ignoring the interruption. "I am stronger. I am faster. I am simply better than you. This will not be a challenge for me. Just very, very painful for you."

"Seven against one. Hardly fair odds."

"You may be right." I place my hands on my hips as I pretend to think. I start to pace again. "So…how about just you and me? No witch protection. No vampire backup."

"Annie." Grace hisses at me. "No."

"You will have to get your hands dirty this time around William. There is no servant to run off and find a hitman for you. I am no longer a weak human girl in a dirty alleyway." I grin at him.

The flicker of understanding that runs through William's eyes tell me that I was right. Corsi may have been the woman that pulled the trigger, the one who betrayed me by spilling my secret, but William was the one who told her what to do. William had been the one who gave her the gun.

"No magical intervention." William muses. His eyes turn on Christiana once again. Elias takes four large strides and stands in front of her. William smirks.

"This place has a strict no fighting rule." Francis interrupts us yet again, throwing a look over at the bartender.

"He doesn't get paid enough to step into a fight between us. Do you?" I smile kindly over at the bartender. He stays silent as he takes a large step backwards to press against the bar's fridges.

"Annie. Be reasonable." Francis persists.

"This is reasonable Francis. I am sure that any woman in here would agree. Now keep your mouth shut before I rip it off." I snap. My eyes are back on William. Francis mutters to himself in French before huddling back into his seat. I flex my fingers at my sides as William walks to the centre of the room. He stays just out of arms reach of me. I smile with my fangs on full display before lunging.

Chapter Seventy-Three

Grace

Thomas puts up a wall to stop me from lunging to Annie's side. Cleo has her hands on both mine and Lola's wrists. If I so much as twitch, then I might end up with it broken. Cleo will be keeping us guarded. Thomas will be keeping us safe. I have the sinking suspicion this wasn't a planned alliance. They just fall into these roles naturally.

Annie hits William in the gut, rushing back and forth around William using vampire speed. Most of them are deflected. William is using some kind of protective hex. I wouldn't be surprised if he had put it on earlier in the day, ready and waiting for whenever we found him. The whole thing smells like a trap.

"You have to stop this." A familiar voice whispers into my ear. A voice that made anything sound like a melody, even the pleads for Annie to come back he had yelled thirty years ago. I turn my head slightly, giving Marcus the briefest of glances as Annie's cruel laugh echoes around the club.

His hair was a different colour, and he had a few more piercings. Under his clothes I imagined he had found some space to cram more tattoos.

"Stay out of this Marcus." Cleo hisses over at him as my eyes once again focus on Annie. William and Annie are once again staring at each other. William's nostrils are flared, and his shirt ruffled.

"You said no magic." William snarls.

"And they are not using any." Annie smirks.

"Then who is protecting you." William twists his hand in her direction and sends a line of white-hot sparks towards her. As soon as they get within an inch of her, they fizzle out and die.

"Cheater!" William booms.

"Maybe you are just losing your edge William. Your dark lord has forsaken you." Annie pulls the final coin from her jacket pocket and holds it up. The coin that was once a dark grey now shines a gorgeous silver and the demonic carvings are clearer than ever before. "I am going to rip your throat out with my teeth and then jam this into your spinal cord."

"Impossible." William stares at the coin and stumbles back until he hits the table. Francis and the other companions stare at the coin with slack jaws.

"I am only going to destroy you, William." Annie says reassuringly. "Everyone else will be free to leave as long as they don't get in my way. Make it easy and drop to your knees."

"I will not." William says proudly, his chin tilted to the ceiling as he appears to accept his fate. Far too easy. Definitely a trap. Annie clearly thinks the same as her steps towards him are slower than before. She twirls the coin around her fingers as she moves.

I find my eyes more focussed on the back of her head than the flashes of light bouncing off the coin. Once this is over, she will be a mess. She will pretend not to be, but she will. I will be there to reassure her, love her and protect her from the voices inside her head that tell her this was a mistake. Maybe I can help her finally have some peace.

Annie takes one more step forward. The large disco coloured floor tile beneath her lights up a bright red and she is thrown backwards through the air, flying over our heads, and heading straight for the back wall full of covered windows.

Chapter Seventy-Four
Cleo

The entire scene plays out in slow motion, like in those awful action movies that Lola enjoys so much. I blink and Annie is still headed towards those covered windows, Grace's mouth is still twisting into a horrified silent scream, and I am still holding back Lola as she tries to rush to catch Annie. No use. No use exposing herself as well. I know the risks, the consequences, the stakes.

Rule number three is annoying but necessary. No killing other vampires. Too much risk of their friends holding centuries long grudges.

Rule number two is what kept our thin strand of our humanity in check. We do not kill innocents. We kill the rapists, racists, and abusers. We kill the monsters that parade as men.

Rule number one. The vital one. The one that Grace had repeated to me over and over for that first year when I would slip up and stand in front of uncovered window or open the door at noon. Never, ever, go out into the sunlight.

The crash is loud and will echo in my brain forever. Annie does little more than grunt as the glass slashes into her skin. Two men have raced after her, arms outreached. One of them is the French one who had pleaded with Annie to stop this. He stands well within the shadows, other supernatural creatures cowering behind him after running out of the way. The smell of burning flesh hits me and I turn to look at the other man.

It's the one with the blue hair. His arm is a ruined mess of peeling black flesh. He is like Lola, fighting against the two vampires that are holding him back. It takes me a second to realise that his scream of Annie's name is the only sound in the room. That crash had silenced everything else.

Even the Bradford's are frozen in place, eyes wide. Maybe they are stuck behind their own spell, the thin hard layer of air acting as a barrier to stop the three of us from rushing to Annie's side on the fight. I have no idea which one of them is behind it. I have no idea why that is the thing I am focussed on as Annie slowly gets to her feet.

The glass crunches beneath her. The sun is set behind her, the stray ginger hairs that frame her face giving her a strange halo. She sets her shoulders and tilts her chin up. She stares right past all of us, stares at William with eyes full of rage and a clenched jaw. Her hands curl into fists as William starts to laugh.

Chapter Seventy-Five

Annie

Shit.

Chapter Seventy-Six

Lola

Annie strides back into the club, wiping glass shards from her shoulders without a care in the world. She walks right past the blue haired man, his mouth hanging open, but the shock has some other emotion mixed in with it. The Frenchman stumbles backwards as do most of the people in her immediate way. I hear faint praying as some of the vampires in the far corners fall to their knees. An elderly vampire tentatively moves forward and his hand hovers inside the shadows as he debates if he should try his own luck.

William's laugh cuts into me, getting louder and louder with each step that Annie takes. I don't want to take my eyes off her. She is glowing as if that brief stint of sunshine has absorbed into her skin and is shining out at us all. She looks like a goddess with an unearthly rage to match. Annie comes to a stop back in the space she had left earlier, nestled between the witches and us. Grace quickly steps closer to her. Thomas does as well. William's laugh cuts off.

"I am Annie Dawson. I can walk in the sun. I have changed the course of nations." Annie's voice is low as she slowly lets her fangs slide out and press against her bottom lip. "I hunt the monsters that parade as men. I avenge women who deserved better. Your cheap little trick does not scare me."

"They see you for what you are now." William growls. I have no idea when he picked up the silver dagger or where he got it from, but the edge visibly burns red.

"Soon they will see your insides." Annie purrs.

I understand now. I understand that Annie does not look at us because she loves us, and she needs to focus. But my entire body screams at me to do something to make her look at me, make her notice that I was there to help, that I had been held back from saving her crashing through that window. I wanted her to acknowledge right then and right there that I had tried. My natural reaction to danger was now proven to be selfish narcissism. How typical.

"You cannot kill me." William twists the blade in his hands as he meets her gaze. "You cannot hold me. I have allies that will rip you apart from the fabric of time itse-urgh!"

Christiana had decided she was done hearing her father talk. She sent a stream of blind white sparks heading straight towards his eyes. The ones that landed burned tiny holes into his skin. Annie lunges forward, wrapping her arms around William and moves them faster than any of our eyes can see.

By the time William's dagger clatters to the ground, Annie is slamming him into the bar. Two seconds later the two of them are crashing through another window causing vampires to scream and scatter to the darker corners. Elias yells as he stumbles into the rest of us and then Annie and William are wrestling on the floor. Annie is slamming his head into the ground once, twice, then screaming as William uses his hands to snap her elbow the wrong way. Annie headbutts him and knocks him out cold.

People are finally starting to react behind us. Those that can run into the sun either via the doors or the now easily climbable window. Some are yelling, trying to find their friends and some are nearly screaming. As I stare at the two bloodied figures on the floor, I wonder how well the glamour spell on this place will work in this kind of situation.

"If no one has any objections." Annie's voice cuts through the noise. "Then I am going to end this now."

"He isn't dead yet." Thomas points out lowly. His words make me tense. We are still in public. How far would Annie go? How long would she take when she needed to be running? We all needed to be running. That was the plan, the guideline, the rule.

"I can handle all of this. If you would like to leave." Annie turns her head slightly to the side, looking at the Bradford's from the corner of her eye. My heart soars into my throat. She was delaying this so they would not have to watch.

"I would like to do it actually." Christiana says in the same bored tone as asking the cashier for a bag. Her eyes move down to look at her father's face. "With his own dagger."

"Christiana." Elias mutters. "Do not put yourself through-"

"I'll flip you for it." Thomas interrupts, his own eyes on the dagger. Elias stares at him in horror.

"You always got what you wanted growing up. You don't get to take this from me." Christiana tells him.

"We could share it." Thomas suggests as if he is talking about splitting a plate of nachos rather than the responsibility of murdering their father. I cannot imagine the emotional and potentially physical damage William must have put them through these past centuries for that decision to be so easy. I could imagine hitting my own parents in certain scenarios, but I could not imagine killing them even now.

"You are using magic." Christiana grumbles as she moves to scoop up the dagger. Annie twists herself off William's body and moves at human pace to stand with the three of us. She wraps us in a tight embrace. Elias remains distant from us. I close my eyes and take a deep comforting breath.

I open them just in time to see Christiana and Thomas both kneeling by William's head. Christiana holds William's silver dagger and Thomas holds one made of ice. They each plunge them into their father's eyes in perfect unison. Elias doesn't look.

Annie waits for the Bradford's to move back to the group before she goes to the body. I close my eyes quickly as I realise where she plans to shove the coin. The squelch sound the coin makes as it enters the gore of the eye socket is almost worse than the sound of the daggers. I open my eyes again when I hear Annie's footsteps.

"Let's go home." Annie whispers to us all as she wraps her arms around Thomas's middle and rests her head on his shoulder. Cleo looks over at the broken window and then raises her eyebrows at Annie.

"Once the sun goes down." Annie fights back a smile. That smile flickers as someone behind us shuffles forward. Annie turns her head and drops her hold on Thomas. The witch does not release his hold on her.

"Marcus." Annie greets the blue haired vampire, her chin held high, but her eyes focussed on his still healing hands. That smile falls. "You…I'm sorry."

"You've been able to do that the whole time. Haven't you?" The man's voice is like a melody, soothing even in this situation. His left eye is a light enough brown to rival Cleo's in beauty, but his right was a light sky blue. My mouth drops as that final piece of information clinks in the hidden part of my brain full of random facts from random lovers. This was Marcus Ramsay, lead singer and guitarist of the seventies punk band The Social Solution.

"Marcus. Please." Grace looks at him with put on wide eyes and a wobbling lip. If she had been allowed, she would have been one hell of an actress. It has taken me decades to know the difference between her genuine and fake innocence. Most of those times were when we were hunting.

Marcus does not look at her for more than a second. I glance over at Elias, to see if he recognises exactly who this is, but he is watching the singer with a clenched jaw and his hands wrapped around Christiana's shoulders as if he was going to yank her backwards.

"I really am sorry." Annie's new smile is soft and sad. "You understand though."

"I do. Are you okay?" Marcus's gaze softens. "That was…"

"I'm fine. I'll be better tomorrow. Always am." Annie hesitantly reaches for his injured hand. "You won't be able to play guitar for a few days now."

"A few days without my strumming or a world without Annie Dawson. I know what I'm picking. Well…I suppose I didn't." Marcus does not take her hand. He does look her in the eye and his lips twitch into a responding smile. Oh. *OH.*

"We should go." Thomas is looking over Marcus's shoulder at the groups of people that were growing more and more bold. Some were still on their knees, others giving us scared glances.

"They cannot go. The sun is out." Annie tells him bluntly. She is still holding onto the backup plan of the backup plan. If one of us is exposed to the outside world, then we act as if it is them and only them that is gifted. It was a plan none of us had ever thought we would stick to. We wouldn't want to.

"There's a back entrance that goes to an underground garage." Marcus interrupts. "Usually only for performers and VIPs. Somehow, I don't think anyone is going to argue with you using it."

Annie looks over at me and winks. I laugh and then before I know it that laugh has turned into sobs. Annie pulls me into her arms, muttering for Marcus to lead the way. The feel of her arms around me makes me sob harder.

Annie is alive. She is here and she is alive, but she almost wasn't. She crashed through that window, and she could have been ripped apart for that reveal, William could have won, we could have been betrayed, Grace and Cleo could have been hurt again. This was one of the best-case scenarios and it still felt like we had lost.

It's okay Lola Cleo's voice is reassuring and loving. *You will be okay.*

I'm not crying for me I hiccup.

I know. Cleo reaches out for my hand and gives it a near crushing squeeze. I squeeze back.

We will all be okay. Annie swears to us all as we step into the back corridors of the bar, lead by Marcus who keeps shooting Annie uneasy glances. *All of us and our prince who is undoubtably waiting for us back home. Let's go see him.*

Chapter Seventy-Seven

Francis

"I am telling you, even William's magic did not work on her. Not properly." I grind out for the thousandth time that hour. Our guest was relentless in his questioning, making me repeat small details in an attempt to catch me in a lie.

I wish I was lying. I wish this sick feeling in my gut was fictional, the stress of my mission causing a bad dream. Annie Dawson could not be the daywalker. Half of the cursed coven could not have been lost. No one had seen Corsi and Mary which meant Annie was telling the truth about what she had done. William's body had disappeared from the safe location our agents had stored it.

"Someone was protecting her." Our guest was clearly amused at the idea.

"Her immortal witch boyfriend, his twisted little sister and their sleazeball cousin." Natalie snaps from her place beside me. She had striped her hair of its colour before reluctantly joining me across the pond. She had no luck following the daywalker trail in America. There is no shock there.

"No witch could have protected her to such extent. She must have drawn power from the coin." The Englishman in front of me has a typical smug grin on his face. It was not nearly as endearing as my friends.

Were they still my friends now? Were they ever my friends? They hid this secret from me for centuries. They hide in the shadows of my Paris townhouse as dawn broke, sharing my blood laced whiskey and worry about if my curtains were thick enough. The betrayal stings my throat as I swallow down my comment. We are not in charge here. This British asshole was.

"That may cause an issue. You say our agents couldn't remove the coin from William's body? Before they lost it?" The man pressed on.

"They couldn't even make the thing twitch." Natalie nodded. "It was like it was a part of his bones only stronger. Nothing could break it or move it. I've never seen runes like that before."

"Well, you are only ninety years old." The man dismisses her with a wave. "There are many things you have never seen. Your boyfriend was too busy failing to give his opinion."

"I am one hundred and ten." Natalie tells him in a deadly calm voice. The betrayal in me is overtaken by panic. Natalie will not win the fight if she chooses to pick it with this man. He is old, I can tell by his stature and the way he talks, the way our boss bows down to him instantly. The stubborn moral streak in Natalie will get her killed. She has never been able to stand for people talking down to others.

"Human years do not count." The Englishman rolls his eyes. He then slams his hand down once on the desk. "Now. Back to the actual business. How do I get into the Palace?"

"You learn how to time travel and be born a royal." Natalie quips. I reach out to place my hand over hers. She moves it away. "I don't think you realise exactly what today means. The *sun* could not kill Annie Dawson. We don't know that anything on this earth will!"

"Annie Dawson is not unbreakable. She just does not burn." The Englishman's voice turns cold.

Unbreakable. Not unkillable. My heart sinks in my chest.

"She is protected by the most powerful witches on the planet." I remind him carefully. "Christiana and Elias know dark magic that I could only have nightmares about. Thomas will never let anyone near her ever again after this. No one will get a chance to *break* her."

"The palace has the tightest security in the country. There is a reason the royal family is protected by infamous witches and now by The Survivors. No one is sneaking in." Natalia continues to rant.

"I do not plan to sneak." The Englishman scoffs. He grins over at us and seems to rejoice in our look of confusion. "I plan on being invited in."

"Oh?" Natalie outright laughs at him. "And who do you think is going to invite you?"

"My little sister of course. She's had quite a day. A visit from me is exactly what she needs."

I feel my mouth drop open, my body understanding three seconds before my brain does.

"You're Teddy Dawson." I croak out. Natalie stills beside me, her own comment dying on her lips. The Englishman settles back into his chair and regards us with a bored expression. I should have realised before. His hair is the exact same shade of ginger and those dark green eyes… If I took a closer look, I would bet there was a gold fleck in the same place as in hers.

"It's Edward actually."

Playlist

The following playlist contains songs listened to during the planning and creation of the characters and world of 'The Survivors'. A more complete copy is available on Spotify.

"Praying" By Ke$ha

"Bad At Love" By Halsey

"The Loneliest" By Maneskin

"Sign Of The Times" By Harry Styles

"Need You Now" By Lady A

"See You Later(Ten Years)" By Jenna Raine

"Brother" By Kodaline

"Just One Yesterday" By Fall Out Boy, Foxes

"Come Back…Be Here" By Taylor Swift

"Till Forever Falls Apart" By Ashe, Finneas

"If We Have Each Other" By Alec Benjamin

"Judgement Day" By Stealth

"Vienna" By Billy Joel

"I Am Not A Woman, I'm A God" By Halsey

"Close As Strangers" By 5SOS

"Who Did That To You" By Geronimo

"Runnin' (Lose It All)" By Naughty Boy, Beyonce, Arrow Benjamin

"Cocaine Jesus" By Rainbow Kitty Surprise

"Got My Mind Set On You" By George Harrison

"Livin' Thing(2012 Version)" By Electric Light Orchestra

"Underground" By Cody Fry

"Starting Line" By Luke Hemmings

"Easy On Me" By Adele

"Boys Will Be Boys" By Dua Lipa

"Things We Lost In The Fire" By Bastille

"The Last Time (Taylor's Version)" By Taylor Swift

"Lost In The Fire) By The Weeknd

"Wherever You Are" By 5SOS

"Downtown- A Capella" By Anya Taylor-Joy

"Malibu" By Miley Cyrus

"Hold On" By Chord Overstreet

"Atlantis" By Seafret

"History Hates Lovers" By Oublaire

"Home" By Edward Sharpe & The Magnetic Zeros

"Everlasting Love" By Love Affair

"Fire on Fire" By Sam Smith

"Infinity" By James Young

"Pretty Woman" By Roy Orbinson

"Do Ya Think I'm Sexy" By Rod Stewart

"Hopelessly Devoted To You" By Julianne Hough

"Hotel Ceiling" By Rixton

"Monster" By Beth Crowley

"When We Were Young" By Adele

"The Family Jewels." By MARINA

"Venus Fly Trap" By MARINA

"Daniel In The Den" By Bastille

"Chasing Cars" By Snow Patrol

"Me Too" By Meghan Trainor

"Not Your Barbie Girl" By Ava Max

"Problems" By Mother Mother

"1973" By James Blunt

"Soldier" By Fluerie and Tommee Profitt

"You Are Enough" By Sleeping At Last

"Look After You" By The Fray

"Look After You" By Aron Wright

"The Night We Met" By Lord Huron

"You're Somebody Else" By Flora Cash

"Viva La Vida" By Coldplay

"More Than A Woman" By Bee Gees

"Whenever, Wherever" By Shakira

"I Will Wait" By Mumford & Sons

"I've Had Enough" By Melina KB

"Cigarette Daydreams" By Cage The Elephant

"Heart Like Yours" By Willamette Stone

"This Is The Life" Amy Macdonald

"Lion" By Saint Mesa

"Lotta True Crime" By Penelope Scott

"Start A War" By Klergy, Valerie Broussard

"Nightmare" By Halsey

"I Was Here" By Beyonce

"Build A Bitch" By Bella Poarch

"Burned" By Grace Vanderwaal

"Way Down We Go" By KALEO

"Notorious" By The Saturdays

"A Daydream Away" By All Time Low

"Fairytale" By Alexander Rybak

"Don't Blame Me" By Taylor Swift

Acknowledgements

As always, I am eternally grateful to every single person who has given this book a chance. While I am touched by the outpouring of love that came from people when they heard about the concept of 'The Survivors' it is horrifying that so many could relate so deeply to these characters backstories. For everyone that has messaged me privately to share their story to tell me about that connection, I see you and I hear you.

To every ARC and Beta reader. I am so grateful for all the criticism and feedback. You helped make this book the best that it could be. The same can and will be said about every person that helped me research everything I needed to know to make the flashbacks as accurate as possible. I may not have needed to write about the intricate details of the Tudor era horse buying markets but it's something I will now know forever.

To my proof-readers. You are sent from the heavens, and I am so sorry about all the clunky sentences, misplaced comma's and broken punctuation rules. When you are going with the flow, grammar takes a backseat until the re-reads.

To Sam, who insists on getting the earliest drafts I will let her read even though I don't have time to put in the trigger warnings, check it over or fix the random capitalisations from when I type too fast. Please never stop telling me that you hate me for making you cry over fictional characters at 4am.

To Charlie. I would beg the devil for you over and over again.

Printed in Great Britain
by Amazon

60769913R00163